Tropical Lies

by
David Myles Robinson

The contents of this book regarding the accuracy of events, people, and places depicted; permissions to use all previously published materials; opinions expressed; all are the sole responsibility of the author, who assumes all liability for the contents of this book.

© 2014 David Myles Robinson

All rights reserved. No part of this book shall be reproduced, stored in a retrieval system, or transmitted by any means without the written permission of the author or the publisher.

International Standard Book Number 13: 978-1-60452-094-1
International Standard Book Number 10: 1-60452-094-9
Library of Congress Control Number: 2014943090

BluewaterPress LLC
52 Tuscan Way Ste 202-309
Saint Augustine Florida 32092

http://bluewaterpress.com

This book may be purchased online at -
http://www.bluewaterpress.com/tropicallies

Printed in the United States of America

Tropical Lies

Chapter One

The sun was high over Diamond Head, and just beyond the mansion's manicured lawn and small strip of beach, Maunaloa Bay glimmered and sparkled.

In the bottom of the blue-tiled pool, a man's head bobbed lazily. Thin strands of hair floated up, waving gently as sea grass, and streams of blood seeped from the bloated neck into diluted shades of pink. His bulging eyes stared upward, as though he could see his armless torso above him, a grotesquely beautiful, weightless dance.

A red-stained chaise lounge faced the view and two arms trickled blood from their cleanly severed stumps on the flagstones nearby, bare, hairy, and oiled with suntan lotion, crumbs of potato chips stuck to one hand. The metal barrel of an air rifle rested against a small koa wood table. On the table, a monkey pod bowl of potato chips spattered with red drops sat next to a quarter-full glass of clear liquid. A greasy iPhone lay on the deck next to the chaise.

Thirty feet from the chaise on a lanai side table, lay a book of matches, the glossy white cover embossed in gold letters: *La Cannelle, 53 quai des Grands-Augustins, Paris.*

Chapter Two

Twelve miles west of the Portlock mansion, Pancho McMartin's hands trembled as he smoothed his tie, the one he wore to every verdict, royal blue dotted with tiny images. He sat at the counsel table facing Judge Wong with his heart pounding, while at the prosecutor's table, Harry Chang's left leg was bouncing a mile a minute. Harry caught his eye and nodded.

Even Drew, the big, astute Samoan, had cautioned Pancho against taking this case. "You can't win, boss. It's a slam dunk for the prosecution. It'll ruin your winning streak, destroy your reputation."

Pancho's client sat rigidly at his side—the new Don Ho they'd called him, his blend of Hawaiian, European, and Chinese features now pale with fear. Pancho had never seen a brown man so white before.

Despite the frigid air-conditioning of the courtroom, beads of sweat were forming on the back of Pancho's neck. *Should he not have gone after Detective Green so aggressively on cross examination? Should he have put his client on the stand?* He ran a hand through his hair and breathed deeply.

The courtroom was packed, not a space left on the spectators' benches.

The jury was just being seated.

When juror number ten took her seat, a middle-aged *haole* with the timid air of a schoolteacher, she glanced at Pancho, and he thought he detected a slight smile.

The clerk pressed a buzzer, and the door behind the Judge's bench opened.

"All rise. The Circuit Court of the First Circuit, Twenty-Fourth Division, the Honorable Terrence Wong, presiding, is once again in session." The bailiff glanced back to confirm that Judge Wong had taken his place on the bench. "You may be seated."

Judge Wong cast stern eyes over the courtroom, nodded to Pancho, then to Harry. "I understand the jury has reached a verdict. Will the foreman please stand?" Judge Wong's voice was sonorous and deep with authority.

A lanky Japanese man wearing an aloha shirt rose nervously in the jury box.

The Judge nodded. "Will you please identify yourself, sir?"

"Leighton Watanabe, Your Honor."

"Mr. Watanabe, will you confirm that you have reached a verdict?"

"We have, Your Honor."

There was nervous murmuring among the spectators. Pancho had been watching the jury, and now juror number ten looked directly at him and smiled. Harry Chang glanced at him, and he could tell Harry had seen her also. Pancho fought to keep his face impassive.

"And is the verdict unanimous?"

"It is, Your Honor."

"Has the verdict form been signed and dated by you?"

"It has, Your Honor."

The bailiff took the sealed envelope and handed it to Judge Wong, who opened and read it slowly, then leaned over and handed it to the clerk of the court.

"Will the defendant rise?"

Pancho stood in the dead silence and steadied his client's shaking arm. Pancho's stomach churned and his heart hammered. There was nothing on earth he hated and loved so much as the moment just before a verdict is read—the competing fear of failure versus the thrill of victory.

The Judge spoke again. "Will the clerk please read the verdict?"

The clerk cleared her throat. "We the jury in the above-entitled cause, as to the charge of negligent homicide, find the defendant —" She paused, as though surprised, "not guilty."

The courtroom erupted.

The great, Samoan bulk of Drew Tulafono was waiting when Pancho led his happily dazed client out of the elevator and into the first floor rotunda. Pancho's green eyes sparkled, his cowboy boots almost springing across the stone tile floor.

"You done good on this one, Mr. PI." Pancho clapped Drew on the shoulder.

Drew snorted in pleasure. "*We* done good, you mean." He gave Pancho a hug, such a big man that even the six-foot Pancho nearly disappeared. "Lucky tie, boss." Drew flipped the end of Pancho's royal blue tie with its rows of tiny images of Lady Liberty, and Pancho laughed.

As the men turned to cross the quiet rotunda toward the courthouse doors where the noise of voices was already building, a movement caught Pancho's eye.

Dr. Padma Dasari, the Medical Examiner, was wearing a tight skirt that showed off her long, nut-brown legs; her black hair, stylish and short, showed off her elegant neck. She seemed to be in a hurry, on her way to the parking garage. She had a cell phone to her ear, but her huge, dark eyes met Pancho's and locked as they neared each other, so that he almost missed her mouth forming the word, 'congratulations.'

He smiled and nodded, then she was gone.

Ten minutes later, Pancho pulled off his linen sport coat and slung it over his shoulder in the glaring white heat that beat off the Honolulu pavement. The last of the reporters and spectators had scattered, while in the distance his client's limousine turned the corner off Punchbowl Street and disappeared, carrying him away from Ka'ahumanu Hale and back into the heart of Waikiki.

Pancho shook his head, the rush of adrenaline still pounding in his temples.

"There goes one happy *kanaka*." Drew's eyes followed the limousine.

"The *tutu wahine* tourists got their King of Aloha back."

"Eh brah, no make fun of da grandmothers." Drew was mock solemn.

Pancho laughed. A souped-up Mazda drove by with the bass so loud he felt it in his body, and the ends of his hair lifted against his collar in the gentle trade wind.

"Pancho! Hold up." Harry Chang, short and squat, lugged his heavy trial briefcase down the courthouse steps.

"Too much time at your desk lately, Harry?"

"Shoots, Pancho, have some respect for your poor victim." Harry put down his briefcase and held out his hand, breathing heavily. "You screwed me again, man."

Pancho smiled and shook his hand. "No, Harry. Justice prevailed."

Harry chuckled. "Gag me."

He turned to shake Drew's hand, and Pancho slapped him congenially on the back.

Harry picked up his briefcase and they walked together down Queen Street. Pancho loosened his tie and swung his brown leather briefcase. It always struck him how ordinary the real world was after the tension and high stakes of the courtroom. How could anyone walk the sidewalks, sit at traffic lights, window-shop, while blocks away inside the cool, impersonal concrete of the Circuit Court Building life and death were being decided?

"Man, you took a big risk in there today when you went after Detective Green." Harry stretched his legs to keep up with Pancho's long stride. "Judge Wong was pissed."

"Why didn't you object? I expected you to jump out of your chair."

Harry snorted. "I was trying to outsmart you, give you enough rope to hang yourself. I figured two more minutes and I'd object, and you'd have made ass in front of the jury."

Drew laughed out loud. "Instead, Pancho made Green fold like a cheap lanai chair, and suddenly Pancho was a genius, yeah?"

"Lucky son-of-a-bitch, you mean." Harry wiped the sweat from his forehead and turned to Pancho. "I got to hand it to you. You take big risks, but I'll be waiting for the day one of those risks blows up right in your pretty *haole* mug."

Pancho looked away. The late afternoon traffic on Queen Street was picking up, but even so, when a blue Toyota honked at a bus, heads turned, the locals surprised to hear such a thing in Hawai'i. The low afternoon sun reflected off a window of the bus, momentarily blinding Pancho, and a coconut palm frond banged against the trunk of the tree with a hollow sound.

He did take too many risks, he knew it, and one of these days one was going bite him on the *okole*. But he also remembered the exquisite pounding of his heart as Judge Wong leaned over the bench and handed the verdict to the clerk of the court.

"Hey Drew," Pancho forced himself to laugh. "Harry thinks I have a pretty mug!"

As Pancho and Drew walked into Pancho's reception area, his secretary, Susan, looked up expectantly from her typing. Drew glanced back to make sure no one had followed them in, then hooted and pumped his fist. Susan laughed, a deep, throaty, smoker's laugh.

"You know you now work for the most famous attorney in Honolulu," said Drew. "I don't know how you'll be able to live with him."

"Don't be a dick, Drew," Pancho said good-naturedly,

Drew and Susan both laughed, then Susan turned to Pancho, and in a quiet and respectful tone, said, "Congratulations, boss man."

Pancho smiled and thanked her and headed into his office. Susan watched him briefly as he walked away, a fleeting look of concern on her well-lined face. Drew pulled up a chair to Susan's desk and began to regale her with highlights, most of which she already knew, but to which she dutifully listened. She knew this was Drew's first homicide acquittal, and she let him savor the moment.

Pancho plopped heavily into his desk chair, the adrenaline high already starting to deflate. He stared through his reflection in the glass window and watched a jumbo jet take off from Honolulu International Airport. It lumbered slowly down the reef runway before becoming a graceful airborne creature, taking sunburned tourists home to their realities. Ordinarily the view soothed and distracted him, but sometimes it had an unsettling effect, as if the tranquility of it was trying to tell him that he was being eaten alive by the law. That's how he suddenly felt.

Pancho sighed, swiveled away from the window, and stared at the files on his desk. He didn't feel like working. Why should he? He had literally just saved a man's life. The sun was beating in through the window, but Pancho couldn't bring himself to push the button that would lower the blinds. He looked out again at Aloha Tower, the deep blue of the harbor, and the aquamarine sky. He felt unsettled and at loose ends, maybe even a little melancholy. Two commercial fishing boats were heading out of the harbor. He could see a huge container ship out at sea, heading to the harbor, Hawaii's lifeline to consumer goods.

Pancho ran a hand through his longish brown hair. He had nothing to be sad about. He was on top of the world, his trial skills in huge demand. After today's victory, he'd be able to pick and choose his clients. He'd finally put his divorce behind him and had recently begun dating. The thought of Paula Mizuno made him smile. They were rapidly becoming serious.

He turned from the window as the door opened, and Susan walked in with a cup of coffee. She was in her early sixties and her skin had begun to show the effects of too much Hawaiian sun and too many years of smoking. The effect worked to create an appearance at odds with the real woman. Clients, mostly criminals, were intimidated by this older, hard-looking woman who talked with a rasp and who could swear with the best of them. But Pancho knew that Susan was a caring and passionate woman, which is why he'd stolen her away from the communal office group she worked for when he'd first started his own practice. Now she was secretary, confidant, and surrogate mother. She put the cup down in front of Pancho.

"You looked like you need this," Susan said softly.

He nodded his thanks. She turned to leave, but then hesitated and turned back to him. "You all right? You just won the biggest case of your life, but you look . . . I don't know, sad, almost."

Pancho looked at her and gave her a wan smile. Only Susan would have picked up on his subtle mood.

"I'm okay," he said. "Just a little out of sorts. Probably just my usual post-trial blues, kicking in early. Everything okay with you?"

Susan laughed. Her light blue eyes sparkled in her brown and wrinkled face. "You think you can avoid telling me what's wrong by asking about me? Like I don't know all your tricks?"

Pancho had to laugh with her. "We've been together too long. You know what I'm going to say or do before I do." He met her gaze and they shared a brief moment of tenderness before she looked away and began to move toward the door.

She said over her shoulder, "Yeah, well, if you need to talk about anything, just holler. I've got to get back to my gossip. I think we're to the part where Drew is just about to crack the case."

Pancho's smile faded as he watched Susan walk away. He realized what was making him melancholy. He had given his life over to the law. He lost his wife, Ellen, because she hadn't wanted to watch the law consume him. She was a producer at one of the local television networks and worked regular hours. She would leave her office and go home to fix dinner with a promise from Pancho that he would be home soon, only to go to bed alone, the dinner still on the table.

Pancho wasn't cheating on her; he always called or texted to explain that he had to finish a memorandum of law or draft a new motion or make notes on a new theory of defense. There was always another crisis, another client, another reason to work. Ellen wanted a life beyond the law and Pancho hadn't been able to give it to her. Now he was falling hard for Paula, and he was scared that he would drive her away as well.

Pancho reached over and turned on his iPod. The soothing sounds of Stanley Turrentine's saxophone filled the office. He opened the bottom drawer of his desk and pulled out a bottle of Patron Silver and a squat, cut crystal glass. He lifted the bottle to pour himself a shot. Then he paused for a second, reached down, and pulled out a second glass. Drew would want a celebratory shot once he was through gossiping with Susan.

He poured himself a healthy shot of the tequila and took a sip. The gentle burn and the earthy taste felt good and Pancho leaned back in his chair, closed his eyes, and let the alcohol and the saxophone work their magic.

Chapter Three

Homicide Detective Frank Nishimoto was at a family picnic at Queen's Beach when his phone buzzed to indicate he had a text message. 'Call office.'

"Dammit," Frank mumbled. He called in. A murder in Portlock. No ID of the victim yet, but a ritzy house. No suspects in custody.

Frank disconnected and went to tell his wife, Mary, to enjoy the rest of the day and have one of the kids drive her home. The 'kids' were all grown, but they were a tightly knit family and had regular outings. Frank enjoyed seeing his three children and his five grandchildren. He saw them all too rarely. It was not unusual for his days off to be interrupted: he was a senior member of the Honolulu homicide squad.

Within minutes, Frank was driving his department subsidized Ford Malibu around Diamond Head and onto Kahala Avenue, past multi-million dollar oceanfront homes. He circumnavigated Waialae Golf Course and entered Kalanianaole Highway, which took him along the ocean all the way out to Hawai'i Kai. Homes lined the highway, offering only occasional glimpses of the inviting ocean to the right.

Frank turned right off Kalanianaole and proceeded into the wealthy area known as Portlock. The oceanfront homes here, with their spectacular views looking toward Diamond Head, were multi-million dollar properties. He pulled into a narrow lane between two houses that were on land long ago subdivided from a main estate. There was a tall oleander hedge on the left and an old, wood panel fence on the right. As he neared the water, he turned left into a driveway of what was a beautifully landscaped estate. He parked under the shade of a large monkey pod tree in the center of the circular driveway.

The house was two stories, wood frame, in the style of an old missionary home. It had large, koa wood entrance doors, leading into an Italian tiled entrance hall. Beyond the entrance hall was an expansive living room, with plush white carpeting. The ocean-side wall of the living room was all glass and glass sliding doors, which opened onto a large lanai, deck, and pool. Beyond the pool was a lawn, then a small stretch of sandy beach fronting Moanalua Bay. In the distance was the backside of Diamond Head, which, in the stark afternoon light, was a surreal silhouette.

It was, to Frank, an awesome sight. As he stood in the entrance hall and took it all in, he'd almost forgotten why he was there. Then he saw a patrolman he vaguely recognized pick something up off a side table on the lanai. Frank took off toward the man.

"Hey! What are you doing there? What'd you just pick up?"

The officer turned, a surprised look on his face. He held up a book of matches. "Just a book of matches," he said, "Nothing important." He tossed them back down on the table.

Frank took a deep breath, trying to control his anger. "You're at a murder scene, Officer—" he paused, reading the nametag, "Lee. Everything's important." Frank saw that most of the activity was out by the pool. He spoke to Officer Lee again. "What're you doing here anyway?"

"I was the responding officer. I got a call to investigate possible gunshots, so I—"

"Go out to the front of the house, then call Bill Hampton and ask him to get over here. When you're done, go back to the office and write your report."

"But—"

Frank ignored him and walked out toward the pool, looking around. A cream-colored chaise lounge sat next to a small matching side table on the flagstone deck. There were rust-colored stains on the chaise, which Frank assumed was blood. A rifle leaned against the table.

On the table was a bowl of potato chips, which were splattered with tiny drops. Next to the bowl was a short glass with a small amount of clear liquid in it. There was a pink droplet on the side of the glass and on the table was a small water spot. A black iPhone lay on the deck. Frank bent down and looked at it closely. It was smeared with grease. Then he saw the two arms lying on the deck near the chaise, about three feet apart. Both arms were bare, hairy, and oiled with suntan lotion. There was something strange about one of the hands. Frank moved closer to get a better look. There were potato chips stuck to the hand. *What the hell?*

He looked around and saw a police photographer taking pictures at the pool. He took a few steps and saw that a head was lying on the bottom of the pool. A torso without arms was eerily bobbing, like it was standing up, in the shallow end.

He recognized Sergeant Russell Cabrillo, pointing out something to one of the photographers. Frank walked over to him. "What's up, Russ?"

They walked back toward the living room, almost instinctively moving away from the death as they talked. Cabrillo referred to his notebook from time to time as he filled Frank in.

"The house belongs to Maynard Laws," Cabrillo paused to look at Frank. Frank's face was impassive.

"Know who he is?"

"Yeah, that investment counselor. One of my aunties has money invested with him. Is that Laws in the pool?"

"Don't know yet. Doc should be here any minute. She was testifying at Circuit Court on a case, but I took the liberty of asking her to come out as soon as she's *pau*." In Hawai'i it was unusual for the Medical Examiner to attend to the scene of a murder, but Frank nodded his approval.

"As soon as the photographers are done," Cabrillo continued, "we'll have the pieces pulled out of the pool. None of my guys are crazy about climbing into the pool to pull the guy out."

"Don't blame them. Let me talk to Doc about how she wants it handled." Frank knew that Dr. Padma Dasari, the coroner, wouldn't want anything damaged by using a hook or the pool net. That could destroy critical evidence.

"Tell the photographers to hurry. I'm sure she doesn't want the body parts under water for longer than necessary."

Cabrillo hurried away to speed up the photographers. He was back in a few moments.

"We should be able to recognize Laws when the head comes out, if that's him. I know what he looks like and so do some of the other guys.

"The forensic team is already at work, dusting for prints. There are a few sets of tire tracks on the driveway, and we got pictures. A plaster mold wouldn't work, too gravelly. I doubt that'll help us any.

"A neighbor called in to say she'd heard a shot." Cabrillo looked at his notebook to check the time.

"A shot?" asked Frank.

Cabrillo nodded, then continued with his recital of information.

"It was at 2:24 p.m. The neighbor was Mrs. Peterson."

"Get someone over to take her statement," said Frank.

"Already being done."

"Okay, go on"

"No one else seems to have been home. No maids, no family. Officer Lee was the first on the scene. He'd been interviewing some burglary victims in the area and got here at 2:55. I got here immediately thereafter, at 2:57. We sealed the area and had homicide call you. I let the photographers and the other forensic guys in, since I knew you'd approve. You got here at 3:33." They both looked up and nodded to Dr. Dasari as she strode directly to the scene of the murder.

Frank turned back to Cabrillo. "Have the forensic men be sure to get fiber samples from the living room rug. Unless the killer came around the side, he'd have had to pass through the living room to get out here." He paused, thinking. "Also, have them check the entry tile for footprints. If the killer took his shoes off, he may have left a print. That marble tile should be perfect for leaving prints."

Cabrillo looked up from his notebook and chuckled. "You think the killer was polite enough to remove his shoes before walking into the living room?" Frank glared at him until Cabrillo nodded and made a note.

"What's up with that rifle by the pool?" asked Frank. "It doesn't look real to me."

Cabrillo nodded his agreement. "It's just an air rifle."

Frank pondered that for a moment, but then moved on. "Don't forget to check to make sure they bag the glass and the iPhone out there. We'll want to check on any incoming or outgoing calls today." He glanced around. "Has anyone noted any signs of forced entry?"

"Nope," Cabrillo answered. "The front door was unlocked. Anyone could've gained access from the beach, and there's only a waist high fence with an unlocked gate at the side of the house."

Frank went over and talked to Doc for a few minutes before meandering back toward the lanai, waiting for the team to pull the body parts from the pool. The lanai furniture looked expensive. The chairs all had plush cushions. Next to one chair was a small koa wood side table, on which he noticed the book of matches. He bent over to read the embossed letters on the glossy white front. "*La Cannelle, 53 quai des Grands-Augustins, Paris*". Frank called out to Sergeant Cabrillo.

"Put those matches in a bag. And make a note that Officer Lee's prints are probably on the cover. The idiot picked it up. Assuming the body is Laws, make a note to check to see if he or his wife had been to Paris recently."

Frank still had matches from his trip to Greece five years ago, but he didn't leave them around for people to use; they were treated more as souvenirs. These matches had been on the lanai table, not thirty feet from the scene of a murder. He made a mental note to talk to Lee's supervisor.

Just then, Frank heard Detective Bill Hampton's booming voice.

"What a pleasant spot for a murder. Howzit Frank, what've we got?" Bill walked past Frank and continued out to the pool.

"Holy shit! What the—"

Despite everything, Frank had to smile. He hadn't seen Bill speechless many times. Bill stood still, looking around but saying nothing for several minutes before he came back to Frank.

"Jesus Frank, we've been on the force a long time, but have you ever seen anything like this?"

Frank had been thinking the same thing. There'd been lots of gruesome scenes, a lot of cases with more blood and guts. There had even been a few dismembered body cases, but for sheer bizarre terror, he had never seen anything quite like this. The eyes staring up from the bottom of the pool; the eerie way the torso seemed to be standing up in the water; the hand with potato chips on it.

"Can't say I have. It's pretty bizarre. But to top it off, I think we might also find that the victim's been shot." Frank filled Bill in on the details he'd been given by Cabrillo.

"Well, I guess if you're going to murder someone, it pays to make sure you got the job done." Bill's famous black humor was coming back.

"How're we going to get him out of the pool?" Bill asked.

"I already talked to Doc about that. I don't want our guys going into bloody water and Doc doesn't want the body to stay in the pool for as long as it would take to drain it. Besides, once the water level got low, the body would start banging around in the pool, so we're trying to get the torso pushed over to the side of the pool as delicately as possible so we can pull it out. They're using the pool net to nudge the head over to where we can get it. Doc doesn't want any more trauma to the body than we can help."

Bill nodded his agreement. "Has someone already taken water samples?"

"Done," said Frank.

They surveyed the scene as two officers worked under the watchful eyes of Dr. Padma Dasari to get the body out. Frank couldn't help letting his gaze linger on 'Doc.' Even at a gruesome murder scene she was drop-dead gorgeous. Her stylish, short cropped hair accented her high cheekbones and her long, elegant neck. Her dark black eyes set off her nut brown skin. Over her blouse, she wore a navy blue, lightweight jacket with 'Coroner' printed in white letters across the back. Somehow, it looked stylish on her. When the head was finally lifted out of the water and placed on a plastic body bag, Frank and Bill walked over. It appeared to be swollen, and the eyes bulged in a horrifyingly vacant stare.

"It's Maynard Laws all right," said Cabrillo, who had come up behind Frank and Bill.

"Yeah, I recognize him too," said Bill. "His picture's been all over the tube and the papers."

"Even so, we've got to get an official identification. The guy was married, wasn't he?"

"Yes, sir" said Cabrillo. "To a local gal, if I remember correctly."

"Bill, get one of your men to locate Mrs. Laws. I'm going to check around the house, see if there's a study or desk somewhere with personal papers. Maybe there's some other family.

"Doc, anything on whether Laws was shot?" She'd been bent over the torso and looked up as Frank spoke to her.

She spoke with a slight accent, which had a rhythmic cadence. "Looks like it. Probably a .38 to the abdomen. I doubt it was a fatal shot, but give me time to do my autopsy." She bent back over the body.

"Now what the hell? Why would someone shoot a guy, not kill him with the gun, then whack off his head and arms?" asked Frank.

"I suppose the killer could've chopped off the head and arms first, then shot him, but that makes even less sense," Bill said.

Bill continued to mumble to himself while Frank went off in search of personal papers. Frank didn't understand any of this. The victim was shot, then mutilated, presumably while he was still alive. The head and the torso were then thrown into the pool, although, he supposed, they could have fallen in at the time of the dismemberment. Doc or the forensic guys should be able to tell whether or not the body had made impact with the deck before going into the pool.

Frank toured the house. By and large it was tastefully furnished, although some pieces of art or furniture were strangely out of place. Frank figured Laws had used an interior decorator, then, thinking they had good taste, had supplemented the designer's work with pieces of their own. Money and taste don't necessarily go hand in hand.

He found a room that looked like it was a personal study. It was small, compared to the rest of the rooms, and contained a beautiful Japanese cherry wood desk, a matching cherry wood bureau, an easy chair made of soft leather, and wall-to-wall bookshelves on two walls. There were no personal pictures. Frank found that unusual, but not necessarily strange.

He opened the center drawer on the desk. Several Mont Blanc pens and some beige stationary with 'Mr. and Mrs. Maynard Laws' embossed in gold across the top were neatly placed in the drawer. That was all.

Frank opened the right hand top drawer. He saw an appointment book. He took it out and leafed to Friday, August 23. He saw a notation, *'Iwalani to H.K.'*

"H.K.," Frank mumbled to himself. "Hawai'i Kai? Hale Koa Hotel? Or someone's name?" He didn't see any other entries that leapt out. Naturally, everyone whose name was in the book would be checked. He placed the book on top of the desk and kept looking.

He found a checkbook in the second drawer down on the right. He stared at the figures he found, amazed by their size. Tarn's Caterers, $15,320. Neimen Marcus, $12,533.20. Honolulu Mortgage, $25,699. A twenty-five thousand dollar a month mortgage? "Yikes."

Then, again mumbling out loud, "What's this?" He read the entry: 'Akamai Travel. 8/20, $4,737.'

Maybe H.K. was Hong Kong, mused Frank. He'd have someone call Akamai Travel.

In the third drawer down, Frank found a ledger book. It was filled with names and figures. *Investors?* He'd look at it later. He saw nothing else of import, but decided that he'd get Mrs. Laws' consent to a more thorough search.

He took the appointments book, check-register, and ledger to the lanai with him and wrote out a receipt for the items he was taking. They were necessary to the immediate investigation of finding family and/or suspects and he therefore had a legal right to remove them from the house.

The body parts had finally been removed. The house had been photographed, and prints had been lifted from everywhere and everything capable of rendering a good print.

Frank ordered the house sealed and posted an officer to stay at the premises in the event Mrs. Laws or someone else showed up. He took another look at the blood stained deck. Then he lifted his eyes to the magnificence of the view beyond. The ocean sparkled. Diamond Head was a beckoning silhouette to this tourist mecca.

He'd have to remember to call Auntie Leona tonight to ask her how much she'd invested with Laws. He then went to the front yard to deal with the growing number of reporters. When he appeared, the reporters began shouting questions at him, some aggressively pushing their colleagues to the side, anxious to get something in time for the six o'clock news, only a half hour away.

Chapter Four

The tall, dignified Eurasian woman had been standing in one place next to her luggage cart for a full three minutes. Iwalani Laws looked around in cold fury for her chauffeur. There were uniformed men with signs outside customs at the cavernous Hong Kong airport, but none bearing her name. She stood next to her luggage cart with two large Vuitton bags and her carry-on, perfectly still in the cacophonous noise, while people pushed past her purposefully, everyone speaking, everyone apparently certain where they were going.

Iwalani was part Chinese, which gave her eyes an exotic look, part Hawaiian, which gave her skin a beautiful light brown sheen, and part *haole*, which took the edge off and seemed to soften the clash of characteristics. She wore a white Chanel two-piece suit with one strand of perfect white pearls. A five-caret diamond wedding band adorned her hand. Her long black hair was pinned up with black lacquer Chinese combs. Her usually sensuous lips were pursed in growing agitation.

As she waited, her dignity began to dissemble, and her usual practiced mask of haughtiness showed the first signs of fear. She was just moving toward a sign for hired cars when a short Chinese man in livery rushed towards her, sweating profusely and breathing heavily, his black suit rumpled, a sign in his hands with her name on it.

She let out a deep breath, her cold eyes glittering.

Forty-five minutes later, spike heels clicked on the highly polished marble floor of the ornate lobby of the Hong Kong Mandarin Oriental Hotel. The smell of the harbor, one block away, and the sounds of the bustling city-central faded as the bellmen fussed over her baggage, speaking to her in rapid fire Cantonese, assuming she was Chinese. Iwalani ignored them, her elegant height rigid, the odor of vodka from the limousine's bar on her breath. She paused at the greeting of an obsequious assistant manager who knew who she was and who spoke to her in perfect English, and allowed herself a self-satisfied smile.

Chapter Five

Two mornings later Pancho was in full post-trial malaise as he rode the elevator to his office. He'd taken a day off after his big verdict to relax and do some surfing, but now it was back to the daily grind. He couldn't have felt less motivated. He instinctively looked around the elevator to see if there was anyone he knew. A mousy looking woman in the elevator reminded him of Maynard Laws' secretary, Elie Watson, who'd been all over the news since the murder. Laws' office was a few floors above Pancho's and when he saw her picture on television and in the papers he realized that he'd seen her in the elevator a number of times. In fact, Pancho was pretty sure that the last time he'd seen her was on the day of Laws' murder. It was when he and Drew were coming from court. She'd been in the elevator, tucked into a corner as she had been every time he saw her. Although she always struck Pancho as being timid and purposely plain, on that day she looked different. She seemed tired, angry, or sad, or, he reflected, maybe all three. He wondered if she'd already known about the murder.

Pancho walked into his office and saw Drew sitting on the edge of Susan's desk. Drew was holding the *Star-Advertiser*. They both looked up as Pancho entered.

"Hey, boss man, we were just getting up to date on that Maynard Laws' murder." Drew shook his head in wonder. "Some weird stuff." He handed the paper to Pancho, who tucked it under his arm.

"Anything important going on?" He asked Susan, who was already handing him several pink, 'while you were out', slips.

She shook her head. Several strands of gray hair had fallen out of her haphazardly pinned bun. "Not really. Lots of congratulations. The Chang hearing's been continued until Thursday. Shorty Gomez is in trouble again and wants to hire you." The derision in her throaty, smoker's voice was obvious. "The usual stuff."

Pancho continued on to his office, tossed the pink slips on the desk and then sat down and opened the paper. His victory for the 'King of Aloha' had been the headline the day before, but since then, it had all been Maynard Laws. New revelations about Laws' business had been coming to light on an almost hourly basis, and it appeared that the mousey secretary was involved up to her ears.

The press had been having a field day with the secretary, Elie Watson. She'd had an affair with Laws, according to 'reliable sources.' She refused to speak to the press on the advice of her attorney, William Chambers, who Pancho knew to be one of the young up-and-comers.

She was also, it was pointed out time and time again, the only living person who'd been close enough to Laws at the office to have extensive knowledge of the way Laws had operated. So far, however, neither she nor the police were revealing much, which simply added fuel to the speculation.

Pancho read today's article.

Laws' Partners All From Mainland

By Les Toguchi
Star-Advertiser staff reporter

The Star-Advertiser has learned that Maynard Laws' partners in the firm of Burling, Woodward, Taniguchi & Laws are all mainland residents who have had no active participation in Laws' business. According to reliable sources, one 'partner,' Alvin Burling, 75, is a retired railroad engineer who lives in Sun City, Arizona, a retirement community. When contacted by this reporter, Burling refused comment, referring all questions to his wife, Gertie, who would only say that "Al done nothing wrong."

The Woodward in the firm name is one Willard G. Woodward, 67, of Cheyenne, Wyoming. Woodward is a retired sanitation worker for the City of Cheyenne. Woodward was unavailable for comment.

It is the same story for the other members of the firm name. It is uncertain how much these people were paid by Laws for the use of their names, which all happen to be surnames of prominent *kamaainas*, local families. Detective Frank Nishimoto refused comment on details, but did confirm to this reporter that all of the partners except for Laws were mainland residents who had no known connection with the actual operation of the firm. Nishimoto also stressed that there is no evidence that any of the prominent *kamaaina* families were in any way involved in Laws' firm.

Laws, who had been touted as a genius investment counselor, was murdered on August 23, while lounging by the pool at his luxurious Portlock estate. No arrests have been made and little is known about the progress of the investigation.

The books and records of Laws' business were seized shortly after the murder, and according to this reporter's sources, it is now clear that Laws' investment counseling firm was a complete fraud. It was yet another Ponzi scheme, similar, although smaller in scope, to the Bernie Madoff fraud in New York. Criminal charges are being considered against various individuals, including Laws' executive secretary, Elie Watson, by state and federal agencies, also according to informed sources.

It is not known whether charges will be pursued against the silent, mainland partners.

Pancho put the paper down and sipped his coffee. He wondered how the investigation was going. Frank Nishimoto was as good a homicide detective as there was, but a case like this with so many angry investors, had too many people with motives to commit murder. Pancho knew from the press that Laws had been dismembered. *That should certainly narrow the list of suspects*, he thought. Even investors who'd lost their life savings wouldn't go so far as to cut off the head and arms. Instinctively, he began thinking about possible defenses, but after a couple of minutes, he shook his head. *I sure wouldn't want to try to defend someone who was capable of that kind of brutality*, he thought.

He rolled up his sleeves and dove into the stack of files on his desk, intent on finishing early and taking Paula out to a fine dinner.

Chapter Six

It was not until the next morning, three days after the murder, when Central Intelligence Agency's Operations Division Chief for the Pacific, Oliver Wilson, heard about Laws' murder. He sat at his desk in his Langley, VA office and gripped the phone tightly as he listened to his agent in Honolulu, Donald Duerden, with a healthy mix of astonishment, anger and alarm.

"Murdered? By whom? Anyone in custody?"

"They don't know who did it; or at least they aren't saying they know," said Duerden. "I'm just letting you know we're fine. There's nothing to connect us to Laws."

Wilson closed his eyes and willed the growing pain in his head to hold off a while longer. "We just ran a fifteen million dollar deal through this guy. Are you positive there's nothing to connect us to him?"

"I'm sure, but just to be one hundred percent positive, I searched his office as soon as I heard about the murder. There wasn't anything obviously incriminating, but I pulled out some records just to be sure. We're completely in the clear," said Duerden. "Nothing to worry about at all, Ollie."

Wilson grunted and hung up. He wished he could trust Duerden, but as far as he was concerned, Duerden was a rogue, a cowboy, who flaunted the rules and cut corners. Duerden had been one of the agents in charge of hiring local militia to help protect the U.S. Mission in Benghazi — militia that failed to show up when the assault on the compound started. Wilson suspected Duerden had screwed the pooch over there, but Benghazi wasn't in Wilson's scope of operations so there was little he could say or do about his suspicions. Then, much to Wilson's chagrin, Duerden ended up in a cushy job in Honolulu, which was in Wilson's scope of operations.

The whole Honolulu operation had sounded shaky to Wilson from the beginning. Not the use of a private citizen to launder money for the Agency, that was done all the time, but the way Duerden had rushed into things bothered Wilson. This dead guy, Laws, and his business, hadn't been properly vetted, but when he'd expressed his concerns to Deputy Director of Operations Randolph Fuller, he was overruled. For some reason Wilson didn't understand, Fuller was enamored of Duerden, who could do no wrong in Fuller's eyes. It was Fuller who had arranged for Duerden to be transferred to Honolulu. Now, just weeks after they'd run fifteen million dollars through one of Laws' corporations to fund a group of African rebels who promised to rid their country of Al Qaeda once they took over, Laws was dead and Wilson knew the authorities would be scrutinizing everything Laws had been involved in.

He stared at the new black phone that had been installed after he cracked the last one in anger, the last time he'd talked to Duerden, and willed himself to relax.

The clock on the wall said it was 3:15 p.m. He was supposed to take his wife to Lee Hing Seafood House for dinner that night, and had planned on leaving early. He pulled out the file on the Honolulu operation from his bottom file drawer and began to make detailed notes of the call with Duerden. At 3:40, he reread what he'd written and began to make notes as to his suggested course of action. Not only did they need to make sure the Agency would not be implicated in the Laws' business, and especially in the murder, they needed to replace Laws as soon as possible. There was a huge deal in Sudan they needed to finalize.

Wilson wrote non-stop for another twenty minutes. When he was done, he closed the manila file and looked at the clock. He let out a breath and rubbed his eyes. He was debating whether he should call Fuller or go downstairs and see him in person. He didn't want to do either. The two men seemed to be in perpetual conflict; their personalities were polar opposites. Wilson was strategic, structured and practical. He'd spent twenty years in the field as an operative. Fuller, the superior, was political, lackadaisical, and soft—except when it came to protecting his own career, when he could become ruthless and hard.

At 4:10, after searching the Internet and reading the *Honolulu Star-Advertiser* stories on the Laws murder, Oliver Wilson rose from his desk and began the dreaded trek to DDO Randolph Fuller's office.

Chapter Seven

Detectives Frank Nishimoto and Bill Hampton were tired and cranky, having spent few hours home with their families since the murder. To make matters worse, on two occasions Frank had to take time away from the investigation to testify in court. He hated testifying.

It didn't help that the cooling trade winds were still missing. The barely discernible wind was southerly, light, and the days were warm and muggy. Frank wiped the sweat from his forehead and prayed silently for the return of the trades. The air-conditioning was out in the building that housed the Honolulu Police Department on Beretania Street. Bill brought in a portable Sanyo fan, but it was kept on low to prevent the reams of accumulating paperwork from blowing all over the office.

The payment to the travel agent that Frank found in the check register had led to a trace of Iwalani Laws at the Mandarin Oriental Hotel in Hong Kong. Frank and Bill marveled at the apparent ignorance of Mrs. Laws when it came to Laws' business and business associates. As far as she knew and was concerned, or at least so she claimed, he was a successful investment counselor. She'd never met Messrs. Burling, Woodward or Taniguchi and had never heard Laws speak of them.

The only person at Laws' office whom she had met was the executive secretary, Elie Watson. Bill told Frank that he detected a bit of coolness when Iwalani Laws talked about Elie, but she said nothing to lead them to believe that Elie was in any way suspect.

Iwalani Laws claimed to be unaware of any money problems and unaware of anyone who would have wanted to see Laws dead. She apparently lived in blissful ignorance of what was beginning to look like one of the biggest con jobs in the history of Hawai'i.

Frank thought that Iwalani Laws was a beautiful woman, but in a hard, cosmetic kind of way. She seemed to hold herself in control at all times. Was she stoic or cold? Iwalani's reaction to the news of her husband's death was hard for the detectives to gauge. She'd been told over the phone, while she was still in Hong Kong, so by the time they met her on her arrival at Honolulu International Airport, she'd had many hours to come to grips with the fact that her husband had been murdered. Despite the daily revelations of potential fraud, the gossip about his secretary, and the growing possibility that she was now penniless, she held herself with an almost regal bearing that deflected pity before it could be proffered.

Iwalani accepted the condolences of Frank and Bill with a nod. She asked few questions, but cooperated in answering those posed to her. She spoke in a soft, but clipped and precise, voice that gave the interrogator the impression that this was all an inconvenience, which she had deigned to tolerate. Luckily, for her, she did not have to identify the body. Had she been forced to do so, Frank wondered how long it would have taken the facade to crumble. One of the attorneys in the law firm that represented Laws, one floor below, handled the identification formality.

Bill had to smile to himself whenever he thought of the young, officious attorney, Wally Jenkins, presenting himself for the identification procedure. The kid was obviously still wet behind the ears, but acted as if he were lead counsel to some corporate giant. He'd not yet realized that the man he worked for was a major swindler. When he was shown the head of Maynard Laws, the kid puked all over the spotless floor of the morgue.

For now, Frank and Bill were accepting Iwalani Laws at face value. She did, after all, have an airtight alibi. She was in Hong Kong when the murder occurred. There was no life insurance, at least that they had been able to find. Although Mrs. Laws thought she and her husband were wealthy, if she'd had him killed for the money she would have been a fool not to make sure how much money there was beforehand. Frank and Bill both concluded that nothing pointed to Mrs. Laws as a suspect.

There were, however, plenty of suspects. All told, according to the ledger that Frank found in Laws' desk at home, there appeared to be over five hundred investors from whom Laws had taken substantial money. The investments ranged from a few thousand dollars to close to a million dollars. The long and arduous process of tracking down and interviewing each investor had been going on for several days and the preliminary reports were disturbing.

None of the investors had seen any return of either principal or profit in months. Many of the investors had begun making inquiries of Laws' office. They'd adeptly been put off either by Laws himself, or Elie Watson. None of the investors had ever seen or met any of the other partners in Laws' firm.

Frank was bent over his desk studying a list he had made of the five biggest investors with Laws based on the notations in the ledger.

> 1. Reggie Bellows - deposits totaling $780,000. $300,000 profits reinvested.
>
> 2. Charles Makuakane - various deposits totaling $1,110,000. [No profits noted].
>
> 3. Hideki Kirimitsu - various deposits totaling $606,000, plus reinvestment of profits.
>
> 4. Walter Heffler - $700,000. [No profits noted].
>
> 5. Joseph Cabrera - $610,000, [No profits noted].

These five individuals, none of whom Frank had ever heard of, must have known or had begun to suspect that they'd each lost a substantial amount of money with Laws. This made them prime suspects.

The ledger Frank found at Laws' house on the day of the murder appeared to be an informal and personal accounting of only the major investors. It listed the investments made by each. For some, such as Reggie Bellows, it also had notations as to "profit reinvested." For Bellows, it was three hundred thousand dollars. Other investors, such as Mr. Makuakane, who had invested over a million, there was no notation as to how much, if any, profits had been paid or reinvested. There was a column for "projected % return" with numbers that varied wildly for each entry. Frank and Bill theorized that these numbers were bogus numbers that Laws would try to sell to each of the investors as to how he expected their portfolio to perform.

Next to Reggie Bellows' name, for instance, it noted "25%???". Frank thought Laws might have been wondering if he would be able to sell this Bellows fellow on the idea that he would see a twenty-five percent return. Judging from the so-called 'profits' that Bellows had already reinvested, Frank figured that Laws took him to be pretty gullible. Most revealing to Frank was the notation at the last entry, which read "get profit statement to RB: will reinvest." RB, Reggie Bellows, could apparently be counted on to reinvest the profits he had made and, Frank speculated, it was therefore safe for Laws to declare that Bellows had made more gains because Laws would not have to produce the money. The ledger was undated, so Frank had no idea as to when the entries were made, or even if they were still relevant.

Frank had consulted with his cousin, a CPA, for some off-the-record input on the ledger. The CPA was shocked at what he'd seen. He agreed with Frank's suspicions: this ledger appeared to be a private working ledger just for Laws. He must have used it to play with the numbers and make notes as to how he might be able to manipulate these big investors. Frank, therefore, obtained a warrant to seize all of the records at Laws' office. Bill and he had taken some perverse pleasure at presenting Jenkins, the attorney, with the warrant. The kid had gone white in the face.

The police sealed the office and began boxing and carting out the files and documents. Because of potential federal violations, Frank had been obliged to inform the FBI of the raid, and had agreed to make all of the material available to the Bureau.

Frank again wiped his forehead.

"Let's get a full background check on these five investors. I want the works, state and national. See if the feds will cooperate."

"You know, Frank, a ten thousand loss to some poor bugga is every bit as heavy a hit as a few hundred grand loss to someone else. Lots of times it's even harder."

"I know. We're gonna have to check out every friggin' person on the investor list, but we have to start somewhere don't we?" The irritation in Frank's voice highlighted his fatigue and frustration.

"Okay, okay, don't bite my damn head off. Jeez."

"Sorry, pards," said Frank. "It's the heat. We're both getting cranky. The press is on our *okole* for a break and we don't have squat. We've gotta take some shots in the dark and hope something turns up."

"You're right. It makes sense to start with the biggest and work our way down. I'll get someone on it. You think we ought to interview these guys now?"

"No. What I'd like to do is get some manpower to put a tail on each of them for a day or two, see what their activities are. While that's happening, we can get the background checks and know who we're dealing with. I don't want someone to cut and run; that is, if they haven't already."

"What about the phone?" asked Frank.

Bill removed a paperweight and rooted around on his desk, sorting through papers. "Laws' cell phone showed five calls out in the three hours before the murder. Two were to the same number, which was answered the second time and resulted in a three minute conversation, and the other three were all to a different number. There was also an uncompleted call to a number starting with nine, which could be 911 or any of the thousands of phones that begin with number nine." Bill paused and looked at his notes again. "The two calls were to a phone registered to a Sandy Foreman. The other three calls were to a blocked number. We're working on that."

"Do we know anything about this Foreman?" Frank asked.

Bill shrugged and gave a half grin. "Not much yet, but from what I've learned he's some two-bit pimp and drug dealer who works mostly out of the Hotel Street area. Not sure what business he'd have with Laws, unless Laws was into skanky ho's."

Frank nodded. Nothing about this case would surprise him at this point. "Keep me posted. What about the air rifle? What do we know about that?"

Bill chuckled. "Apparently our boy Laws liked to go down to the ocean and shoot things, little *a'ama* crabs mostly. We talked to the neighbor who called in the shot. She didn't hide the fact that she despised Laws. She thought he was, and I quote, 'a fat, arrogant pig'. She routinely called the cops about hearing gunshots at Laws' house."

"What took Lee so long to get there? He was just a few blocks away."

"I asked him," said Bill. "He looked kind of sheepish when I confronted him, but he said he'd responded to so many supposed gunshots at the Laws' residence that he assumed it was just the neighbor calling in about the air gun again."

Frank shook his head in disgust. "He needs to be reprimanded, Bill. That fool may've blown the whole investigation by making an assumption and not responding in time. If Laws had been shot, then hacked up, that would've taken some time. Lee might've gotten there while the murderer was still there."

Bill nodded in agreement. "No shit. Think what McMartin could do with that tidbit if he turns out to be the defense attorney on this case."

Frank rolled his eyes. "Yeah. He took Billy Green apart piece by piece on cross a few weeks ago in that negligent homicide case. I would've bet the farm against him getting a defense verdict on that one."

"You know, when McMartin first showed up on felony cases I thought, 'what's up with this guy?' Long hair, cowboy boots, jeans, and a name that sounded like a Mexican-Irish restaurant. But I gotta say, he turned out to be the real deal, the bane of our existence." He gathered his notes and stood to leave. "I'll go check on the tails."

As Bill left, Frank looked around at the boxes piled up against every wall in the office. This was going to be a long, slow process unless they got a break.

Frank turned his attention to the autopsy report from Dr. Dasari. Laws had been shot with a .38 caliber handgun in the abdomen. It was not a fatal shot and Doc's opinion was that Laws would probably have retained consciousness after the shooting, at least for a while. The killer had then amputated the head and both arms, not necessarily in that order, with a sharp, thick-bladed sword or machete, most likely a machete. According to Dr. Dasari, this was not an easy task, and it tended to rule out a woman, at least as a sole perpetrator.

Although there was evidence of some hacking, especially on the neck, Doc noted that whoever had performed the dismemberment would seem to have had some knowledge of anatomy and/or some special combat training.

Death would have been caused either by the complete severance of the spinal cord at the base of the skull or by massive blood loss, depending on what was amputated first. There was bruising on the head at the posterior occipital region, which led her to opine that the head had struck the deck before rolling into, or being thrown into the pool.

Frank closed his eyes and tried to get the picture of the grotesquely swollen eyes out of his mind. He could see them, magnified by the water, staring up from the pool. The heat in his office and the mental image of the corpse were combining to produce a slight nausea, but he forced himself to read on.

The right upper extremity had bruises on it at or about the forearm area, where the killer had apparently held on to the arm, presumably to stop the body from falling over after the decapitation. There were no other significant abrasions on the arms. Frank summoned up a grotesque image of the murderer holding hands with a headless torso.

The arms had apparently been left where they fell or had been placed where they were found immediately after amputation. The potato chips stuck to the left hand were a result of chips having stuck to suntan lotion. The stomach contents showed that Laws had been eating potato chips just prior to his death. His blood alcohol was .14, drunk but probably not out of it. Time of death was placed between 1:00 p.m. and 2:45 p.m.

Frank checked his notes again. The neighbor had called in the shot at 2:24 p.m. and the first officer was on the scene by 2:55 p.m. *Damn that Lee*, mused Frank. If the neighbor was telling the truth about calling a few minutes after hearing the shot, and if the dismemberment occurred after the shot, that meant the killer had to work pretty damn fast to cut off the head and both arms.

'*Shoots, it takes me longer than that just to carve a damn turkey,*' thought Frank.

He put down the autopsy report and cover letter from Dr. Dasari, which set forth opinions, which she did not feel comfortable including in the official report. Frank knew that over the course of the investigation he would read and reread the autopsy, the statements, and the forensic reports to see what otherwise trivial pieces of information had suddenly become important in light of some new evidence.

He looked at the forensic report. The importance of the information from the labs would not show itself until later. There were numerous fingerprints in the house, but other than Laws, his wife, and that idiot, Lee, none that had so far been identified. No one expected to find the killer's fingerprints anyway. Ten-year-old children knew from television that criminals wore gloves. This was clearly a case of premeditated murder. One doesn't go calling on someone for purely social reasons carrying a gun and a machete.

They had fiber samples, but so far, nothing to match them to. The only bare footprints on the entry tile matched the footprint taken of Laws. The glass from the poolside table had only Laws' fingerprints on it. The matchbook from Paris held only Lee's prints. Someday, Frank hoped, all this evidence would come together. He hoped it was sooner rather than later.

Chapter Eight

Elie Watson stared up into Donald Duerden's sweaty face as he thrust into her again and again. She didn't dislike the sensation, but just wanted him to get done with it. She had other things on her mind.

They were in a condo on the beach at Po'ipu on Kaua'i, and although the lanai door was open, it was hot as a sauna. She could hear the surf crash on the beach. There was no air-conditioning; only an overhead fan. It swirled the hot air around and spread the musky scent of sex throughout the room.

Donald had come over to meet Elie that morning. On Donald's instructions, she had taken the room under an assumed name. It had been his idea for them to meet on Kaua'i. She'd been bugging him to meet with her, but he'd refused to do so in Honolulu. So far, Elie had not mentioned Donald or the CIA to the police, or even to her attorney.

Elie heard Donald grunt and could feel the convulsions of his orgasm. She was relieved he was finally finished. She hadn't felt romantic. How could she? Her employer had been murdered. He'd been a fraud and she'd been an accomplice. No matter how much she told herself that she'd been an unwilling accomplice, she was not foolish enough to believe that she would be protected from the wrath of the law. There were hundreds of people out there who'd been swindled by Laws. Some had placed their entire life savings with him in the hopes of making their old age more comfortable.

Laws hadn't cared and he didn't discriminate. He stole from the rich and the poor alike. She'd had vicious arguments with him about taking investment money from people who couldn't afford to lose, but he'd just laughed at her.

"These people are greedy," Laws said, waving off her concerns. "They want to make a fast buck. Well, there're risks involved in making a fast buck. Sometimes you win, sometimes you lose. Only I'm the one who controls who wins and who loses." He beat his fist on his chest, and he reminded Elie of a big, arrogant gorilla. "If any one of these people could make a fast buck at the expense of someone else, they'd do it in a heartbeat."

Donald rolled off her and the separation suddenly made Elie want to cry. She felt exposed and vulnerable. Just seconds ago, she'd wanted him out of her and off her. Now she wanted to crawl back into the safety of his arms. She thought about all the pain that she'd helped cause. She'd been the one most investors had personal contact with. She'd taken their money. She'd covered for Maynard. These people, who had trusted her and had trusted Maynard, were going to want blood, and someone had already gotten Maynard's blood. She was the only living target. What was going to happen to her now?

She told herself that's why she needed Donald. He could help her. He could fix things, he was CIA. He would take care of her. But first, she had to let him have his way with her. Well, she thought, she'd been screwed before and it was pretty clear she was going to get screwed again.

"So who do you think killed Maynard?" she asked, watching Donald slip on his boxers.

He shrugged. "Wellll," he drawled, "my guess would be any one of the hundreds of investors he fucked over." He flopped himself back on the bed beside her and looked at her. "Who do you think did it?" He smiled, a cruel looking smile. "It wasn't you, was it, Elie?"

Elie gasped, but then saw the smile on Donald's face and knew he was just being an ass. "Was it you?" She tried to imitate his mean sarcasm, but it just came off as a timid query.

Donald laughed out loud. "I've got too much invested in the prick to have killed him," he said. "Although, that's not to say I hadn't thought about it."

Elie was taking the discussion more seriously than Donald and she pulled the sheet up over her breasts as she sat up in bed. "At first I thought maybe his wife killed him," she said, "but then I heard about how it was done. She could never have done that."

"She could've had him killed," prompted Donald.

"Yeah, I guess, but I suppose you're right, and it was one of the investors."

Donald climbed out of bed, signaling an end to the conversation about the murder. He walked out to the lanai. Elie got up and wrapped a *pareo* around her, Tahitian style. She went out to the lanai and sat next to Donald. A child on the beach squealed with delight as she ran from the breaking surf. Elie watched her run back and forth, daring the ocean to get her.

"So what'm I going to do?" she finally asked. "Can I run away? Can you get me a new identity or anything like that? I'll go away with you if you want." She knew she sounded childish and pleading.

"Whoa, hold on, babe. Let's talk this out and discuss your options. Calm down." He patted her arm as he would a child.

Donald got up and uncorked a bottle of chardonnay and poured two glasses. He wore only his boxers. Both of them still glistened from the sweat of their lovemaking. He set the wine on the glass-top of the lanai table, then he sat in a chair opposite Elie. He took a sip.

"One, you can run, but, as the saying goes, you can't hide," he said. "I can't help you officially. Obviously, I can tell you where to get fake ID's and shit, but getting out of Hawai'i would be difficult. Besides, if you run, you go from being a potential defendant in a fraud and theft case, to a number one suspect in a murder case. If you run, you'll be assumed to be the murderer." He took another sip of his wine before continuing.

"Do you want the world to think you murdered Laws?"

"Well what the hell, Donald, the world is already going to know I helped him steal from little old ladies." There was venom in her voice, and it rose in pitch. She could feel the tears, so far, held at bay.

"I said calm down. You need to start thinking rationally."

"Yeah, fine. Easy for you to say." She took a gulp of her wine, watched the child play. "Okay, I'm calm," she said.

"Good. Okay. So, my best opinion is that you shouldn't run away. You'd be caught in a matter of days. The flight from the murder jurisdiction could be used in court against you, I think. They'd try to tie you to the murder.

"If you stay, they're probably going to be able to implicate you in Laws' thievery. I suppose you could lie and say you didn't know he wasn't actually investing the money, but from what you told me, they'd be able to bust you on that in no time."

She didn't say anything. She didn't like any of the options Donald was laying out for her so far. The tears started. She couldn't help it. She wiped her eyes.

"If you plead guilty to whatever the theft or fraud or conspiracy charges that they come up with, you'd probably go down fairly light. You don't have a record and you could argue coercion, or something. I don't know, I'm not a lawyer, but it seems to me that you'd even have a shot at probation. If you cooperated with the police and did plead guilty, I'd think they'd go pretty easy on you."

The short time Elie had spent lying in the sun before Donald arrived had cast a pink tint to her face, highlighting tiny freckles. She closed, then reopened her eyes, looking straight at Donald.

"Why'd you have me make that call?" she asked.

The change of topic seemed to have caught Donald off guard. "No reason," he said stiffly. After a beat, he said, "You didn't make that call Elie. That never happened." His voice was stern and he stared hard at her. "Got it?"

She frowned, wondering what that was all about. For a moment, she debated whether to ask him to explain, but then she nodded meekly.

"What do I say about you? About the CIA?"

Donald took a sip of his drink. She watched him carefully. She could sense that he was working hard to choose his words carefully, as if she already knew that she'd be thrown to the wolves.

"You can't say anything about me or who I work for. I don't exist. You were sworn to secrecy on this. If you pull us in on this mess it'd do you no good, and it would do serious damage; not just to me personally." He paused dramatically. "There's national security involved here."

Elie's face was a mess. There were tears and sun oil and mascara smeared on a sorrowful canvas of skin. She took a sip of wine and stared at Donald without saying anything. She made no attempt to wipe her face.

"Let's look at it this way," Donald continued. "The records of the business are clean of any reference to the CIA. We didn't run Laws or tell him how to do his business. Shit, I didn't even know he was out-and-out stealing all the freaking money until I started going out with you. The fact that we may've used his corporations from time to time has nothing whatsoever to do with whether he was ripping people off." He paused and took a deep breath. He kept his eyes glued on her, as if he was trying to measure how she was reacting to his spiel.

"Believe me Elie, disclosing our connection would only hurt you . . . seriously." She knew a threat when she heard one. She looked out at the ocean. The tears blurred her vision.

"Besides," he said softly, "when you came to Africa with me, I told you to get the hell away from him before the shit hit the fan. Remember?"

Donald stopped talking and waited for Elie's reaction. She sipped her wine and looked out at the ocean again. The tears streamed down her face. Donald kept his mouth shut, and didn't push any further.

Finally, Elie turned back to Donald. She smiled a sad smile.

"Yeah, I remember." Her voice was sarcastic and sounded tired. She'd accompanied him to Kenya as a kind of vacation. She knew he was transferring money from Laws' Hong Kong corporation to somebody in Africa, but she didn't know any details. Laws knew she was having an affair with Donald and he'd urged her to take some time off and go with him.

"You could use a little vacation," Laws had said, unnaturally nice. "And while you're at it, you can let me know when the money transfer is *pau*. When it's done our commission will be huge, and we're in desperate need of a cash infusion right now." Even though Laws had asked her to spy on her new lover, she jumped at the chance to get away.

Now she said, "I'll go back, Donald. I don't know yet if I'll plead guilty to whatever they charge me with or fight it. I'll have to talk to my attorney first. But I won't say anything about you. Or the CIA. You're right. What would it get me except more publicity?" She paused and seemed to think some more.

"In fact, as I think about it, I could see you assholes denying everything, making me out to be some whacko. You'd do that, wouldn't you?"

Donald didn't answer. He stared down at his glass of wine.

"Answer me dammit! That's exactly what you'd do, isn't it?" The pitch and the volume of her voice rose and the anger flashed in her eyes. She'd been literally fucked into committing crimes for Maynard Laws and now she'd been fucked into keeping silent about the one thing that she'd tried to rationalize as having legitimized Laws' operation.

Donald's soft, almost gentle, response made it all the more menacing.

"Yeah, Elie. That's exactly what we'd have to do. You've no evidence of our involvement. You'd be made to look like a psycho. The Agency would have no choice but to protect itself."

Elie laughed. It was a short, staccato laugh of derision. A trail of slime hung from her nose. She wiped at it carelessly.

"Everyone has to protect themselves. Laws is protected: the son-of-a-bitch is dead. You're protected because the CIA will protect you. But Elie can hang. That's about it, isn't it?" She held her wine glass in front of her face and seemed to talk to it.

"You know, after Laws had used me and manipulated me so that I was part of the shit he was doing, I was afraid to run away. I didn't know who to turn to. I know I should've left. He couldn't have done anything to me without busting himself. I mean, I knew some day, when he got busted, they might've come after me too, but I would've had a chance. I could've said I left because I didn't want to be a criminal." She swiped at the tears, which smeared the oil and the mascara. She looked like a crazy woman.

Donald said nothing.

"I was too afraid to go to the police because Maynard had convinced me that I'd be arrested too. I realize now that I could've cooperated with the police and gotten, whatchacallit, immunity, but even then, I would've been humiliated and ridiculed. People just don't voluntarily ruin their lives.

"Maynard kept telling me we were going to be protected, that this was all a CIA cover. I didn't believe him until I met you." She directed her gaze at Donald briefly, but she looked back at her glass when she resumed talking.

"God, I was so vulnerable, Donald. I suppose you knew that. That's your business after all, isn't it? I don't know what you wanted from me.

Just the sex?" She held up her hand as if to warn him off attempting any answer. She shook her head from side to side. "When I think about how I threw myself at you. I thought you really wanted me. I thought you cared about me." She snorted a derisive laugh. "Hell, I thought you even loved me." She looked at him again.

"When I knew for sure who was working with us, it allowed me to regain a little bit of my self-esteem. Maybe I wasn't such a rotten person. After all, you guys know everything. You must've known that Maynard was stealing all that money. So it must've been kinda okay. I mean, it was like I was really working for the CIA. Know what I mean?" Her eyes were pleading.

"Yeah, Elie, I know," Donald said softly,

"You should've left me alone. Maybe I'd a gotten out. You sucked me further and further into Maynard's toilet until I was completely covered with shit, just like you said I'd be, didn't you?"

Elie went silent, still staring into her glass. She sat like that for several minutes. Donald stared out to sea. The little girl and her family were gone. Finally, Elie wiped her face again and looked at him.

"Go away now, Donald. I'll do my part. I'm the sacrificial whore."

Donald didn't move, like he wasn't sure if it was over.

"I said go away, goddammit!" She flashed to anger and her face looked hard and ugly.

"Get out—now!" Her voice was loud, shrill. Donald got up, went inside and dressed. He ventured one last glance as he was shutting the door. Elie was bent over, sobbing.

Chapter Nine

Pancho was slowly digging out from the backlog of work that had piled up during the last trial. Long days and nights at the office were finally paying off. As he strolled back to his office from a motion at circuit court, he decided it was too beautiful an afternoon to spend in the office. Instead of spending the rest of the day immersed in files, he'd return a couple of calls, then head back to his Diamond Head condo, do a quick change, and surf for as long as he wanted. He and Paula had a date to go to dinner in Waikiki that night.

When he walked into the office Susan was on the phone, but she smiled at him as she handed him the stack of pink 'while you were out' slips. He leafed through them as he walked to his office. There were three calls from Brian Flannigan, an attorney he knew slightly from Bar Association meetings. If Pancho recalled correctly, Flannigan did mostly business law. He dialed the number as soon as he was seated at his desk.

"Yeah, Brian, it's Pancho, what's up?"

"Oh man, I've got a biggie for you, Pancho." Flannigan's voice was excited. "How'd you like to defend the man accused of murdering Maynard Laws?"

Pancho unconsciously sat up straight. His pulse quickened. This *was* big. It was more than big. It had all the earmarks of Hawaii's case of the century. He kept his voice under control, hiding his excitement.

"Who's been charged?"

"A man named Reggie Bellows. Nice guy. I represented him on some corporate stuff. He's in jail now. He doesn't sound so good."

"Who would? What do you mean jail? Is he at cellblock or O triple C?"

"What's what?"

"Cellblock is at the police station. It's where he'd be if he was just arrested. It's too late today for him to go in front of a judge if he hasn't done so already. In that case, he'll stay in cellblock until tomorrow morning. O triple C is Oah'u Community Correctional Center, the prison, which is where he'd be if he'd already had his initial court appearance."

"Must be cellblock then, because he just got arrested this afternoon. Can you go see him?"

"Sure. Do you know anything else?"

"About why he was arrested? No, except that he said bail is set at two million. That's pretty high isn't it?"

"Not that high, considering the crime and the high exposure of the case."

"Well, thanks. Let me know if there's anything I can do. I don't know if he killed Laws or not, but I always liked Reggie."

"Okay, thanks Brian, I appreciate the ref—"

"Oh, Pancho, one more thing I guess I should tell you, although I suppose Reggie will anyway."

"Yeah?"

"Reggie lost a ton of money with Laws. I don't know the exact amount, but I'm under the impression it was around a mil."

"A million dollars?"

"Yup."

"Yikes. I guess they got the motive part covered. Okay, thanks again, Brian."

Pancho hung up, the thoughts of surfing gone in the new rush of adrenaline. Losing a million dollars would certainly be a reason to murder someone. He wondered if this guy, Bellows, had any money left. This one would have to cost big dollars. Although the press Pancho would get on the case would be worth big bucks, he had just received an enormous amount of press and didn't need to be working for the publicity. A case like this would take huge amounts of time, and time was all Pancho had to sell.

He picked up his phone and pressed the intercom button.

"Yes, master?" Pancho smiled. Obviously there were no clients in the reception area.

"Is Drew still around?"

"No, he left. What's up?"

"I've got to go down to cellblock. They picked up a guy for Maynard Laws' murder and he's asking for me."

Susan grunted ambiguously. "Who is it?"

"Guy named Reggie Bellows. Ever hear of him?"

"No. But it sounds like it could be a lot of work." Pancho didn't know if she meant that in a good way or bad way. He knew exactly what it would have meant if he'd still been married to Ellen. Susan hadn't hidden the fact that she'd agreed with his ex that he worked too hard and too long, but when the marriage had finally failed, Susan stopped lecturing and was there for Pancho every difficult step of the way.

"Yeah, well, first things first. I can't be doing this for free and I don't know if this guy has any money."

Pancho hung up and gathered a notepad, pen and a retainer agreement to take to cellblock. He tried to keep his excitement under control. There was a lot to talk about and consider before he would take a case like this. Besides the money, which was a reality that could not be ignored, there was the question of guilt and character and circumstances. While he couldn't very well refuse to represent guilty defendants, since the vast majority *were* guilty, Pancho nonetheless had his own personal criterion as to which new cases, particularly murder cases, he would take. He'd never tried to verbalize it, though. Much of it was gut instinct.

Despite his unshakable belief in the criminal justice system, which required that all defendants be represented by qualified counsel, he was finally in a position where he could pick and choose his cases. Forgotten was his previous conviction that he wouldn't want to be the one defending Laws' murderer. It was exactly what he wanted.

Pancho walked to his car and smiled as he thought about how he decided on which cases to take. It was almost ridiculous to try to explain. How did he, how *could* he, draw distinctions between murderers? Were some better than others? Would he represent a murderer who seemed nice but who was nonetheless guilty?

More times than he could count over the years, he'd been confronted by people who couldn't understand how he could represent criminals. He remembered one particularly contentious dinner party at which several of the men and women had all but called him a sleaze-ball. He'd drunk too much wine, and so rather than appease and diffuse, he pontificated.

"My heroes in the law, and they should be yours, too," he had said, pointing with his wine glass to his antagonists, "are the career public defenders who spend their lives representing the scum of the earth. Every day these men and women are in the trenches, providing their clients with the protection the Constitution requires. Think about it: if we didn't have these people doing that dirty work, and believe me, it isn't easy or nice or fun, our whole system of criminal justice would grind to a halt." He paused and took another sip of wine before continuing.

"They may not be on the side of the angels. They may not be able to go to dinner parties like this and say they're the good guys, like the prosecutors who're putting the bad guys in jail. But without them we would not have the best and the fairest criminal justice system in the world, because without someone to provide the criminals with effective representation, our laws would require us to set them free."

In the end, of course, no one's mind was changed and Pancho happily knew that there were several more parties to which he could count on not being invited.

As he drove down King Street from his downtown office, Pancho tried not to get too far ahead of himself. He could feel the excitement he always felt at the prospect of a big new case, but, at the same time, he knew what a huge undertaking it would be. He'd just come out of a long trial. He didn't feel fully rejuvenated yet. He was just starting his relationship with Paula. There were any number of reasons not to get involved in this one.

By the time Reggie Bellows was led into the interview room to meet with Pancho, he'd been in custody for two hours. He was a squat, solidly built man, with salt and pepper hair. He looked as if he'd been in custody for two days. His hair was disheveled and his expensive linen shirt was wrinkled and soaked with sweat. His eyes looked dazed. He'd been arrested and booked too late to have his initial appearance in court. Now he would have to wait until tomorrow.

When they were seated and alone in the small, drab room, Pancho introduced himself. "I'm the attorney that Brian Flannigan recommended."

"Yeah, yes, you gotta get me out of here. Can you?" The daze in the eyes was replaced by a look of pleading desperation. Pancho shook his head.

"Not today, unless you got some significant spare change lying around."

The desperate hope left Reggie's eyes as fast as it had appeared. He looked down at the top of the scratched metal table. Then he looked up at Pancho.

"What's happening to me?" Pancho couldn't tell if Reggie meant why was he in jail, or why was he falling apart.

"You're being charged with murder in the second degree. Even though that may not sound as bad as murder one, it's pretty much as bad as it gets without murdering a cop or a judge."

"You trying to cheer me up?"

"I'm trying to get you to get your act together. You're in serious trouble, and I'm going to need your help. Are you okay?"

"Yeah, I guess. Jeez, I've been in a lot worse dumps than this and called it a hotel, but for some reason I just can't handle this." He made a sweeping gesture with his right arm. "I'm sorry. I—" Reggie swallowed and breathed deep. "This is a frigging nightmare, man. I can't believe it. I was just about to board a flight to Bangkok when the cops arrested me." He stopped and stared at Pancho. "Are you good?"

"They say I am. I think I am." Pancho coughed into his arm and then pulled the legal pad in front of him. "Let's get down to business. I'm going to tell you what's going to happen. I don't want you to tell me whether you did or did not kill Maynard Laws right now. When I ask the question, I'll expect a truthful answer. Okay?"

"But I—" Pancho held up his hand to cut him off.

"Okay?"

"Yeah, okay."

"Fine. One more thing before we start. I want you to understand that even though I'll be with you tomorrow, and even if you decide you can afford me and want to hire me, I will not make my final decision on whether I'll represent you until after you and I have a more comprehensive meeting, which we can do after court. Once I make that decision, I'm all in—unless you violate one of my golden rules, that is. Are you good with that?"

Reggie nodded tentatively. "You mean you may not take my case?"

Pancho smiled. "You wouldn't want me to take your case unless I believed in you, would you?"

Reggie half-heartedly shook his head.

"Well I won't know that until we talk in detail tomorrow. Fair enough?"

"I guess so. I mean, sure, I understand."

Pancho smiled again, wanting to put Reggie at ease. "Don't worry. My initial impression of you is good and that goes a long way with me. I just need to keep my options open until I learn a little more about you and what evidence they have against you." He paused. "Besides, we don't even know yet if you want me."

The two men looked at each other for a moment before Pancho continued. "So, tomorrow morning you'll be taken to district court for an initial appearance. It'll be at 8:30. I'll be there to lend you moral support, but there's nothing that either you or I will do. You'll be handed a written complaint of the charges against you. You will not be asked to plead guilty or not guilty. Do not say or do anything other than to acknowledge that you understand the charges. Okay?"

"Okay."

"You will then be taken to O triple C, the prison. You'll be kept in a separate area from the inmates who've been convicted. Within two days, you'll have a preliminary hearing, again at the district court. You still won't be asked to plead guilty or not guilty. The prelim is to find out if the State has enough evidence to bind you over to circuit court on the charges." Pancho paused, watching Reggie closely.

"Are you following me?" he asked.

"Yes."

"At the time of the prelim we can learn what kind of evidence they have against you. I can ask questions of the witnesses, but we will not put on any defense."

"Why not? If we win that, I go free don't I?"

"First, I won't have a defense to present, not yet. Second, even if the charges are tossed out at the prelim, the prosecutor can still go to the grand jury and get an indictment against you. I don't even get to go into the grand jury room, let alone examine witnesses. A halfway decent prosecutor with a few shreds of evidence could indict Mickey Mouse if he wanted to." Pancho studied Reggie for a moment to make sure he was getting it all. Reggie looked to be listening intently, so Pancho continued.

"All I can do at the prelim is attack their witnesses as best I can. If I can shoot enough holes in the prosecutor's case, the judge may not find probable cause to bind you over. You'd be free until, or unless, they indicted you. But realize here and now that the chances of a judge not finding probable cause are slim. I'll know more what our chances are after we talk in detail about the case tomorrow. Got that?"

"Yeah, I got it. Meanwhile, I rot in jail?"

"We'll be filing a Motion to Reduce Bail as soon as we can. Which brings us to money. I don't work cheap and a murder case will mean I'll have to turn down a lot of other cases for a while. You'll also need money and collateral for bail. Do you have money?"

"Some. How much do you charge?"

"Two hundred fifty thousand. I'll spend up to fifty in expenses out of that. Thereafter, the expenses must be paid on top of the two fifty by you. If I spend less than fifty thousand in expenses, the balance is not refunded, but is additional fees. Can you handle that?"

Reggie had rolled his head back and was staring at the ceiling.

"No," he said. It was almost a whisper. "I don't think so. I . . . I have money in a bank in Switzerland. Depending what the franc is at right now, I have somewhere around two hundred thousand, I guess. I have twenty-five thousand in traveler's checks that they took from me when I was arrested. I have five thousand in First Hawaiian Bank. I have a penthouse condo in Makiki worth about seven fifty, but I have a big mortgage on it that has to be paid. I don't know how much I could borrow on it under these circumstances. And I have about thirty thousand dollars' worth of furniture in a warehouse on Sand Island Road.

"That's not enough is it? And if I were to get out, I've got to live."

"Do you have any family?"

"No."

"No one?"

"Not a soul. My parents are dead and I'm the only kid. Whatever other relatives I have, I don't know."

"Any friends who could take you in while this is going on?"

"No. Just acquaintances who wouldn't want to have anything to do with me now. An ex-girlfriend who hates my guts." As he answered the questions, Reggie's voice had gone softer and softer, as if he were only now realizing how empty his life was.

Pancho had been doing some mental calculations. He made a decision.

"Okay, look, if we take the two hundred K for my fee, we can use the twenty-five thousand in traveler's checks for bail money, if we can get the bail down to two fifty or less. Your condo can be collateral for that. I have to tell you, though, that with no family or other strong connections to Hawai'i, the chances of getting bail reduced anywhere near that level is a real longshot.

"If we do get bail down and you get out, the five grand in the bank can go toward your living expenses and you can sell the furniture and apply the money to legal costs or living expenses; we can work that out. You may be able to get some kind of small loan against the condo to cover the mortgage while this is going on. I can also take a lien for the balance of my fees against the condo." Pancho looked up from his notes and looked Reggie in the eyes.

"I know that takes everything you've got, but I can't work for less than that. I can give you some names of good attorneys who'll represent you for around a hundred to a hundred and fifty grand."

Reggie looked like he wanted to vomit, but he nodded.

"All right. I want to go with you." He let out a nasty sounding half-grunt, half-chuckle. "It's like that prick, Laws, is reaching out from the grave to pick me clean of whatever he didn't already get."

Pancho ignored the remark and brought Reggie back to business. Reggie gave Pancho his Swiss account numbers and instructed him on how to accomplish the withdrawals. Pancho would have a power of attorney drawn up to give him the ability to deal with the rest of Reggie's affairs while he was still in jail.

Pancho got up to leave.

"Aren't you going to ask about me and Laws?"

"Not today. We'll have plenty of time. I want to start doing some background checking, on both you and Laws, and I want to get things rolling on these money transfers. I want you to get past the shock of all this so we can talk in detail. Okay?"

Reggie was silent for a moment. Pancho had seen the look of panic on his clients' faces when he left them in jail the first time, and he could see it on Reggie's face. He waited patiently for Reggie to work things through. Finally, he nodded to Pancho. "You're the boss. I'll see you in the morning?"

"I'll be there. See you."

Pancho left the cellblock and decided to head back to his office. It was too late to go surfing. He might as well get some work done before his dinner date.

As he drove, his thoughts returned to Reggie Bellows. Most clients proclaim their innocence the moment Pancho meets them, before Pancho can stop them from saying anything. Reggie hadn't done that, which was fine. Pancho didn't want to hear what Reggie had to say about guilt or innocence until he was ready for it. If there was to be a confession, Pancho wanted to be sure that it was in a controlled situation, and only after Reggie fully understood the implications of making a confession.

He turned onto Bishop Street and drove the rest of the way to his office garage thinking about his probable new client. It was not a good situation in which to form first impressions and Pancho had a feeling that there was much, much more to Reggie Bellows than what he'd seen so far. There was an underlying toughness about the man that belied the sensitivity and self-pity to which he seemed to have fallen prey. Nonetheless, Pancho felt sure that he'd be willing to take him on as a client.

When he reached his office, the usually unflappable Susan looked at him with what he took to be a mixture of relief and irritation. All the phone lines were buzzing.

"Please hold." She looked tired. "Thank God you're back. The phones are going nuts. Every reporter in town, plus some from out of town have been calling. Word sure gets out fast on the ol' coconut wireless. That Flannigan guy must have spread the word that you were involved. What do you want to do?"

"Tell them I have no comment at this time." He looked at his watch. "It's almost quitting time anyway. Why don't you deal with whoever you have on hold now, then get out of here?"

"I was hoping you'd say that." She returned to the phone.

Pancho went into his office, immediately picked up his phone, and punched in some numbers. "Hello Drew? It's . . . yeah, geez, how'd you hear so quickly?" The speed at which things spread around this town never failed to amaze him.

"Well, I need you. Can you be here tomorrow at 1:00? I have the initial hearing at 8:30, then I want to spend the rest of the morning with Bellows." He paused, listening. "Good, see you then."

Drew Tulafono had played professional football with the San Diego Chargers until his knees gave out. He'd moved to Hawai'i ten years ago and hooked up with another ex-football player who ran a successful private investigations firm. Drew found that he had a knack for the work and enjoyed the challenges each case presented. Pancho hired him to work on a money laundering case six years ago and they'd immediately hit it off. They quickly became best of friends and Pancho now used him exclusively whenever he needed an investigator.

Pancho then called Brian Flannigan and asked for his help on drawing up the power of attorney and arranging the financial transactions. There wasn't much more he could do until tomorrow. He tried not to think of his new client sitting in the holding cell at HPD.

* * *

Three hours later Pancho pulled into the parking lot on Seaside and walked to the Suntory restaurant. Ordinarily, he would have parked at his condo on Diamond Head and walked into Waikiki, but he'd gotten involved in writing a motion and lost track of the time. *So what else is new*, he thought, and he had a brief, guilty vision of Ellen, his ex. She'd always seemed to be waiting for him. He'd vowed to himself not to make the same mistake with Paula. He glanced at his watch and took a deep breath. He was only a few minutes late.

The tourists were out in full force in their shorts and Aloha shirts. Sunburns abounded. He walked past a golf shop in which everything was advertised in Japanese. A male and female duo on a small stage were singing the *Hawaiian Wedding Song*.

The Royal Hawaiian Shopping Center had been built on Kalakaua Avenue in front of the Royal Hawaiian Hotel. It blocked the beautiful old 'pink lady,' so that it could no longer be seen from the street, but the Center had recently been renovated to open up and show off the expanse of lawn and gardens between the Center and the Hotel. He climbed the stairs to the restaurant and saw Paula sitting in the bar, to the right of the entrance.

"Hey, sweetness, howzit?" Pancho bent down to kiss her.

"I'm fine, now that I'm here and have a drink. Wasn't that traffic awful?"

"Yeah." Pancho sat and ordered a chardonnay from the kimono-clad waitress. Paula was *hapa-haole*, part Japanese and part Caucasian, with some Hawaiian and various other ethnicities mixed in for good measure. She had big oval eyes, jet black thick hair, cut short, and sensuous, full lips. To Pancho, her body was perfection. She was about 5'7", had a tiny waist, and had perfectly shaped medium-sized breasts. Seeing her, and feeling the physical effect it had on him, confirmed again to Pancho that he was falling in love with her. They'd been seeing each other for four months, and the relationship had gotten progressively more serious. Neither had dated anyone else after the first two weeks. Both of them had, however, been married before, and were cautious about acknowledging the commitment they each knew was forming.

Paula was a stockbroker with Morgan Stanley. She'd been born and raised in Honolulu and her father was a successful businessman. She had no brothers and sisters and her father spoiled her rotten as a child. Somehow, however, she'd come through it as a charming, frugal, and, most astonishingly, humble person. Pancho had always figured that it must be hard for a beautiful woman to be humble.

Paula was thirty-four years old, a few years younger than Pancho. She and Pancho had met at a wedding reception for a mutual friend at Oah'u Country Club. Pancho had seen her from across the lanai, where the reception was being held, and immediately decided that he had to meet her.

Despite being fearless in court, however, Pancho was relatively shy with women to whom he had not been introduced and to whom he was attracted. He still wasn't used to being single. Pancho didn't see anyone he knew talking to Paula and therefore couldn't count on an introduction. He decided to take the direct approach when he saw she was alone.

"Hi, my name's Pancho McMartin, and I'd like to meet you." He had held out his hand to shake. Either that would commit her to make contact with him or force her to be rude, and he couldn't conceive of this gorgeous woman being intentionally rude.

"Hi. I'm Paula Mizuno." Her smile showed amusement.

"What's funny?"

"I like your direct approach. It's refreshing. Besides, I already know who you are. You're the attorney, right?"

"That be me. It's good to know my infamy is spreading. What do you do?"

"I'm a financial consultant with Morgan Stanley, otherwise known as a stockbroker. Can I interest you in some stocks, T-bills, mutual funds?" Her smile was captivating.

"Oh, give me one of each, to go."

They chatted on and on until they noticed there were only a handful of people left at the reception. The shadows from the tall paper-bark trees lining the third fairway were fading into the dark green of the grass. The Honolulu city lights were beginning to twinkle in the view down the valley toward the ocean. Their banter had been light and amusing. Pancho surprised himself at the ease with which he was able to communicate at this level of the relationship. He was horrible at small talk, but the thrust and parry of the conversation with Paula had clear, discernible undertones. They were, in a way, like two fighters, feeling each other out. *'Yes, there is wit there'*. *'Hmm, intelligent'*. *'Oh yeah, great sarcasm'*. The deeper things would have to wait for a more intimate setting.

Pancho asked Paula to go out following the reception, but she had to decline due to prior commitments. She didn't wait for him to ask about another time, however, as she volunteered that the next night was free.

One of the things that impressed Pancho was that Paula didn't ask him about his name within the first five minutes of meeting him. It wasn't until they were having dinner on their first official date that she raised the question.

"So, I'm guessing that you're pretty sick of having to explain it, but you have to admit that the name Pancho McMartin, for a *haole* guy, is pretty intriguing." Her eyes sparkled and, to Pancho, her small smile seemed mischievous.

Pancho took a sip of wine and smiled back at her.

"Yeah, there was actually one point in my life that I think I had a real chip on my shoulder about having to explain my name to every person I ever met, but I'm over that now . . . mostly." He didn't say more, instead taking another sip of wine while he watched her face.

Paula played along, taking her own sip of wine while maintaining eye contact with Pancho. The silence was deafening.

Finally, Paula said, "Sooo, how about those Giants?"

Both of them cracked up.

"You gonna make me beg?"

Pancho laughed again. "Nah. As long as you promise never to make me beg."

Paula nearly spit out her mouthful of wine.

"*Mister* McMartin," she said in mock shock, with a hint of a blush on her face. "Why this is only our first date."

Pancho held up both hands in surrender.

"Sorry, I couldn't resist, the set-up was so good." He could see she was fine with his risky joke.

"Anyway," he said, "I was born in Taos, New Mexico. My parents were kind of strange, especially my Dad. They were pretty much original hippies. Taos has a big Hispanic and Indian population and I think Dad had some bizarre notion that if my name was Latino sounding, I would get along better in school." Pancho couldn't help but laugh and shake his head. "That, or they were both stoned on acid when they named me.

"So here I was, some *haole* kid with a last name that couldn't be more white, going to school with the name Pancho. Poor Dad had no idea what an idiotic idea it was. I was beat up with regularity until I became fluent in Spanish and learned to fight. By high school, most of my pals were the same guys who'd beaten me up in elementary and junior high school." Pancho shrugged and smiled.

"And, to top it all off, I've been explaining my name ever since."

Paula smiled. "Well, if it's any consolation, I like the name. It's weird, I know, but I like it anyway. Where are your parents now?"

Pancho could feel himself falling hard for this beautiful woman.

"They live in Santa Fe now. They got over their hippie phase and Mom wrote a self-help book that sold millions. Now they collaborate on pumping out these ridiculous self-help books and e-books and make a shit-load of money. They sold-out completely. They live in a million dollar adobe style house in the foothills, just outside of town." Pancho ran his hand through his long brown hair and scrunched up his tanned, sharp featured face. He gave Paula a half-grin.

"If they start voting Republican, I'm going to disown them."

They talked some more about Pancho, and how he had ended up in Hawai'i. He'd known he was going to be an attorney from elementary school. He wasn't quite sure how he'd known. Maybe he'd felt the injustice of being beat up over a stupid name. Maybe he took his mother seriously when she'd say that he should become an attorney because he loved to argue.

When Pancho graduated from high school in Taos, he knew he wanted to get out and see more of the real world. He went to UCLA and majored in political science. From there he went to law school at Boalt Hall at Berkeley. He was thirty-nine years old, and had been practicing law for fifteen years.

By the time that first date was over, it was a given to both of them that they would be seeing each other again.

"So, how'd it go today? How'd the market do?" Pancho asked. They were seated in the *tepanyaki* side of the Suntory restaurant, looking at the menus.

"Nothing much, down twenty points. How about you? Good day?"

"Great. I may be representing the accused murderer of Maynard Laws."

Pancho could see the look of surprise on Paula's face. "Wow." She tilted her head slightly and smiled. "That's a good thing, I assume?"

"Well, it'll be a huge case. Whether it'll be good or bad for me remains to be seen."

She nodded. "I lost two clients to Maynard Laws. Both of them gradually withdrew their entire accounts to go with Laws. I tried to caution them about putting everything in one place, but they both kept raving about the huge returns they were getting." She shook her head at the memory. "There was no talking to them."

Their attention was diverted by the chef preparing their meal on the grill built into their table. The chef worked without the theatrical flourish of the Benihana chefs, but with speed, precision and skill. First, he cooked the zucchini, potatoes and onions. Then the cubes of Chateaubriand and, finally, the scampi. He covered both the steak and the scampi with a pepper sauce and gave them each a helping.

As they ate and chatted on about their respective days, Pancho thought about Reggie Bellows. A million dollars lost. The man responsible brutally murdered. Pancho was looking forward to hearing Reggie's story.

The next morning, after the initial appearance in district court where the formal charge of Murder in the Second Degree was read, Reggie was transported to the Oah'u Community Correctional Center, commonly called O triple C, which was on Dillingham Boulevard in Kalihi. It was not one of the more scenic parts of Honolulu.

OCCC itself was a combination of the real old and the fairly old. The original facility looked like the classic prison, with concrete walls topped by barbed wire and guard towers. It was a hideous shade of dirt red, which was peeling in more places than not. Built adjacent to it were the newer modules, which at least gave the appearance of a more civilized outlook toward corrections. But OCCC was overcrowded and rife with drugs and weapons. Rape and assault were not uncommon.

Reggie was placed in Module 5, the holding area for pre-trial felons. He met with Pancho in an interview room.

"Time to get down to business, Reggie. How you doing?"

"Much better than I was yesterday. This morning was a bitch, with all those reporters in the courtroom. It's all so embarrassing. Thanks for being there with me."

Pancho could see that Reggie would be all right. He was clearly a resilient man, and had worked his way through the mental stress of the arrest and booking procedure.

"Okay. What I want to do first is give you my standard rap on our relationship. It will be the most important relationship in your life, and we can't screw around with each other. There isn't time.

"You and I have what is called an attorney-client relationship. That means everything you tell me is absolutely confidential unless you authorize me to release it. If you tell me you shot Laws and cut his head and arms off, there isn't a damn thing I can or will do about it except figure out a way to provide the best possible defense for you."

Reggie nodded and looked as if he were about to say something, but Pancho held up his hand to stop him.

"When you tell me something, I'll expect you to tell me the truth. Do us both a favor and don't lie to me. It'll only haunt you later. A defense built on lies will come crumbling down as surely as a sand castle. Do you read?"

"Yeah, I read you," he said, "but what if you decide not to represent me after we meet today? Does the privilege still exist?"

Pancho gave Reggie a crooked smile. It was nice to have an intelligent client. He nodded. "As of right now I represent you and the privilege exists and cannot be undone even if one of us terminates the relationship."

Reggie nodded his head in understanding. When he said nothing further, Pancho continued.

"If you tell me you killed Laws, I'll defend you as aggressively as if you'd said you were innocent. You're entitled by law to such a defense. But I will not put you on the witness stand to testify. I will not have a client of mine commit perjury. Got it?"

"Got it."

"All right then. First, I want to hear your life story. Tell me who Reggie Bellows is. Start with your childhood and stop with your investing with Laws. I'll want to take you through that part carefully. Give me the good and the bad of your life. I'll interrupt as little as possible."

Slowly, and guarded at first, Reggie told Pancho about his childhood in the Bronx, the street gangs, and about his mother and father. He talked with some emotion about his service in Vietnam, how he loved it and feared it at the same time. After Vietnam, he fulfilled his duty to his father by taking care of him until he died. He was restless then. He missed the rush and the camaraderie of military life, and so he signed up with an agency that sent him out to work as a mercenary in Africa, South America, and even a short stint in the Philippines.

Reggie talked with pride about eventually getting out of the war business and starting the import-export firm that had made him a millionaire—almost. He thought he'd found the love of his life in Marcelina, a young, beautiful Filipina who, it turned out, ditched him as soon as he began having money problems.

Pancho listened, fascinated. Reggie's past was the stuff of books. Pancho could see how the effect of an arrest for murder could have such a devastating effect on someone who took pride in having gone through so much and survived. Reggie was tough, though Pancho suspected there were a few layers of complexity to the man that would take some time to unravel.

There seemed to be a kind of 'push/pull' aspect to Reggie's life that made him different. He survived Vietnam, only to get out of the service and put his life in peril again as a mercenary. He survived the life of a mercenary and became successful at business only to put most of his money at risk with a scam artist. He'd created a relationship with a younger woman, a relationship destined to fail if the money ever gave out.

"All right. We're running out of time now. I know you invested a lot of money with Laws. Let me ask you some direct questions. We'll go into details when I see you again."

Reggie nodded. The telling of his life story appeared to have taken a lot out of him. Pancho suspected that Reggie had just revisited parts of his life he'd meant to keep private.

"Did you know or suspect your money had been lost before Laws was killed?"

"Yes."

"Had you confronted Laws?"

"Yeah. I made a few scenes, rather nasty ones at his office over the last month or so before he was killed."

"Did you ever go to Laws' home?"

"No."

"Where were you on the day Laws was killed?"

"I went driving. I went to Haleiwa, had a beer at Jameson's, then went to Waimea Beach. I hung out there for a couple of hours, then took the long way back, through Kahuku and over Likelike."

"You were alone?"

"Yes."

"Did you meet or talk to anyone?"

"Just the bartender at Jameson's."

"Do you think he'd remember you?"

"He might, I don't know."

Pancho looked down at his notes, then back up at Reggie. "You were leaving town when you were arrested at the airport, yes?"

Reggie nodded.

"And you had twenty-five grand on you at the time?"

Reggie nodded again. "Yeah, I had to go on a buying trip to Thailand. I was seriously low on inventory. I would've had to shut the store down if I didn't go. The money was to buy inventory. That's how I always traveled on buying trips."

Pancho made a couple of notes. "Where'd you get the twenty-five grand? I thought you were out of money."

Reggie snorted dismissively. "That was it, man. That's all I had. If I didn't get some new stuff into the store and sell it quickly, I was going under."

Pancho looked Reggie in the eyes. It was time to wrap it up. Time for the question.

"You're obviously telling me that you didn't kill Laws. Is that right?"

"That's it. I did not kill Laws." Reggie did not blink or look away.

Pancho nodded. It was too early for him to personally decide if he believed Reggie or not. He didn't like the fact that Reggie had said the sentence slowly, without contractions: 'I did not kill Laws.' That was often the way guilty men tried to sound innocent.

He would proceed on the theory that Reggie had told the truth, but he'd been around too long to believe every client who proclaimed his or her innocence. He hoped Reggie was telling the truth. He liked him and tended to believe his story, at least so far, but Pancho knew the police wouldn't have arrested Reggie unless they had something concrete. Either it was something that Reggie knew nothing about, or else he had begun their relationship by lying.

Chapter Ten

Pancho was surprised to see Harry Chang at the prosecutor's table. Harry was a high-level trial attorney and usually didn't do preliminary hearings.

"Hey, Harry, bringing out the big guns on this one, huh?" Pancho placed his soft leather briefcase on his table as he spoke.

Harry grinned back at Pancho. "I just didn't want to miss getting my picture on the tube." He glanced into the gallery and saw the reporters and the camera. On motion, the television media could ask for, and usually received, permission to place a camera in court. Only one camera was allowed, and the media would have to share the video. It was to be expected that there would be cameras at all future proceedings in the case of State of Hawai'i vs. Reginald Bellows.

The sheriff's deputies brought Reggie into court through the side entrance, where he'd been brought up from the district court holding cells.

"All rise, the District Court of the First Circuit, Honolulu Division, is now in session, the Honorable Linda Murchison presiding."

The Judge entered from behind the bench and took a seat. She was in her mid-thirties and healthy but plain looking. Pancho had known her when she was first starting out at the prosecutor's office and knew she started every day with a jog and finished most days paddling an outrigger canoe with the Outrigger Canoe Club. She'd been on the bench for a year and had developed a reputation for fairness. Pancho hoped that one day she would be elevated to the circuit court.

"Be seated."

Pancho made sure Reggie was sitting, while he remained standing, as did Harry Chang. The bailiff called their case and the judge asked counsel to enter their appearances.

"Good afternoon, Your Honor, Harry Chang for the State."

"Good afternoon, Your Honor, Pancho McMartin for the Defendant, Reginald Bellows, who is also present."

"Good afternoon, gentlemen. Mr. Chang, are you ready to proceed?" The Judge's tone was pleasant and polite.

"The State is ready, Your Honor."

"Call your first witness."

"The State calls Sergeant Russell Cabrillo." Harry waited while the bailiff went out to the corridor to call Sergeant Cabrillo.

Cabrillo described having received the call of a possible gunshot. He'd gone to the residence in Portlock and found Officer Lee, who'd been in Hawai'i Kai interviewing witnesses for a burglary case, already at the scene. Together they determined that no one else was on the premises — no one else alive, that is.

He then described the scene at the pool. The courtroom was hushed as he spoke, his official police language making the scene seem almost as gruesome as it really was.

Pancho had Cabrillo pin down the time of the call, the time of his and Lee's arrival on the scene, and the time of the arrival of the lead detective.

A preliminary hearing was like a game. The prosecutor wanted to give away as little as possible about what their case consisted of, offering up only enough to establish probable cause to bind the defendant over to circuit court to stand felony charges.

The defense, on the other hand, wanted to take the opportunity to conduct discovery, to see what kind of evidence the prosecutor actually had. Pancho also wanted the prosecution witnesses to commit themselves to as much detail as possible, so that their testimony would be locked-in for trial.

"Did you find any gun, knife, sword, or machete at the scene, Sergeant Cabrillo?" Pancho asked when it was his turn to question the sergeant.

"No, sir I—" Cabrillo stopped. "Strike that, I did find an air rifle at the scene, but it could not have been the murder weapon."

Pancho's expression turned curious. "An air rifle? Where did you find that?"

"Actually, it was right at the murder scene, leaning up against a side table next to a chaise lounge." Cabrillo scratched his head. "Apparently the decedent liked to shoot at targets with the air rifle."

Pancho thought for a moment. He couldn't see how it would be relevant.

"Did you find any instrument known or suspected to be the murder weapon at the scene?"

"No, sir I did not."

"Thank you Sergeant, that's all I have."

It was ironic, but true, that real life lawyers lived in the shadow of television lawyers. In fact, many attorneys routinely talked to juries about TV lawyers and cop shows during *voir dire*, or jury selection, discouraging any notion that the jury was going to witness a courtroom confession.

The reality was that the defense usually knew little or nothing at the time of the preliminary hearing. It had to be held within forty-eight hours of the initial appearance. No discovery was provided to defense by the prosecutor yet. The defense attorney examined witnesses in court completely in the blind as to what their testimony would be. All the defense attorney had was whatever his client had told him.

Pancho had met with Reggie twice more before the preliminary hearing. They talked in detail about the money invested and presumed lost. Reggie was angry, he said, but he hadn't killed Maynard Laws. He told Pancho he didn't know anything about it except what he'd read in the papers or seen on TV.

Reggie's ignorance troubled Pancho. The police and prosecutors were no dummies. They felt they had enough evidence to charge Reggie with murder. They'd be made to look like idiots if they didn't have enough in a case like this.

The coroner, Dr. Padma Dasari, took the stand next. She was conservatively dressed in a blue linen pantsuit with a white silk blouse. She took her seat in the witness stand and glanced at Pancho. Their eyes met, so fleeting as to be undetectable to everyone else in the courtroom.

Pancho and Dr. Dasari first met several years ago at a charity function at Washington Place, the Governor's mansion. They'd been introduced by the Lieutenant Governor, a mutual friend, and the chemical attraction was immediate and overwhelming. Pancho was still married to Ellen at the time, and he was completely monogamous, his only mistress the law, but his fidelity had nothing to do with the chemistry between him and Dr. Dasari, over which he had no control.

Their eyes had met as they shook hands and the eye contact and the hand shake lasted moments longer than normal. Pancho had been shaken by the impact she'd had on him and he knew with absolute certainty that she felt the same. As they engaged in the usual small talk with several other people present, the two would make occasional eye contact, and each time it was as if each had been pulsed with an electrical current.

"So, what do you like to do besides cut up dead bodies?" Asked one of the men who had been hanging around, clearly trying to be humorous. She glanced at the man, but her look returned to Pancho as she answered the question.

"Actually, I have an interest in the science of Human Factors." She nodded toward Pancho with a coy smile. "I'm sure Mr. McMartin knows what that is."

Pancho smiled back and turned slightly to the man who'd asked the question. "Basically it's the study of human social behavior. We use it sometimes in the law to try to show how someone would react in a given situation." He turned back to Dr. Dasari. "Maybe someday, when you retire from the Medical Examiner's office, I can use you as an expert witness."

Their eyes met again and she smiled, broadly this time. "I'll look forward to the day."

As Pancho was preparing to leave the event, he took Dr. Dasari aside to say goodbye. "It saddens me that the next time we meet will probably be in court as adversaries," he said. "So I want to apologize in advance if I ever upset you or make you uncomfortable by my cross-examination of you."

Dr. Dasari looked at his serious face, still holding his hand, and laughed aloud, her dark eyes sparkling with good humor. She spoke with a singsong, but clipped accent. "Yes, I suppose most, if not all, of our future meetings will be in court. But don't worry, I'm a big girl and I understand how the game is played. If you ever catch me up in court, I'm thinking that I'll probably deserve whatever I get." Her voice softened. "It was a pleasure." And with that, she gently withdrew her hand and walked away.

The two had never spoken privately again, yet over the several times they'd met in court since, there was always the ephemeral eye contact before getting down to business, each time affirming for both the inexplicable magnetism.

Dr. Dasari turned her attention to the prosecutor. She testified that the probable cause of death was the decapitation. She described the amputation of the head and the arms and rendered her opinion that the amputation had been accomplished by a sword or machete, wielded by a man or exceptionally strong woman. She further testified that Laws had been shot in the abdomen first, with a .38 caliber bullet. This shot would not have been fatal, except over the passage of a long period of time if untreated, but would have had the effect of rendering Laws disabled, so as to accomplish the amputation.

"Dr. Dasari," said Pancho, a shade more deference in his tone than he'd shown for the other witnesses, "you can't state with specificity when the gunshot occurred in relation to the amputation, can you?"

She answered in her clipped, rhythmic accent, pleasing to the ear and easy to understand. "Well, I can state with reasonable medical certainty that the shot was first. There were gunshot burns on the abdomen that suggested a shooting on dry land. Our best analysis is that once the arms and head were severed, the torso fell or was pushed immediately into the pool. This is based on various factors, including the large blood loss in the pool. Our conclusion was that he had been shot prior to the amputations."

"Couldn't it have been possible to shoot the victim immediately after the amputation, while the torso was still being held, and to then allow it to fall into the pool?"

Pancho could see her think about the question before answering.

"Yes, it would be technically possible. I think that would require the use of an accomplice though."

"Why?"

"Well, the gunshot appeared to have been from a range of approximately five feet. Had the amputations occurred first, the torso would have been incapable of standing on its own. This means someone would have had to hold the torso while someone else shot it. Shooting a person without a head or arms doesn't make any logical sense."

"Dr. Dasari, as you and I both know, murder doesn't always fit into a clear logical pattern, does it?"

"Objection, argumentative."

"I withdraw the question, Your Honor." Pancho noticed a glancing smile cross Dr. Dasari's face.

"Dr. Dasari, have you ruled out an accomplice?"

She shook her head. "From a purely medical perspective, I have not and cannot. From any other evidentiary perspective, you will have to ask the police detectives." Pancho knew Dr. Dasari could thrust and parry with the best of the best on the witness stand. Putting aside the attraction that Pancho had long ago acknowledged to himself, he also admired her professionally, both from a medical and an ethical point of view.

"Doctor, let's assume that the victim was shot before the amputations. Can you tell us how long before the arms and head was severed that the victim was shot?"

"Not with any certainty. Again, although it is not purely from the medical perspective, we sometimes do take into consideration extrinsic factors to assist us in our forensic analysis. In this case, we have the fact that a neighbor called in a shot sound at 2:24 p.m. The first officer was on the scene by 2:55 p.m. There is no evidence, medical or otherwise, that I am aware of, to contradict the conclusion that the victim had been shot and dismembered between 2:24 and 2:55 p.m."

"But to answer my question then," interjected Pancho, "it is possible that the victim had been shot one minute before being dismembered?"

"Yes."

"Five minutes?"

"Yes."

"Fifteen minutes?"

"Yes, I suppose."

"Thirty minutes?"

"I start to have trouble with that time period, solely from a logical perspective, although it is technically possible."

"Thank you doctor, no further questions."

Pancho sat down and couldn't help watch Padma Dasari as she left the stand, walked past counsel table and out of court. Other than the brief encounter in the circuit court rotunda on the day of his murder verdict, which was the same day Laws had been killed, this was the first time he'd seen her since he'd broken up with Ellen, and he couldn't help the slight tightening in his chest. He'd thought about calling her, asking her out on a date, numerous times in the months following the divorce, but so long as he was a criminal defense attorney and she was the coroner, they would be professional adversaries. Then he'd met Paula, and thoughts of Padma retreated to the far corners of his mind. He looked down at his notes, forcing his mind back to the business at hand.

Pancho hadn't the slightest idea what he'd learned or gained except that he'd bought himself some potential expanded time frames. You never knew what was going to be useful later.

"The State calls Detective Frank Nishimoto." Harry Chang looked over at Pancho and smiled. Pancho knew this would be the big one. Whatever they had, it was going to come from Nishimoto.

Harry took Frank through the initial investigation of the scene and the subsequent investigation of Laws' business affairs.

"Based on your investigation and interviews with witnesses, including investors, is it your testimony that Maynard Laws was stealing from his clients?"

"Objection. Leading, calls for conclusion, lacking in foundation, and speculative."

"I agree, at least as to a couple of your objections," Judge Murchison smiled at Pancho. "Sustained."

Harry sighed.

"Detective Nishimoto, let's be specific then, shall we? I show you what has been marked as State's Exhibit 12, and ask you if you can identify it."

Frank took the book from Harry and looked at it.

"It's a ledger that I took from the victim's house on the day of the murder."

"What does the ledger contain?"

"What purports to be a listing of some of the investors with Laws. The amounts of their investments, and notations as to profits."

"All told, how much does the ledger reflect as having been invested by the defendant with Maynard Laws?"

"Principal investments are noted as being seven-hundred-and-eighty thousand dollars."

There was a noticeable gasp from the audience.

"The ledger notes profits to the defendant too, does it not?"

"Yes it does. Profits are noted as being three-hundred-thousand dollars."

"Does the ledger reflect any payment to the defendant of these profits?"

"No, sir. The ledger notes that all of the profits were reinvested."

"Correct me if my addition is wrong, Detective, but I come up with almost one million dollars of principal and profits which the defendant, according to the ledger, had on deposit with the victim. Is that correct?"

"Your Honor, I object and move to strike the previous testimony pertaining to this ledger. It's hearsay. There has been no proper foundation laid to establish the authenticity of the ledger and the truthfulness of the information contained therein. The prosecution is calling the victim a crook, but is then asking this court to believe everything that's written in some ledger found at his house."

"Overruled. This is just a preliminary hearing, Mr. McMartin. Proceed, Mr. Chang."

"Thank you, Your Honor. Detective Nishimoto?"

"Your addition is correct, sir. It is one million eighty thousand to be precise."

"And does the ledger reflect any payments made to the defendant in the last year, before the victim was murdered?"

"No, sir it does not. It doesn't reflect any payments ever having been made to Mr. Bellows."

"Detective Nishimoto, do you have any evidence indicating that the defendant had ever been in the home of the victim?"

"Yes, sir I do."

Pancho shot Reggie a look, but Reggie averted his eyes.

"At the time of Mr. Laws' murder, our forensic team took fiber samples from the living room carpet of Mr. Laws. On the day of the defendant's arrest, his home was searched incident to a warrant and his shoes and clothes were vacuumed. Fiber samples matching those of Mr. Laws' living room carpet were found on rubber slippers found in the defendant's closet."

Pancho was fuming, but forced himself to keep his eyes on his legal pad as he made notes.

"Go on Detective," prodded Harry.

"In addition, a book of matches found on the lanai table at the victim's home was from a restaurant in Paris called *La Cannalle*. Subsequent investigation has shown that the defendant was in Paris a little over a week before the victim was murdered. The reservation manifest at the restaurant contains a reservation under the name of Reggie Bellows during the time the defendant was in Paris.

"We interviewed the housekeeping staff of the victim the day after the murder. The staff swears that no such matches were on the lanai table the morning of the murder. The staff had been excused by the victim that morning, which explains why he was home alone."

"Detective, did your department ever find any of the weapons used to assault and or kill Maynard Laws?"

Pancho stared down at the documents in front of him. He was still, he wasn't even breathing. A part of him knew what was coming, and he didn't want anyone to see his reaction. There had been no leak that a murder weapon as having been found.

"Yes, sir. Two days before we arrested the defendant, a boy who'd been fishing at Koko Marina in Hawai'i Kai, which is less than a mile from the victim's home, found a handgun wedged in the rocks. Subsequent ballistic tests have proven the gun to have been the same gun used to shoot the victim in the abdomen."

"Do you know who that gun belonged to?"

"Yes, sir it was registered to Mr. Reginald Bellows, the defendant."

The courtroom erupted with chatter, forcing the judge to demand silence. Pancho did not look at Reggie. So he'd lied, what else was new?

"Mr. McMartin, your witness."

"Thank you, Your Honor." Pancho rose slowly, trying to calm himself and regain his composure before proceeding.

"Detective Nishimoto, the fibers found on the defendant's rubber slippers do not tell you when he had been in the victim's home, do they?"

"No, sir they do not, only that he'd been there."

"Detective, can the housekeeping staff state with certainty that the matches from Paris were nowhere in the Laws' house prior to the day of the murder?"

"No, I don't think anyone could say that with certainty."

"So, if the matches had been left there earlier, and retrieved by Laws or a guest of Laws on the day of his murder, you would be unable to rule out that scenario, wouldn't you?"

"Yes, I guess I would."

"Were there any fingerprints on the matches?"

"Yes, there were." Pancho wondered why Frank Nishimoto was turning red.

"Were they identified?"

"Yes, they belonged to Officer Lee. He was the first police officer on the scene. At one point, I observed the officer pick the matches up off a lanai table. He shouldn't have done so and I immediately ordered the matches to be bagged and for it to be noted that Officer Lee's prints would probably be found."

Pancho could see Nishimoto's jaw was tight and pulsing. "It's pretty embarrassing, actually."

"Were any other prints found on the matches?"

"No, sir"

"Were any prints of the defendant's found anywhere in the Laws' house?"

"No, sir."

"Where was the gun found, exactly?"

"In the rocks, at the bridge between Koko Marina and Moanalua Bay. The tide was exceptionally low. The gun was below the high water mark."

"I assume there were no prints found on the gun."

"That is correct."

"Was the sword or machete found?"

"Not yet. We naturally conducted an extensive search of the area, including having sent divers down, but it would appear that the machete, or whatever, was discarded elsewhere."

"But we are all in agreement that the machete or sword was the instrument of death, is that correct?"

"Yes, that is correct."

"Thank you, Detective, I have no further questions."

After hearing oral argument, Judge Murchison found that there was sufficient probable cause to bind Reggie over to circuit court to stand trial on the charge of Murder in the Second Degree. A hearing date for arraignment and plea was scheduled and court was adjourned.

Pancho turned to Reggie before they took him away. In a whisper, Pancho said, "I could keep my retainer and dump you right now for lying to me." Pancho looked around the courtroom, making sure no one was in earshot, but also trying to get his temper under control. "In fact, I may do just that."

Reggie's whisper was panicked. "I'm sorry, when can I see you? We've got to talk."

Pancho responded through clenched teeth. "No shit we've got to talk. I'll see you in a day or so. I've got some stuff to do." Pancho grabbed his briefcase and walked out of court without looking back. He 'no commented' his way through the mass of reporters and walked to his office. He was fuming.

Yes, tell me lies, thought Pancho. *Tell me lies upon lies.*

Chapter Eleven

When Pancho left the district court building and walked down Alakea Street toward his office, the sky was a faded blue with only a few cloud crumbs ahead of him. It was warm, and, as he usually did, he took off his sport coat and slung it over his shoulder. He began to feel rain drops on his head and he turned to look back toward the Ko'olau's, the jagged mountain range that splits the Island. Dark rain clouds had slipped down from the Pali into town so that it was raining lightly at his back, yet sunny ahead. The traffic was thick and the noise, heat, and the stress made him feel dizzy. He was sweating profusely.

Pancho knew he should not have been surprised at the preliminary hearing. Obviously, the police and prosecutor would have had some strong evidence or they wouldn't have risked an arrest and public display. They could have gone the more secret route of a grand jury indictment without exposing any evidence to the public yet.

But there'd been something about Reggie Bellows that had made Pancho feel he could trust him. It wasn't the first, and certainly wouldn't be the last time, that Pancho had been duped by a client, but it never felt good. Sometimes it made it damn hard to keep going, to keep caring.

Pancho entered the elevator, illogically half expecting to see Laws' secretary. The elevator was empty, and he as he rode it to his floor, he felt a dull pain in his chest. He felt dizzy and faint. He stared at the digital read-out of the floor numbers, willing the elevator to get to his floor before he passed out.

Susan glanced up at him as he entered the office. She saw immediately that he was in trouble. She jumped up and rushed to him.

"You okay, Paunch? You look ill." Susan's voice followed him as he made his way to his office.

Pancho threw his briefcase onto his couch and tossed his coat over the back of his chair. His armpits were soaked with sweat, as was the back of his shirt. He sat down heavily in his chair. The pain in his chest eased a little. Susan had followed him and now put her hand on his forehead.

"You're flushed and sweating, but I don't think you have a fever. What's going on? Talk to me."

Pancho waved his hand dismissively. "Just feel a little faint, probably nothing." He tried to smile at Susan, but it was a weak, pathetic looking smile.

"Bad day in court," he said.

Susan backed away, unconsciously wiping her hand on her pants. "I assume they have some pretty good evidence against our client?" Her tone made the statement a question, and Pancho nodded.

"How about the murder weapon being his gun?"

Susan nodded judiciously. "Yeeesss," she drawled out, "I would say that's pretty decent evidence." She looked long and hard at Pancho before finally speaking again. Her tone turned motherly. "Look Pancho, don't you think you should maybe take a pass on this one? You worked yourself to death on the last trial and it hasn't been long enough for you to catch up with work, let alone physically and emotionally recover. Now you've got another client lying to you who's probably guilty as hell. You don't need the money right now. You've had tons of great publicity lately. There'll be plenty of clients knocking on the door." She paused and sighed. "I just don't want you to kill yourself over these scum-buckets."

Something inside Pancho ached as he listened to Susan. Even as the pain in his chest and the feeling of dizziness dissipated, he knew she was right. He knew this case would be hard on his burgeoning relationship with Paula. He didn't want to blow that. But trial work was his passion, his addiction. It was his drug, just as surely, and probably as dangerously, as cocaine or heroin or meth were the drugs of choice for others.

He ran his right hand through his sweaty brown hair and smiled again at Susan. It was a better effort this time. "We'll see, mom," he teased. "I'll go see what Reggie has to say for himself before I make any decisions about whether to stick with him or not." He paused for a second before continuing, his voice soft and gentle. "But thank you for caring. You know that means a lot to me."

Susan laughed, a throaty, loud laugh that sounded like it might turn into a cough. "Blah, blah, blah. You'll go see Reggie and he'll tell you why he had to lie to you and he'll apologize and he'll beg, just like a husband who beats his wife and wants another chance. And you," she pointed at him, "just like the abused wife, will take the jerk back."

She turned and walked to the door. Over her shoulder she said, "Don't forget you're supposed to go surfing with Drew this afternoon."

Pancho stared after her, then down at his desk at the work waiting for him. His right hand rubbed his chest where he'd felt pain. "Just the stress," he mumbled to himself and picked up the phone.

A little over an hour later, Pancho and Drew were sitting on their surfboards at Queens, a break almost directly out from Pancho's condo. Pancho's board was a nine-foot Velzy, a classic. Drew's board was an eleven-foot Ben Aipa. The big boards made it easier to paddle out, a good thing when one went for months at a time without surfing, as Pancho did. Or if you were a huge Samoan ex-NFL player, as Drew was. The big boards allowed them to catch the waves faster and easier, also a good thing when competing against the young bucks on the shorter boards. Once on a wave, there were unwritten rules about 'dropping in' on another surfer.

Pancho saw Drew take off on a decent four footer. He watched the big man's head and shoulders move gracefully above the wave. Watching him, Pancho almost missed the nice wave that was forming. He lay down on the board and began to paddle, needing to get up to speed to catch it. He felt the wave lift and propel him forward and he jumped to his feet and felt the board drop downward as he surfed the face. He made a wide, elegant, sweeping left turn at the bottom of the wave and climbed halfway back up the face. He was ahead of the break, so he used his right foot at the back of the board to turn back toward the break. Then, when he was almost back to the whitewater break, he wheeled the board around to the left. He was in a good position. He saw that the wave, which he guessed to be a little over four feet, was about to break. He moved forward on the board, which caused it to accelerate, and shot across the face of the wave as the break curled on and over him. It wasn't a full tube, but it was close and it felt real, and he knew that he and the wave had worked well together. A moment later, he saw that the wave was about to close-out. He moved back on the board and kicked out. The wave that a moment ago had been a part of him, rolled in toward shore, dying in a confusion of whitewater.

When he got back out to where Drew was once again straddling his board, Pancho sat up and grinned. He saw that Drew already had a huge smile pasted on his face. They didn't need to say anything. It was a perfect moment between friends, men as boys.

When the surfboards were stowed and the two men were back in Pancho's condo, sitting on his lanai drinking Patron and lime on ice, Pancho reluctantly returned to business. He briefed Drew on the preliminary hearing. Drew listened impassively. When Pancho was done, Drew smiled and lifted his glass in a toast.

"Bungholed again."

Pancho laughed and clinked his glass to Drew's. They sipped and looked out to sea. The light was starting to fade into a surreal pinkish glow, but there were still quite a few surfers out.

"So, Big Man, did you make any progress on the background checks?"

Pancho and Drew had met on the afternoon of the initial appearance to discuss the case and, since there wasn't much to work with yet, Pancho asked Drew to do some initial digging on the main players: Laws, Bellows, and the secretary, Elie Watson.

Drew took another sip before putting the drink down on the side table. He wiped the condensation on his hands off on his bright orange T-shirt, then he picked up his small pocket notebook that had been sitting on the table. He made a big show of leafing through the pages, then closed the notebook, carefully placed it back on the table, and turned to Pancho.

"No."

Pancho cracked up. "What a dick," he said,

"That's a fine thing to say to your ace investigator." Drew chuckled and picked up the notebook again. "Not a whole lot. Our client's backstory checks out pretty much as he told you. Born in New York, rough and tumble youth, saw plenty of action in Vietnam. Seems like the dude couldn't, or didn't want to, give up the action hero lifestyle, so he signed on as a mercenary with several campaigns. Let's see," said Drew, turning the page, "Three stints in Africa and one in the Philippines. I think the Philippines was the last, but I could be wrong. I talked to the recruiting agency that he worked with and the owner remembered him. His comrades-in-arms supposedly spoke highly of him. Stand-up guy and all that. Damn proficient with all kinds of weapons." He paused.

"You mean like with a machete?" Pancho broke in. He wasn't expecting an answer and Drew knew it.

"Let's see, it was in 1981 or so; Ferdinand Marcos was grossly exaggerating the communist insurgent threat and his buddy, Ronald Reagan, showered him with foreign aid. Although Marcos' secret police were brutal, and quite adept at killing, apparently our esteemed CIA thought it would be helpful to send some mercenaries with jungle fighting experience to teach a special unit Marcos had created to specifically hunt down and kill the commies hiding out in the jungles." Drew paused again and looked over at Pancho. His dark eyes glistened with humor, "And so, while Marcos and his cronies were stealing the Philippine treasury blind, our boy, Reggie Bellows, was part of a team paid for by the CIA to teach jungle warfare to soldiers who had grown up in the jungles. Brilliant."

Pancho smiled and shook his head in wonderment.

"After that, Reggie seems to have mellowed with age. He settled in Honolulu and used his money to start an import-export furniture business. He bought most of his stuff from Thailand, Bali and the Philippines. For a while, he sold to retailers, but eventually he opened his own place, selling both wholesale and retail. He did well." Drew stopped for a moment and looked at Pancho again. "That is, until he invested with Maynard Laws."

Pancho grunted and sipped his Patron. "Yeah, we know he has motive. Any love interests? Best friends? Enemies who'd want to frame him for murder?"

Drew acknowledged the sarcasm with a slight 'hmmph' and reached over to turn on a lamp. It had gotten too dark to read.

"He had a live-in girlfriend named Marcelina, a Filipina." Pancho couldn't see Drew's expression, but he knew damn well his friend was smiling.

"Seems she was quite a bit younger than Reggie. And very much a looker."

"How much?"

"How much what? I said 'looker', not 'hooker'."

Pancho sighed theatrically and looked skyward. "What I put up with. How much of an *age* difference?"

"Ohhhh," Drew drawled out, as if just understanding the question. "Twenty-five years or so."

"Yikes! When did they split up?"

Drew chuckled dryly. "I'm sure it was just a coincidence, but it appears she left him when he started having cash flow problems. He stopped taking her on the trips to Southeast Asia. Their fancy dinners at Alan Wong's and Roy's became more and more scarce."

The two men sat in silence for a few moments, staring out at the sparse lights at sea and, to their right, the glistening spectacle of Waikiki.

"Anything else on Reggie?" Pancho finally asked.

"Only that I did confirm he'd gone to Paris a little over a week before the murder. His round trip ticket was to Geneva. He apparently changed it at the last minute to include a stopover in Paris." Drew paused and looked at Pancho. "Has he said anything to you about that trip? Seems like an odd thing to do when you're having money issues."

Pancho shook his head from side to side. "I haven't talked to him since I found out about it at the prelim this morning. I see him tomorrow."

Drew ran a hand over his short, nubby hair. His face was strangely handsome considering that his nose was bent and flattened from having been broken three times. He had a four-inch scar on his right cheek and another one-inch scar on his chin. His eyebrows were a little bushy and his hairline was receding, yet there was a Polynesian elegance about the man that defied all the imperfections.

"I don't have anything to speak of on Laws yet. I found out he was born in Nebraska and left home while still in his teens, but I suspect he'd been using fake names for most of his life, because I just haven't been able to dig up anything on him. A guy like that, you expect him to leave a trail of felonies. We'll see. A work in progress."

"And the secretary?"

"Just that she was born in Hilo and worked for Laws since he started the company. I don't think we'll find much on her. I talked to a few of her old friends from Hilo and, to a person, they say she was always a shy, timid, insecure little thing. One of her old boyfriends called her 'needy', but who knows, that could've just been sour grapes. Everyone was pretty surprised when she up and moved to Honolulu and started working for the high-roller Laws. Naturally they were all shocked by her role in Laws' Ponzi scheme."

Pancho absently rubbed his neck. After a minute, he looked over at Drew. "It bums me out that Reggie lied to me like that. A part of me wants to tell him to go fuck himself." He looked back out to sea, staring at nothing. Drew didn't say anything. They each took a sip of their drink.

"Did I ever tell you about Walter, one of Dad's old ski buddies in Taos?" Pancho looked back at Drew, who shook his head.

"Sometimes I'd go ski with Walter, just the two of us. He was a pretty cool guy."

"Was he a hippie too?" Drew asked. He knew the story of Pancho's parents.

Pancho chuckled. "He was, but he got tired of it long before my parents did. He opened a health food market, buying produce when he could from the communes. He did well." He paused. "I think Walter may've been my parents' inspiration to finally do something with their lives. Anyway, Walter knew me well. If my parents had believed in such a thing, Walter would probably have been my Godfather."

Pancho turned a little in his seat to face Drew. "So this one time, Walter and I are up skiing at Taos Ski Valley, and we were riding the lift to start the hike up to Kachina Peak. It's kind of a long lift and we were talking about my wanting to become a lawyer, and out of the blue Walter turned to me and said that he thought I'd make a shitty lawyer."

"Huh?"

"Exactly," said Pancho. "I was shocked. Here was my parents' best friend and a guy I looked up to, telling me I'd be a shitty lawyer. I mean, what's up with that?

"Walter could see I was upset and offended and tried to explain. He told me not to get all pissed off, that I was plenty smart and all, but he said I'm too emotional. That if I see an injustice, I get too angry and upset. 'An attorney has to be cold, calculating, and non-emotional,' he told me. He said there's way too much injustice in the world to take it all to heart."

"What'd you say?" asked Drew.

"Nothing, really. We got off the lift and hiked to Kachina Peak and never talked about it again. But every once in a while, I think about what

Walter said and I wonder if maybe he was right, maybe I do take too much on myself." He paused. "Maybe that's why I lost Ellen."

Drew grunted. "And maybe that's why we love you, man. You care. Everyone who knows you, knows you care, and I don't think it's anything to be ashamed of. You're who you are—a fucked up son of hippies who cares about what he believes in."

Drew started to get up, his face grimacing in pain from his knee. "And you lost Ellen because she wasn't willing to share you with your life's passion, simple as that. And with that fine speech, I need another drink."

"Want to grab dinner someplace?"

"You buying?"

Pancho laughed. "No, Reggie Bellows is."

Chapter Twelve

Sandy Foreman and Ricardo Baguio sat in a window booth at the Filipino restaurant on Hotel Street owned by Ricardo's parents. They made an odd-looking pair. Sandy was tall, black, and big. His hair was cut short and there was a balding spot at the crown of his head. His dark eyes were deep set, hard looking, and there were dark, purplish patches under the eyes.

Ricardo was a short, tightly muscled, Filipino man. He was older than Sandy, but it would have been hard for anyone to determine how much older. His face was weathered and lined, but his eyes looked clear and young, and gave him a kind of innocent look. He had a habit of pausing to look out the window every few minutes. Ricardo knew pretty much everything that went on in this part of town and he liked to keep an eye on things.

The two men were eating bowls of menudo, slurping as they ate without talking. A plate of shared lumpia sat between them on the scarred and scratched orange Formica tabletop. The blue Naugahyde booth was cut and torn and patched with duct tape, and the window looking out onto Hotel Street was pasted with hand printed daily specials that hadn't changed in months or years. The window itself was pitted and streaked.

As Ricardo checked the outside activity again, he sat upright and moved his head closer to the window.

"What's up?" Sandy asked.

Ricardo grunted. "You see the *haole* in *da kine* blue shirt over there?" His head nodded toward the opposite side of the street. The Caucasian man was short, solidly built, and he walked slowly, holding a cheap iridescent green plastic bag like he would have gotten from any of the fruit or vegetable vendors in Chinatown. Sandy looked him over.

"Yeah, what about him?"

"He looks like the guy they arrested for the murder of your boss. For one minute I thought maybe he got out on bail, but it's not him."

"You knew him?"

Ricardo nodded. "Last time I wen see the guy was in the jungle, in Philippines. We was fighting communists. Long time now."

"You fought communists in the jungles in the Philippines?" Sandy knew his friend had worked for Marcos in the old days, and had even followed him to Hawai'i when Marcos was exiled, but he didn't know much more.

The haole man disappeared from sight and both men turned back to the table. Ricardo laughed. "Like I wen say, long time now." He went back to slurping his menudo, but after a moment, he looked up and saw his friend looking at him as if he was waiting for the rest of the story. He thought for a second and looked around, checking to see who was in earshot.

"My grandfather," he nodded his head toward the kitchen, "was one old fren of Ferdinand Marcos. My family wen come from Ilocos Norte, where Marcos come from. Grandfather get one job as territorial administrator when Marcos get elected." He grinned cunningly. "Plenty good *kine* bribes. But I neva wen like country life, so Grandfather get me one job with Marcos' secret police."

Ricardo had been trained to kill, and had done so in the name of his country more times than he could count. Much of the time, those he killed had been communists, but once in a while, there was the liberal political opponent who had to be taken care of. While his relatives wielded machetes on the farms of Ilocos Norte, he had wielded Marcos' ruthless justice in the cities and jungles of the Philippines. He nodded toward the street where the *haole* man had been a few minutes before.

"Pretty funny *kine*. The guy Reggie, an' about ten more was sent by American CIA to train us dumb Flips how to fight in the jungle." He shook his head in recollected wonderment. "They was good, but we was just as good, maybe mo' betta. Thing is, Marcos wanted America to think it was fighting the commies right along with him." He paused, remembering the times.

"But that guy Reggie was real good." He smiled. "He was like one maestro with a machete. Even I wen learn some shit from him."

"How'd you end up here?" Sandy asked, pushing aside his empty bowl.

His friend snorted gleefully. "When Marcos had to leave, we had to leave." He drew his index finger across his throat, like a knife. "Plenty *kine* enemies."

Ricardo warmed to the telling of his story, which he didn't share with most people. He talked faster, accentuating his accent and pidgin English, and Sandy had to lean in and concentrate. Ricardo explained how he'd used his position to become moderately wealthy. The easiest was when he went to arrest a dissident at his home. He would help himself to whatever money or valuables were lying around the house. "Who was to complain?" His grin widened.

As Ricardo became savvier, he learned to use his advance knowledge of the impending arrest or disappearance of a businessman to turn a profit by wisely placed investments that were bound to appreciate when the businessman was arrested and his business would be lost or seized.

Ricardo smiled broadly and opened his arms to take in the restaurant. "I wen bought my parents this restaurant when we first moved here. Now I no can get them for retire."

Just then, Ricardo's grandfather, stooped, gray haired, and tired looking, approached their table. The old man made a telephone gesture with his hand and was talking in a fast, rasping Ilocano, the names Donald and Ricky and Mexico the only words spoken that Sandy could understand. Without waiting for a reply from his grandson, the old man turned and shuffled back into the kitchen.

Ricardo excused himself. "Gotta take this." He grinned. He was back in less than five minutes.

"What's up?" asked Sandy.

"Nothing important," answered Ricardo. "Just one guy I do some *kine* work for sometime." He smiled and winked. "CIA," he whispered theatrically. Sandy smiled at the joke.

The two men ate in silence while they finished the meal. When Ricardo had swallowed the last of his tripe and broth, he looked up from his bowl at Sandy. His friend didn't look good.

"So what you gonna do now your boss is dead?" asked Ricardo. He could see, even in the shadows of the restaurant, that Sandy's eyes were pinned.

Sandy tried a smile and shrug at the same time, as if the death of the man who supplied him with cash to buy hookers and drugs for the both of them was no big deal. Ricardo knew better.

Ricardo and Sandy had met several months before at the restaurant, and Ricardo found that he liked Sandy. He'd known of Sandy as a small time pimp and drug dealer—he knew pretty much everything that went on in the four-block area around Hotel Street—but he thought Sandy had a certain style, and he could see Sandy was smart, much smarter than Ricardo expected. They'd become cautious friends, eating late night dinners at the family restaurant, while Sandy's girls worked the street.

Then, one night after they'd eaten and were standing on Hotel Street talking about nothing in particular, some drunk Marines started talking about the thin 'Flip.' There were five *haole* Marines. They ignored Sandy, choosing instead to pick on the smaller of the two, apparently assuming the big black man wouldn't intervene. They started pushing Ricardo, taunting him, but then, before anyone knew what was happening, Ricardo had a knife out and cut one of the Marines. Ricardo was fast and brutal, but even he couldn't take on all four drunk Marines, and the others charged him and pinned him against the wall. Ricardo cut two more, but the odds were against him, and it was clear to Sandy that Ricardo was about to get his ass kicked, possibly worse.

Moments later the Marines were peeled off Ricardo, one by one, as Sandy, in a rage, intervened. Ricardo was able to break free and the two of them proceeded to pummel the Marines who were still standing. Ricardo looked like he was ready to stab them all to death, but Sandy pulled him back. They got away, moments before the police came.

To Ricardo, this sealed their friendship for life. He would do anything for Sandy.

Over time, the two shared more and more about their lives and their past, as Ricardo had just done over lunch. Sandy had already told Ricardo about Maynard Laws, 'the rich *haole* dude', and about how he'd known Laws from the old days on the mainland. Ricardo had heard of Laws. Just last year, his grandfather proudly told Ricardo that he'd invested a hundred thousand dollars with Laws, pretty much everything the old man had. So far, his grandfather boasted, he'd already made twenty grand.

When Ricardo heard about Laws from Sandy, he tried to convince his grandfather to get his money out, but his grandfather refused to believe that Laws was anything but the financial genius his old Filipino cronies claimed him to be. Now, it appeared his grandfather had lost everything.

"I used to work for Maynard in his credit card scam in Miami—of course he wasn't Maynard Laws then. When I moved to Hawai'i, I wanted to clean myself up and get my act together," Sandy said one night over drinks in a seedy bar on Maunakea Street. "I'd heard Maynard was doing well, and since I'd once been a securities broker in Iowa and Illinois, I thought he could use me. So I went to meet him and asked him for a job, a legitimate job." The bitterness in his voice was clear and strong.

"He blew me off at first, but then I guess he figured out I could sabotage him pretty good, and he offered to put me on retainer as his kind of personal assistant." He snorted a kind of laugh. "Except that all I assisted with was getting him whores and drugs. The money was great. Shit man, I was making a grand or two a week again. I started running a few girls on my own, I dealt a little bit. Then I got into drugs again myself, which was stupid, but shit, look what I was doing." He stopped then, and looked at Ricardo.

"You ever do heroin, Ricardo?"

Ricardo shook his head, no.

"Well it grabs you hard man. It's got my ass now. If I try to stop, it'll be hell." He shrugged then, as if it didn't matter.

He looked at Ricardo, and instead of the hard look Ricardo had grown used to, Sandy's eyes had become sad and even scared looking. It shook Ricardo to see his friend like that.

Sandy became drunk telling Ricardo the story that night, and eventually Sandy started crying and confessed that he despised Maynard Laws more than any other human being in the world.

Sandy and Ricardo never again talked about that night, and Ricardo knew that Sandy was thankful for that, but now Ricardo saw that Sandy had given himself over to Laws. Sandy's submission was total and complete. He'd been mercilessly used by Laws and now, with Laws dead, Sandy was nothing more than an abandoned piece of trash.

"I'm gonna have to figure something out fast," said Sandy, his voice soft, almost a whisper. "I don't have any girls working for me anymore — at least none worth a damn — and I have no money coming in. As soon as my little stash runs out I'm gonna be in deep shit."

Chapter Thirteen

Pancho's head felt like it had been used as a ball by a group of Argentinian soccer players. He hadn't slept well. Thoughts of Reggie's lies, and Susan's admonitions, alternated for attention in his overworked brain. He cranked up his air conditioning and kept the radio off as he contended with the traffic on Dillingham Boulevard on his way to the prison. Other than a few wispy clouds, the sky was a clear, baby blue. There was little wind, and the ocean, as seen from his apartment before he left, was a still, beckoning blanket. He would've preferred to go for a swim to clear his head, but instead he was on his way to see what Reggie had to say for himself — why he had lied, why he had risked losing his attorney and his retainer.

Driving through Kalihi, it was impossible not to reflect on the disparity between the haves and have-nots of Hawai'i. Industrial warehouse space competed with old wood frame houses or concrete block apartments with louvered windows. Colorful clothes and white underwear dried on lines stretched across tiny lanais. When it was hot, the small apartments would be stifling and cramped, and even the cockroaches would get listless.

Homeless people built makeshift lean-to's out of blue tarps tied to fences. Pancho passed a great number of discount shopping centers, auto repair shops, Korean bars, and fast food joints. Kalihi was the true melting pot of Honolulu. Hawaiians, Samoans, Tongans, Micronesians, Filipinos, Puerto Ricans, Koreans, Vietnamese, Laotians, Chinese, Japanese, and every other Asian and South Pacific culture was represented. It was this area that many of his clients resided when he worked as a public defender.

While many well-known Honolulu lawmakers, attorneys, businessmen, and even a Governor, came from Kalihi, it was obvious to Pancho why so many more did not make it out and turned to crime.

A few short miles away people lived in multi-million dollar estates, or, like Pancho, in expensive condominiums overlooking the ocean and the beaches that had once been the exclusive domain of the native Hawaiians, whose descendants were now all too frequently relegated to the prison-like tenements of civilization.

In many ways, Pancho preferred the days of the public defender's office, when he represented defendants who were poor. Much of what he saw, many of whom he defended, he could understand, if not justify.

As he became successful in private practice, he began charging a lot of money for his services. His clientele changed. These were criminals who did not have to be criminals. Many of his clients had come from well-off families and had plenty of opportunities, legitimate opportunities, available to them. Other clients had found their way out of the slums of places like Kalihi by using their innate intelligence for crime. Wasted energy. Wasted intelligence. Like Maynard Laws.

Pancho went through the check-in process at the prison, including a comprehensive pat-down search, and was shown to an interview room where Reggie was waiting. Pancho sat, took out a legal pad, and studied Reggie, saying nothing.

There were dark circles under Reggie's light blue eyes. His nose was a little flat, and his lips were a touch too thin. He was not a particularly handsome man, yet there was something about him that in better days would be called character.

He was not large, but he was clearly solid, about 5'7", and although getting on in age, he was not someone to mess with. Pancho didn't think he'd have to worry about his client being overly harassed in prison.

"You look pretty shitty," said Pancho. "You trying to get my sympathy?"

"Look, I'm sorry about lying to you. I've been awake all night trying to figure out how to explain it to you."

"Explain it, or come up with more lies?"

"Come on, give me a break here. I was scared, okay?"

Pancho's voice turned harsh. "Didn't you listen to anything I said the other day? I have a good mind to walk." The ensuing silence was palpable.

Reggie stared at Pancho. Neither man said anything. Finally, Reggie backed down, looked at his hands, then looked back up at Pancho with a change in his eyes, a resignation.

"All right. I'm going to tell you the truth. When I'm done, you tell me whether you would've believed me had I told you it from the beginning, ok?"

"Fair enough." Pancho kept his eyes glued to Reggie's face.

Reggie exhaled deeply and rubbed the back of his neck with his left hand before beginning.

"As you know, I lost a lot of money with Laws. Except for what I told you about, it was everything I had. Everything I'd built up from my business. I was to the point where I needed capital to finance a new buying trip in the Philippines and Thailand.

"I went to Laws in June, asking him to cut me a check for fifty thousand dollars from my account. He gave me some bullshit story about how all the funds were tied up in investments. Nothing was liquid.

"I went nuts. I was in his fancy office and I started yelling at him. I guess I got pretty loud, because his secretary, Elie, came in and asked if everything was all right.

"He had about a million dollars of mine and I couldn't get out a measly fifty thousand. You can imagine how mad I was."

Pancho nodded, wrote some notes, but said nothing.

"I went back to Laws' office day after day. Elie wouldn't let me see him. He wouldn't return calls. I began to realize that something was terribly wrong. All that money, all that work." Reggie shook his head as if he still couldn't believe what was happening.

"In early August, I decided I had to go to Switzerland and meet with my bankers, and probably withdraw some money to keep my business alive. Just before I left, I received a weird note from someone named D. Kendall. The note said to meet him at the steps of the Sacre-Coeur, in Paris, on August 14. It said that it could be financially beneficial to me if I kept the meeting."

"Did you know who Kendall was?"

"No, never heard of him."

"But you went to Paris on the basis of this note?" Pancho's tone was incredulous.

"Look, I was in a desperate situation. I didn't know what the hell this note was all about, or who it was from, but someone knew I was in financial trouble and apparently had some proposition for me. Whoever it was knew all about me: my business, how much I'd invested, even that I was going to Switzerland to withdraw money from an account that no one in the world but me knew anything about. Yes, I went. I was desperate."

"Why'd you have to go to Switzerland to withdraw the money? Couldn't you have done it by wire?"

Reggie nodded and rubbed the side of his face. "Yeah, but I'd lose the secrecy of the account if I did that. That was money I'd earned as a mercenary. I hadn't paid taxes on it. It was my secret stash."

"Okay, what happened?"

"Well, I went to the Sacre-Coeur at the appointed time. I was a few minutes late, and I thought I'd blown it, like I'd blown everything else. I didn't see anyone beckoning to me, so I sat down on the steps, just below the entrance to the church. After a few minutes, this guy came up and asked if I'm Reggie Bellows. I said yes. He introduced himself as Kendall. I'd never seen the guy before, or since.

"He told me he knew Laws had ripped me off and that I was in serious shit. He even knew my girlfriend had left me. I asked him how he knew all that, but he waved it off, said it didn't matter.

"He said Laws had screwed him over too, and that he thought it was time we did something about it. I asked him what that meant. It was beginning to get pretty weird." Reggie stopped for a beat and looked around before continuing.

"So Kendall said, 'We should kill him.' Just like that. He didn't even dick around with it. He said, 'We should kill him,' like he was talking about taking a trip to the market, or something. I told him he was fucking nuts. I said I'm not a murderer.

"Then Kendall looked at me, a real cold stare, and said 'You sure as hell've killed a lot of people for not being a murderer.' I mean, Jesus, Pancho, this guy knew all about me; knew that I'd been in 'Nam and had been a mercenary.

"Anyway, so then Kendall said that he has some money left and would be willing to use it to see that Laws was off'd. He told me he'd pay me fifty thousand bucks to kill Laws." Reggie shook his head from side to side.

"It didn't escape my attention that it was the same amount of money I needed, and had tried to withdraw from the account with Laws. I don't know why I didn't just get up and leave at that point, but I tried to talk some sense into this guy. I said that killing Laws wouldn't get our money back. He said it would stop him from spending whatever was left.

"I said that I wouldn't want to go to jail for killing some asshole like Laws. He said that anyone who's careful could get away with a basic execution. That's the word he used, 'execution.' I mean the guy was fuckin' nuts, and there I was, discussing murder with him.

"Finally I told him no, I didn't want any part of it. So get this," Reggie straightened up and leaned in toward Pancho, "Kendall then told me he'd already deposited twenty-five thousand dollars in my bank account in Honolulu. He didn't want the money back. If I chose to kill Laws, I'd have another twenty-five grand deposited. If I didn't do it, then I didn't have to return the money, or anything.

"I said I didn't want his twenty-five K, but he said it was already there, that there was nothing I could do about it. Take it and enjoy it, he said. But he told me to think about Laws. If I killed him soon, there might be money left that Laws hadn't already spent and, on top of that, I'd get another twenty-five grand.

"It was all so bizarre. I mean, what d'you do? I left and called my bank in Honolulu. Sure enough, twenty-five thousand bucks in cash had been deposited in my account."

"Is that the twenty-five grand you had on you when you were arrested?" asked Pancho.

Reggie looked down at his hands again.

"Yeah. I waited to hear from this guy Kendall, but he never contacted me again. The money was sitting there, and I needed to save my business, so I was going to use it to buy new inventory, then put it back and hope to return it later." His tone sounded like he was imploring Pancho to believe him.

"Well, what did you think when Laws was murdered?"

"A lot of stuff ran though my head. I figured that either Kendall killed him or hired someone else to do it."

"What about your gun?"

Reggie shook his head insistently. "I keep that gun in the dresser by my bed. I didn't even know it was gone. I never go in that drawer."

"You did go to Laws' house, though?"

Reggie nodded, looking contrite.

"Yeah, I did. I'd been trying for days to confront him again about my money. I got tired of being stonewalled, and decided to take a chance on catching him at home. So, yes, I went to see him that morning he was murdered. He answered the front door and I followed him through the living room to the lanai. He'd been drinking, pretty heavily, it looked like. We yelled at each other for a while. There was no one else around. Finally, I got frustrated and told him to get fucked, and I left. He was alive when I left . . . I swear it."

"Wow." Pancho said, then sat silent, staring at his pages of notes.

Finally, Reggie broke the silence. "Well, would you've believed me?"

Pancho looked at Reggie a long time before answering. Reggie held his gaze.

"I don't know. It's a pretty farfetched story. I can't tell you what I would or would not have believed. Why didn't you go to the cops as soon as you got back to Honolulu?"

"With that story? I didn't think there was anything there. Except for the twenty-five grand, which was in cash, I only had this bizarre tale of meeting some guy in Paris. I know damn well that Kendall was not a real name. I also didn't have any reason to believe that Laws would be murdered if I didn't do it. Frankly, I wasn't particularly concerned with Laws anyway, the asshole deserved to be killed. It never occurred to me that I was being framed."

"What about the matches, did you smoke at Laws'?

Once again, Reggie shook his head vehemently. "No, I've no idea how the matches got there."

"So where were you at the time Laws was murdered?"

"Driving out to the north shore, like I told you."

"Alone?"

"Yeah, alone."

"Describe this man Kendall to me."

"Well, it was getting dark and we were outside, but I'd say he was about six feet or so, trim, about 180 pounds, medium length brown hair. I couldn't tell what color his eyes were. No scars that I could see on his face. Not a bad looking guy."

"Do you still have the note he sent you?"

"No, I threw it away."

A fly landed on Reggie's nose as he looked at Pancho. He did not bat it away.

Pancho watched Reggie watching him. It looked like Reggie was waiting for a word of encouragement, like a child who had just confessed to his parent and now wanted absolution. Pancho wondered why Reggie didn't bat the fly away. He knew that Reggie wanted Pancho to tell him that it was all going to be okay, but he didn't see how it was. If the prosecution found out about the twenty-five thousand, the motive would go from anger over losing money, to that and murder for hire. Murder for hire is Murder in the First Degree: life without possibility of parole.

When Pancho spoke, his tone was cool. "I don't know what to think right now, Reggie. You're in deep kim chee, but you don't need me to tell you that. I'll get my investigator on this, though we don't have much to go on. The chances of finding this guy, Kendall, are slim to none without more information. I'm sure the money's a dead end.

"You start doing some serious thinking. Who could've seen you on the north shore? What more do you remember about Kendall? Could anyone have seen you leaving Laws' house earlier in the day? If you think of anything, call me.

"In the meantime, I'm preparing a motion to reduce bail. We'll see if we can get you out of here, but don't get your hopes up."

Reggie nodded, somewhat dumbly. He'd not been given any reason to be optimistic. He finally batted the fly away and stood to leave.

Chapter Fourteen

Elie sat on the orange crushed velvet sofa at her uncle's home in Aiea Heights and watched as the huge Samoan man named Drew explain who he was. She was awed and intimidated by his size. She drew her legs up under her on the couch, an unconscious act of closing in on herself. She was wearing a plain blue pleated skirt and a long sleeved white blouse. Her blonde hair was pinned carelessly up in the back. She wore no makeup.

She'd been surprised that this man had found her. She'd given up her apartment; she needed all her money to pay for legal fees. She had not yet been indicted on anything. The police and the federal agents all seemed to want to keep that threat looming over her. Her attorney, Bill Chambers, told her not to say anything to anyone until the authorities decided on whether or not she was to be prosecuted. He'd been trying to get immunity for her, but the prosecutors were having none of that until they knew what she had to offer. After all, she could be the only one left to prosecute. Against her attorney's advice, she had decided to cooperate, and had been giving endless statements and answering endless questions for weeks. Some days the FBI would question her, some days the HPD would question her, other days agents from various law enforcement branches would have at her all at the same time. It was a long and frightening circus of a nightmare.

Now there was this man, who said he was an investigator working for the attorney who represented Reggie Bellows. She knew she should call Bill Chambers and ask him what he thought she should do, but she also knew that she wouldn't necessarily follow his advice. All he ever told her to do was to say nothing, but she wanted this whole thing to be over. If there were any chance whatsoever of not going to jail, she'd take it. She figured that cooperating without any strings attached would give her that chance. Then she could go back to Hilo and get a secretarial job somewhere and sink back into anonymity. She rubbed her face with her right hand, and then absently smoothed her unruly hair. *Why had she left Hilo to come to Honolulu in the first place? What had she been thinking? Had she ever really thought she could become someone other than the meek, insignificant person she thought she was?* For a while, after she had gone to work for Maynard, who'd become the darling of all Honolulu, she thought that's exactly what she'd done. Then Maynard had taken her to bed and she'd become the mistress of one of Hawaii's most powerful men. But all too soon, it became clear to her that Maynard was nothing more than a cheap, perverse, low-life fraud, and once again, her self-esteem plummeted.

Then came Donald. The CIA was working with Maynard, and Donald wanted her. She let herself be romanced. She thought she was in love, and she thought she was helping with a CIA mission. Of course, once again, it had all been bullshit. *Now what?* She had to protect Donald and the CIA; but mostly she had to protect herself.

But what could this investigator do for her? He could offer her nothing that would help keep her out of jail. She asked him why she should talk to him.

"Because you may be able to help a man falsely accused of murder." Drew's voice was surprisingly gentle for being such a big man.

"Falsely accused? It sounds to me like the case is open and shut against Mr. Bellows."

Drew's mild expression didn't change. He nodded. "There's some damaging evidence, but our client maintains his innocence and you may have some information that could be of help. I assume you've already told the police all you know."

The last was more of a question than a statement, and Elie recognized it as such. She nodded tenuously.

"Then what's the harm in answering some of my questions?" Again that gentle, prodding voice. He looked her straight in the eyes. His voice and his calm demeanor belied the force she felt him exerting on her.

"What d'you want to know?"

Drew smiled, and opened his notebook.

"You know who Bellows is, of course?"

"Sure, he was one of the biggest investors. I've talked to him on the phone quite a bit, and I met him when he came to the office."

"I understand he made quite a scene at the office before the murder."

"Yeah, he sure did. The first time was about a month before. For a while, he started coming practically every day. He was mad as hell. 'Course, who could blame him? Then, about a couple weeks before Maynard was murdered he just stopped coming."

"Did he threaten Laws?"

"Well, more or less. I mean he said 'I'll get you" or 'you'll get yours,' or something like that."

"Did he say he would kill Laws?"

"No."

"Did he say anything about going to court?"

"Oh sure, he said he was going to get an attorney and sue Laws, that kind of thing."

"Did you or Laws fear for your life as a result of what Bellows was saying or doing?"

"No. I don't know about Maynard, but he never said anything about being afraid of Bellows." Elie absently picked some lint from her skirt.

"Did Bellows call a lot?"

"Oh man, did he. On the days he didn't come by, he called every day, three or four times a day. I felt sorry for him, but what could I do? I just told him that Mr. Laws was not available."

"Did you ever hear of a man with the last name of Kendall?"

Elie appeared to be considering the question, searching her memory banks.

"No. Was he an investor?"

"We don't know. You never heard the name?"

"No."

"Were there any other investors who were mad, like Bellows?"

"Oh shoots, by early summer, there were about ten that had decided Laws was a crook and were pestering us all the time. Maynard was trying to figure out a way to get some money to the troublemakers, to buy some time."

"Did Laws have any partners, backers, anyone behind the scenes?"

Elie thought of Donald. She'd kept her promise to him and had never mentioned him.

"No, not that I know of."

"Did you ever hear Laws' life threatened?"

"No, not really, just stuff like Bellows, saying 'I'll get you'."

"Can you give me a list of the ten or so other investors who were angry at Laws?"

"Sure, give me a piece of paper and I'll write them down for you."

Drew tore out a piece of paper from his notepad and handed it to Elie with a pen. He smiled at her when she handed the paper back, and she returned the smile briefly before looking away.

"When was the last time you spoke to Laws before he was murdered?"

"The day before. He called me at home and asked me how much had come in. He was trying to get some money together to pay some dividends. He wanted me to get five-thousand dollars to each of the more troublesome investors. You know, keep the wolves off his back for a while longer. Probably your client would have gotten something, although I doubt he would've been happy about it."

Drew nodded and wrote something down. He looked around.

"This your uncle's place?"

Elie nodded. "How'd you know where to find me? I haven't given out this address to anyone, except the police of course."

Drew smiled. "I'm a private investigator. Finding people is the easiest part of my job.

"Well, thanks for talking to me," said Drew, getting up. "I'll try not to bother you anymore."

"Have I been of help?"

Drew smiled again. "Hard to say."

Elie did her best to control her breathing as Drew let his intimidating gaze dwell on her. She looked down and wiped at some wrinkles on her skirt. When she looked back up at him, he nodded his goodbye and walked out the door. She let out a deep breath and covered her eyes with both hands.

Chapter Fifteen

Pancho stared out his office window, wondering if it was ever going to stop raining. It had been coming down in sheets for five days straight and people were starting to get depressed. Some people had more reason to be depressed than others. It seemed like every day the media had another tragic story about one of Laws' investors. On KITV the night before, Pancho watched a story about an eighty-seven year old widow who could no longer afford to stay in her assisted living building. No one could say for sure what would happen to her.

Reggie Bellows had been arraigned in circuit court the day before, and his bail was reduced to seven hundred fifty thousand dollars, which was about half a million dollars more than he could afford. He would remain in jail until his trial, which was still ninety days away.

Pancho filed his request for 'discovery' immediately after the arraignment. It was a *pro forma* pleading, wherein he requested everything under the sun. The prosecution would eventually be required to give the defense everything it had, with the exception of 'work product,' things like the investigation notes. Additionally, the prosecution had an affirmative duty to give the defense anything that might be considered exculpatory. In other words, if there was an eyewitness who said she had seen Reggie Bellows at the market at the time of the murder, that would have to be disclosed to Pancho.

Pancho knew the gamesmanship played in the discovery phase, and knew the evidence would be dribbled in to him over time. So far, all he'd received was the basic police report, which included some follow-up reports by investigating officers, and the autopsy report. He didn't see anything earth shattering that he hadn't already learned the hard way at the preliminary hearing.

Drew had no luck in finding the mysterious Mr. Kendall, who'd allegedly lured Reggie to Paris to ask him to kill Laws. Drew put in day after day locating and interviewing other Laws investors. All expressed extreme hostility toward Laws, but none stuck out as a potential candidate to replace Reggie as the prime suspect.

Drew filled Pancho in on his conversation with Elie. After a few moments of silence, Pancho said, "What else have you got?"

"Not much. I talked to the bartender at Jameson's who was on duty that day, and showed him a photo of Reggie. He'd already seen Reggie's picture on television, so it made him unsure. He thought that maybe he'd seen him, but he said he couldn't remember when it would've been."

Pancho frowned. Another dead end. Pancho had been racking his brains for a viable defense, but so far, he had nothing. Although he could ethically put Reggie on the stand to testify in his own behalf, as things now stood, the prosecution would decimate him on cross-examination. His story was unsubstantiated and almost ludicrous.

Pancho turned back to stare at the torrent of rain that washed over his office window as Drew went through his notes of interviews. They were missing something, somewhere.

It was like his view, thought Pancho. He could barely make out the forms of buildings and structures, which he knew were there, but were almost totally obscured by the monsoon rain and darkness. Had he not known what was there, by virtue of his seeing the same view day after day, he would not know what the shapes and shadows were.

He didn't know what was 'out there' in the Laws case, but he knew there was something, something presently obscured by their inability to find the right people and ask the right questions. He turned his attention back to Drew.

"Look man, we're all over the farm on this. We're stumbling around in the dark without any focus. We've got to re-think this thing."

"I'm listening."

"Let's look at what we've got. We have a ton of investors, including Reggie, who're pissed at Laws. We have Laws' wife, who doesn't seem to know jack, and thinks, or at least, thought, her husband was a damned genius—except that, according to the police report, she was busy robbing him blind behind his back. We have Elie the secretary, who knew that Laws was ripping people off, but was scared to turn herself in because she was in too far. And we have a mysterious Mr. Kendall, who wants Laws dead, but who doesn't match a description of any of Laws' investors."

"Assuming Kendall exists."

"Right, but can you see what we're missing, Drew?"

Drew folded his arms across his chest. He shook his head.

"What players in this game are we missing?" asked Pancho.

The big man wrinkled his brow. After a few moments, a smile spread across his face.

"Friends, cronies, accomplices. No man is an island, as they say"

Pancho smiled. "As who says?"

"You know, 'they.'"

"Oh,'*they*,' why didn't you say so? You're right, though. Laws had to have someone he confided in, besides Elie. There must've been someone who knew what he was up to. There must've been someone he hung around with, screwed around with, drank with. That's who we have to find. We've got to get to the real Maynard Laws if we're going to find out who killed him."

"Assuming, of course, our man didn't do it." Drew smiled.

"My friend, my clients are always innocent, even when they're guilty."

"Ri' on, ri' on."

"So, all you have to do is find this person or these people." Pancho held up a hand, then rifled through some papers. When he found what he was looking for, he read for a moment, then looked back at Drew.

"Remember the police report noted that Laws had called two numbers in the hour before the murder? One was a blocked number, and there's no indication that they located the subscriber. But the other call, the one that went through, was a guy named Sandy Foreman. I don't see any follow-up on that. See what you can find out about this guy, Foreman." He dropped the paper to the desk. "Also see if the wife will talk to you. She may know who his friends were. Go see Elie again if you have to."

"Okay." Drew rose slowly. "I'm outta here." He stuck his notebook in his back pocket, gathered up his raincoat, and turned to leave. Pancho noticed that Drew's limp was more pronounced. Drew had once told Pancho that rainy weather made the knee pain worse.

When he got to the door, Drew turned back to Pancho.

"Oh, there's one semi-bizarre thing that came up in the interview of two of the bigger investors, you know, from that list Elie gave me of the ten who were pissed."

"Yeah?"

"Apparently Laws, in trying to calm these guys down and stall them, had made some reference to government contracts, or government backed investments, or some such shit. They had nothing specific, but they seemed to think that Laws was telling them that their investments were safe because of this ambiguous 'government involvement.'"

Pancho put his elbows on the desk and rubbed his temples with his hands, visibly thinking.

"Probably just more hype by Laws to stall. Maybe he was trying to give the impression that he had their money tied up in government bonds, or securities, or whatever. Elie didn't say anything about government contracts, did she?"

"Nope."
"Well, back burner it, but I doubt if it's anything."
"Nor did I, buddy, nor did I. Ciao."
"Later."

Pancho watched his best friend limp out before he swiveled back to his window. He knew Aloha Tower was out there, but he saw nothing, nothing at all.

Pancho and Paula were lying in bed in Pancho's Diamond Head condominium. Paula's workday ended early, since it was mostly timed to the stock exchanges on the East coast. Pancho had given up trying to solve the puzzle of Reggie Bellows for the evening and had called Paula to meet at his condo and go for a swim. They never made it to the ocean. Instead, they made love, and were now reluctant to remove themselves from bed. Pancho switched on the television to catch the evening news. Another 'human interest' story about one of Maynard Laws' victims led the slow news day.

"Well," said Paula, "you can't say there aren't a ton of people out there who would probably have liked to kill the SOB." The covers had fallen from her breasts as they talked and Pancho began to be more interested in the brown, protruding nipples than in the subject of Maynard Laws. He reached out for her.

"Just what do you think you're doing?"

"You're always telling me I watch too much news. This seems like a good time to start weaning me from it."

They kicked the sheet off, and let the overhead fan and the trade winds coming through the open lanai door cool them. Their passion was still that of the passion of new lovers, and they found the exploration of each other's bodies wondrous and rewarding. Pancho loved the firm smoothness of Paula's rich brown skin. Her waist was tiny and her stomach was perfectly flat. He traced the outline of her cheekbones and her mouth with his fingers, reveling in her beauty.

Paula had told Pancho she loved the fact that he adored her body, as she his. His six foot frame held little fat. He was naturally muscular, not the developed look of body builders. His buns were round and hard. His face was handsome, yet sharp featured, which she'd said made it full of character. His smile was crooked and cynical and made her laugh.

They made love, occasionally hearing the laughter of the evening beachgoers.

Chapter Sixteen

At CIA headquarters in Langley, VA, Oliver Wilson looked across the desk at Donald Duerden. Wilson thought of Duerden as a smug, pompous, asshole. Oliver Wilson was used to dealing with smug, pompous, assholes, although usually they were his superiors, and he was required to defer to their inane pomposities. He didn't have to take shit from Duerden.

"Sir, I believe the situation in Honolulu is completely under control." Duerden's tone was patronizing and irritating to Wilson.

"There's absolutely nothing to connect us with Laws. I have a new system set up to provide us with the dummy corporations we need. I think we can have it in place in time for the Sudan operation. I say goodbye and good riddance to Laws. He was a loose cannon."

"Your new set-up is in Singapore, is that right?"

"Yes, sir."

"Why not Hawai'i?"

Duerden smiled an ingratiating smile that Wilson wanted to punch.

"Hawaii's was too hot right now, what with this Laws deal and all."

"If there's nothing to connect us to Laws, what's too hot about it?" Actually, Wilson had no problem with using a Singapore corporation, but he wanted to bait Duerden a little to see what came out. He had a feeling there was more to this whole Laws thing than Duerden was telling, a dangerous feeling for a CIA Division Chief.

"Just playing it safe, sir. No other reason." Duerden crossed his legs and smiled again. Wilson thought he detected a slight tic in Duerden's right eye.

"Donald, had Laws been alive and decided to go public with a claim we were using his corporations to launder money, was there anything to connect us to Laws?"

Duerden didn't hesitate. "Absolutely nothing, nothing at all. Why do you ask?"

"Then why your big concern over Laws being a 'loose cannon,' as you call it?" Wilson made quotation signs with his hands.

Duerden looked at Wilson as if he were a four year old.

"All the deniability in the world wouldn't have undone the adverse publicity we'd have gotten if Laws had been exposed and started claiming he was backed by us."

Of course, he was right, thought Wilson, but there was something—he could feel it.

"You were in Hawai'i when Laws was murdered, weren't you?"

Duerden's eyes narrowed and Wilson could see the wariness on his face, and there was that tic again.

"Yes, sir I was. Just what're you asking?"

"What I'm asking, and quite deliberately, is whether you had any involvement in the death of Maynard Laws?"

Duerden's face remained impassive, although his right hand moved to his right temple, as if he was aware of the tic and could somehow make it stop.

"You can safely assume that at no time did I act outside of my authority."

Wilson almost laughed out loud. "So that would be a no?"

"That would be a no, sir." Duerden uncrossed his legs and smoothed his gray wool dress pants before looking up at Wilson again. He picked at an eyebrow and one corner of his mouth turned up in a kind of snarl. "I'd like the record to reflect that I've answered all of your questions and have cooperated fully with you despite what I consider to be insulting and unprofessional behavior on your part, sir." He paused, but before Wilson could reply, he said, "If you'd like to take this discussion downstairs to Mr. Fuller's office, I'd be happy to cooperate there as well."

Wilson felt tired all of a sudden. His legs ached and he felt the beginning of one of his infamous headaches. He was sure that the loose cannon in this whole mess was Duerden, but he acknowledged to himself that it was all gut feelings. He had no reason to relieve Duerden of his position. If he did so, he would have to answer to the administrative complaint Duerden was sure to make. Wilson knew Duerden relished his field position. If Wilson transferred him without cause, there'd be hell to pay. He reminded himself that Duerden was Fuller's fair-haired boy.

Wilson leaned forward onto his elbows and stared hard at his subordinate.

"I'm going to be watching you, Duerden. If any of this shit comes back to haunt us, you can kiss your career goodbye. Do you read me?"

Duerden glared at Wilson for a couple of seconds, then broke into a smile. "Yes, sir I read you."

"All right, get out of here."

Duerden stood and turned to leave.

"Oh, Duerden, one more thing."

"Yes, sir?"

Wilson shuffled some papers on his desk.

"What's this requisition for expenses for a trip to Paris? What possible business did you have in Paris?"

The question seemed to catch Duerden off guard. His eyes shifted to the paper on Wilson's desk, then back to Wilson.

"I was on my way back from Africa and I wanted to meet one of my arms sale contacts in Paris before I returned to the Pacific."

"Oh? Which one?"

"Well, sir, I'd rather not give his name. It's one of my personal contacts. You know how it is."

Wilson looked at Duerden as if he were a piece of lint. Finally, he said, "Yeah, I know how it is."

Chapter Seventeen

Sandy Foreman's regular table in the Paradise Lounge was in the far corner, the one near the bathrooms. It was dark and private, and that's the way he liked it. He'd become inured to the smell of urine, Clorox, roach spray, and God knew what else.

"You okay, honey?"

Sandy's drooping and clouded eyes moved toward the sound, his expression dull and vacant. He felt a hand on his shoulder.

"Sandy? Baby? It's me, Tiffany." The voice was scarred and hoarse. He tried to focus.

"Tiffany."

"Jesus, Sandy, you're all fucked up. You sure you're okay?"

Sandy's jaw was slack and his forehead showed beads of perspiration. He ran a hand over his scalp. He felt like he was moving in slow motion. He made a guttural sound, which could have meant anything, but to him it was an ironic laugh. To think that Tiffany thought he was fucked up was funny as hell. She was a walking corpse.

He brought her into marginal focus. Her dirty blonde hair was matted, she was missing two upper teeth, and the ones she had left were rotten brown. Her lips were crusted white. There were dark circles under her eyes. He looked down at the hand still resting on his shoulder. It was bony, like the rest of her body. The meth had consumed her. She hadn't turned a trick for him in weeks.

"I'm fine," Sandy managed to say. "Jus' coming on is all." He felt the hand withdraw and he heard her say something as she walked away, but it didn't register. Amy Winehouse was singing about not going to rehab — 'no, no, no'. He closed his eyes and let himself nod for a while, waiting for all the pain to vanish; waiting for the payoff.

Sandy let his mind float from thought to thought. His mind's eye saw the huge Samoan man who'd tracked him down here at Paradise. *Man, that dude was big, but I worked him hard*, he thought.

He was feeling good now, painless; pain he didn't even know he had, was gone. It was perfect now. *This is how life is supposed to be lived*. Things slowly began to come back into focus. He could see Tiffany sitting at the bar, trying to talk to a fat man who was trying to ignore her. He heard the toilet flush behind him. He heard a shrill laugh. He could smell the piss and the sweat and the staleness of the room.

He wouldn't talk to the Samoan dude without getting some cash in return. They'd danced around and around, and when Sandy saw the Samoan start to push the three hundred bucks back into his jeans' pocket he made the deal. *Worked him good.*

Pancho was sitting on the floor of his office working his way through a new box of documents that had just come in from the prosecutor's office. He was disappointed. It looked like a bunch of corporate documents, articles of incorporation, things like that. He couldn't see how they had any relevance to the investigation, but he sorted them in piles, hoping that Harry Chang had tried to pull a fast one by inserting something important in the middle of a bunch of crap so that Pancho would miss it. Harry could later claim in all innocence that he'd provided everything to the defense. It was an old trick, one that could still work if he got sloppy.

There was a knock on the door, and then it opened without waiting for a reply,

"I found that guy, Foreman," Drew announced as he entered. Pancho could hear the whoosh of the couch as Drew plopped himself onto it.

"And?"

"Some pretty interesting stuff, although I'm not sure how helpful any of it is in the end."

Pancho unwound his six-foot frame and got off the floor. He wore old jeans and a polo shirt. He was barefoot. When he was seated behind his desk, notepad at the ready, his look told Drew to talk to him.

"Foreman's a black guy," Sandy said. "He was Maynard Laws' go-to guy for drugs and whores. Apparently Laws was pretty weird."

"In what way?"

"He got off on all sorts of different stuff. Girls, the younger the better, men, the younger the better, public sex, coke, hash, uppers, some downers, and whatever prescription shit Sandy could get for him."

Pancho nodded but said nothing. The wheels were turning in his head. They'd had so little so far that anything new got him excited.

"But here's one of the interesting things," Drew continued. "This Foreman guy's no dummy. He was born in Kansas City, Missouri. He did well in school, got a scholarship to the University of Iowa, got his

Bachelor's in Philosophy, then went on to get an MBA. He had a securities license in Iowa and Illinois. He worked for a Wall Street firm in Iowa City after graduating, then decided to try to move up to the big time. He moved to Chicago, but times had gotten tough and he had a hard time finding a job, so eventually, he went to work for a guy by the name of—" Drew looked down at his notes, "Brian Wells.

"Wells had this penny stock boiler room, where his people, like Foreman, would make cold calls to people on lists they were given. According to Foreman, they were mostly old people looking to supplement their retirement. He'd talk up the stock and explain how only a dollar gain on a fifty-cent stock would triple their money. Of course, the stocks had about as much chance of tripling as I have of winning the lottery. You know the routine."

Pancho nodded.

"Foreman claims he tried to quit a bunch of times—that he was disgusted by what he was doing. But the money was too good and Wells kept talking him into staying. Foreman was living the high life, making upwards of five grand a week. He had an apartment on Lakeshore. He had a three-hundred dollar a day coke habit. He wore Armani suits, pussy by the bushel, blah, blah, blah.

"So anyway, Foreman had completely sold out. He was a top producer. He quit thinking about ethics and morals and all that pesky stuff. Then, one day the shit hit the fan. The consumer protection office moved in, the SEC moved in, the police were investigating. Foreman lost his license and hit the road before any indictments came down. He moved to Miami, but he couldn't sell securities anymore. He drifted from job to job until one night, when he was bartending at a spot in Coconut Grove, who should be sitting across the bar from him but his old boss, Brian Wells. He's with a guy named Mike Thornton, who, it turns out, is none other than our boy, Maynard Laws."

Drew heaved himself off the couch and walked over to the credenza where a pitcher of water and four crystal glasses sat on a Chinese lacquer tray. He poured himself a glass and sat in one of the client chairs at the desk. He grimaced as he lowered himself into the chair.

"Wells and Laws were running a credit card boiler room scam. They talked Foreman into coming to work for them. More big money, more coke, nice clothes. *Plus ca change, plus c'est la meme chose.*" Drew smiled and Pancho laughed. *The more things change, the more they stay the same.*

"Let me guess, the feds move in, Chicago all over again," said Pancho.

"Pretty much, except that Wells was doing some chick who worked at the U.S. Attorney's office who was able to alert them in advance, so they all left town. No arrests. Laws ended up in Hawai'i, using his own name for the first time. Foreman kicked around the East Coast for a while, then heard about Laws in Hawai'i and decided to come check it out."

"I'll bet Laws was pretty happy about Foreman showing up on his doorstep," said Pancho.

Drew chuckled. "Not so much. According to Foreman, he asked Laws for a job. After all, he'd been a legitimate securities broker at one point in his life. At first, Laws shined him on. He didn't exactly say so, but I'm assuming Foreman made some noises about exposing Laws, because next thing you know, Laws offered him a job as a 'personal assistant,' which turned out to mean pimp and drug dealer. Foreman had spent everything he had getting to Hawai'i, so he was desperate."

Drew looked up from his notes. He smiled. "As Foreman so eloquently put it: 'he turned me into his nigger.'"

"Hmmm, motive to murder?"

Drew's look turned serious. "Don't know, but there's a lot more to it than just whores and drugs," he said. "I got the feeling that Foreman and Laws became kind of friends. Foreman never said that," Drew quickly added, "but he told me how they used to drink and party together, and how Laws would sometimes open up to him."

Pancho looked up from his notes. "You mean Foreman knew about Laws' business?"

Drew waved a hand, dismissively. "Oh sure. He knew that almost immediately, remember, he's no dummy. It took him no time to figure out that Laws was working a Ponzi scheme. He even tried to get Laws to rein things in a bit."

Drew used the arms of the chair to push himself up and walked to his leather backpack, which was sitting on the couch. He pulled out a small tape recorder and walked back and set it on the desk. "I want you to listen to this part." He turned on the tape.

Sandy Foreman's voice on the tape was deep and smooth.

" — but he was getting out of control. I told him he was going to fuck up the whole gig. He was spending way too much on himself. He wasn't getting anything back to the investors. For a Ponzi scheme to work, you gotta keep getting money back to the early investors. Use the new to pay the old, while skimming off a reasonable cream. He also wasn't saving anything. I told him to open an offshore account and put something away for the day the whole thing would inevitably come down on him.

"But Maynard had convinced himself he was infallible. I mean, shoot, he was putting his money into shit like real property. He got married for Christ's sake. Now, how the hell do you pick up a house and lot and split town when the heat gets turned up?

"One night, when we were shit-faced on Wild Turkey, and I was going after him on how he was fucking up, Maynard turned to me and told me he had an ace-in-the-hole. He had protection, I think he called it.

"Now get this," there was a slight pause on the tape. "Maynard said he was a CIA operative. That's the exact word . . . 'CIA operative.' He said he was doing work for the CIA and that they'd guaranteed him he'd be protected. I pressed him for details, but he kind of clammed up on me after a while.

"I wrote it off as the ramblings of a scared and drunk man, but on several other occasions, always when we were fucked up on something or other, Maynard referred to his protection and his work for the CIA."

Drew turned the tape recorder off and sat back in his chair, looking at Pancho, who was staring at the tape, saying nothing. Finally, Pancho shook his head, bewilderment showing on his face.

"CIA? Seriously? I think Foreman was right: drunken ramblings."

Drew gave a half shrug. "Maybe," he drawled. "That's what I thought at first, and it's probably right, but remember how I told you about the other investors telling me about some kind of government connection? What if there's something to it?"

Pancho rubbed his neck, scrunching up his face as he did so. "Doesn't make any sense," he said finally. "Why in the world would the CIA work with some bozo like Laws?"

Drew bent over, massaged his knee, and sighed.

"But," said Pancho, "Foreman does open up a whole new arena of investigation for us: drugs, women, gay sex. Think of all the potential suspects that brings into the picture. Someone burned, someone humiliated, someone jealous, someone stoned out of their mind." He paused. "How'd you find him anyway?"

"Not so tough for an ace investigator like me."

Pancho rolled his eyes.

"We had his name and cell phone number from the police report. From that, I found an address for him, some dump on Maunakea Street. There was no answer every time I showed up at the apartment, so I tracked down the manager, some old Chinese dude. He told me Foreman still lived there, but was rarely home. I asked him to describe Foreman for me, and it was only then I learned he was black. So that made it easier to walk around Chinatown asking for some black guy named Sandy. A waitress at a Filipino restaurant on Hotel Street told me he comes around there a lot, even eats with the owner's son from time to time. I tried to find him, the owner's son I mean, some guy named Ricardo Baguio, but no one seemed to know where he was. The waitress said Foreman hangs at the Paradise Lounge down the street."

Drew smiled and spread his hands. "Sure enough, that's where I found him, just sitting in the bar, nursing a beer. He didn't look so good. He's clearly heavy into drugs himself. I think he may be on the junk. He hit me up for three bills to get him to talk. I got the feeling he was hurting for a fix."

Pancho made a face. "So, even if he had something helpful to testify about, he's an unreliable junkie? Is that why he was so willing to talk about his supposed friend for three hundred bucks?"

"Yeah, pretty much, although I think it was probably more of a love/hate relationship. Laws was his gravy train, but Foreman hated him for, as he called it, turning him into Laws' 'nigger.'"

Pancho looked up at the ceiling. "What was the timing in terms of the call from Laws to Foreman and the time of death?"

Drew looked down at his notes again. "Not sure. The timing is all screwed up, as you discovered at the prelim. Plus, the call was to Foreman's cell phone. Who knows where he was at the time of the call? He could have been sitting in Laws' driveway for all we know."

Pancho clasped his hands behind his head. "Okay, let's see if we can find out where Foreman was at the time of the murder. Hopefully, the cops are exploring this angle too, but I don't want to presume. They think they have it all locked up with the evidence against Reggie."

Drew chuckled. "Can't say as I blame 'em."

Pancho ignored him. "Let's also explore the dope and prostitution angle a bit, see what you can come up with."

Drew rubbed his hands together in mock anticipation. "This is getting good. A drug addled gay prostitute, whose life savings are invested with Hawaii's premier investment counselor, first falls in love with the counselor, then murders him when he finds out that his money has all been lost."

Pancho shook his head and ignored Drew's slow exit.

Chapter Eighteen

Pancho jerked awake, his pulse racing, his body moist with sweat, the sheets thrown aside. The dull pain in his chest was back. He opened one eye and peered at the clock on the Oceanic cable box by the TV. Three twenty-six. He wondered if he should go to the emergency room. He was sure that whatever was going on was just stress related, that he was too young and in too good shape to be having a heart attack, but, he thought, it would be pretty stupid not to check it out.

He climbed out of bed and went to the bathroom. He peed, then dry-swallowed an aspirin. The pain had subsided and he could feel his pulse slowing. *Could've been the nightmare I'd been having*, he thought, another one of those running dreams where someone he knew was in grave danger. Paula maybe? Or a client? He tried to run to help, but his legs felt like he was running in quicksand.

He decided to wait until morning and swing by his doctor's office on the way to work. When he climbed back into bed, he immediately knew he was going to have a hard time getting back to sleep. Now his mind was racing. The trial date was looming and he had no defense. He began to second-guess himself for having taken the Bellows case. It looked like he was going to get his *okole* handed to him on a platter.

Pancho could hear the surf breaking on the reef outside. Last night's news had reported that a South Shore swell was coming in. He tried to stop thinking about the case. He tried to stop thinking about whether he'd had a heart attack. He tried thinking about surfing. It didn't work. At quarter-to-five, he climbed out of bed and made coffee. The first birdsongs of the morning had tentatively begun in the *hau* tree below his lanai.

He downed his coffee, put on a pair of faded jeans, soft brown leather boots, and a light blue cotton shirt. This was a workday; no clients, no court. He decided he'd go to the office for a while, then try to see Dr. Ginsberg sometime that day.

Twenty minutes later, he was at his desk. He stared out at the harbor. The bay was flat and glassy. He rubbed his face with both hands. He had to figure something out. He was at a loss over how to defend Reggie; he had nothing. All he could do was to try to knock holes in the prosecutor's case and argue reasonable doubt.

For a while, he and Drew had been excited over Drew's find in Sandy Foreman. Here was someone who had intimate knowledge of the decedent and his seamy alter ego. Drew's jokes aside, there were an unlimited number of potential suspects, including Foreman himself. Couldn't Laws have been murdered by an abused and angry whore? Or a gay lover? Or a burned-out doper who'd found where Laws lived, had tried to hit him up for money, then killed him in a rage when rebuked? The permutations were endless, but the hours spent by Drew on the street had come up empty.

The overriding question was Bellows' gun. No scenario that Pancho came up with using the underworld characters as the bad guys explained the coincidence of Laws being shot with Bellows' gun. To argue that the same person who killed Laws broke into Bellows' apartment and stole his gun was pushing any hypothetical beyond reason.

When Drew tried to interview Elie Watson again, she reluctantly let him in, but when he asked her about the CIA connection, she denied knowing anything and had cut the interview short. It was suspicious, but so what?

Although unwaveringly skeptical of the information, Pancho nonetheless contacted the CIA and was passed from clerk to clerk, with nothing learned. He wrote a letter to the Director of the CIA, inquiring into the CIA's knowledge and involvement with Laws and/or his firm. He received a polite generic response, which said that the CIA had a policy of not responding to any such requests for information.

Pancho and Drew talked at length about putting Sandy Foreman on the stand to testify about his conversations with Laws, but decided that without any corroboration, such testimony would sound absurd, and would be interpreted as the defense grasping for straws, which, of course, it was.

At ten o'clock, Pancho called Dr. Ginsberg's office. Ginsberg was Pancho's primary care physician and friend. Pancho told Cecelia, the nurse, what was going on and, after putting Pancho on hold and talking to the doctor, she told Pancho to come in right away. As Pancho walked by Susan's desk, he told her he'd be back in about an hour. She nodded to him and didn't ask where he was going.

Dr. Ginsberg's office was in the Physician's Office Building next to Queen's Hospital. It was less than a five-minute drive from Pancho's office. Two people were seated in the reception area when Pancho walked into the office, but Cecelia had been standing next to the receptionist and she motioned for him to come directly back to the examining rooms.

Dr. Ginsberg looked like a stereotypical professor. His dark, curly hair seemed to be perpetually wild. His brown eyes were alert and in constant motion as they took everything in. He had deep laugh lines that made him look like he found everything humorous, but as he listened to Pancho's account of the symptoms he'd been having, it was clear he didn't find anything funny.

"Jesus, Paunch, you're supposed to be a smart guy. I can't believe you didn't come in or go to the ER the first time you had these symptoms." He shook his head in apparent disgust as he put the stethoscope buds in his ears.

Twenty minutes later, after having listened to Pancho's heart and lungs, and reading the results of the EKG test Cecelia had administered, Dr. Ginsberg took Pancho into his office.

"Everything looks normal," said Ginsberg. "But these were just basic tests. I wouldn't mind getting a stress test done. We'd have to do that over at the hospital; I don't have a treadmill here."

Pancho was smiling from the relief of hearing that he hadn't had a heart attack, or at least *probably* hadn't had a heart attack. He nodded, "Sure, but I'll need to figure out when I can do it. I've got this big trial coming up."

Ginsberg chuckled. "Yeah, I know, but I don't want you putting this off too long. Those symptoms mean something."

Pancho stood and put his hand out to shake. "I'll have Susan call your office to set it up as soon as I get back." He smiled broadly. "I promise."

Chapter Nineteen

CIA Operations Division Chief for the Pacific, Oliver Wilson, walked down the long, fluorescent-lit hallway. He paused at a door for a brief moment before knocking and entering. Deputy Director for Operations, Randolph Fuller, looked up from his massive wood desk across the expanse of royal blue carpet, then, seeing who it was, looked back down at some paperwork. There was a trail of worn carpet leading from the door to the desk. Wilson followed the trail and stood in front of Fuller, waiting for an invitation to sit.

Fuller started talking while still looking down. He didn't invite Wilson to sit.

"Just what the hell's going on in Hawai'i, Ollie?"

Wilson shifted on his feet. The bad back that had forced him out of the field and into a desk job caused sciatica to flare when he was forced to stand. "What do you mean?"

Fuller finally looked up. The veins in his throat stood out and his temples visibly throbbed. The tiny capillaries in his nose and cheeks were pinker than usual. His thin lips were curled downward. He held up a piece of paper. "Do you know what this is?"

"No, sir. If I did, maybe I'd know what you were talking about."

Fuller let the paper drop theatrically to the desk. "This, Ollie, is our careers falling into the shitter. This is—"

Wilson interrupted, keeping his voice calm. "I presume this has to do with the Laws case in Honolulu? If you'd cut the drama and tell me what the hell's going on maybe we can better assess the situation." His back was killing him, but he refused to ask to sit.

Fuller stared at him, as if debating whether to be angry at the insubordination, or to get to the point. He finally chose the latter.

"This is an official inquiry from an attorney in Honolulu asking the CIA to comment on allegations that it was involved in business dealings with that Maynard Laws fellow."

Wilson felt a sharp pain shoot down his left buttock and into the back of his thigh. He cringed. He tried to keep his voice level and in control. "Do we know the source of the allegation? I mean, do we know where this attorney got his information?"

Fuller shook his head. "Obviously it wasn't from Duerden. You've got him running around on some half-assed mission in Mexico, don't you?"

"Yes, sir I thought it best to get him out of the area for a while. So I'm at a loss as to where this information is coming from. Duerden assured us both there were no loose ends."

"Hmmm. Well someone's talking and we need to nip it in the bud, now. Get—"

Wilson cut him off. "I'll call Duerden and try to find out if there's anyone else over there who knew about us. But I'll tell you again that I don't trust him, and I've been against this whole operation from the beginning."

"Save the excuses and blame-game for later, Ollie. Right now, I've got the Director all over my ass and we need to get this under control. If this goes public, heads are going to roll." Fuller waved his hand dismissively and looked down at the papers on his desk. Wilson looked at him for a hard beat, then turned and walked away. He felt like someone was stabbing him in the butt with an ice pick.

Chapter Twenty

Pancho listened to the soft thud of his New Balance running shoes as they struck the sidewalk pavement alongside Kapi'olani Park. He hated running, but Paula was into it, and, from time to time, he allowed himself to be talked into going for a run. He had passed the stress treadmill with flying colors and Dr. Ginsberg had finally decided on a diagnosis of stress-induced panic attacks, which can manifest similar to a heart attack. Ginsberg suggested that Pancho get more exercise and reduce his stress levels, a suggestion that made Pancho laugh out loud. He knew that as long as he was involved in a murder trial, he wouldn't be able to reduce his stress any time soon. So he figured he might as well kill two birds with one stone by making Paula happy and increasing his exercise level.

His hamstrings felt tight, his low back ached, and he knew he should stop, but they were almost back to the condo. Paula had given up trying to stay back with him, and he now watched her beautiful *okole* move in rhythm to her stride. It motivated him to continue the chase.

It was a picture-perfect winter morning in Honolulu. There was a slight chill to the air and the morning dew was heavy. It felt clear and fresh, and Diamond Head had recently turned green from the more plentiful winter rains. Most mainlanders were surprised when they were told by Hawai'i residents that there really were seasons in Hawai'i. Pancho told mainlander friends that the longer he lived in Hawai'i, the more pronounced the seasons became.

They ran by a plumeria tree, and the heavy scent of the flowers in the morning stillness was pleasing. Pancho put out a burst of speed for a strong finish and had almost caught up with Paula by the time they reached the building where Pancho lived.

"I had a hard time holding myself back for you," Pancho said between pants.

Paula grinned. "Next time I'll try to pick up the pace a little."

"You do and you run alone." He pulled her to him and brought their sweating bodies close. Her sensuous lips still smirked, so he covered them with his mouth and they kissed a long, lingering kiss, enjoying each other's wetness and clean smells of sweat.

"A swim? Or do you just want to go up and shower?" he asked when they finally broke their embrace.

"I've got to get to work."

"Okay, if you're worn out, I understand."

Paula gave him a punch to the stomach and trotted into the building foyer. Pancho caught up as the elevator arrived.

As they rode in the elevator, Pancho caught Paula studying him.

"What?"

"What what?"

"What you looking at?"

"Just checking you out. I love you, you know."

They showered together and Paula rebuffed Pancho's attempts to get her to go back to bed and make love.

"Don't you have a trial starting tomorrow?"

"Yeah, but it's only a murder trial, and I don't have shit for a case, so I may as well stay home and make love. If you aren't interested, perhaps you could refer me to someone?"

"You'll need a hospital referral when I get through with you," said Paula, as she threw another punch that actually kind of hurt, but which Pancho pretended he barely felt.

Paula was dressed and ready to leave for work before Pancho, who seemed to be taking his time with just about everything this morning. She kissed him, took his tongue, and lightly brushed his penis. When she felt it grow hard, she broke off the embrace.

"Have a nice day."

Pancho stood in the middle of the bedroom with a hard-on. He gave her a mock look of shock, looked in astonishment at his penis, as if he didn't know what to do with it, and looked back at her like a child who'd just had a toy taken away from him. Paula laughed.

"I love you, you dumb shit. See you later." Then she was gone.

As Pancho dressed for work, he thought about how best to approach Harry Chang to broach the subject of a deal. Reggie continued to maintain his innocence, but Pancho was at a complete loss how to put together any kind of a defense. This case had plea bargain written all over it. The thought of trying the case with no defense theory was terrifying. All the hard work Pancho had done to build up his reputation was in peril.

When he walked into the office, later than usual, Susan gave him a knowing, sympathetic look. He knew she understood the anguish he was putting himself through. When he'd asked her to make the stress-test appointment, he'd finally confessed to her that he'd been having chest pain, but he reassured her that all the tests so far, were negative.

Pancho tried a bright smile for her, but he knew it fell short, so he just kept on walking. Drew was waiting in Pancho's office. He'd been poring over the police and autopsy reports, looking for missed clues, new directions of investigations, anything that would give them some measure of optimism. He looked up when Pancho came in.

"Pancho, glad you could make it, buddy."

"Bite me. Anything new?"

"Yeah, a little bit. I decided to interview the neighbor who called in the shot to the police. I don't know why, just desperate, I guess. Anyway, there may be a few things you can play with. She got a subpoena to appear as a witness at the trial, but other than her statements to HPD, she hasn't been contacted by anyone to discuss her testimony. I guess the prosecutor feels it's a slam bam, in and out, witness. Heard a shot, called the police, and that's it."

Pancho sat behind his desk. "Yeah, and?"

"Turns out she waited after hearing the shot to call the police. This is pretty funny in a bizarre kind of way," said Drew. "Laws apparently liked to take his air rifle out to the edge of the Bay and shoot at poor little defenseless *a'ama* crabs. Blow 'em out of the water, so to speak. The neighbor lady didn't like that, so she started calling the cops every time she heard Laws shoot his air rifle. She knew damn well it was only an air rifle, but she called it in as a possible gunshot." Drew paused and took a sip of coffee.

"So, long story short, a kind of feud develops, with the cops, mostly this guy . . ." Drew checked his notes, "Officer Lee, Jason Lee, caught in the middle. According to the neighbor, Officer Lee never actually did anything, even though Laws wasn't supposed to be shooting at crabs. On the day of the murder, she heard Laws shoot his air rifle, but there was only one shot so she didn't call it in. A little later, she heard another shot. She's not sure, but she thinks it sounded different. Again, there was only one shot, so she thought she'd let it go. But it nagged at her that it sounded different, and she finally called it in. She isn't sure, but thinks she waited a good fifteen to thirty minutes. She was embarrassed about having waited so long once she found out Laws had been murdered, which is why she didn't volunteer the information to the cops.

"It may also explain why it took the police so long to respond. She said that when she called it in, she was pretty wishy-washy about whether it was a gunshot or not. If the police dispatcher conveyed that attitude to the patrolmen in the vicinity, and particularly if it was Lee, which, according to the police report, it was, I can see him not making a beeline to the address. He probably finished up whatever he was doing before responding."

Drew watched Pancho for his reaction to the new data. Pancho said nothing, mulling over the implications of the information. After a few minutes, he spoke.

"I'm not sure what to do with this. I suppose we could argue that if the jury's inclined to believe that because the gun belonged to Bellows, and they believe he must have been the one to pull the trigger, then they should consider a lesser offense of assault, or attempted murder, because Bellows could have shot Laws, which did not kill him, and then someone else came along and whacked off his head and arms, which did kill him."

Pancho and Drew looked at each other, then laughed at the same time. *That sounded about as preposterous as anything else they'd come up with*, thought Pancho. He closed his eyes and rubbed his temples.

"Good detective work, Drew, but I think I'm still stuck with a pure reasonable doubt argument. The fact that Bellows might have killed Laws a half hour earlier than the State says probably isn't going to impress the jury."

"Hey man, I'm just the detective. I detected shit, now you do your magic."

Pancho laughed, but he wasn't feeling particularly funny. "Did you go see Bellows?" Pancho asked.

"Yeah. I took him a suit to wear to court tomorrow. He didn't look too bad. He's pretty strong."

"Did he have any more thoughts, any leads, anything to help us?"

"No. He knows he's in deep shit, but he hasn't come up with anything new."

Pancho sighed. He knew his case, or lack of case. He knew what he would have to argue, but he liked to have something to work with, and everything he pursued led to a big dead-end. He had no meat to his case at all. In fact, he was ninety percent sure at this point that he would present no case, would not even put Reggie on to testify.

He decided to spend a few hours going over the jury pool list. At least he could try to get a good jury.

Chapter Twenty-One

Elie Watson was trying to watch TV, but she kept glancing over at the subpoena sitting on the side table. Her throat felt tight and she couldn't seem to catch her breath. She tried to concentrate on something Oprah was saying, but it wouldn't register.

Elie and her attorney, Bill Chambers, had met with Harry Chang, who explained that her testimony should be brief. She'd be asked about Bellows' investments and his anger and confrontations at the office. Harry told her she was an important witness for presentation of motive.

What Elie didn't tell Harry Chang or her own attorney was that she'd been interviewed twice by Drew. She didn't mention that Drew had been asking about CIA connections.

Elie didn't know what to do. She'd been trying for weeks, since Drew had reappeared with the questions about the CIA, to get hold of Donald. She left repeated messages for him at the CIA headquarters in Langley, but there had been no response. It was almost as if he didn't exist.

Elie couldn't stop thinking about whether or not Bellows' attorney would ask her questions about the CIA and about Donald. She'd convinced herself that the authorities would go easy on her for her role in the investment scam, which is why she had ignored all the expensive counseling of Bill Chambers, but perjury was a different matter. So far, she'd kept her promise to Donald, but how far should she go? What did she owe him? Nothing, she thought, not a damn thing. Then why did she have this irrational need to protect him? Why did she so desperately wish that he was with her?

If only she could talk to Donald, she would tell him she was sorry she told him to get out of her life. She would tell him that she'd do whatever he wanted, if only he would protect her, make her safe. Then they could be together. They could leave Hawai'i. She wouldn't have to go home to Hilo with her tail between her legs.

She looked again at the subpoena, and she knew in her heart she was kidding herself. She wiped at her tears with her bare hand. If only she'd taken Chambers' advice from the beginning and refused to answer any questions, then she wouldn't be in this bind. Now, as her attorney explained it, she'd given so many statements that she had effectively waived the privilege against self-incrimination.

Elie willed herself off the couch and walked to the bathroom and stared at herself in the mirror. There were dark circles under her eyes. Except where the tears had trailed, her skin seemed dry and taut. She smeared some collagen cream on her face and rubbed it in.

If only she had someone to talk to.

She brushed her hair, slowly and methodically.

If only she had someone to hold her and tell her it would be all right. If only she'd run away like she first wanted to do. If only she'd never left Hilo and come to work for Maynard.

Elie thought about how briefly happy she'd been when she was in Africa with Donald, so far away from all this mess.

She went to the mirrored medicine chest and took out the plastic bottle of Halcion, her sleeping pills. She poured them into her hand and counted them: fifteen.

If only she could go to sleep and wake up and this would all have been a nightmare. Or, maybe it would be better not to wake up at all.

She walked to the kitchen and took a glass from the cupboard. She filled it with tap water and started taking the pills, two at a time. When she had taken all fifteen, she went into the living room and lay down on the orange crushed velvet couch. She changed the channel with the remote control.

Judge Judy was on. It was a case about a person suing her veterinarian for having put her pet rabbit to death without consent. The rabbit had been riddled with cancer, and had only days to live. The person called the vet a murderer.

Elie shut her eyes and listened to the bickering, Judge Judy interceding in a nasty tone every once in a while. She was beginning to feel less scared. It was going to be okay. She could sleep now. Sleep without nightmares.

Chapter Twenty-Two

Pancho sat at his desk, flipping through reams of documents from Laws' business. He was searching for new directions, new possibilities, new angles. Both he and Drew had been through all the records before. The late afternoon sun poured in through his floor to ceiling windows, winning the war of temperature dominance with the air-conditioner. *What had happened to winter?* Pancho's armpits were sweat stained, but he refused to close the blinds. He felt tired and useless. He put his head down into his arms on the desk. He felt the onset of chest pain, slight, but clearly noticeable. He closed his eyes and tried some deep breathing.

He jerked his head up moments later when Susan flew into the office without knocking and turned on his television set. Shelly Chen, the court beat reporter, was standing in front of Queen's Hospital with a microphone to her mouth.

"In a dramatic late-breaking development in the Maynard Laws murder case, this reporter has learned that Elie Watson, Laws' executive secretary, has taken an overdose of pills, and is in guarded condition at Queen's. The police have not confirmed that it was a suicide attempt, although from everything this reporter has heard, all indications point to that being the case.

"Watson was scheduled to testify in the trial of Reginald Bellows, the man accused of murdering Laws. The trial starts tomorrow in circuit court. We do not know what impact, if any, this development will have on the commencement of the trial.

"Watson herself may be facing criminal charges for her role in the Laws investment swindle, although no charges have yet been filed—"

Pancho switched off the television.

"The poor thing," said Susan. "Imagine what she's been going through."

Pancho nodded and rubbed his chest reflexively. His mind was racing. He knew that Elie was scheduled to testify. What was she afraid of: the possible criminal charges against her or something else?

"You think Harry will ask for a continuance?" Susan kneeled down to the floor and began straightening the stacks of paperwork.

Pancho shook his head. "Doubt it. She's pretty much a motive witness. I reckon she'll be able to testify in a couple days."

Susan finished what she was doing and lingered for a few more moments before she wandered back out to her desk. Pancho took some more deep breaths. The fact that he knew he wasn't having a heart attack whenever he felt the onset of symptoms was a relief, but it was still scary. All he had to do was wait it out, and eventually the pain, the sweats, and the dizziness would go away. He swiveled his chair to look out the window. The January sun was finally sinking into the ocean. Shades of orange and red were creeping in to take over from the blues.

Pancho's guts and brain were in complete agreement that he had missed something of great significance in this case. Unfortunately, they failed to tell him what it was.

He had tried many a case with no real defense, arguing only reasonable doubt. He'd won a good many cases that way. But this case was different. This was murder. The stakes were as high as they could be. His intellectual and intuitive systems were screaming at him, but he couldn't make out the words. It was like a cacophony of warning alarms going off in his head and stomach. What could Elie's suicide attempt mean beyond the obvious?

Pancho rubbed his chest and turned back to the desk. He pushed the documents he'd been reviewing aside and pulled a yellow legal pad in front of him. He began to write.

Hypothesis:
- *Laws starts up scam investment firm.*
- *CIA somehow learns of him and asks him to do some favors for them*
- *government blackmail???*
  - *government subsidized fraud???*
- *Laws starts to go out of control, even for CIA.*
- *CIA needs to cover its ass. Kill him?*
- *CIA knows investors have lost $.*

Motive for Murder?
- *Easy to find right investor to set up.*

> –Bellows good man to set up: ex-vet; ex mercenary; has own gun; in the financial hurt locker.
> –Someone (CIA?) steals Bellows gun; offer to have Bellows kill Laws; puts $ in Bellows account (why do this?); kill Laws, plant gun where will be found.
> "Problems/Questions re Hypo:
> why not just kill Laws w/o setting anyone up?
> why hack off Laws' head and arms?
> why ask Bellows to kill Laws, even if setting Bellows up?
> why waste $ by putting it in Bellows account?
> why not set up a whore or druggie? CIA didn't know of Laws' sexual forays?
> –would CIA kill Laws????
> what would CIA be using Laws for anyway???
> wouldn't someone else in Laws' co. know about CIA?
> if someone else knew: Elie??
> is Elie afraid of someone or something? (besides going to jail?)

Pancho put down the pen and studied his list. There were some pretty strong assumptions that had to be made for the CIA hypothetical to work. Most disturbing was that if the theory was correct, how could it ever be proved? Going up against the CIA would be impossible. They never answered anything, even if they were innocent.

Elie was the key. If anyone other than Laws knew the CIA was using Laws for some kind of work, it had to be Elie. She would know what Laws was being used for. If she testified to that knowledge, Sandy Foreman's testimony could then be used as corroboration. Pancho didn't have to prove the CIA murdered Laws. All he had to do was put up enough reasonable doubt.

Pancho scratched his head. Some dandruff fluttered to the desk, landing on his work sheet. He absently brushed it aside. He picked up the pen and twirled it in his fingers.

Did Elie know, or suspect, that the CIA had killed Laws? Is that why she'd never admitted to CIA involvement, and why she'd now tried to kill herself? Was she afraid that if she implicated the CIA, her life would be in danger?

Pancho stuck the end of his pen in his mouth and chewed it.

He was still nowhere unless Elie testified as to CIA involvement. He was beating his head against the brick wall that had haunted him from the beginning of this case.

He called Susan on the intercom and asked her to call Drew to come in. Drew had been going twenty hours a day and had gone home to shower and catch a nap.

Pancho tossed the legal pad on the credenza to the left of his desk. He would let the questions and the hypotheticals rumble around in his brain for a while, let his unconscious work on it.

He returned to the documents. There was no record of payments received from the CIA. That would not be expected, anyway. But if the CIA had used Laws for something, more than likely it wouldn't be Laws as a person. They had trained operatives, and Laws was an amateur and a crook. So what would they want?

Pancho was holding a document entitled "Articles of Incorporation of Platte River Corp., a Hong Kong corporation." Pancho smiled to himself, remembering that Laws had grown up in Nebraska, which was where the Platte River was.

"What a sentimental guy," Pancho said aloud to himself.

He was about to set the document aside, for he'd seen scores just like it, with different names and different places of incorporation. He froze. Corporations. That's what the CIA would want.

Pancho had read somewhere that the CIA sometimes used dummy corporations for its covert dealings. In fact, he thought, didn't those guys captured in Nicaragua work for corporations that were reputed to be CIA fronts? Didn't they even have CIA documents, or something, on their person? Pretty sloppy work, if true. After that whole Iran-Contra fiasco, would the CIA still be doing the same old thing?

Pancho got up and began pacing. Laws' operation would have been perfect for setting up any number of corporations around the Pacific. Pancho wondered why someone like Laws would have been attractive to the CIA. Obviously, they thought he'd be willing to play fast and loose with the law, but would they have used him if they knew he was a complete fraud? He shrugged, maybe so. Maybe that's exactly what the CIA was looking for — someone they could use and discard at will.

When the CIA learned that Laws was on the verge of being exposed as a fraud, maybe they decided they needed to do some house cleaning, which included killing the host.

It was preposterous. It was absurd. It was scandalous. But it was actually starting to make sense.

An hour later, Drew walked into Pancho's office wearing cargo shorts, an old Aloha shirt, and a pair of worn, brown flip-flops on his feet. He saw Pancho sitting on the floor, surrounded by stacks of papers.

"What's happening?"

Pancho addressed Drew without looking up; placing a document he'd just pulled from a box onto one of the stacks.

"I think I've got some things figured out. I think there really might've been a CIA connection here. Did you hear about Elie?"

"Yeah, poor girl." Drew lowered himself down onto the couch. "So, fill me in."

Pancho proceeded to run through his thought processes, his working hypothetical, his questions, and his theory about the corporations. As he verbalized his thoughts, he realized that it was still farfetched, yet he'd heard of real life scenarios just as crazy.

"Who in the world would ever have thought we would sell arms to Iran, despite an embargo, to finance rebels in Nicaragua?" asked Pancho.

"Yeah," said Drew, "but that was a long time ago. Don't you think they learned their lesson by now?"

Pancho chuckled. "You'd have thought so," he said, "but just recently we had a CIA Director who was a retired General, having sex with a woman who was a totally loose cannon. We had the CIA sending emails back and forth to the State Department after Benghazi, trying to make itself not look as incompetent as it apparently was. We had revelations from that Snowden guy that the CIA and NSA routinely used outside contractors." He paused, looking at Drew. "Think about all of that, and this scenario doesn't seem so farfetched, does it?"

Drew scrunched up his face while nodding. "Good point." He nodded at the stacks of paperwork that surrounded Pancho on the floor. "What're you doing?"

"I'm pulling out all of the various corporations which Laws had set up. I'm separating them by location of incorporation. Then I'll want to go through the financial records to see if any money went through any of these corporations. If so, where did the money come from and where'd it go? If not, what was the corporation used for? We'll want to check with the prosecutors tomorrow to see if there're any other corporate documents that we don't have."

"Are you nuts? Do you realize you have a whole supply room full of boxes of documents on Laws, not to mention the ones filling up this lovely office? You got trial starting tomorrow, in case you've forgotten."

Pancho looked impatient. "I haven't forgotten. That's why you're here. You and Susan are going to keep doing this while I start the trial. I'll hire a paralegal to help. I want you to call Glenn Hubbard, the economist I usually use, to help answer any questions on the financial side."

Pancho stopped working a moment and looked up at Drew.

"I can't count on getting Elie to testify about any CIA connection voluntarily. I either have to prove a connection exists, or I have to come up with enough stuff so she'll have to admit it." Pancho ran his hand through his hair. There was a gleam in his eye. He could feel the start of an adrenaline rush. It might be the day before trial, but he finally felt the rumblings of a possible defense.

"Don't you see, once I get the CIA involved in the case, the jury will believe anything. After all the crap the CIA has pulled over the years, the jury would be receptive to a scenario of the CIA setting up Bellows to take the fall for Laws' murder. I don't have to prove jack. I just have to get the CIA in there heavy enough to cause total confusion."

Drew smiled. "Does it help your confidence if I were to tell you that you confused the shit out of me?"

Pancho smiled back, easing off his intensity for a moment. "You're an easy audience, you confuse easily. Now, let's get to work."

Chapter Twenty-Three

Pancho sat at the defendants' counsel table, alone in the courtroom. The walls from were paneled with beautiful local koa wood, as was the raised judge's bench. There were no windows and no pictures. On one side of the bench was an American flag and on the other was the Hawaiian flag. The koa-paneled jury box held fourteen seats, two for alternates. The clerks' desk and the court reporter's station fronted the judge's bench. Behind Pancho was the wood railing with a swinging gate that separated the court from the spectator section. It was eerily quiet.

Pancho had long ago developed a habit of coming early to the first day of trial to sit alone in the courtroom. The various judges' staffs accommodated his whim, and unlocked the court ten minutes earlier than usual on such days. Pancho did not work—he had not opened his briefcase, he simply let his gaze wander around the room and allowed his mind to drift. This was his real office. This was his version of an operating theatre. To Pancho, this was sacred ground to which he was driven to pay homage before the battle for justice began.

Pancho closed his eyes and listened to his controlled breathing. This was the first trial he'd be involved in since his panic attacks had started. What if he had an attack and passed out in court? The thought of it caused his pulse to race. He forced himself to breathe, deep and slow. He'd be fine. It was just another day in court, on the stage he loved. *I'll be fine.*

At two minutes before nine, Harry Chang bustled in, out of breath under the weight of his trial briefcases. The two warriors barely had time to say hello before the sheriffs walked Reggie into the courtroom, shackles removed for now.

"You okay?" asked Pancho.

"Yeah, I'll be all right."

"I have some stuff to discuss with you, but it'll have to wait. All we're doing today is picking the jury. I'm going to give you a pen and paper. If you want to pass me any notes, go ahead. Otherwise, keep quiet at all times."

Reggie nodded.

"And remember what I told you, look interested. This is your life. Look at the jury, but don't stare anyone down. Don't overreact to things, but don't be a cold fish either. You're a human being, and I want the jury to feel that, okay?"

Reggie nodded again. He looked at the empty jury box. Soon it would be filled with people who would decide his fate. They would be picked from the jury pool, the group of people now filing into the courtroom, a few talking in hushed tones. The spectators would be admitted only after the jury was in place.

From the jury pool, individuals were called to take a seat in the jury box as their names were pulled out of a box. In a short time, the jury box was filled. The process called *voir dire* began. The attorneys for each side posed questions to the jury as a whole or to individual jurors. The purpose was to determine whether the person would be a fair and impartial juror. Of course, fair and impartial to the prosecutor meant a juror that would be likely to convict. Fair and impartial to the defense meant a juror who was likely to acquit. The theory being that after both sides had a shot at the jurors, the result would be a group of twelve men and women, plus alternates, acceptable to both sides.

Both Harry and Pancho made a big show of talking about fairness and impartiality.

Harry's style was formal, almost officious. He was not an imposing figure. He stood at about 5'5" and was overweight. He was in his late thirties. His hair was jet black, and his round, Chinese-American face, was too soft to be imposing. His less than complimentary nickname among the Bar was 'Pillsbury Dough Boy', but Pancho knew that any defense attorney who underestimated Harry would find themselves in serious trouble. Harry was as formidable an adversary as there was. He wore the ubiquitous blue blazer and gray pants that so many attorneys in Honolulu wore. Besides picking jurors he thought would be prone to convict, Harry's other goal during *voir dire* would be to set himself up as an authority figure.

The good thing about Harry, thought Pancho, was that Harry knew himself. Harry knew that he came across somewhat aloof, and rather than be someone he wasn't, he had adapted his style to his personality. He didn't try to be overly friendly or play the 'local boy' card that many local attorneys tried to do when they came up against a *haole* like Pancho. Juries were not dumb, and were more than capable of seeing through an act.

Pancho's style of *voir dire* was to try to get the jurors to be as comfortable as possible. He was selling himself, and he had an innate ability to relate to almost any jury, regardless of its ethnic makeup. If he could convince the jury of his credibility and fairness, he would not have as far to go to convince them of Reggie's innocence.

Pancho quickly memorized the jurors' names as he filled them into his jury chart. He had a little more time to do that, since Harry went first. When it was Pancho's turn, he stood, holding nothing in his hands. He left the counsel table, but did not use a podium. He stood in the middle of the courtroom, not so close to the jurors as to intimidate them, yet not so far away as to seem distant.

He asked the first prospective juror, Mr. Watanabe, about his hobbies and the magazines he subscribed to. One could tell a lot about a person from the magazines he read. He made a golf joke to Mr. Watanabe before moving on, reluctantly breaking off the intimate conversation they had been having, or so he made it seem.

Mrs. Chinn was married to a police officer, and Pancho knew he was going to use one of his peremptory challenges to bump her, so he used her to do a little lecturing, not fearful of hurting the feelings of a juror who would not be on the panel.

"Mrs. Chinn, you are married to a police officer, is that right?"

"Yes." Her voice was meek and nervous.

"I'm sure all of us in this court would agree that the police do a wonderful job, your husband included," he said, evoking a pleased smile from Mrs. Chinn.

"Because you're married to a police officer though, Mrs. Chinn, would you feel that you're going to have a hard time with the proposition I'll be suggesting that the police made an honest but terrible mistake in this case?"

"No, I'm willing to listen to what you have to say."

Well said, Mrs. Chinn, thought Pancho. No chance of bumping her for cause, although he never really expected to be able to anyway.

"Would you agree that police officers are human beings, sometimes overworked human beings, and may sometimes make mistakes?"

"Yes, I guess I'd have to agree that mistakes can be made."

"And you wouldn't assume that just because my client has been arrested, that he must be guilty, would you?"

Mrs. Chinn glanced at Reggie, as did several of the jurors.

"Well, I'm willing to listen to what you have to say about it."

Oh, Mrs. Chinn, thought Pancho.

"Well, ma'am, does that mean you're inclined to think my client guilty, but that you're willing to have me convince you otherwise?"

Pancho was quickly evaluating his position. Should he push her and try to get her off for cause, now that she'd started to show her true colors, or should he settle for using a preempt? He was afraid of seeming to badger Mrs. Chinn in front of the other jurors, thereby making him look bad, but if he could get her off for cause, he wouldn't have to waste a preemptory challenge.

"Well, I guess if I'm going to be truthful about it, I would say that the police must've had a good reason to arrest your client." She paused for a beat, then added, "But I agree with what you said about mistakes, and if you can convince me that he's not guilty, I'll vote not guilty."

Pancho backed off, both literally, moving to a new location, and figuratively. When he spoke again, he addressed all the jurors.

"Ladies and gentlemen, forgive me if you think I'm giving good Mrs. Chinn here a hard time. But what all of us in this trial must remember at all times is that by law, by the very Constitution of the United States of America, by everything that we Americans hold fundamental and dear, my client, Reginald Bellows, is presumed innocent. He is an innocent man under the law. I don't have to prove Mr. Bellows innocent. Mr. Chang here must prove him guilty. And he must do so beyond a reasonable doubt, beyond any shadow of a doubt."

Pancho had addressed the panel, not wanting to embarrass Mrs. Chinn. He made a mental note of those prospective jurors who had watched him intently and had nodded, as if schoolchildren who already knew the right answer.

"Now, Mr. Watson, do I have your assurance, your contract, if you will, that if Mr. Chang does not prove to you that Mr. Bellows is guilty, guilty beyond any reasonable doubt in your mind, that you will set Mr. Bellows free?"

Mr. Watson had been one of the ones nodding at Pancho's little speech.

"Yes, sir you do."

"Mrs. Simpliciano, do I have that same assurance from you?"

"Yes, sir you do."

Pancho elicited the assurance from several more jurors, then addressed the rest of the panel and obtained a mass affirmative response.

They broke for lunch at noon. Susan brought Pancho a deli sandwich so Pancho could spend the lunch hour with Reggie.

"How you holding up?" Pancho asked Reggie when they were settled in their small, private conference room.

"I'm okay, I guess. How's it going?"

"Not too bad." Pancho talked between bites of his turkey on rye. "Not a bad panel to work with. There'll definitely be a few we want off. There're a couple of great ones that I expect Harry will bump."

They talked about the individual jurors for a bit. When they were done, Pancho filled Reggie in on his CIA theory. Reggie looked dumbfounded.

"Pancho, I appreciate what you're doing for me, I really do, but don't you think that maybe you're grasping at straws here? CIA? I mean, come on. Laws was a two-bit con man who got aced by someone he ripped-off and who framed me."

Pancho nodded and swallowed.

"Look, twenty-four hours ago I would've agreed with you. I know it sounds ridiculous, but it all fits. Besides, we've interviewed just about every investor, certainly every investor who'd lost more than a few grand. The police have done the same. No one comes across as a good suspect. It also had to be someone with some intelligence. I don't mean brains, I mean data. You were picked as the fall guy. Someone had to know about your investments, about your past, about your military experience. Someone had to know how to break into your apartment; know about your gun. And whoever killed Laws knew a thing or two about cutting people up. Your everyday investor, or whore, or druggie, or whoever, just wouldn't have those kinds of knowledge and skills."

Reggie was silent for a full minute. Pancho let him think.

"Okay, I see your point," Reggie finally said. "So how do you prove it?"

"Ah, therein lies the rub. Not easy, my friend. I need you to put your mind to work. Anything more on this man Kendall that you can think of? More description? What about his bearing? Did he seem like a police or military type?

"I want you to think long and hard and tell me tomorrow what you come up with. In the meantime, we're working our *okoles* off, trying to find something to use. I sure wish you were out so we could use you. We're low on manpower for this late in the game."

The *voir dire* continued into the late afternoon, with many of the questions focusing on pre-trial publicity. Few people ever admit to being biased, and such biases had to be gently extracted by roundabout questioning. These weren't witnesses who could be cross-examined. Insult one juror and you ran the risk of insulting them all. Scare one and you may scare them all.

Judge Ramos was giving the attorneys wide latitude in *voir dire*. It was a murder case that had received a great deal of publicity. He didn't want to be accused of error before the jury even got impaneled.

By five o'clock, they had a jury of five men and seven women. Because the trial was not expected to take more than a week or two, they chose only one alternate. Both Pancho and Harry had used all of their peremptory challenges, bumping people they thought would not be receptive to their respective positions, asking questions anew of the replacements. Pancho bumped Mrs. Chinn; he had not even tried to bump her for cause. He figured that the judge would rehabilitate her by asking her if she could be fair, to which she would certainly say yes. He decided not to risk having the judge say he was satisfied she could be fair, forcing Pancho to bump someone whom the judge had already pronounced as fair.

He said goodbye to Reggie as they led him away. He yawned and stretched, thinking about the long night ahead. He nodded to Harry Chang as he left, avoiding the reporters by throwing out 'no comments' as he walked. He was too tired to be interviewed.

It was calm and warm outside. The late afternoon sun cast long shadows. The *pau hana,* after work, traffic had already begun. As always, after spending a full day in the unreal environment of a courtroom, it felt strange to return to the real world. People were leaving work, going about their routine lives—far removed from the drama of a court battle over a man's freedom.

Chapter Twenty-Four

"The police won't let anyone in to see Elie. I tried this afternoon," Drew said to Pancho. He took a bite from his plate lunch of teriyaki chicken, rice, and macaroni salad.

"Then I'll have to take some chances on cross," said Pancho. "You have some grease on your chin."

Drew wiped his chin with a paper towel. "Isn't that pretty risky?"

"Risky isn't the word for it. I could end up looking like a complete lunatic." Pancho ran his hand through his hair. "Shit, can you imagine what this'll do to my career if I bring up the CIA angle and have nothing to back it up?" He paused for a few beats. "Not to mention pretty much guaranteeing a guilty verdict for our client."

Drew shook his head. "I just wish we could understand what all this stuff means." He gestured to the reams of paper, representing scores of corporations incorporated in various countries.

"I mean," Drew continued, "if Laws didn't do any investing, what did he have all these corporations for? There's no way we can figure this out. The FBI would be lucky if it could come up with something, but that's the kind of resources it would take."

Pancho sighed. Drew was right, of course. They had stacks of corporations. Most of the check registers and bank statements of the corporations were not in the documents they had, if they even existed. Perhaps Laws had done some investing, or had planned to.

There was a joint venture agreement, for instance, with some company to do studies for business opportunities in southeast Africa. There were other similar types of agreements, proposals, ventures, but no indication that anything had come of them.

It was Susan who came up with the idea.

"What if the CIA cleaned out Laws' office after the murder?" she said. "I mean, I personally think this CIA connection is *shibai*, but if you're gonna go there, wouldn't it be logical to think they'd clean up after themselves? Obviously there's stuff missing."

There was silence. Pancho looked at Drew, who looked back at him. Susan looked from one to the other.

"I didn't see anything in the police records to indicate that anything had been removed," said Drew, "but then again, why would there be, if it was done on the sly?"

Pancho yawned and leaned back in his chair, his thinking position. When he finally spoke, it was slowly, as if he were still finishing the thinking process.

"Drew, go down to the security office and see if they have video surveillance in the building and, if so, how long they keep the tapes."

Drew smiled, pushed himself up, and was gone without answering.

"Good idea, Susan."

She smiled at him, patted her tight gray hair bun to make sure it was still in place, and returned to examining the documents.

Fifteen minutes later, Drew still hadn't returned.

"Hey, look at this," said Susan, who'd been rummaging through one of the boxes pulled from the supply room. She held up a file marked 'travel.'

"This file has all the trips that Laws or the staff took on business. There are airline receipts, hotel receipts, rental car receipts, that sort of thing here. Any help?"

"Let me have a look," said Pancho. He took the file from Susan and scanned through it.

"Now what do you think Elie Watson would be doing for Laws in Hong Kong or Nairobi?"

"Nairobi?"

"Yep. Think it was just some sort of boondoggle?"

"Alone? I can't see a woman travelling alone to Nairobi just to spend a few days," Susan said. She brushed dust from the files off her dark skirt.

"I tend to agree."

Just then, Drew walked in with a smile on his face and a mini-cassette in his big hand. Both Pancho and Susan looked at him expectantly.

"This, my dear friends, and colleagues, is the loading dock tape from the night of the murder. It shows that at around ten o'clock that night, some guy in coveralls and a ball cap pulled up to the dock in a white van and entered the building with a push dolly. An hour and a half later he came out with a box, which he loaded into the van."

"Is the man identifiable?" asked Pancho.

"Negative, which, in and of itself, makes it suspicious," Drew said. "The guy was clearly hiding his features."

"Any way of telling which office he went to?"

Drew shook his head. "Unfortunately, there aren't any cameras in the halls or in the elevator. All we know is that there was no report of a break-in at any of the offices in the building that night."

The room went silent as the three thought about what the tape meant and whether it could be of help.

"One more imponderable for now," Pancho finally said. "I can't see what we get from this other than the assumption that someone entered and cleaned the office out after hearing that Laws was murdered. But we can't even prove that whoever is on that tape went to Laws' office, or what was taken."

"Maybe you'll get something out of Elie if you ask her about missing documents," said Susan.

"Yeah, maybe. We'll see." Pancho smiled at Susan. "Still, it was a hell of an idea." He turned to Drew. "In the meantime, while you were gone, our lady Sherlock found these travel documents. It appears that Elie might've traveled to Nairobi not long before the murder."

Drew took the documents from Pancho and peered at them. He looked puzzled. "Alone? When the company's in deep financial crisis?" He shook his head. "Doesn't make a lot of sense to me."

Pancho smiled and snatched the travel document from Drew's hand. "Just what we thought. Get on the horn to the . . ." Pancho checked the records, "Norfolk Hotel in Nairobi. See what kind of room Elie had and whether there was anyone registered with her. Also see if there's any way you can get the name of whoever sat next to her on the plane trip between here and Hong Kong and from Hong Kong to Nairobi and back."

Drew chuckled. "Man, we've already grasped at so many straws we may as well not stop now." He looked at his watch. "If my calculations are correct, it should be about a twelve hour time change between here and Nairobi, so I can try right now." He got up to go into another room to use the phone.

Pancho looked through the rest of the file. All of the other trips were taken by Laws himself: Tahiti, Fiji, Australia, and Hong Kong. He had corporations set up in each of those countries. Maybe all the corporations were just a way to create write-offs for travel.

Exhaustion crept over Pancho like a San Francisco fog. He needed to get some rest. The doc told him rest was essential to controlling his attacks. But that was easier said than done. He was starting a trial without a game plan, and he'd never done that before. Even in his no-defense cases, he'd always had things well orchestrated, his cross-examination questions ready to make the points he needed.

As things stood now, he didn't know how to cross-examine Elie. He didn't know what to do with a potential half-hour lag time between the shot and the call to the police. He didn't know whether he was going to put Reggie on the stand, or even if he was going to present a defense.

The weariness washed over him, and he decided that he had to go home. The best he could hope for was five hours of sleep.

"I'm going home," he said to Susan, who was still looking through papers. "Good work. Tell Drew that if he comes up with anything, to let me know first thing in the morning."

"Night, boss."

Pancho was so tired he almost pulled over to the side of the road on his way home. He took Ala Moana Boulevard to Waikiki, then Kalakaua Avenue through Waikiki. The sidewalks of Kalakaua were crowded with tourists and bar hoppers at 1 a.m. The clubs were open until 4 a.m. Pancho looked at the people on holiday.

Which was real: the resort atmosphere of Waikiki, or the world of murder, the CIA, and the law? Going into Waikiki was like walking out of court into the bright sunshine of Honolulu, different layers of the same world. Sometimes Pancho felt trapped in his particular layer. The law had taken over his life, slowly and subtly, like a parasite that grew within one's body until it assumed the shape and being of the body.

Pancho hadn't had a vacation in over two years; since Ellen had left him. He'd had over fifteen jury trials in the last two years, a high amount for a private attorney. *And now these damn panic attacks*, thought Pancho. It had been a huge blow to his ego to know that he was diagnosed with panic attacks. It sounded so weak. He rubbed his chest, a new habit he'd fallen prey to, even when he wasn't having any pain.

He could see the shadow of Diamond Head as he passed the last hotel on the Kalakaua strip. The zoo and the beginning of Kapi'olani Park were on his left. To his right was the Aquarium and Queen's Beach.

Pancho wondered how many high-powered attorneys and executives felt like he did, as if they were just playing at being a grown-up. Inside, hidden beneath his facade of maturity, was himself as a kid. What he felt when he walked to court to start a trial was not very different from what he'd felt as a child, walking to the first day at a new school. What he felt when he saw an injustice occur was not all that different than what he'd felt as a college student, demonstrating against the cause *du jour*.

The difference was that as a child he could get away with pretending to be sick to avoid an event that scared him. As a child, he had a mother to take him to school or to hold him when he cried over something that was terribly wrong with his young life.

Now he was a grown-up, a mature adult. Now he was expected to deal with stress, to work within the system against injustice, to be responsible; responsible for his life and the lives of all of his clients.

He turned into his driveway. As he parked and walked to the building entrance, he thought about responsibility. That was the key, that word, that perceptual burden, which was so overpowering. Pancho had accepted the burden of responsibility, and, in so doing, it was as if he had checked himself into a vast and empty prison, doomed to wander the corridors and dorms behind bars made of letters: r-e-s-p-o-n-s-i-b-i-l-i-t-y.

Chapter Twenty-Five

The packed courtroom was hushed as Harry Chang rose to deliver his opening statement. He stood away from the podium, sometimes letting his left arm rest against it. He was dressed in his trial 'uniform,' a lightweight wool blue suit off the rack from Sears, a white dress shirt, and red 'power' tie. His hair was rumpled from the wind on his walk to court and there were flakes of dandruff on the back of the suit.

The opening was good. It was a straightforward recital of the facts that the State intended to prove. Opening statements were not meant to be argument. Opposing counsel can and will object, interrupting the flow of the oration, if it goes beyond a recital of the evidence and into the realm of argument.

Harry's style lent itself more to the opening than to closing, which was argument. Because he was not a theatrical person, he played up the dry, narrative style of an authority figure ticking off the evidence against the accused.

As his opening drew to a close, Harry addressed the character of the victim.

"As most of you already know, Maynard Laws was not a particularly nice or sympathetic man. The evidence will show that Maynard Laws was a cheat and a thief, preying upon innocent men and women, squandering life savings. Maynard Laws caused a great deal of tragedy and human suffering. But Hawai'i does not have the death penalty for theft. Maynard Laws was still a human being, and the evidence will show that he was brutally butchered by this defendant," he pointed at Reggie Bellows.

"The defendant was cheated. His money was stolen from him. He had a right to be angry with Maynard Laws. While you consider the evidence in this case, I ask that you follow the law, and put aside any feelings of anger or hatred of Maynard Laws or sympathy for Reggie Bellows. You will find from the evidence that the defendant had a clear motive to murder Maynard Laws, but the defendant had no right to be judge and jury and sentence Laws to death.

"For this reason, based on the evidence that will be presented to you, I will ask that you find the defendant guilty of murder in the second degree."

Harry returned to his seat and all eyes turned to Pancho. The courtroom was quiet, as if the collective of individuals was savoring both the impact of the prosecutor's opening statement, which was impressive in his account of the overwhelming evidence against Reggie, and the anticipation of Pancho's opening.

"Mr. McMartin?" Judge Ramos spoke with a slight lisp, which Pancho knew to be the result of surgery to correct a hair lip when he was a baby in the Philippines. The Judge was a former prosecutor, but he'd been on the bench for almost ten years. His hair was cut short and was gray, not yet white. He sported a long, scraggily moustache, also gray, which covered the scar on his upper lip. Pancho and he went way back, and, although Pancho still considered the Judge to be more prosecution than defense oriented, Pancho thought Judge Ramos to be one of the fairest and brightest of the judiciary.

Pancho stood, slowly. He buttoned the front button of his black linen sport coat and straightened the royal blue silk tie. His black Tony Lama boots matched the color of his coat. He enjoyed the drama of these moments and he made a pretense of shuffling some papers while he let the impact of the prosecutor's opening remarks fade. After a few moments, he left his counsel table and approached the podium without any papers or notes.

"Your Honor, Mr. Chang, ladies and gentlemen of the jury. As you know by now, I represent Reginald Bellows, a man accused of murder, a man presently presumed by law to be innocent." Pancho stood to the side of the podium, facing the jury head on.

"The purpose of opening statement is to preview for you what the evidence is expected to show. What I tell you now is not evidence, just as what Mr. Chang has told you was not evidence. But we do agree, as a matter of fact, that the evidence will show, conclusively, that Maynard Laws suffered a grizzly, Friday-the-13th type murder."

Pancho stopped for a pause, looking to the faces of the jury.

"Don't dwell on that for one second. That is an uncontested fact and is not an issue for you in this trial.

"Consider, as you sit in judgment on this case, not just what the evidence *does show*, but what it *does not show*. The evidence will *not* show that my client killed Maynard Laws." Again, Pancho paused for a moment, making eye contact with the jurors.

"There is no question that the evidence will show that my client had every reason to be angry with Laws. Maybe he even wished Laws were dead, just as so many of those who invested with Laws must have secretly wished Laws dead. The prosecution tells you that is evidence –"

"Objection, that is argument, Your Honor."

Pancho looked wounded, wanting the jury to think he was being picked on.

"But, Your Honor," said Pancho, "a case is at least as much about what the evidence won't show as what it will."

"Overruled."

"Thank you, Your Honor." Pancho wanted it to look like the Judge had agreed that Harry was being unfair, as if Harry were trying to hide something from the jury. He repeated the objected to phrase.

"The prosecution tells you that this is evidence that the defendant committed murder. This is *not* evidence; it's a *substitute* for evidence.

"Mr. Chang tells you that because my client lost money with Laws, that because my client made a scene in Laws' office, and because my client was a mercenary, that he must be a murderer. But ladies and gentlemen, it is precisely that evidence that will force you to conclude that Mr. Bellows did not kill Maynard Laws. That very evidence will show that Mr. Bellows' training was such that he would never have killed Maynard Laws in such a manner.

"Mr. Chang's own evidence will show that if Reggie Bellows intended to kill Maynard Laws, it would have been swift, clean, no evidence of murder." Pancho decided he'd better move on before he drew another objection. He was, in fact, arguing the case.

"I ask each one of you to remember the promises that you made to me during jury selection, and listen carefully to what I have to say. This is not a television show where I would stand here and promise to prove to you who killed Maynard Laws. No one is going to pop up in the audience and confess to murdering Maynard Laws during this trial . . . at least I'm not expecting that to happen." Most of the jurors smiled. "The defense will not prove to you who killed Maynard Laws, but neither will the prosecution."

Pancho pointed at Harry. "He promised you that he would, that he could, and he has to. Mr. Chang must prove to you beyond any reasonable doubt that Reggie Bellows is guilty. Hold him to that promise he has made, he has promised to prove his case beyond any reasonable doubt.

"Never, ladies and gentlemen, never let those two words leave your mind while you listen to the evidence presented in this case. Reasonable doubt."

Pancho talked for a while about the meaning of reasonable doubt, stressing the strict standard imposed upon the prosecutor by law.

"As I advised you during *voir dire*, Reggie does not have to take the witness stand in his own defense. There are many considerations as to whether or not he will do so. As of this moment, I don't know whether Reggie will testify. If he doesn't, you are not to draw any conclusions, or form any opinions based upon his failure to do so. You are prohibited by law from doing so. Nor do we have to present any defense on his behalf, and, again, you are not to draw conclusions from that. The prosecution has the burden of proving its case against Reggie Bellows.

"If Reggie does take the witness stand, however, you are not to rule out his testimony just because he is the defendant. You may assign whatever credibility you feel appropriate to any of the witnesses in this case, and Reggie should be afforded the same analysis of credibility that you would give any witness.

"I thank you in advance for your patience and for your commitment to the contract that we entered into. Just as this isn't any of the lawyer shows you may have watched on television, where the trials are fast paced and always interesting, there are many boring, technical parts to a trial. If you would be so kind as to listen to everything and assume nothing, I'm sure that you will come to the only proper conclusion, a verdict of not guilty. Thank you."

Pancho returned to counsel table and sat down. There had been no stunning revelations, but he hoped that he'd made it clear that there didn't have to be. All he'd intended was to stress the significant burden of proving guilt beyond a reasonable doubt, and to recall for the jurors the contractual commitment he had elicited from them during jury selection. He found over the years that psychologically, the contract he made with the jurors was taken very seriously.

He was relieved to have gotten through the rest of his opening statement without further objections. He hated having to give reasonable doubt openings, preferring instead to give the jurors something they could sink their teeth into. He liked to promise them hard evidence, then have them reward him for delivering the evidence as promised, especially after having indoctrinated the jury during *voir dire* that he did not have to give them anything at all.

But today he could give them nothing except the canned opening of reasonable doubt, trying to drive it home so they would begin to feel that if there were anything at all to give them pause about the prosecution's case, they had to acquit.

"Mr. Chang, is the prosecution ready to proceed?"

"We are, Your Honor."

"Call your first witness."

"The State calls Sergeant Russell Cabrillo of the Honolulu Police Department." The bailiff rose and walked to the hall outside the court to call Sergeant Cabrillo.

Cabrillo's testimony was to set the murder scene, since he'd been one of the first to reach Laws' house. He testified that he had arrived at the scene immediately after Patrolman Lee. He recounted what he observed and described the floating torso, sunken head, and arms lying on the deck.

It was a graphic description, and from what Pancho could read on their faces, the jurors listened in fascination and repulsion.

The question of the admissibility of photographs of Maynard Laws had been the subject of a pre-trial motion *in limine*. Pancho had filed a motion to exclude the photographs of Laws as being too grotesque, and therefore highly prejudicial. Harry argued that the photographs were relevant because the fact of the dismemberment tended to show that the perpetrator was, in all probability, a male.

Judge Ramos had reviewed the photographs and agreed with Pancho that they could serve no purpose but to inflame the jury. Dr. Dasari would testify as to the dismemberment and opine that the killer was most likely a male, due to the strength needed to effect such clean amputations. Therefore, Judge Ramos reasoned, the prejudice outweighed the probative value. The pictures were out.

What Judge Ramos did allow, however, was photographs of the scene after Laws had been removed. These had no prejudicial effect and would aid the jury in visualizing the scene of the crime. Pancho had no objection to such pictures, and they were now identified by Sergeant Cabrillo as the home of Laws and the scene of the murder.

They broke for lunch before Pancho's cross-examination. Pancho decided to return to his office during the break to see if there were any developments. He hadn't heard from Drew since he'd left his office the night before.

Drew and Susan were both on the phone when Pancho walked into the office. Pancho went to his desk and unwrapped his fast-food chicken sandwich. Drew was the first to get off the phone, and he sauntered into Pancho's office, smiling.

"Well?"

"Well, it looks like our girl Friday was not alone in Nairobi. She shared a double room with a man named Matthews. No description available. We'd have to send someone there to interview staff to see if anyone remembered them, long way to go for another longshot. Elie probably got a paid business trip and decided to take a lover along."

Susan came in as Drew was finishing. "The name of the passenger in the seat next to Elie from here to Hong Kong was Peterson. The name of the person next to her on her legs to Nairobi was Matthews. From Nairobi to Frankfurt, it was Matthews again. From Frankfurt to New York, the seat was empty. New York to Honolulu was a woman named Craven." She smiled.

"Good work," said Pancho. "It looks like we have a guy named Matthews to find."

"I tried to get in to see Elie again," said Drew, "but she isn't seeing anyone. I can't figure out if it's her, the police, the doctors, or her attorney who's keeping us away."

"Have you started any local checks on Matthews? You do have a first name, I assume?"

"Only from the Norfolk Hotel," said Drew. He looked at Susan to verify. She nodded her head in agreement.

"Dennis. And yes, I've already checked phone books and DMV. There are three Dennis Matthews in Honolulu. I've talked to two of them and they claim never to have heard of Elie and had never been to Kenya. One is a State employee with the Department of Agriculture, and the other works for Kentucky Fried Chicken as a store manager. Even if they lied about Elie and Kenya, they certainly aren't CIA, which is what we're looking for, I guess. Right?"

"Yeah, but we're open to new angles too," said Pancho. "Any Matthews on the investor list of Laws?"

"Nope," said Susan. "I checked it first thing."

"What about the third Matthews?" asked Pancho.

"Don't hold out much hope. The guy works for Xerox as a service technician. I have a call in to him."

Pancho frowned. "Of course, if the guy we're looking for is CIA, the odds are he wouldn't have been travelling under his own name."

Pancho gulped down the rest of his sandwich. It seemed they were making some kind of progress. He just wasn't sure what kind. He was due back in court in twenty minutes.

"Okay guys, great job. Drew, keep on it and keep trying to get in to see Elie. Call her attorney. Let Susan know what you need her to do. I've got to make some notes for cross-examination."

He turned to his notes of Cabrillo's direct testimony and reviewed his notations in the right hand margin. He'd jotted notes or made stars next to areas of testimony that he wanted to pursue on cross. Now he reviewed and expanded them.

Pancho didn't have time to dwell on the fact that a new player had entered the game. A mysterious traveler, Elie's lover? He'd think about it later.

Harry Chang wrapped up Sergeant Cabrillo's testimony soon after the lunch break. Pancho rose quickly and approached the podium, though he again didn't stand directly behind it. He had his legal pad on the podium for easy reference.

"Sergeant Cabrillo, when you arrived at the Laws' residence, you didn't see any vehicles other than Laws' and Officer Lee's in the driveway?"

"No, sir."

"And you saw no car leaving the Laws' residence?"

"Correct. I did not see any vehicles either at or leaving the Laws' house. Other than Laws' Rolls Royce and Officer Lee's patrol car, that is," he added.

"What time did you say Officer Lee arrived at Laws'?" Sergeant Cabrillo consulted his notebook.

"2:55 p.m."

"And what time did you arrive?"

"2:57, right after Officer Lee."

"And the call from the neighbor came in, when?"

"2:24 p.m." Cabrillo shifted his body in the witness chair and glanced at Harry.

"Where were you when you got the call to check out the Laws' residence?"

"I was on the road, heading back to Hawai'i Kai station."

"Do you know where Officer Lee was?"

Cabrillo consulted his notebook again. "He was at 5672 Lunalilo Home Road."

"That's in Hawai'i Kai, isn't it?"

"Yes, sir."

"In fact, by car, that's about three minutes from Laws' house, isn't it?"

"I guess, about that."

"Sergeant, would you explain to the court why it took you and Officer Lee almost one half hour to respond to a call of a possible gunshot?"

Cabrillo glanced at Harry Chang again before answering.

"Well, to be honest, I was in no hurry, since Officer Lee reported that he'd attend to the call. He was familiar with Mr. Laws and had responded to possible shooting calls there on a number of occasions." Cabrillo looked uncomfortable. "By the time I was in Hawai'i Kai I hadn't heard anything further, so I decided to go to the house to make sure someone had responded to the call and that everything was okay."

Pancho put his hand on his chin, like he was pondering the situation. "Do you have knowledge as to why it took Officer Lee so long to respond?"

Harry Chang was on his feet. "Objection, hearsay."

Pancho looked to the Judge. "May we approach?" The Judge nodded and the two attorneys walked to the side of the bench as far away from the jury as possible. Cabrillo stayed seated in the witness chair. The three men waited while the court reporter made her way to the bench so that she could record the conversation.

Judge Ramos looked at Pancho to begin. "Your Honor, I'm not sure why the prosecution isn't calling Officer Lee. He's not on their witness list, but from what I read in the police report, Lee didn't respond quickly because he'd responded to calls at the Laws' house for possible gunshots so many times, each of which turned out to be air rifle shots, that he took his sweet time. He assumed it was more of the same." He looked at Harry. "Is that correct, Harry?" Chang nodded.

"So Sergeant Cabrillo knows all this. I realize it's hearsay, but I need to get this in. The time delay in responding is critical, so I can either call

Officer Lee, make him my witness, and make things more complicated than they need to be, or we can let Sergeant Cabrillo testify as to why Lee took his time in responding."

Judge Ramos thought for a moment before turning to Harry Chang. The Judge had a sly smile on his face. "Mr. Chang, as a former prosecutor myself, I suspect you don't want one of the police officers made to look like he's a defense witness. It all sounds pretty innocuous to me. Any chance of you withdrawing your objection?"

Harry expelled some air and Pancho could tell the prosecutor was running through all the possible scenarios. "Agreed," he finally said.

Judge Ramos smiled and shooed everyone back to their places before addressing Harry, once more in open court. "Mr. Chang?"

"Your Honor, the State withdraws its objection to the last question to Sergeant Cabrillo."

The Judge turned to Cabrillo, who had been patiently watching the silent show play out. "Would you like the question read back, Sergeant?"

Cabrillo shook his head, "No need, Your Honor, I know what it is." He turned back to Pancho. "We get a lot of calls on possible gunshots. Car backfires, firecrackers, all sorts of things can sound like a gun to a layperson. In this particular case, the neighbor lady who called had a repeated history of reporting possible gunshots at the Laws' residence. Mr. Laws apparently liked to shoot an air rifle in his back yard, which irritated the neighbor, so she'd call in a possible gunshot, even though she knew it was probably an air rifle."

Cabrillo looked at the jury and shrugged good-naturedly. "Officer Lee was the usual responder to these calls. He thought this was just another false alarm, so he finished up with the witness on Lunalilo Home Road before heading over to Mr. Laws' home."

"But Sergeant," said Pancho, "if the call really was about a gunshot, someone could have been shot, isn't that true?"

"Yes, that's true."

"Is it departmental policy for the dispatcher and the responding officer to make a judgment as to whether a call is legitimate or not?"

"No, sir, it isn't."

"Your Honor, I object. This line of questioning is irrelevant and immaterial. The time of response and the reasons for any delay have no bearing on the issues relevant to the charges against the defendant."

"Your Honor, I disagree," said Pancho. "While Officer Lee's error in judgment might have been an honest mistake, it was a mistake nonetheless. Had he followed police procedure and responded quickly, he had every chance of catching, or at least seeing the killer of Maynard Laws. There are other mistakes of the police that I intend to show. Compounded, these mistakes add up to an erroneous charge against my client."

Harry Chang had allowed Pancho to make a speech in front of the jury. He'd made a mistake, and Pancho had scored points off nothing.

"Overruled, I'll allow it." Judge Ramos looked at Harry, and Pancho could see the Judge give Harry the subtle look that told Harry he'd goofed.

Pancho turned back to Cabrillo. "Sergeant, did Officer Lee in fact violate departmental policy in failing to respond to this call in a timely fashion?"

"Yes, sir, I guess he did."

Pancho let it drop. He'd made his point.

"And, just so we're clear, you arrived on the scene before Officer Lee had entered the premises?"

"When I arrived, Officer Lee had already rang the doorbell and received no answer. He knew that Mr. Laws usually shot his air rifle down by the water, so he was just about to walk around the house to head to the back yard when I arrived. We came upon the murder scene together."

"So as far as you know, Sergeant, there is nothing Officer Lee knows about this case and the scene that you don't know?"

"Objection, calls for speculation. How can Sergeant Cabrillo know what Officer Lee knows or doesn't know?"

Pancho could see Judge Ramos nodding and he jumped in. "Your Honor, Mr. Chang is correct, let me withdraw and rephrase." He turned back to Cabrillo. "Sergeant, to your knowledge, did Officer Lee have any investigative responsibilities at the scene?"

Cabrillo glanced quickly at Harry Chang to confirm there was no objection before responding. "Not that I'm aware of."

"To your knowledge did Officer Lee venture anywhere on the premises outside the scope of the murder scene?"

"Not that I'm aware of."

"How long did Officer Lee stay at the scene?"

Cabrillo looked down at his notes. "He left within minutes of Frank Nishimoto's arrival," he said, then added, "Frank Nishimoto is the lead homicide detective on the case."

"Which was when?"

"3:33 p.m."

"No further questions of this witness, Your Honor."

"Redirect?"

"No questions, Your Honor." Sergeant Cabrillo left the witness stand. He looked none too happy. Pancho knew Cabrillo to be a good cop, and had felt bad about making him the whipping boy for Lee's mistakes. *Blame Harry Chang for not putting Lee on to take his own medicine*, thought Pancho.

"The State calls Detective Frank Nishimoto."

Harry took Frank through his arrival at Laws' house and his observations of the scene, again reminding the jury of the horrible nature of the crime. Frank described in details not elicited from Cabrillo the nature of the wounds inflicted upon Laws: gunshot to abdomen, amputation of the arms, and the detachment of the head from the body.

Frank then testified about seeing Officer Lee pick up the matches and how he'd ordered them bagged. *No wonder Harry isn't calling Lee*, thought Pancho. *What a screw-up.* Harry obviously wanted to take the wind out of any cross-examination on this point.

The revelations about Laws' fraudulent investment company, about Laws' past, then about Reggie's heavy investments with Laws, followed.

It was almost five o'clock when Judge Ramos adjourned court for the day. He admonished the jury about watching the news or reading the press accounts of the trial before discharging them.

Pancho said goodbye to Reggie, who asked for another suit to wear to court, before heading back to his office.

It was drizzling outside, and the trades were blowing their usual ten miles per hour. The misty rain felt good on his face as he strolled leisurely to his office.

"Hey, Pancho." Pancho turned to see Harry Chang walking toward him.

"How you doing?"

"About the same as you, Harry. Working my *okole* off until the wee hours every night, sleeping three to five, then coming to court to listen to your pretty voice every day. What a life."

Harry smiled. "Nice work today. You screwed me on that objection. I should've approached the bench."

Pancho waved him off. "Could've happened to anyone. It was just a relevancy objection. How were you to know the Judge would let me make a damn speech in response? I expected him to overrule before I said a word."

They walked for a few moments in silence. Harry's shorter legs working hard to keep up with Pancho's loping stride.

"Your man is bugging the shit out of one of my witnesses, Pancho. She's getting pissed off, her attorney's getting pissed off, and I'm getting pissed off."

Pancho looked at Harry. He didn't look pissed off.

"Elie Watson is not your witness, Harry. She's a witness whom I presume the State intends to call. I have every right to attempt to interview a potential witness. You guys have interrogated her to death. She's waived her right against self-incrimination. No one has a right to keep her from my investigator except her, and she didn't seem to mind talking to Drew until your people got their hands on her."

Harry stopped walking and looked up in surprise. "Drew already interviewed her?"

"Hell yes. Do you honestly think I'd wait until the start of trial to interview a witness? What's the matter, Ms. Watson's not coming clean with you? She didn't tell you about her talks with Drew?"

Harry was silent. Pancho started walking again. Harry followed.

"Don't pull this intimidation shit with me," said Pancho after a few strides. "We've always dealt pretty straight with each other, at least I have on my end."

"I know, I know. Look, Elie's saying she doesn't want to talk to Drew. So call him off, okay?"

Pancho could tell Harry was trying to recover from the shock of learning that Elie had already talked to Drew. He'd be trying to figure out what she'd said — whether Pancho had been given any advantage.

"You make my life hard, Harry. Someone's got Elie suddenly clamming up. Is it you? Your boss? The cops? The feds? Who is it, and why?"

Harry looked at Pancho and didn't answer. Pancho didn't expect one.

"See you in court," Pancho said, as he turned down Alakea Street.

Chapter Twenty-Six

There was a note from Drew when Pancho arrived at his office. He still couldn't get in to see Elie, which Pancho already knew, and the third Dennis Matthews was apparently clean. A dead end on Mr. Dennis Matthews, travelling companion to Elie Watson.

Pancho didn't know when Harry would be putting Elie on to testify, but it was becoming increasingly clear that he would be doing some blind cross-examination when the time came. He had no choice but to violate the age-old precept of trial examination, 'never ask a question to which you don't already know the answer.' Well, he was going to have to ask a lot of questions to which he didn't know the answer. Even if his working hypothesis about the CIA was correct, all Elie needed to do was lie, and Pancho would have a great deal of egg on his face and on his reputation. His entire defense theory would fly out the window.

Pancho took three aspirins and lay down on his couch. For the millionth time he reviewed the CIA theory. He had no solid facts to support it. Drunken ramblings to Sandy Foreman; a surplus of foreign corporations; documents taken from Laws' office in the middle of the night—which he couldn't prove; an offer to Reggie to pay to have Laws killed; and a mysterious travelling companion on Elie's trip to Africa.

Pancho rubbed his eyes. He didn't have time to properly investigate. He'd just formed the working theory the other night. There were too many things that didn't make sense. Too many things that could easily be explained away.

If only he could come up with a reasonable explanation for Reggie's gun being the murder weapon. That was the whole case against him. Then he wouldn't even have to go into the CIA connection. He could get his reasonable doubt by a logical explanation of the gun. He could avoid looking like a conspiracy theory crackpot.

Nevertheless, he could think of no serious explanations other than what he was now convinced was the truth: Reggie Bellows had been framed, and someone stole his gun. It was laughable without some supporting evidence. Which brought him back to the CIA. Circles. Circles within circles.

Pancho finally got up off the couch. It was dark outside. He decided to take a night off. There wasn't anything he could do except think, and he knew that he was pretty much doomed to do nothing else. He could do that over a nice dinner with Paula. He dialed her number, doodling on a yellow legal pad as he waited for her to answer.

"Paula. Dinner. You, me, tonight, now, Chiang Mai."
"Is that any way to invite a lady to dinner?"
"Is it going to work?"
"You bet. Want to meet there?"
"Sure. About twenty minutes?"
"Fine."
"Aloha."

A half an hour later they were seated at Chiang Mai Thai restaurant, on King Street. They ordered spring rolls and white wine while they studied the menu.

"Shall I ask how it's going?"
"The same. I'm at a complete loss. Do I go with the CIA connection and face getting burned and ridiculed, or do I ignore it and try to come up with lame reasons as to how Reggie's gun happened to be the one that shot Laws and happened to have been thrown into Koko Marina?"
"Since when did potential personal embarrassment stop you from doing what had to be done for a client?"

Pancho looked at her across the table. The soft light from the candle flickered on her face. She was beautiful.

"Would you still love me if I was publicly humiliated and my practice fell to shit?"
"First, you won't be publicly humiliated; at least I don't think so. Second, your practice won't fall to shit from just one case; at least I don't think so. And third, if you were publicly humiliated and your practice fell all to shit, you'd have to get yourself another cookie because this one sure as hell wouldn't stick around."

Pancho laughed out loud.
"Well I certainly appreciate your support." They toasted.

When Pancho and Paula returned to his apartment, he opened the sliding glass doors onto the ocean. They made love on the living room floor so they could feel the cooling trades and hear the soothing surf. It was a long, slow, sensual lovemaking.

They held each other in silence for a long time, he still inside her. Pancho listened to the gentle lap of waves on the beach. He felt at peace and he knew it wouldn't last, so he savored every moment of it. After a while, his penis shrank and her vaginal muscles bullied it out of her. They shifted positions slightly, but continued to embrace, neither wanting to break the spell. They held each other until Pancho drifted off to sleep.

Pancho felt refreshed as he sat in court the next morning, listening to Detective Frank Nishimoto's continued direct examination. More financial records, both Laws,' and Bellows.' It was clear that Reggie was in deep financial trouble because of Laws. The motive was being well established. Harry was intent for the jury to see just how desperate Reggie had become.

Background. Reggie's military records and history as a mercenary.

"Detective Nishimoto, did you conduct any research into Mr. Bellows' stints as a mercenary?"

"Yes. We found the company he worked through. It was called Soldiers of Fortune something or other." Frank leafed through some pages in front of him. "Mr. Bellows served two tours in Africa and one in the Philippines."

"Did you learn what his assignment was in the Philippines?"

Pancho considered objecting, but he had an idea where this was going and worried that he could end up highlighting something he didn't want to look important.

"Yes, he was sent with a small team to help train Filipino jungle fighters who were fighting communist insurgents." Frank didn't wait for another question before continuing. "As such, according to the owner of the company, he was involved in training involving small arms and hand-to-hand combat, including the use of machetes as weapons."

Pancho jumped to his feet. Frank had gone much further than he'd anticipated. "Objection, move to strike, Your Honor. The testimony is lacking proper foundation. It's also hearsay." Pancho was kicking himself. Harry and Frank had probably rehearsed the testimony so that Frank could get the machete part in before Pancho knew what the question was.

Judge Ramos absently played with one end of his moustache. He gave Pancho an amused look. "A little late on the objection counsel, but you are correct, the objection is sustained and Detective Nishimoto's last statement will be stricken." The Judge then turned to the jury to explain to them how they were now supposed to ignore and disregard what they had just heard.

"Thank you, Your Honor." Pancho refused to let the jury see how badly he'd screwed up.

Harry asked a few more questions about Reggie's mercenary activities. He wanted to show Reggie as a violent man, capable and willing to kill for money; knowledgeable about the human body, and able to wield a sword or machete. Pancho had known Harry wanted to highlight the mercenary activities, and knew he wouldn't be able to keep it out, but he'd erroneously assumed that there would not be any direct testimony about Reggie's expertise with a machete as a weapon, since there were no known witnesses who could have direct knowledge of such. But there it was, stricken from the record, but not from the minds of the human beings who made up the jury.

Harry and Detective Nishimoto then moved on to the gun, the kid who found it, and where. The connection would require the ballistics expert to tie it all together, but Frank established that it was Reggie's gun, and of the same caliber as used to shoot Laws.

The capture. Arrested at the airport with twenty-five thousand dollars in cash. Implication: flight to avoid arrest.

Pancho watched the jury as they listened. They appeared fascinated by the detective work as Frank painted the picture of the jigsaw puzzle he and his partner had so skillfully, and, in the case of the gun, luckily, pieced together.

It was after lunch when Pancho was given the witness. Frank eyed him warily. The two men had been through a number of contentious courtroom encounters. Pancho moved slowly and deliberately, as if he was reluctant to put the detective through a cross-examination, but once he got to the podium and put his notes down, he started in immediately. He'd decided to use a shotgun approach, hitting at different subject matters, out of apparent order, hoping to make it appear as if the jigsaw puzzle was still scrambled and incomplete.

"Detective Nishimoto, you are aware of Mr. Bellow's occupation?"

"Yes, sir, he imports and sells furniture and household items."

"And from where does he import most of these items?"

"My understanding is Thailand and the Philippines."

"Your understanding? Surely you checked that out."

"Yes, I did have it checked out. He imports primarily from Thailand and the Philippines."

"Do you know how he usually pays for his purchases in Thailand and the Philippines?"

"Yes, sir. Mostly cash, from what we can determine."

"Where was Mr. Bellows going when you had him arrested?"

"He was about to board a plane bound for Thailand."

"Where he buys much of his merchandise, correct?"

"Correct."

"And did your examination of his business records indicate whether or not twenty-five thousand dollars was an unusual amount for him to spend on a buying trip?"

"No, sir it was not unusual."

"So there is absolutely no indication that Mr. Bellows was doing anything when he was arrested other than commencing a usual buying trip, correct?"

"Yes, I suppose that is correct."

"You suppose? Is there any indication to the contrary?"

"No, sir there isn't."

Pancho didn't understand why intelligent officers like Frank Nishimoto fell into the same trap as rookie cops when testifying. By being recalcitrant, and refusing to give up the point on an issue of little merit to the State's case, they made themselves look shady, like they were out to get the defendant.

"Thank you, Detective. Now, it is correct, is it not, that by picking up the matches on the lanai table at Maynard Laws' house on the day of the murder, Officer Lee may have smudged or covered the fingerprints of whoever murdered Maynard Laws?"

"Objection, Your Honor, argumentative, speculative, assumes facts not in evidence."

Judge Ramos waved Harry Chang off as Pancho began to speak. "Overruled, the witness will answer."

All eyes turned back to Detective Nishimoto, who was none too happy about having to answer the question.

"Would you repeat the question?"

Pancho sighed and asked the court reporter to read the question back.

"Anything is possible, counsel."

Pancho let a glimmer of frustration show on his face. He wanted the jury to see that Frank was playing games with him.

"Well now, Detective Nishimoto, it's my understanding that the State is going to argue that because the matches were from a restaurant in Paris, and because my client had been to that restaurant a month or so before, that my client must have therefore obtained the matches in Paris and carried them to Maynard Laws' house, where he then left them at the scene of a grisly murder. Is that your understanding of the State's position?"

"Objection, argumentative. Detective Nishimoto is not the prosecutor. What is or is not the State's position is not Detective Nishimoto's domain."

"Sustained. Rephrase the question, Mr. McMartin."

"Yes, Your Honor. Detective, in the course and scope of your police investigation, did you not trace the matches in question to a restaurant in Paris?"

"That is correct."

"And did you not then determine that Mr. Bellows had dined at that very restaurant?"

"That is correct."

"And did you not then make a determination as a police detective that this book of matches may be evidence of Mr. Bellows' presence at Maynard Laws' house?"

"Yes, sir, I did feel that it was evidence of the defendant's presence at the decedent's."

"Please, sir, just answer a yes or no question with a yes or no, otherwise we could be here for days. Mr. Chang will have an opportunity to allow you to have your say on redirect. All right?"

"Yes, sir." Pancho could see Frank's jaw tighten, a sure sign he was becoming irritated.

"And if the match book is potential evidence of the murderer's presence at the scene of the crime, would not fingerprints found thereon likewise be competent evidence?"

Frank hesitated, but there was no helpful objection from Harry Chang.

"Yes, sir, fingerprints would have been evidence. But I think it would have been unlikely for the defendant to have left fingerprints on the matches as he was most likely wearing gloves."

Pancho blinked. It was a good point.

"So you're saying that Mr. Bellows was smart enough to wear gloves and not leave fingerprints, but stupid enough to leave matches at the scene of a murder?"

Frank cocked his head slightly. "We usually catch criminals from the small mistakes they make."

Pancho knew this exchange was getting away from him. He had to reel it back in.

"But the fact is that we will now never know whose fingerprints were on that match book, will we?"

"No, sir."

"Other than Officer Lee's, of course."

Frank's voice was tight, controlled. "That is correct."

Pancho wrote a quick note to himself for possible use in closing argument. 'Two chances to catch the real murderer blown: time of arrival and matches.'

"Detective Nishimoto, were there any other objects found at the immediate scene of the murder?"

Frank frowned. "Like what?"

"Well," said Pancho, "how about a cell phone?"

"Uh, yes, there was a cell phone on the table near the chaise lounge."

"Right. I presume your office determined the ownership of the phone?"

Frank sat up straight, the muscles in his face still tight. "Of course we did. The phone belonged to Maynard Laws."

Pancho looked in the direction of the jury as he said, "Thank you, Detective," as if it had been an ordeal to get this small piece of information out of him. "And I presume your good office checked out any recent calls made from the phone?"

"Of course."

"Would you share your finding with us?"

"There were two complete numbers called in the two hours before Maynard Laws was murdered. One number was to a cell phone and had been called multiple times, but there was no response and no voice mail. The cell phone was a pre-paid phone, purchased out of State, so we were unable to identify who Mr. Laws had been attempting to call. The second number did result in a phone conversation. The called number belonged to a man by the name of Sandy Foreman. The final number showing on the phone was simply the number nine. We don't know if it was an attempt by Mr. Laws to call 911 or to some other number that began with nine."

"Did you or your detectives talk with . . ." Pancho walked to the podium and picked up a piece of paper, "Mr. Foreman?"

"Yes, my partner, Bill Hampton, and I both met with him. According to Mr. Foreman, he'd been having a late lunch at the Mabuhay Filipino Restaurant on Hotel Street between 2 p.m. and 3 p.m. on the day of the murder, which, as you know, counsel, is within the time frame the coroner has concluded the murder took place. Mr. Foreman's alibi was independently corroborated by the restaurant personnel."

"Detective, what does Mr. Foreman do for a living?"

Frank Nishimoto shot a glance toward Harry Chang before responding. "Not much that we can tell. He has no regular employment. He told us he does odds and ends."

"In fact, Detective, isn't Mr. Foreman a pimp and drug dealer? Wasn't he supplying drugs and prostitutes to Maynard Laws?"

Judge Ramos called for quiet as the courtroom exploded into chatter.

Frank looked uncomfortable. He shifted in his seat and glanced again at Harry Chang, who was not offering any help. "Well," he finally said, "he's never been arrested for those offenses, so I'm naturally hesitant to agree categorically with your statement, counselor. But, that said, Mr. Foreman himself admitted to us that his relationship with Maynard Laws was to drink and party with him. He said he would sometimes bring girls to the parties. He did not admit to drug use or to procuring for money."

"Did he say he brought both girls and boys to party with Mr. Laws?"

Frank Nishimoto shook his head. "He didn't say."

"Did you or your team investigate any of the people, boys or girls, who Mr. Foreman took to party with the decedent?"

"No, sir, we had no reason to do so, Mr. Foreman's alibi checked out and we had . . ."

Pancho interrupted. "Once again, Detective, please, just a yes or no when the question calls for it." Frank glared for the briefest second, then nodded in compliance.

Pancho consulted his notes. "What time was the call to Mr. Foreman?"

The Detective looked at his own notes before responding. "Two oh seven."

"Thank you, Detective. Now, the weapon used to dismember Maynard Laws was never found, is that right?"

"That is correct, only the gun was found."

"Please sir, I haven't asked about the gun yet. The weapon to dismember Maynard Laws was not found?"

"Correct."

"You searched Reggie Bellows' apartment?"

"Yes."

"No weapon?"

"I hardly . . ." Pancho held up his hand and Frank got the message.

"No weapon was found at the apartment."

"Any bloodstained clothes?"

"No bloodstained clothes were found at the apartment."

"Or anywhere else, isn't that correct?"

"Yes, that is correct."

"When you searched Mr. Bellows apartment, did you look for any indications of forced entry?"

"You mean at Bellows' apartment?"

"That's exactly what I mean."

"Why would . . ." Frank caught himself and cut himself off. "No, sir we did not."

"Any fingerprints found on the gun?"

"No, sir."

"Detective Nishimoto, how many people lost money as a result of Maynard Laws' scam operation?"

"Oh, I don't recall offhand the exact figure."

"Hundreds?"

"Yes, I would say hundreds."

"And some of these people lost their entire life savings, isn't that correct?"

"That is correct."

"How many of these people served in the military?"

Frank glanced over at Harry Chang, then looked back at Pancho.

"I have no idea."

"Yet you seem to be implying that my client is a murderer because he served in Viet Nam?"

Frank was clearly angry. Harry was on his way out of his chair, but Frank began to answer before Harry had a chance to object.

"I'm not implying anything, counsel. I investigate and present the facts to the prosecutor. Your client was in the armed forces and also served as a mercenary, a gun for hire."

"Ah yes, Mr. Bellows did indeed serve other causes in other countries for money. He fought in wars, is that right?"

"That's right."

"And does fighting in wars make someone a murderer?"

"Objection, Your Honor, this is . . ."

Judge Ramos cut Harry off. "Sustained."

"Detective Nishimoto, did you personally oversee the review of the voluminous documents found in Maynard Laws' offices?"

"Yes I did."

"And did you happen to notice that there were at least a dozen foreign corporations set up by Laws, in various countries?"

"Objection, relevancy."

"Your Honor, I hope to tie in this line of questioning through later testimony."

"I will allow it. Overruled."

"Detective?"

"Well, no, I didn't pay much attention to them."

"Do you now, sitting here, as one who is most intimately familiar with the documentation of Maynard Laws, have any reasonable explanation why a man who did no investing needed to have a dozen or more corporations, spread out through the Pacific region?"

Frank thought about it. He was clearly wary of Pancho. A quick glance at Harry Chang told him nothing.

"No, sir, I can't say that I do know of any reason for those corporations."

"Did you direct any inquiries or conduct any investigations into the purpose or scope of those corporations?"

"No, I didn't see the relevance."

"Detective, did you order anyone from your office to go to Mr. Laws' business office on the night of the murder and remove documents?"

Frank looked confused. He looked at Harry Chang, then back at Pancho. "No, of course not."

"Are you aware of any other governmental agency that might have done so?"

"No."

"Thank you, Detective, I have no further questions."

They broke for the day. Pancho hoped the jury was wondering why Maynard Laws had a dozen corporations that didn't seem to serve any purpose.

Chapter Twenty-Seven

Pancho sat on the beach in front of his condominium, legs drawn up to his chest, watching a couple trying to right a Sunfish they had capsized four times. Drew sat to his left, his surfboard beside him. It was Saturday. The first week of trial was behind them.

After Frank Nishimoto testified, the rest of the investigating officers were paraded onto the stand. The forensic officer testified about the fibers from Laws' carpet on Reggie's flip-flops.

Pancho scored the obvious points. The matches could have been left on the lanai table by anyone, including Laws himself. He used the forensic man to again remind the jury of the lack of fingerprints.

The ballistics officer connected the gun that was found and registered to Reggie to the gun that had been used to shoot Laws. The kid who found the gun was on and off the stand in less than fifteen minutes. Pancho scored no points on the gun, except to again point out the lack of fingerprints.

The neighbor who called in the gunshot had not been put on the stand. The prosecution didn't need her, but Pancho worried that she'd been left off because the prosecution had discovered the sloppy police work in the taking of her statement. Not only had Officer Lee delayed his response to the call, but the neighbor admitted to Drew that she had delayed calling in the shot, adding even more time to potential scenarios. Now, she would not testify unless Pancho called her as a witness, and to do so, it would mean that he would be presenting a defense. He still hadn't decided if he was going to do so.

Pancho shifted his attention to Drew, who was telling him about Sandy Foreman.

"'No fucking way.' That's all he kept saying, over and over, 'no fucking way.' I told him we could subpoena his ass and he'd have to testify, but he just laughed." Drew shook his head, his big body tight with frustration.

"What happened?" asked Pancho. "Did you explain to him we would want to call him only if Elie admitted to a CIA connection?"

"Sure, but we aren't exactly dealing with Mr. Solid Citizen here. He kept asking what's in it for him, and I had to explain that we couldn't pay him to testify. Then he started in about how his picture would be all over the papers and on the tube. It was one thing after another."

Pancho flicked a fly off his leg. "Did he still look like he's on drugs?"

"Yeah, I'd say so."

"Well, then he probably wouldn't be much good to us anyway." Pancho took a deep breath, then exhaled. "Let's play it by ear. If Elie does her thing, we can see about subpoenaing him. If she doesn't admit the CIA connection, I'm toast anyway."

They sat silent, watching the Sunfish, now sailing nicely. An outrigger canoe from the Outrigger Canoe Club next door was working its way out through the waves. A DC-10 streaked across the sky, looking like an advertisement as it passed over the sailboats and surfers.

Pancho closed his eyes, taking in the sounds: the soft slap of the small waves on the beach, the cries of delight of children playing in the shallow surf, the rustle of the palm trees at the edge of the sand.

He didn't open his eyes when Drew announced he was going surfing. He heard the big man rise, actually heard his knee crack, and heard him pick up the board and walk off.

Pancho stretched his legs and lay down on the sand. He let the sun warm his eyelids. Despite the peacefulness of the moment, his stomach churned. He was about to take one of the biggest gambles he had ever taken in court. He thought about what Harry Chang had said after the negligent homicide trial, about how he would someday be there to pounce on a Pancho gamble gone bad. Was he pushing his luck by pursuing this CIA thing?

Chapter Twenty-Eight

At CIA headquarters in Langley, VA, Oliver Wilson stared at Deputy Director Randolph Fuller with an open mouth.

"You did what?" He sputtered.

Fuller's body straightened, a clear body language hint to Wilson to remember who he was talking to.

"I paid him."

"Holy fucking shit." Wilson didn't care who he was talking to, not anymore. He couldn't believe what he was hearing. "You paid Foreman off? Why the hell didn't you just have him killed? Wouldn't that be cleaner? No muss, no fuss, what's one more dead pimp?"

"Now just wait one goddamn minute, Ollie. You've no right to talk to me like that."

"I've every right in the world. You've just committed God knows how many crimes. You surely don't have the DCI's approval for this. You've already had Duerden running around practically on his own, not answering to any Station Chiefs or operations officers. Now you've circumvented the Division Chief. Don't tell me I don't have a right. Jesus H. Christ." Wilson was dumbfounded, and couldn't think of what else to say.

"Look, Ollie," Fuller's tone turned conciliatory. "When Duerden found out that the only link between Laws and the CIA was this man, Sandy Foreman, and that he might be called to testify, it was clear we needed to take action. Duerden seems to have everything else under control. If Foreman were to testify that Laws had confided in him that he was working for the CIA, regardless of whether the jury, the court, or the public believed him, it would've been all over the papers.

"For ten thousand dollars, we pay Foreman off so that he refuses to testify. The guy's no dummy. He had it all figured out. He's a small time crook. Pretty much anything he says incriminates himself in something, so he just takes the Fifth if he's called to testify.

"Chances are he won't even be called after he tells the attorney he won't help his case." Fuller smiled. "It's clean Ollie; it's the last thread to us."

Wilson shook his head in wonder.

"Don't you think you should've talked it over with me first? I am the Division Chief after all."

"Well, I just thought you might've gotten too close to the whole thing. I know you have some kind of animosity toward Duerden. I made the decision after I talked to Duerden, and we agreed that it was a smart and effective move."

"You talked to Duerden about this?" Wilson's voice rose several octaves.

"He was the case officer. I trusted his opinion. Someone had to arrange the pay-off. Duerden said he had a man in Honolulu who could do it for us."

"Would it alter your opinion any, *Deputy Director*, if I told you that I suspect Donald Duerden of killing Maynard Laws?"

It was Fuller's turn to be shocked. His face turned white, then pink.

"Please explain that."

Wilson responded that he'd been suspicious almost from the first moment that he'd heard of Laws' death.

"Why didn't you tell me?"

"I never had anything concrete. I didn't even have enough to pull Duerden from the field. The best I could do was to assign him to some bullshit job in Mexico, to keep him away from Hawai'i and the Laws' case. Now I find he's still meddling in the case, only on an invitation from high."

"Well, as you say," said Fuller, "you have nothing concrete. You can't prove Duerden did anything and neither can anyone else. All the more reason, though, to keep the Agency out of the picture altogether. As far as we know, Foreman and Laws were the only civilians who knew of any CIA business with Laws, and Laws is dead. With the Foreman angle covered, we should be fine."

Fuller got up from his desk and came around to Wilson. Wilson rose and allowed Fuller to put his arm around his shoulder and edge him to the door.

"Don't worry. It's covered. Duerden's in Mexico; Foreman isn't talking; and Laws is a goner. Think about it and you'll feel a lot better."

Wilson squirmed away from Fuller's arm and faced him as he reached the door.

"One last thought," said Wilson. What if Foreman was setting you up? What if he plans to testify anyway and now will testify that the CIA tried to buy off his testimony for ten grand? What if this whole thing was a trick by that defense attorney to prove the CIA had something to hide when he had no evidence until now?"

Fuller's face had gone ashen again as Wilson spoke. He said nothing.

"Did you get any leverage to make him keep his bargain?" asked Wilson.

"Uh, no, not really."

"Jesus . . ."

"No one should be able to trace the money," said Fuller, his tone now clearly defensive. "It came from some offshore corporation, three or four times removed from us. We still have deniability."

"Deniafuckingbility my ass. I'll show you deniability. I'm going to my office to draft the strongest worded cover-my-ass memo you've ever seen. I'm not going you let you dump this one on me when the shit hits the fan."

He looked directly into Fuller's eyes. "And it will, Randy, it will."

Chapter Twenty-Nine

"Call your next witness, Mr. Chang."

"Thank you, Your Honor. The State calls Dr. Padma Dasari." As the bailiff left the courtroom to make the call for the coroner, Harry glanced over at Pancho, who nodded to him. Harry frowned and returned to his notes.

Court had started late this Monday morning, as Judge Ramos had to hear some motions from other cases before trial resumed. Before court, Harry tried to get Pancho to tell him what was up with all that stuff about foreign corporations, but Pancho shrugged him off.

Dr. Dasari walked into the courtroom. Pancho watched her as she passed his table and took the stand. She wore a slightly flared black dress that came to just above her knees. It was longer than the miniskirts she usually wore. She had on a matching jacket, presumably to ward off the freezer-like temperature of the courtroom. To Pancho, even her movements of taking a witness stand in a murder case were sensual. As always, when she sat and faced the courtroom she glanced first at him. He smiled, but she had already looked away, expectantly facing Harry Chang.

Although Pancho had offered to stipulate to her expertise, Harry took Dr. Dasari through her impressive credentials. Pancho didn't really want to stipulate, but he knew that Harry wanted the jury to know that Dr. Dasari was one of the major players in the field of forensic pathology, whose opinions were respected, and Pancho knew that if he objected, Harry would insist on taking the doctor through her credentials.

The recital of Dr. Dasari's observations of the scene was straightforward and did not conflict with the various police officers' accounts.

"Doctor, would you please tell the jury what kinds of wounds were inflicted on Maynard Laws."

"Yes." She turned slightly so as to speak to the jury, her melodic accent belying the nature of her testimony. "The decedent was shot in the abdomen by a .38 caliber handgun. The bullet entered the large intestine and lodged in the spine. In addition, the head of the decedent was severed from the body at the neck. Naturally, this severed the spinal cord and the major arteries, such as the carotid artery, to the brain. Most of the blood loss was from this wound. Both of the arms of the decedent were severed at the shoulder joints. The amputations appeared to have been accomplished by a sharp machete, or sword, most likely a machete.

"In addition, there was a bruise at the rear base of the skull, which I have concluded is most likely due to the head striking the pool deck prior to it rolling, or being pushed, into the pool, where it was ultimately found."

"Doctor, do you have an opinion as to the distance from which the shot was fired?"

"Yes. I believe, within reasonable medical and forensic certainty, that the shot was fired from five to eight feet from the body. This is based upon the analysis of the entry burn and the angle at which the bullet entered and rested in the body." Dr. Dasari drew a diagram and explained her opinion further. The jury and spectators alike listened intently.

"What is your expert opinion as to the cause of death of Maynard Laws?"

"I would say that the severance of the spinal cord at the base of the skull was the cause of death. He was brain dead immediately following that event. There was a simultaneous massive loss of blood."

"Do you have an opinion as to the sequence of wounds?"

"Yes I do. I believe he was shot first, then dismembered. It's possible, not probable, but possible, that he was shot after being dismembered, but that would require someone holding up a headless and dead body for someone else to shoot."

"Do you have an opinion as to the gender of the assailant?"

"Yes, sir. I believe the assailant was in all probability, a male. This is based upon the extreme force necessary to sever the head and arms. It is, however, possible that it was a strong and well-trained female."

Harry paused to check his notes. The cause of death was not in dispute and he couldn't think of anything else to cover. He thanked the Doctor and turned the witness over to Pancho.

Pancho rubbed his hand through his long brown hair and slowly rose to the examination of Dr. Dasari. Pancho's body language made it clear he respected the doctor and was reluctant to cross-examine her.

"Doctor Dasari, how are you?"

"Fine, thank you, counsel." A flicker of a smile, so fast Pancho thought he might have imagined it.

"Just a few questions."

Dr. Dasari dipped her head with a slight smile, suggesting that whenever an attorney said 'just a few questions,' she could expect to settle in for a long examination.

"The gunshot was not a mortal wound, is that right?"

"Yes, that's correct. The gunshot would not have killed the decedent unless he had gone untreated for quite some time."

"And for 'quite some time,' I assume you mean a matter of hours?"

"Oh yes, depending on blood loss."

"Can you state with medical certainty how long before the dismemberment Mr. Laws was shot?"

"No, I can't."

"Could it have been an hour?"

"Well, yes, I would say that it could, although it is my understanding that the neighbor called in the gunshot about a half hour before the police arrived."

"Your answer, though, is that the shot could have occurred an hour before the dismemberment?"

"Yes."

"Doctor, the decedent had potato chips stuck to one of his hands, is that correct?"

"Yes. There was a bowl of chips beside the chaise lounge, and he had apparently been eating just before the murder."

"Forgive me, Doctor, I'm not sure if you can answer this. Could the potato chips have been wiped from Laws' hand if he had slapped his two hands together, like this?" Pancho demonstrated how someone would ordinarily wipe their hands. He then described his actions for the written record.

Dr. Dasari bowed her head slightly. "I'm rather sure he could have. The chips were stuck to the hand because of suntan oil the decedent had rubbed on himself, presumably with that same hand. Had he wiped his hands together, most, if not all of the chips would have come off, I should think."

"And, Doctor, again forgive me if you can't answer, just tell me if this is outside the scope of your expertise." Pancho glanced at Harry, who looked poised for an objection,

"If a person is relaxing, eating potato chips, some of which are actually stuck to his hand, and he has a hostile visitor, would it not be human nature for the person to wipe his hands before dealing with the visitor?"

"Objection." Harry was on his feet. "This is outside the scope of Dr. Dasari's expertise. This is a human factors question."

"Ah, but Your Honor," interjected Pancho before the Judge could rule. "Mr. Chang is forgetting that in the long list of qualifications of Dr. Dasari that he *insisted* on parading by us, was Dr. Dasari's Ph.D. in psychology? And her membership in the Human Factors section of the

American Psychologists Association? I also point out the published articles by Dr. Dasari on forensic ergonomics, which is the fancy name for human factors."

Judge Ramos allowed himself a slight look of amusement. "Mr. McMartin, are you moving to have Dr. Dasari qualified as an expert in the area of human factors?"

"Yes, I guess I am, Your Honor."

"Mr. Chang?"

Harry had a sheepish look on his face. Pancho and the Judge knew that if Harry didn't agree to it, then he would have to try to impeach his own expert's qualifications. He would be in the position of having to argue to the jury that his expert was qualified to say what he wanted her to say, but not what Pancho wanted her to say. He decided that it wasn't worth it.

"No objection, Your Honor, except to the fact that it is outside the scope of direct." The defeat in Harry's voice was obvious.

"I find Dr. Dasari qualified by stipulation in the area of human factors. All other objections are overruled. The Doctor may answer the question if she can."

All eyes turned back to the witness stand and Dr. Dasari. She smiled, and her dark eyes glowed, as if she'd enjoyed the repartee. Pancho loved the way her eyes crinkled at the sides when she smiled.

"That isn't a particularly easy question to answer, counsel. In certain situations, I would agree with you that someone meeting a hostile person would almost instantly and unconsciously clean an embarrassing mess off themselves before dealing with the hostile individual. That assumes time to do so, however. It is equally likely that there was no time for Mr. Laws to wipe his hands."

"Let's back up a minute, all right, Doctor?" The Doctor nodded. Pancho went to the easel and pulled out the blown-up photograph of the scene.

"According to the testimony of the police officers, this is the scene of the murder exactly as found, except for the removal of the body, is that your understanding?"

"Yes."

"And could you tell the court the direction in which the chaise lounge is facing?"

"Well, it's kind of sideways to the pool."

"So that a person laying on the chaise lounge would have a view of the pool and the ocean beyond, as well as a view of the lanai and living room, to the left. Correct?"

"Yes, that would be correct."

"Now, let us assume for a moment that someone enters the house who is known to Mr. Laws and poses no known threat. Laws remains seated, maybe waves to the person and asks him what he's doing there. Suddenly, that person pulls a gun and orders Laws to stand and raise his hands. He then shoots Laws. Is that a reasonable scenario given the basic assumption that Laws knows and does not fear the visitor, at least at first?"

"Yes, I guess it's one of many potential scenarios. As it goes, it's reasonable."

"And," continued Pancho, "let us now assume that the intruder is not a friendly person, but someone known to be hostile to Laws. Laws sees him in the living room. He rises from his chaise to deal with him, wipes his hands almost simultaneously, and begins to converse with the intruder. At approximately five feet, the intruder pulls a gun and shoots Laws. Reasonable given the scenario of a hostile intruder?"

"Another reasonable scenario, but again, one of many permutations."

"Thank you, Doctor, I have no further questions."

Harry rose to re-direct. He looked confused.

"Doctor, as you testified, there are many different possible scenarios, isn't that correct?"

"Yes."

"For instance, the defendant, whom I would assume we are classifying as a hostile intruder for the purpose of this very strange exercise, enters the house, points a gun at Laws immediately and tells him to stay where he is. Laws rises and is shot."

"Yes, quite a reasonable scenario."

"And in that scenario, there would still be potato chips on Laws' hand, correct?"

"Yes."

"Thank you, nothing further." Harry took his seat.

Pancho rose again and looked at Harry. Harry furled his brow.

"Doctor, what would you do if you saw someone known to be hostile to you coming at you with both a gun *and* a machete?"

"Run like hell." The courtroom erupted into laughter. Dr. Dasari, who had laughed also, quieted when she realized what she'd just said. She glanced at Harry, whose face was an expressionless mask, then she turned back to Pancho, and this time he knew he hadn't imagined the slight nod from her.

Pancho could see Harry was fuming. He'd been suckered into the whole smoke-screen about potato chips, while all the time Pancho was setting the Doctor up to say she would run from a hostile intruder with a gun and machete.

The State's case was premised upon Reggie being known to be hostile to Laws, ready to do him harm. Yet Laws had clearly been murdered at or near where he'd been relaxing on the chaise lounge. He'd made no attempt to flee. Had Harry not done redirect examination, the trap Pancho set would never have closed on him. It would have backfired on Pancho, leaving him with twenty minutes of testimony about whether someone would or would not have wiped potato chips off their hands.

Chapter Thirty

Pancho took a bite of his chicken ravioli and sipped the heavy Barolo wine he'd ordered. Drew's cannelloni was almost finished, and Pancho watched with amusement as Drew began to eye Paula's veal saltimbocca. Paula saw him too, but pretended to ignore him. It had become something of a routine between them, and Paula would inevitably end up passing her half-eaten dinner to Drew.

It felt good to be having dinner, with a good wine, talking to his two best friends. He watched the interplay between Drew and Paula, half-listened to the banter, and allowed himself an inward glow of satisfaction. Pancho had multitudes of acquaintances, but few close friends. It pleased him that the two people he loved most dearly in the world had also become close.

Finally, with a theatrical flourish, Paula offered Drew the remnants of her dinner. Drew acted surprised, as if he'd not been expecting it.

"So," said Paula, turning to Pancho, "what would you have done if you'd seen someone coming at you with a gun and a machete?"

"I like to think that I would've run, leapt for cover, something like that, but who knows? I imagine a lot of people would have frozen in fright."

"Then what made you so sure that Dr. Dasari would answer the way you wanted?"

Pancho smiled. "I wasn't sure at all. I do know she loves the theoretics of behavioral psychology, especially after the more pure science of forensic medicine. I guess I figured that if I could get her wrapped up in talking about what a person would do about potato chips stuck to their hand when confronted with a hostile versus friendly person, when I finally threw in the fact of the machete, she'd come up with the quick response of first inclination, which would be flight — to run."

Drew shook his head and grinned while swallowing a bite of veal.

"What are you smiling about?" Pancho asked.

"The vision of a greased-down Maynard Laws, getting drunk by his pool, with goddamn potato chips stuck to the suntan lotion on his hand." Drew let out a belly laugh, which infected Pancho and Paula, who laughed with him.

"What I don't understand, though," Paula said, "is why the Judge let you go into all that stuff. Isn't that speculative, what someone would do?"

"You should've been an attorney," said Pancho. "You're right on. It was highly speculative. But the Judge is going to give the defense in a murder trial a lot of leeway. Ramos doesn't want to leave me any opening to overturn him on appeal, and the best way to do that is to give me everything I want, within reason." Pancho took another sip of wine.

"What about Harry, did he object?" asked Drew.

"Oh, sure. Harry objected, but when the Judge asked him if he was objecting to the doctor's qualifications to testify about human factors, Harry was faced with the unenviable quandary of whether to agree to her qualifications, or try to say his own expert is only qualified in the area he wants him to be. It would've looked bad to dispute the good doctor's qualifications."

"I don't understand this human factors stuff anyway," said Paula. "I mean, I don't care what kind of training someone has, who can say what someone would, or would not do, in a particular situation?"

"Well, there are some in the field who would agree with you, at least when talking about this kind of a situation. The field was originally called ergonomics, and many of the experts deal with design of products, and how people will react to and use certain products. What's the best layout for a dashboard in a car, for instance? Or what types of warning signs people are most responsive to.

"But the field has evolved to the point where there are many experts who will testify as to predictable human response. Frankly, I've listened to some experts, charging about five hundred dollars an hour, say some of the most outrageous bullshit you'd ever want to hear. Hired guns, we call them."

"Well," interjected Paula, "that's what you are, isn't it?"

Pancho and Drew laughed.

"Right on. I admit I've heard myself utter some of the most outrageous bullshit you'd ever want to hear, but not at five hundred bucks an hour."

"Yeah, only three-fifty," said Drew. More laughter.

"The question is, what're you going to do with any of this?" asked Paula.

"Good question. On the point of whether Laws would have run or not, I've left myself room to argue that if Bellows were the intruder, known to Laws as being real hot about not getting his money and he strolls in holding a gun and a machete, Laws wouldn't have just hung out at his chaise lounge waiting to be murdered. I mean, some guy doesn't come into your house with a gun and a machete, wanting to talk story. Laws would've tried to run, at least so I'll argue.

"But if the intruder is a friend, or Laws thinks he's a friend, the guy could be holding a howitzer and Laws would be curious, but not necessarily afraid. The place of the shooting and dismemberment, i.e. right next to the chaise lounge, is more consistent with that scenario than with a known enemy intruder."

Paula looked skeptical. "I sure wouldn't want my freedom to hang on that argument."

Pancho smiled. "Neither would I. But it's just a point to make. If I can make enough of them, I can build a bridge of reasonable doubt for Reggie to walk away on. I'm certainly open to suggestions on how else to use the facts in Reggie's favor."

There was no response, although Pancho could see that both Drew and Paula were working the puzzle through in their heads.

"I also left the door open to do something with the timing. I'm not sure why, just an instinct that it might be useful."

"You mean the time from the shot to when the police came?" asked Drew.

"Yeah."

"Jeez, it seems to me you've just given the murderer more time to whack off the head and arms. It was going to be pretty tight using the police times."

"You're right, I guess. I don't know, there's just something that nags at the back of my mind about the timing. I can't put my finger on it."

Drew put down his fork and patted his stomach. "Man, am I full."

"I certainly can't understand why," said Paula.

Drew grinned at her. "I need to power down some coffee. I've got to head on down to beautiful Hotel Street to find Sandy Foreman tonight. I've been trying to keep tabs on him until we subpoena him, but now I've lost him. I've been in every sleazy bar in Chinatown and even on Keeamoku for the last two nights looking for that mother, but he hasn't been around. I'm beginning to fear he pulled a disappearing act on us."

"Don't even talk like that," said Pancho. "You're giving me an ulcer."

"Then you shouldn't be drinking wine, my man." Drew took Pancho's wine glass and drank the remaining contents.

"Hey, I was saving that last sip."

"Ah, when will you *haoles* ever learn? Sometimes saving is counterproductive. Spend it while you can. Look what happened to poor

Reggie. He wouldn't be in prison right now if he hadn't done such a good job at saving all his money."

"You know, Drew, I usually learn something from every case. I'd been wondering what the lesson to be learned from this one was. Now I know. Don't save it, spend it."

The night was overcast, but warm for January. The slight trades were soothing. Pancho had decided to tag along with Drew in their search for Sandy Foreman, and they'd been in three bars, including Paradise Lounge, but there was no sign of Laws' former pimp. If Pancho could get Elie to admit to even the slightest involvement of the CIA, then Foreman's corroborative testimony would be crucial.

They passed a group of three Japanese sailors, looking to get laid or robbed or both. Half-broken neon signs glared from the bars in reds and greens and yellows. Drew saw a hooker he thought he recognized as having been one of Sandy's, standing on the comer of Maunakea and Hotel Street. She was trying to look sexy, but she looked like a skeleton. Pancho wondered how she was able to stand on the matchstick legs. She had several runs in both of her black stockings, which drooped loosely. Drew approached her, Pancho held back.

"Hey, seen Sandy around?"

The hooker eyed Drew, as if trying to remember if she recognized him. Drew figured she was on meth. She kept tilting her head back to look at Drew's face. She was missing two front teeth.

"No man, I ain't seen him. Not for a while."

"What's a while?"

The hooker looked at him as if he was irritating her.

"A while is a while. Fuck off, I'm missing customers."

Drew pulled out a twenty dollar bill. He tried to be subtle with it, but the hooker's eyes were so glazed that he ended up having to unfurl it six inches in front of her face before she could figure it out.

"I tol' you. I ain't seen him." She tried to grab at the twenty. Drew jerked it away.

"Honey, I don't know what you be charging, but from the looks of you, I figure you got to be doing about five blow jobs for a twenty. That is, if you could find the customers willing to let you touch any part of their body. There's no dick attached to this one. Just answer my question and it's yours."

Drew stood patiently as he watched her try to think.

Finally, she said, "'Bout two days. I ain't seen him for 'bout two days. Don't know where he is neither, so don't ask." She grabbed for the twenty again and Drew let her take it.

The hooker's answer was consistent with whatever other information he'd been able to gather from the inherently guarded personalities of Hotel Street.

Drew signaled to Pancho and they continued toward River Street, stepping into a bar now and then to look and ask around. They entered a brightly lit restaurant that served Filipino food. This was the restaurant Sandy had used for his alibi, and Drew told Pancho that Sandy often came there to have a bite to eat late at night. He walked up to the old man behind the counter, who grinned a toothless smile at him.

"You seen Sandy?"

"Who?"

"Come on old man, you know, Sandy. Black man."

"He no stay." The toothless man gestured around the restaurant.

"I know he no stay. You seen him?"

"He no stay."

"Where he stay?"

"He no stay here."

Drew gave up, and he and Pancho walked out. The toothless man's grin faded, and he snapped his fingers. A slender Filipino man in shorts and a T-shirt came out from behind the curtain to the kitchen. The man followed them out onto the street.

Pancho was fed up. This was a dead end. He should have gone home to try to get a good night's sleep. Sandy had obviously decided to lay low until the trial was over so he wouldn't have to testify; couldn't even get served with a subpoena. He and Drew walked across River Street and leaned on the rock wall above the stream.

"I'm not sure where to try next. Maybe we should go to the police," said Drew.

"And say what?" said Pancho. "That we may need this guy to corroborate Elie's testimony about the CIA that she might or might not..."

Just then, a shot rang out and they heard the crack of a bullet hitting the rock wall, inches from Drew's right hip. He turned and saw a shadowy figure of a short, thin person across the street. The figure took off running *makai*, toward the ocean. Drew took off after him, and Pancho took off after Drew.

The shooter was fast, and Pancho could see that Drew's knee was too painful to keep up. Pancho's pulse was already racing from the near miss of the gunshot. He could feel his blood pressure rising, a pounding in his head. He wondered what the hell they were doing chasing a man with a gun. The shooter turned on King Street. Drew stopped as he approached the corner and Pancho caught up with him. *Jesus, his pulse had to be about two hundred*, thought Pancho. He watched as Drew rubbed his knee as he edged around the corner carefully. When Drew signaled, he followed. There were few people on the street, and no one paid them any attention.

"He must have dodged into a building," said Drew, breathless. "I don't think the shooter could've made it to the next block already."

It was time to retreat. They were too easy a target. King Street was too quiet at this end and Drew decided to take the chance of going back up to Hotel Street, which was well lit and more crowded.

Their walk down Hotel Street, back to the car, was frightful. Drew limped painfully. Pancho imagined he was having chest pain. It was sinking in that someone had just tried to kill them. Pancho looked with suspicion on just about everyone he passed. He watched as Drew slowed at the corners and alleys, assuring himself that it was safe before he opened himself up as a target.

Both men were sweating heavily by the time they reached their car at Hotel and Pauahi. Just as Drew started the car, the rear window shattered in a mighty roar. Pancho thought he heard a thud, but he wasn't sure what was going on. "Get down," yelled Drew, who was already sunk below the seat level. Pancho watched as Drew put the car into drive, swinging the wheel away from the curb as he accelerated, pulling himself up just enough to see over the dash. Pancho braced himself for another attack. If his heart was pounding before, now it was about to jump out of his chest. Thankfully, there were no more shots.

After about twenty yards, Drew straightened up in the seat and Pancho followed suit. He could feel the crunch of glass dig into his thighs and back as he did so. They drove fast up Pauahi toward Beretania Street.

"I don't know if we're being followed or not. I don't see anyone." But he turned left on Beretania without stopping. Pancho heard a squeal of tires, and he saw that a car travelling on Beretania had just braked hard to miss them. Drew cut across the street and turned up Nuuanu to Vineyard Boulevard. This time he checked the traffic on Vineyard before he turned right. He watched his rear view mirror constantly as he drove toward the freeway. It was hard to see. Some of the shattered glass was still in the window frame. Car lights glared without definition.

Neither man said anything as they entered the freeway. The odds were that the assailant had not been in a car. Nonetheless, Drew didn't take any chances. He got off the freeway at King Street and took a cautious, circuitous route to Pancho's apartment at Diamond Head.

They both sat still for five minutes after Drew parked. There was no one else around. Pancho took a few deep breaths to expel the fear and calm his still racing heart. Then he turned on the interior lights and looked around. He found the bullet hole in the headrest of the driver's seat, inches from where Drew's head was resting as he stared out into nothingness.

"Son of a bitch," Pancho said aloud.

Chapter Thirty-One

Pancho handed Drew a snifter of brandy and helped himself to one. They sat on the lanai, listening to the muffled rumble of waves breaking on the beach below and the more ferocious reef break further out. It was late, and their fear had been replaced by an overwhelming exhaustion. They'd spent the last fifteen minutes talking everything through.

Naturally, it should be reported to the police immediately. By the same token, what exactly were they to say? Not spoken, but considered by each, was the scary question of who to trust.

"It's possible that it was some kid trying to hold us up," said Drew. He didn't sound like he meant it.

"It's certainly possible, and it's probably what the police will say, but I personally don't believe that for a minute. That's not how you rob somebody, let alone two people. You don't start shooting from across the street. And when it goes bad, you don't track the victims and shoot at them again when they're in a car.

"No, man, somebody tried to kill us, or at least scare us. That's what I believe."

Drew took a sip of his brandy.

"Yeah, me too."

Pancho tried to figure things out. As far as they knew, the only people who knew about Laws' alleged involvement with the CIA were the CIA, Laws, Elie, and Sandy Foreman. Foreman spilled what he knew to Drew, then got shy about testifying. That made sense, given who Sandy Foreman was and what he did for a living. But then Foreman disappeared, and when Drew and Pancho went looking for him, someone shot at them.

"Well, we have to report this," said Pancho. "I'm going to call Frank Nishimoto."

"What'll this do to your cross-examination of Elie tomorrow?" Drew asked.

Pancho hadn't moved to make the call yet, and he took another sip of his brandy while he pondered the question.

"It will take the element of surprise out of it if Harry figures out my only way to the CIA connection is through Elie, but I'm not sure he'll be able to piece all that together in time. I also don't think he'd do anything unethical, but I worry about Elie being prepared for my questions. The element of surprise is pretty much all I have going for me."

The two friends listened to the ocean and thought their own thoughts.

"What worries me more," said Pancho, after a while, "is the danger you may be in. I think I just happened to be in the way. I have a hard time believing any of this, but the most logical conclusion to draw if our working hypothesis is correct, is that the CIA arranged for Foreman to disappear and for you to be shot at—either killed or scared away. If the CIA thinks the only way to prove the CIA connection is through Foreman, then it would make sense for them to get him out of the way and for you to quit looking."

"Yeah. I've thought about that. It scares the hell out of me to think it could be true. If it is, though, we can't rule out danger to you either."

Pancho nodded. He'd already thought of that.

"Well, I've got to call." He got up and went into the living room. He found his phone directory and called Frank Nishimoto at home.

Frank was none too pleased to hear from Pancho, especially at that hour, but when he heard that he and Drew had been shot at, he agreed to come right over.

"And, Frank?"

"Yeah?"

"Do us a favor, don't call anyone else yet or bring anyone else with you. Security may be an issue."

There was silence on the line for a few moments until Frank assured Pancho that he would go along with Pancho's request.

Pancho went back to join Drew and wait for Frank.

Frank Nishimoto's look of skepticism hadn't left his face for more than a few seconds since he'd arrived at Pancho's. A few times, the look was replaced by a frown of consideration as he mentally chewed on a piece of information, but each time his skeptical look returned.

Pancho told Frank about tracking down Sandy Foreman, and what Foreman told Drew about the CIA. He told him how they didn't think anything of it until they began to wonder about the shell corporations Laws had incorporated around the Pacific region. When Drew went to talk to Sandy about testifying, Sandy had suddenly done a reverse, and refused to cooperate. Now he had disappeared and Pancho and Drew had been shot at while looking for him.

Pancho couldn't tell Frank about the man who'd contacted Reggie and met him in Paris. That would have been violating attorney-client privilege. He also didn't tell Frank that he thought Elie would be the key to this whole thing.

As he concluded, he realized how little he had.

Frank wasn't buying any of it. "You guys have lost it, you really have. What the hell kind of story is that? Some drunken scam artist bragged to his good friend, a pimp and drug dealer, that the CIA was backing him? When you wanted the drug dealer and pimp to testify in court, he ran scared and got some little turd to shoot at you? That's giving you the benefit of the doubt that it wasn't some completely unrelated thing." He shook his head, as if he felt sorry for Pancho and Drew.

"CIA. Unbelievable. You guys have been reading too many novels."

"Yeah, you're probably right, Frank. You know how it gets in a trial. Sometimes we grasp for straws. Just write it up. Drew's not going looking for Foreman again, but we'd appreciate it if you'd have your people do a look-see for us. No matter what, it's still a serious thing."

Frank nodded. "Yeah, I'll do that." He packed up to leave, still mumbling about the CIA.

Pancho walked him to the front door. "No hard feeling about court, yeah?"

Frank gave Pancho a hard look for a few beats before he allowed a half-grin.

"No hard feelings, Pancho. You piss me off every time, though. I never learn. Boy, was Harry pissed." They both laughed at that.

When Pancho rejoined Drew on the lanai, Drew was nodding out. Pancho went and got a pillow and blanket and prodded Drew into the living room and onto the couch. It was a matter of seconds before Pancho heard the gentle roar of Drew's snores, interspersed by the slap of the waves.

He walked back out to the lanai and sat down, propping his feet up on the railing.

It was 4:30 a.m. He had to be in court in four and a half hours. Today he had to make the big decision. When his turn came to cross-examine Elie, he had to either play his hand on the CIA thing or forget it. He still didn't know what to do.

Pancho had handled a lot of cases. Many were complex and intriguing. None were as bizarre and shapeless as this. That defined it perfectly, thought Pancho: shapeless. There was no form to this case.

The State's case was better only because of the gun. That was Harry's handle, that he could and would go back to time and time again, confident that any attempt to argue that Reggie's gun had been stolen from his condo by some unnamed and unknown person, with an unknown motive, would be scoffed at by a jury.

That's why Pancho needed the CIA connection. It could give the jury some semblance of a plausible theory. It provided motive and stealth.

Pancho ran his hands through his hair, yawning as he did so. He needed to sleep. He couldn't make a decision now. He wasn't sure he could ever make a decision. He'd shoot from the hip, deciding what to do as he stood up to cross-examine; a hell of a way to run a trial.

He checked to make sure the deadbolt was locked on the door before he went back to bed.

Chapter Thirty-Two

Elie Watson did not walk to the stand like someone who had tried to kill herself only a week before. She was a different woman than Pancho remembered. She stood tall, her chin up, her eyes straight ahead. She was wearing makeup, which hid her freckles, and her blonde hair had been styled. *Someone's been working with her*, thought Pancho.

Harry brought her along slowly, letting her get used to testifying, making her look good in front of the jury. He let her testify that she hadn't known what Laws was up to until she'd been working with him for a while. By that time, they'd begun having an affair. She'd been infatuated with him because she thought he was a genius, a rich and powerful man.

She testified unabashedly, letting the jury know she was a fool who fell for a married man with money and power. Only occasionally did she begin to revert to her old submissive self, but then it would be as if she'd remembered her role, and she put herself back on stage. When she'd learned Laws was a crook, he threatened her and told her she'd be arrested too. She'd be humiliated and embarrassed; and so she got sucked into the con game.

Harry set her up to answer a question about her financial gain from working with Laws. Pancho figured she or her attorney must have insisted on Harry asking this question, so Elie would be able to testify that she was paid nothing over her regular salary of forty-five thousand per year.

Finally, Harry brought her to Reggie. She testified that she knew Reggie had a large sum of money invested with Laws. She told how he kept putting more and more in, all the while drinking up Laws' lies of the enormous gains he'd made; "Like some little kitten lapping up milk," she said. Pancho wondered who'd fed her that line.

When Reggie started to figure out he wasn't going to get his money back, he became angry. "He'd swear and yell at me on the phone, using cuss words I hadn't even heard before."

"Did he ever come to the office?" asked Harry.

"Oh, yes, sir he sure did. He came in a bunch of times. It seemed like every time he came in he was madder than before."

"Objection."

"Sustained."

"What did he do when he came into the office . . . say, on the last time before Mr. Laws was murdered?"

"Well, as I said, he was real mad. He demanded to see Maynard right then and there. I had to tell him Mr. Laws wasn't in. He called me, well, he called me a name."

"What name, Ms. Watson?"

She looked up at the Judge, who nodded to her to answer.

"He said, 'You lying cunt, I know he's in there.'" Elie's face turned pink, and she looked down at her lap.

"What else did he say or do?"

"He said he was going to sue the shit out of us. He said, and I quote, 'I'm going to get that dirty prick if it's the last thing I do, and you tell him that for me.'"

"How long was that before Mr. Laws was murdered?"

"I'd say a few weeks. We didn't hear another word from Mr. Bellows after that, which was kind of strange."

"Thank you Ms. Watson, no further questions."

"Mr. McMartin?"

Pancho glanced at the clock. It was only eleven. He didn't want to be interrupted.

"Ms. Watson, when Reggie Bellows called for Laws, or came to the office asking for Laws, was Laws ever in his office?"

"Oh yes. He just didn't want to see or talk to Mr. Bellows."

"And so you lied to Mr. Bellows for Mr. Laws?"

"Well, yes, I guess I did. I did an awful lot of bad things for Mr. Laws."

"Yes, we know, Ms. Watson. But you understand you're now in court and under oath?"

"Yes, sir I certainly do."

"And you understand if you fail to tell the truth now, you would commit an additional crime of perjury, which carries a possible jail sentence?"

Elie made a face and looked up at the Judge, who remained impassive. Then she looked at Harry before turning her attention back to Pancho. "Mr. McMartin, everything I've said is absolutely true."

"Ms. Watson, I don't doubt that at all. In fact, I believe everything you have said so far."

Elie looked mollified, as if her dignity had been upheld despite all the lies and crimes to which she had recently admitted.

"I just want to make sure you understand your responsibility to this court and to yourself."

"I do."

"Fine. Then can you please tell this court who you went to Nairobi, Kenya with in early August of this year?"

Elie immediately turned scarlet. She looked panic-stricken. It was obvious to everyone in the courtroom. She glared at Harry, who tried to help.

"Objection, Your Honor. Relevancy."

"Overruled."

All eyes turned to Elie.

"Ms. Watson?"

Silence.

"Your Honor, would you please instruct the witness to answer?"

Judge Ramos leaned toward Elie. "Ma'am, I am going to have to order you to answer that question."

Elie looked at him, a pleading look in her eyes. Finally, she looked back to Pancho.

"A friend."

"Well now, ma'am, I'm going to need a name."

Elie's eyes roamed the courtroom, as if looking for someone to help her. Tears started streaming down her face. She made no attempt to wipe them.

"Ms. Watson? The name?"

"It . . . it was Matthews."

"And the first name?"

Elie frowned. She looked confused.

"Donald."

"Donald?"

"Yes. It was Donald, I think."

"You think? You *think* Donald was his first name?" There was some tittering in the audience.

"Yes, that's what I said." The pitch of her voice was noticeably higher.

"You travelled with this man on an airplane from Hong Kong to Nairobi. You stayed for a couple of days in the same room with him at the Norfolk Hotel in Nairobi. You flew with him from Nairobi to Frankfurt, and you *think* you remember his first name?"

Elie was sobbing. "Yes, that was it, it was Donald. I'm just confused, is all."

"Your Honor, perhaps a break might be in order." Harry was going to try to stop whatever was going on.

"Your Honor, with all due respect, I don't think a break is appropriate at this time. I've asked a simple question that has obviously caused a great deal of consternation on the part of the witness and I believe I should be allowed to proceed."

"Counsel will approach the bench."

Pancho and Harry went to the bench, as did the court reporter. The jury would not be allowed to hear the exchange.

"What's going on, counsel?" Judge Ramos looked at Pancho.

"Your Honor, I'm asking some questions in an area that I believe the witness will do everything in her power to avoid answering, to the point of feigning a breakdown. I believe that to allow her to leave the stand now would be to give her the opportunity to fabricate a story."

Harry exploded. "Now hold on a minute Mr. McMartin, that's—" Judge Ramos held up his hand to cut Harry off.

"That's a serious allegation, Mr. McMartin. I don't like leaving a witness on the stand who is out of control. I'm going to go along with you for a few minutes, but I will call a recess if I believe one is appropriate. That's all."

Pancho and Harry walked back to counsel table.

"Would you like a second to wipe your eyes, Ms. Watson?"

Elie glared at Pancho with a cold look of hatred. She looked up at the Judge. It was clear she wasn't going to get a break. She shook her head, no.

"What does your friend . . ." Pancho made a point of looking at his notes, "Donald Matthews, do?"

"I'm not sure."

"What did you say?"

"I . . . I'm not sure."

"Please bear with me, ma'am, but do you often go away to foreign countries with men whose first names you aren't sure of and whose occupation you don't know?"

Elie looked down at her hands in her lap, her voice was soft. "I don't do that."

"Do what?"

"What you said."

"You don't go to foreign countries with men whose names you don't know and whose occupations you don't know?"

"No."

"Well then, what does Donald Matthews do?"

"I'm not sure exactly. I think he works for the government."

"He works for the government. What branch? What does he do?"

"I'm not sure."

"What do you *think* he might do?"

"I don't know."

"Where does this man live?"

"Back east, I think."

"You're not sure of that, either?"

"No."

"How did you meet this man, whose name you're not sure of, whose occupation you don't know, and whose residence you don't know?"

Elie was breathing hard, sucking in air. She again looked around the courtroom, a look of panic on her face.

"Met him through Maynard." She said it so soft it was almost a whisper.

"Pardon? I couldn't hear you."

She looked right at Pancho, her face harder and nastier than he could ever have imagined. She spoke through clenched teeth.

"I met him through Maynard."

Pancho held his elation in check.

"What was this man's relationship with Maynard?"

"I don't know for sure. They may have had some business."

"You need to speak up, ma'am, so the jury can hear you."

"I don't know for sure. Some business."

"You don't know that either?"

"No."

"You were Maynard Laws' executive secretary, his right hand person, weren't you?"

"I was just a secretary."

"Since when does 'just a secretary' fly to Hong Kong and Nairobi on the company tab, to have a liaison with a government man?"

"It was a kind of bonus."

"A bonus? Oh, so when you testified earlier that you got nothing from the con Laws was running but your salary, you forgot about a little trip to the far east and Africa?"

Elie tried crying again. She started sobbing, her body heaving. Judge Ramos had a record to protect. He called for a ten minute recess.

Chapter Thirty-Three

Elie sipped some water. Harry was talking to her a mile a minute, asking her what was going on, what Pancho's line of questioning was all about. She ignored him.

She looked at Harry, babbling away, red in the face.

"Just shut up, will you?" Gone was the pretty, innocent woman who had testified on direct. Her face was tight and hard.

Harry backed off. He sighed and walked away. He would have to wait for the story to unfold like everyone else.

He watched from a distance as Elie took several deep breaths, shunned a reporter who tried to ask her some questions, and walked back into court.

Judge Ramos noted they were back on the record and the jury was present. He indicated that Pancho could proceed with his examination.

"Ms. Watson, isn't it true that your friend Donald worked for the CIA?"

Elie visibly gasped, as did virtually the entire courtroom, including Harry.

Pancho figured Elie had forgotten what first name her travelling companion had used, and that she guessed he'd used his real name. Pancho therefore avoided using Matthews, and instead called him Donald, making him more real to Elie. It also served to keep Elie guessing as to how much he knew.

"I . . . I don't know for sure."

"But you think he did work for the CIA?"

"It's possible, I guess. I think he worked for the government. I said that already, didn't I?"

"Yes, you did. In fact, didn't Donald's business with Maynard Laws involve CIA work?"

"I don't know."

"Are you sure you don't know?"

"Objection, Your Honor. Argumentative. I also object to this line of questioning on grounds of relevance."

"Overruled." Judge Ramos was obviously as fascinated as everyone else. He was hunched over, listening intently.

"Are you, Ms. Watson? Are you sure you don't know?"

"I'm not sure of anything. You're confusing me."

"Oh, well, I'm terribly sorry. Perhaps we should start all over again, shall we?"

"No, no need for that," she said quickly. "Just let me think."

"Yes, you do that." Pancho no longer felt the need to be too careful about being civil to Elie. She'd lost his sympathy for her long ago, and he hoped the jury felt the same. He thought it was now safe to go after her without mercy.

There was dead silence for several moments in the courtroom. All eyes were on Elie as she looked first to Harry, then the Judge, and finally back to Pancho. She was on her own.

"I don't know any details. I think Donald and Maynard may've had some business together. That's how I met Donald, we kind of had an affair, but that's over now, and I haven't seen him since."

"The affair with Donald was after you had the affair with Maynard Laws?"

Elie nodded.

"You need to answer out loud, Ms. Watson."

"Yes."

"The business that Donald had with Laws involved foreign corporations that Laws had set up, didn't it?"

"Yes, it might have."

"And did the CIA use those corporations set up by Laws?"

Again, the stunning silence. Elie looked like a trapped animal. Her eyes darted everywhere.

"I'm not sure, I guess so."

The courtroom erupted. Judge Ramos called for silence. It took a few minutes for things to quiet down.

Harry was on his feet. He looked confused and angry. He waited to be heard.

"Your Honor, may we approach the bench?"

Judge Ramos nodded, and Harry, Pancho, and the court reporter again walked up to the bench for a conference.

"Your Honor," began Harry, "this is a development of which the State was completely unaware. If this witness is saying that the CIA was somehow working with Maynard Laws, then I submit that we should recess and make contact with appropriate officials in the Federal government. There's the possibility of national security issues involved here." Harry's voice was pleading.

The Judge looked for a long moment at Pancho, toyed briefly with his moustache, then sighed. "I'm going to excuse the jury and empty the courtroom so that we can have an on-the-record-discussion without having to whisper." In moments of stress, his lisp became more pronounced.

Judge Ramos asked the jury to leave and ordered the courtroom empty. Journalists bolted for the door. As the bailiff herded the jury into the jury room, Harry and Pancho walked to their tables. Harry looked at Pancho and shook his head in astonishment, as if Pancho had really stepped in it this time.

Judge Ramos spoke. "Now, we are back on the record, the jury is not present and the courtroom is empty of all spectators. Mr. McMartin, I would like some kind of offer of proof as to where you are going with this."

Pancho stood up. "Your Honor, I would like to have the witness excluded during this discussion."

Everyone had forgotten about Elie, sitting on the witness stand, silently sobbing, while the courtroom was being cleared. Judge Ramos looked embarrassed that he hadn't noticed her still sitting there.

"Yes, of course. Ms. Watson, please step down and wait outside to be recalled." There was silence as they watched Elie go.

"Your Honor, it came to my attention during the investigation of this case that there might've been some connection between the decedent and the CIA. There is a witness, a Mr. Sandy Foreman, who has recently disappeared, who gave us this information. If you will recall from Detective Nishimoto's testimony, Sandy Foreman was the man Maynard Laws talked to in the hour before he was murdered. Last night, my investigator and I were shot at while trying to locate Mr. Foreman." He ignored the shocked looks on the faces of Judge Ramos and Harry Chang.

"The scores of shell corporations were suspicious to us. The records, provided to us by the State, showed that Ms. Watson had travelled to Nairobi with an individual in August of this year. That also struck us as being strange. I figured if anyone knew of this alleged CIA involvement, Ms. Watson did. Our working theory was that this stranger she travelled with was indeed the CIA agent with whom Laws worked."

"Her testimony today has, I believe, confirmed both of these theories: that the CIA was involved with Laws and the CIA agent was someone named Donald. I believe the last name, Matthews, was a fake."

Both Judge Ramos and Harry looked stunned, despite having heard the testimony of Elie. Judge Ramos turned his attention to Harry.

"Your Honor," said Harry, in a strained sounding voice, "the whole thing sounds preposterous to me. Ms. Watson's testimony was anything but decisive. She said over and over again that she didn't know, that she was unsure, that such and such might be the case. I think this whole line of questioning should be stricken, and Your Honor should grant a motion, which I hereby make, to have any future reference to the CIA excluded as being speculative and prejudicial."

Judge Ramos looked down at Harry. "Well, I'm not going to do that, so what's your next position?"

"Then we should contact the CIA or the U.S. Attorney's office immediately and advise them of this development so they can have the opportunity to intervene in the event of national security issues."

"Your Honor," said Pancho, "had there been national security issues, the CIA would have shown itself long ago. I have personally written to the CIA, which blew me off. This is a national exposure case. If the CIA's involved, we can all rest assured they know exactly what has happened."

"I still don't know where you're going with the whole CIA thing," the Judge said to Pancho.

Pancho took a deep breath; here it was.

"Your Honor, I believe that the CIA had Maynard Laws killed, that my client was framed. I believe that when my investigator tried to push the only known witness to CIA involvement other than Elie into testifying, the CIA tried to have him killed. I think I just happened to be in the way."

Judge Ramos and Harry stared open-mouthed at Pancho.

"You've got to be shitting me!" Harry realized what he'd said. "I'm sorry, Your Honor, I'm so shocked I didn't know what I was saying."

Judge Ramos grinned. "Mr. Chang, you took the words right out of my mouth." He looked at Pancho. "Mr. McMartin, are you proposing to prove this?"

"No, Your Honor. That would be virtually impossible. I do intend to argue it as a reasonable inference."

"How much more of this witness do you have? It's noon now."

"I'm not sure. I wasn't sure how far Ms. Watson would go toward telling the truth about all this. To me, she's obviously trying to walk the thin line between protecting this Donald fellow and not being hit with perjury."

Judge Ramos was quiet as he sat back and thought about what he should do. Finally, he made the safe call.

"We're going to break for lunch until 1:30. Mr. Chang should feel free to contact anyone he wants in the Federal government. If there's no attempt to intervene by then, I will allow Mr. McMartin to proceed. Court stands in recess until 1:30."

Pancho looked at Reggie. Reggie grinned at him and whispered. "Goddamn, Pancho. You did it, goddamn."

"I didn't do it yet, Reggie, we'll see." He patted Reggie on the shoulder and watched as the sheriff led him out of the court.

Chapter Thirty-Four

Harry virtually ran back to his office, his short legs pumping, ignoring the heat as the sweat soaked through his shirt. As he flew into the office, he told his secretary to find Ron Shigemura, the head prosecutor, and ask if Harry could see him immediately. He also told her to get Bill Hart, the U.S. Attorney for Hawai'i on the phone.

Three minutes later he was talking to Hart, telling him what had happened in court.

"Look Bill, I know there's no way I could get to anyone in a position of authority in D.C, especially at this time of day. You must have some connections. Find out what they want to do. If you do nothing, the case proceeds."

Hart didn't sound happy about having this dumped in his lap.

"C'mon Harry, that's all bullshit and you know it. I'll try to make some calls, but it's after 5:00 p.m. there now."

"Yeah, okay, Bill. Do what you can. I'm just trying to be careful."

They hung up. *A less than fulfilling conversation,* thought Harry. He looked up as his boss walked into his office.

"What's going on?" Ron Shigemura was a good-looking, fiftyish, local Japanese. He stood just over six feet tall, had a distinguished dusting of gray at his temples, and had a deep, smooth voice that had enraptured many a jury in his day. He was a born trial attorney cum politician.

Harry filled him in on the morning's events in court. Ron's reactions were about the same as everyone's.

"That frigging McMartin's gone too far this time."

Harry shook his head. "Hey boss, I'd do the same damn thing. Pancho's not making up this CIA thing. Elie Watson virtually admitted that Laws was working with the CIA."

Ron frowned. "What're you going to do?"

Harry told him about his call to Hart. Ron nodded in agreement. Harry knew the politician in Ron would like the idea of dumping it on the Feds.

"Assuming we go ahead with the trial, I'll just try to make it sound absurd and inconceivable. Not much else I can do, is there?"

Ron thought a few moments and stood up, nodding as he did so. "Not that I can think of. Keep me posted."

Harry watched Ron leave. *Well, that was a big help.* Idly, he thumbed through his messages. There was a call from Frank Nishimoto. It was noted as having come in at 7:00 a.m. He called Frank, who filled him in on last night's events at Pancho's.

"And get this Harry, you're not going to believe it—"

"Let me guess," Harry interrupted, "Pancho and Drew think the CIA tried to have them killed."

"Damn, Harry, how'd you know that? Pancho tell you this morning?"

Harry laughed. "More or less." He told Frank what had happened in court. He was getting tired of telling the story.

"You mean it might be true?" Harry could hear the astonishment in Frank's voice.

"Draw your own conclusions, Frank. I don't know jack anymore."

Chapter Thirty-Five

Oliver Wilson was just packing up to go home for the day when his secretary announced an emergency call from Mr. Bernard Farrington, Assistant United States Attorney.

"Wilson here."

"Mr. Wilson, my name is Bernard Farrington, Assistant U.S. Attorney. A strange set of events seem to be occurring in Hawai'i, which have some relevance to your firm."

"Mr. Farrington," interrupted Wilson, "please give me your number and I'll call you back." Oliver wanted to be sure he was actually talking to someone from Justice.

When contact had been reestablished, Farrington told Wilson of the phone call from the U.S. Attorney in Honolulu. Oliver listened without comment until Farrington was through.

"I thank you for your call Mr. Farrington. I'll check with my superiors on this matter. Of course, as I'm sure you're aware, the Agency's position has always been to neither confirm nor deny."

"Yes, sir, I'm quite aware of that," said Farrington. "I've made a memo of our conversation. Should your firm require the assistance of the Justice Department, please don't hesitate to call."

Oliver hung up and swore to himself. It was coming unraveled, just as he'd feared. He picked up his phone and buzzed Deputy Director Fuller. He'd gone for the day. Oliver told his secretary to track Fuller down. Then he sat down to think and wait.

Donald Duerden stepped out of the shower in his hotel room at the Zona Rosa Holiday Inn in Mexico City. He was going out to dinner at the San Angel Inn. He had a date with a good-looking woman who was an expatriated American who'd moved to Mexico City after her divorce. She'd found that she could live well on her alimony in Mexico. But she was lonely, and was receptive to Duerden's advances.

His cell phone rang and Donald picked it up on the first ring. He heard the crackle and static of an overseas connection moments before hearing the Pidgin English of Ricardo Baguio.

"Donald? That you?"

"Yeah, it's me. What's up?"

"The shit wen hit the fan here."

"Just tell me what's going on."

"Okay, okay, no get pissed. The girl, Elie, wen go and say about CIA and you. She say Donald . . . uh, Donald Matthews, that you, Donald?"

"Just tell me what happened." Donald could feel his stomach tightening.

"She say you and her wen sleep together; go to Africa together; and that you wen work for government. Attorney ask if you CIA and she say maybe, possible, I'dat"

"What else? What else?"

"Not much else. Attorney wen ask about some corporations and the CIA. Elie say she not sure; she think maybe you and Laws work on 'em."

That bitch, thought Donald. She'd turned on him. He'd deluded himself into thinking that she'd never offer him up. *What had gone wrong*?

"What happened? How did that attorney know what questions to ask?"

"I don' know. I wen try for shoot the Samoan man who ask so many questions, but miss him. Sorry."

"You did what? You dumb fuck!"

Ricardo was silent. There was nothing to say. When Oliver Wilson ordered Donald to stay away from Honolulu, Donald hired Ricardo to keep any eye on things. Ricardo had been doing odd jobs for Donald since the two met following Donald's transfer to Honolulu. It had been a good gravy train for Ricardo, and he knew how to be a good soldier.

"Where's Foreman?"

"Don' know. He no stay. He leave Hawai'i. That's good, yeah?"

"Yeah, that's good. At least they don't have him. Okay, keep your eyes and ears open. Keep me posted, but don't do any more stupid shit, okay, Ricky?"

There was a pause on the line before Ricardo answered. "Okay. I let you know."

They hung up and Donald sat on the bed, water dripping onto the bedspread and onto the floor. He felt helpless. His career was spinning away from him. He looked at his limp penis. He should cut the damn thing off, he thought. He'd thought taking Elie as a lover would be a good way to keep an eye on Laws, but all it had done was make him more vulnerable. If he got thrown out of the CIA, he didn't know what he'd do. It was his life. It was all he'd ever wanted to be. He knew in his heart that he'd be nothing without his CIA persona. He got up off the bed and started to dress. He may as well keep his date, he thought. Maybe a good dinner, some wine, and some pussy would cheer him up.

Chapter Thirty-Six

Pancho was back in court at 1:20. He couldn't remember the last time he'd been so nervous in court. He silently prayed he wouldn't have a panic attack. Then he thought about how fucked up it was that he was even thinking about it.

Drew was spending the day in Pancho's office, making calls, re-reviewing documents, and basically making work for himself. They'd decided it would be best for him to stay off the streets for a day or two. If it was the CIA that tried to kill them, they should be safe now that it was out in the open.

Harry bustled into court at 1:28. He looked a little ragged. He nodded to Pancho and took his seat. The clerk came up to the attorneys and told them the Judge would see them in chambers.

They left the courtroom through the side door, walked across the security hallway, and entered Judge Ramos' chambers. Pancho and Harry both nodded to Beatrice, the Judge's long-time secretary, who waved them into the Judge's office.

Judge Ramos sat behind a spacious oak desk, which had a matching table extending out from the front, perpendicular to the desk. He waved Pancho and Harry to take a seat, and they placed themselves on opposite sides of the table. The judge was holding an unlit cigarette. Even he wasn't allowed to smoke in the courthouse.

"Well, Harry, any developments?"

"No, Judge. I called Bill Hart and he promised to call Washington. I haven't heard anything since."

"You told him of the deadline?"

"Yes, Your Honor."

"Okay then, I see no choice but to proceed." He looked from Harry to Pancho. "Anyone have anything to say?"

Both Pancho and Harry shook their heads.

"Okay then, let's get this mess over with."

The attorneys went back to court while Judge Ramos absently played with his cigarette, waiting for the buzzer that would tell him the court was ready for him.

Elie was on the stand again. Pancho studied her for a moment. She'd pulled herself together as best she could. Most of the make-up had been removed, cried into smears, then wiped off. Pancho knew the advantage of surprise was gone. He'd shown his hand. He'd have to tread carefully again, at least until he could assess where she'd be coming from after having had time to think about things.

"Ms. Watson, is it still your testimony that your friend, Donald, may or may not have been with the CIA?"

"Yes, sir. He never showed me identification. He could've been a plumber for all I knew."

Pancho nodded, mainly to himself. Obviously, she hadn't given up yet. She was still intent on trying to protect this man.

"What was your business in Hong Kong?"

"I went to check on one of the corporations Maynard had set up. I had power of attorney to arrange for the transfer of money from that corporation to a bank in Nairobi."

"Why were these funds being transferred?"

"I don't know. I just followed orders."

"Where did the money in the Hong Kong account come from?"

"I don't know that either. I think there was some joint venture with a company to check into business opportunities in Africa."

"Didn't that strike you as strange, since Laws wasn't doing any investing?"

"Maybe he decided that it was time to start, I really don't know."

"Why did this CIA man accompany you to Nairobi?"

"I didn't say he was CIA."

"Okay, why did Donald, who might have been CIA, go with you to Nairobi?"

"To be with me. We were having an affair."

"That's the only reason?"

"To my knowledge."

"Where did he go after he left you in Frankfurt?"

"I'm not sure, probably home to Washington."

"Ah, now you remember that his home is Washington?"

Elie looked flustered. She brushed some imaginary lint off her dress. "I'm assuming he lived in Washington, since he worked for the government."

"I see." Pancho's words dripped with sarcasm. "Didn't he go on to Paris?"

Elie squinted at Pancho. "I don't know."

"Did you and Donald talk about Laws?"

"We must've."

"What was said?"

"I can't remember."

"Was Donald angry at Laws?"

"What for?"

"You tell me."

"I can't say whether Donald was angry at Maynard, or anyone else, for that matter."

"Did Donald say he was upset with Laws for stealing his investors' money?"

"He might've indicated something like that, you know, like, Maynard was going to get himself in trouble one of these days, that kind of thing."

"How long had Laws been doing business with Donald?"

"I'm not sure, a year or so, I guess."

"And Donald knew that Laws was pulling a scam?"

"I don't know that."

"Ms. Watson, you just testified that Donald said that he thought Laws was going to get himself in trouble because of his thievery."

Elie blanched. "Yes, well, I guess Donald knew Maynard wasn't exactly on the up-and-up."

"Did you ever see Donald with a gun?"

"No, not that I remember."

"Is it your testimony that if you wanted to reach Donald, you would not know where to call or write?"

"Yes, I don't know where he is."

Pancho picked up a piece of paper and approached Elie. "Ms. Watson, I show you a document that has been marked for identification as Defense Exhibit 21." He handed her a set of papers.

"Do you recognize this document?"

"Yes, it's the Articles of Incorporation for Platte River Corporation, a Hong Kong corporation. It's one of the companies Maynard set up."

"And was it this corporation that received the money which you had transferred to a bank in Nairobi?"

"Yes."

"Your Honor, I move that Defense Exhibit 21 be placed into evidence."

"Mr. Chang?"

"No objection, Your Honor."

"Ms. Watson, where are the rest of the documents that pertain to this corporation? You know, the check registers, financial records, those kinds of things?"

Elie looked confused. "I don't know."

"Were those records kept in the office?"

"Yes."

"Did you remove them?"

"No, I certainly did not."

"Do you know if your friend, Donald, removed them?"

"No, I don't."

"But you'd agree that if those documents aren't there, then someone removed them?"

Elie's eyes narrowed, as if she was trying to figure out if this was yet another trap. Finally, she nodded tentatively. "I guess that would be correct. Those documents should have been there in the office."

"Ms. Watson, isn't it true that your government friend, Donald, was becoming irritated with Laws, that he was scared the CIA connection would be blown if it came out that Laws was a fraud?"

"I don't know what Donald thought. He may've expressed concern over Maynard's handling of the business, as I've already said."

Pancho took the Exhibit from Elie, placed it on the clerk's desk, walked to his table, and picked up another piece of paper. He appeared to examine it before turning back to Elie.

"Ms. Watson, I take it that Donald was your friend's real name?"

"What do you mean?"

"Well, does it refresh your recollection any that the name Donald used in Nairobi was Dennis?"

Elie blushed.

"Maybe."

"And Matthews was not his real last name, was it?"

"I don't know, he didn't show me his birth certificate."

"Cute, Ms. Watson. Was it because Donald worked for the CIA that you didn't think it strange he used different names when he travelled?"

"Lots of people travel under different names."

"Sure they do, Ms. Watson, sure they do."

Pancho decided that he'd gotten everything he could from Elie.

"I have no further questions of this witness." Pancho took his seat. Reggie beamed at him.

Harry rose slowly and stood behind counsel table as he commenced re-direct.

"Ms. Watson, you aren't sure that Donald was CIA or not, are you?"

"No."

"And you aren't sure what his business, if any, with Laws was, are you?"

"No."

"Thank you, no further questions."

The court watched in silence as Elie walked from the witness stand out of the courtroom, a very different appearing woman than the one who had entered that morning.

"Your Honor, the State rests." Harry sat down. He wished he had a witness left to put on the stand. He didn't like resting on such a low note. But Elie's suicide attempt had delayed her taking the stand so she was all he'd had left.

"Your Honor, since it is relatively late in the afternoon, the defense respectfully requests that it be allowed to proceed tomorrow."

"It has been a long and interesting day," said Judge Ramos. "I see no problem. Court is recessed until nine a.m. tomorrow."

Pancho and Reggie sat in silence at counsel table as the courtroom noisily emptied. Pancho waved the sheriff off, telling him he wanted to talk to his client for a few minutes.

"Well, Reggie, this is it. We have to decide what to do. I don't think you should take the stand."

"But what about the man in Paris? Won't that look like more CIA stuff?"

"Possibly, but consider what else you'd have to testify about. You admit it was your gun, but claim you don't know how it disappeared, and, most damaging, you'd have to admit having been at Laws' house that morning. I think we're in better shape resting immediately and let me argue the CIA connection."

"I know all that stuff about my not having to take the stand, but won't the jury assume I'm guilty if I don't stand up and deny it?" asked Reggie.

"A lot of people would agree with you. I can only tell you that I've won a lot of cases without ever putting the defendant on the stand. I give juries a lot of credit for following the law. If I can give them a reason to doubt the State's case, I can get an acquittal. I think we have a shot at it.

"Once you take the stand, it's a whole new ball game. If they don't believe you, or don't like you, you're screwed. Simple as that."

Pancho let Reggie think about it. No one likes to think they were not believable, or that a jury would not like them.

"I just don't know."

"Look Reggie, it's a gamble not to put you on the stand. I know that. But I don't like having to admit you went to Laws' house. I don't like having to admit that some guy asked you to kill Laws—paid you money to kill him—and you didn't report it to anyone.

"My strong recommendation is that you let me rest tomorrow."

Reggie nodded. "Okay. You made a case out of nothing, so I guess I'll trust you all the way."

"All right. But no illusions on this. This thing could easily go against you. If we do as I say and still lose, I don't want you coming back at me.

Okay? This is a judgment call. I don't have a crystal ball and I don't give guarantees, okay?"

"I understand. Just do the best you can, that's all I ask."

Pancho had Reggie sign a form which acknowledged that Reggie would waive his right to take the stand in his own defense, and which stated that Pancho had told him of the risks involved in doing so. The form was essentially the same form that the judge would also have Reggie sign. In Hawai'i it was referred to as 'the Tachibana form', after the Supreme Court case in which it first became required. Pancho felt that by having the client already sign the form, the process in court would be less fraught with tension and doubt. Besides, Pancho reasoned, it never hurt to cover his *okole* in as many ways as possible.

Reggie signed it.

"See you tomorrow, Reggie. Dress nice, it could be all *pau*, all finished."

Chapter Thirty-Seven

The story hit the late news on the east coast. It only covered the allegations of CIA involvement with Laws, but it was enough to cause a fair amount of commotion.

Deputy Director Fuller had been back at Langley since shortly after Oliver Wilson's secretary tracked him down at a chic French restaurant in Georgetown. He hung up the phone and turned to Wilson, who was slouched in Fuller's black leather reading chair where he'd been waiting for Fuller to finish covering his ass with the Director.

"Any suggestions?" asked Fuller when he hung up the phone.

Wilson did not alter his position. He looked relaxed and at ease. It'd been kind of fun watching Fuller squirm. "Well, there's nothing we can do except refuse comment. That's why we have that policy. But I think it'd be a good idea for me to pick someone to leak to the press that the story is totally ridiculous."

Fuller nodded. Wilson thought he looked somewhat shell-shocked.

"What about Duerden?" asked Wilson. "He never told us he was having an affair with Laws' secretary. That compromised the whole operation."

Fuller nodded again, but said nothing.

"I want to bring him in immediately. I want him suspended pending investigation."

Fuller put his head into his hands and rubbed his face, as if he were washing. "Okay," he finally said.

Wilson rose to leave. "God knows what other loose ends Duerden's left. Let's just hope the witness, Foreman, doesn't show himself. If he goes public about a CIA payoff to keep his mouth shut, we can deny or refuse comment to kingdom come and have no credibility at all. Just don't forget he's out there."

Wilson left Fuller sitting in silence. He didn't feel sorry for the pompous ass. He'd stuck his nose in an operation that he should've left to the Division Chief. Fuller deserved whatever he got.

Wilson strolled down the carpeted corridor and took the stairs to his floor. He ordered his secretary to make contact with Duerden in Mexico City, then called one of his assistants whom he knew to have a contact with the *Post*. He'd do nicely as the leak.

Pancho, Drew and Susan watched the six o'clock news in Pancho's office. It was the lead story, and the reporter, who'd been present in court all day, not only gave an account of the allegations, but also had courtroom footage from the morning session in which Elie was clearly being evasive while seemingly admitting the CIA connection.

They all knew an acquittal was still a longshot, but at least the gamble of going after Elie had paid off. They were now convinced their working hypothesis was correct, that Laws had been killed by the mysterious Donald.

"Do you think Elie knew that Donald killed Laws?" asked Susan.

Pancho shook his head. "I doubt it, which is why I chose not to ask her about that on cross. She would've denied it either way, and even if she did know, I don't think I'd ever get that admission out of her."

Drew and Susan were excited, and had been jabbering to each other about the case and about Elie since the news broadcast was over. Pancho watched them and felt good. They were a good team, and had given him the support he'd desperately needed to do battle in court.

In some respects, thought Pancho, being a trial attorney was like being an actor. He had to get up and perform day after day, even if he bombed out or had completely embarrassed himself. He had to pick himself up and go back into the arena. But unlike the theatre, in trial the lines were not scripted. A trial was fluid, and could change from moment to moment. A ruling by the judge could suddenly exclude whole segments of planned testimony, and he had to be ready to adapt immediately. And, underlying everything, of course, was that human lives were at stake.

Susan had asked Pancho a question. He came out of his reverie and asked what she'd said.

"Are you going to put Reggie on?"

"No. I think that can only hurt us."

"So you're going to rest first thing?" asked Drew.

"Yep. Without Foreman, we have no witnesses. I don't see any point in putting the neighbor on. That'll just confuse the jury about where I'm going with the case. I'd rather put on no defense than just one witness who doesn't add much to the scenario I want to present.

"For a while I thought the timing could be important, but now, all I want to do is raise enough smoke to take the jury into the realm of reasonable doubt."

Drew nodded his understanding.

"Besides, if I don't put on a case, the prosecution doesn't get any rebuttal. And so, my dear friends, if you'll excuse me, I want to put together some notes for closing."

Chapter Thirty-Eight

Elie had gone from court to bed, from which she hadn't stirred. Her aunt and uncle looked at her with something between disdain and sympathy. She hadn't heard from her parents. Reporters followed her home, and were now camped outside her uncle's Aiea Heights house. She shuddered when she thought of them screaming questions at her as she left the courthouse.

She intermittently cried and watched television, masochistically watching each of the news broadcasts. She could hear the phone ringing in another part of the house. It had rung almost constantly since she'd returned home.

A few minutes later, there was a knock at her door and her aunt stuck her head in.

"Elie, there's a man on the phone who insists on talking to you. He says he's not a reporter." Her aunt's face looked drawn and worried. Elie wished she hadn't come to stay with her aunt and uncle. She'd brought nothing but shame on them.

"I don't want to talk to anybody."

"He's very insistent and rather rude. He says you know him, but he won't give me his name."

"Oh, okay." Elie picked up the phone beside her bed and plugged in the cord, which she'd disconnected so she wouldn't hear the constant ringing.

"Hello?"

"You fucking bitch." Elie gasped.

"Donald? Is that you? Donald?"

"They didn't have shit, you know. They had nothing but guesses until you opened your big mouth." His tone was venomous and somewhat slurred, as if he'd been drinking.

"Donald, I tried." Her voice was pleading, whimpering. "I really tried. I practically committed perjury for you. Please, I tried. I don't want to go to jail, Donald. I tried to say as little as possible."

"They didn't have shit."

"They knew, Donald. I swear to God, they knew."

"Okay, okay. They still don't have my last name. You give them that and you're dead. Do you understand me, Elie? You're a fucking dead woman if you give them anything else."

"I understand. Oh please, Donald, I need you. I tried to call you, write you. I'm all alone."

"Just remember what I said." There was a click on the line, then a dial tone.

Elie began crying. She held the phone to her chest and cried until her aunt slipped into the room, took the phone from her hands, and hung it up. She left her niece weeping alone in the dark, her sympathy all used up.

Donald hung up the phone. His hotel room seemed claustrophobic. He'd already listened to Oliver Wilson ream him a new asshole and order his immediate return to D.C.

He was sweating, even though the air conditioning was on and the room was cool. He picked up the bottle of Scotch sitting by the phone and took a long pull. He wasn't completely sure why he'd called Elie. It was a stupid thing to do. He knew that logically, but he hadn't been able to help himself. He wanted her to pay for her broken promise. He wanted her to know that all she had to do was deny everything and it would've been all right. He wanted her to suffer like he was suffering. And he wanted to scare her into not giving his real name to the police.

Donald figured the CIA would protect him as long as it was in their interest to do so. They would have to try to deny involvement with Laws, and as long as they did that, he'd be protected from the police and a public investigation. He should've had her killed.

He decided to go out and have a real cocktail, maybe hit some clubs. Tomorrow he'd be headed home to face the music. He had to get some explanations ready.

It hadn't been a good night. First, the call from Ricardo, then he'd been unable to get a hard-on after taking his date back to her luxurious apartment in San Angel. She tried to tell him it was all right, but he wasn't in the mood to be patronized and he had left her lying naked on her bed, condemned to spend another lonely night. He visualized her masturbating after he left, laughing at him, at his inadequacies, as she successfully brought herself to a lonely climax.

Donald figured his career was over. That asshole, Oliver Wilson, had it in for him. It just wasn't fair, he thought, as he shut the door on his Holiday Inn room.

Chapter Thirty-Nine

Reggie was already seated when Pancho threaded his way past reporters and spectators and entered the courtroom. Pancho put his briefcase on the table and squeezed Reggie's shoulder.

"Not much longer now."

Reggie gave Pancho a nervous smile. There were deep circles under his eyes.

Harry came into court with another deputy prosecutor. Apparently, Harry wanted some moral support, thought Pancho. They nodded and smiled briefly at each other. When the courtroom was filled and quieted, the bailiff pressed the buzzer for the Judge to enter. The attorneys, knowing the signal, rose, followed by the rest of the courtroom. The bailiff said, "All rise," as the Judge's door began to open, but everyone was already standing.

Judge Ramos greeted the attorneys and asked Pancho if he was ready to proceed with the defense. The jury was not yet present.

"Your Honor, at this time I move to dismiss the case against my client on the grounds that the State has failed to meet its burden of proof." Pancho argued his motion for a few minutes.

Harry rose to argue, but Judge Ramos waved him down.

"For such a motion, the Court must weigh the evidence in a light most favorable to the State. Doing so, the Court finds that there is a sufficient question of fact and basis for a jury to find guilt. The motion is therefore denied."

This was an expected and routine procedure. The Judge ordered the jury to be brought into court. When the jury was seated, Pancho rose to address the court.

"Your Honor, the defense rests."

There was a general murmuring among the spectators and reporters in the courtroom. Neither Judge Ramos nor Harry Chang looked surprised.

"Is counsel ready to proceed with closing?"

Harry and Pancho stood and advised the Judge that they were ready to do so. Pancho sat down and watched as Harry nervously tugged at his rumpled blue blazer and coughed into his hand.

Harry assumed the same dry, factual approach he'd used on opening. He discussed the charges, and some of the jury instructions that the Judge would give to the jury before they began deliberations. He made it sound as if he were privy to what the Judge would be doing, not pointing out that the attorneys meet with the Judge to go over the jury instructions ahead of time, trying to come to agreement on which instructions were to be given. The Judge ultimately decided the content of the instructions, and each attorney had a right to note his objection to such instructions for the record. This was all done in chambers, but on the record, outside of the presence of the jury.

Harry then started ticking off the facts that supported the case against Reggie, culminating in the gun.

"This is a case of murder, ladies and gentlemen. Not a case of spies and intrigue. It is simple, brutal, malicious, premeditated murder. Whether the decedent, Maynard Laws, did or did not have some kind of arrangement to provide corporations for the CIA is an interesting theory, but it's irrelevant to this case. This case isn't about the CIA, it's about murder — murder in its most violent, horrible, ghoulish, form.

"Yes, it would've been nice if we could have located the sword or machete that was used to viciously cut off the head and arms of Maynard Laws. It would've been nice to have had all sorts of additional evidence."

Harry gave a rare smile. "It would have been nice to have a confession, but the reality of premeditated murder, ladies and gentlemen, is that the murderer tries to hide his weapons, destroys evidence, proclaims his innocence. If he didn't, we wouldn't need a trial. Unfortunately, for the defendant, a small boy, out fishing, found the gun that the defendant had used to shoot the decedent before dismembering him. That gun was registered to the defendant. The defendant had never reported that gun as missing." Harry paused, keeping eye contact with the jurors. "That gun is the link, ladies and gentlemen. It is the incriminating link between the murder of Maynard Laws and the defendant.

"The defendant had been in Laws' house. The fibers from Laws' living room carpet were found on the defendant's rubber slippers. Matches from a restaurant the defendant was known to have eaten at in Paris just a few weeks before were found on the lanai, near where Laws was murdered. You heard the testimony of Laws' maids, that the matches had not been there that morning, and had not been seen around the house before the day of the murder.

"Coincidence? Anything is possible, ladies and gentlemen, but I submit to you that it is stretching the realm of coincidence too far to say that matches from a Paris restaurant where the defendant had been shortly before, found their way to Laws' lanai from a source other than the defendant."

Harry paused, letting the heart of his case sink in. He coughed and took a sip of water.

"Don't let my esteemed adversary mislead and confuse you. The facts are in evidence, and they speak loudly for themselves. All this hullabaloo about the CIA and corporations is an interesting diversion, but that's all it is, a diversion, a card trick, a sleight of the hand to make you look from the facts to a hazy scenario of confusion and intrigue. I trust that you will consider the evidence, listen to the Judge's instructions, and bring back a verdict of guilty. Thank you."

Harry sat down and looked at Pancho, expelling air, letting himself wind down as he did so. He had only rebuttal left. Since the State had the burden of proof, it was given the opportunity to argue first, then to rebut the defense argument. The defense had only one shot at the jury.

Pancho rose without papers. He put his hands in the pockets of his jeans, looking thoughtful, as if he were only now considering the evidence Harry had just laid out for them. He wore black cowboy boots and a black linen sport coat that set off the red tie with the tiny figures of lady justice. He nodded to the Judge, then to Harry, and then faced the jury head on.

"Interesting diversion? Is that what it is? When the evidence points to the fact that the Central Intelligence Agency of the United States of America is working with a person whom they know to be a liar and a thief, my colleague calls it an interesting diversion. This interesting diversion," Pancho made air-quotes with his fingers, "has thrown a blanket of doubt over the State's entire case.

"Remember during jury selection, what we call *voir dire*, there was a woman whose husband was a police officer? Remember when I asked her if she thought that the police were capable of making mistakes? She acknowledged that anyone could make a mistake.

"Well, ladies and gentlemen, this case, this investigation, is rife with mistakes. I'm not here condemning the police, please do not think that. The police do a wonderful job for us most of the time. But they do make mistakes, and unfortunately they made a bunch of them in this case.

"Had the police responded to the call in a timely fashion, there would've been a strong chance of catching the culprit, so that my client would not be sitting here today.

"Had Officer Lee not picked up the match book without thinking, the police may have been able to find fingerprints of the culprit on the book so that my client would not be sitting here today.

"Had the police, with their enormous resources, been able to find what we found, that Laws had been working with the CIA, then other, more appropriate avenues of investigation would have been pursued so that the true murderer would have been caught and my client would not be sitting here today."

Pancho's voice was low and even-paced, a voice of reason. He stayed a respectable distance from the jury box, but he prowled the courtroom, not using notes and not using the podium.

"But, what about the gun? What about the match book? What about Reggie Bellows' anger and lost fortune?" Pancho paused. "Ladies and gentlemen, I told you at the outset of this case that I would not be able to prove who actually murdered Maynard Laws. I don't have the resources of the police, and I certainly don't have access to the CIA.

"Consider, however, Elie Watson's less-than-voluntary testimony. A man named Donald, who works for the government, and probably for the CIA, had been working with Maynard Laws for a year or more. Laws set up dummy corporations, certainly for no legitimate purpose having to do with investments, since it's been shown he did no investing. Consider that it's a reasonable conclusion that these corporations were set up as dummy corporations for the CIA to use in their worldwide operations."

"Objection, Your Honor, this is nothing but speculation."

Pancho sighed theatrically, as if exasperated by the interruption.

"Your Honor, I submit that this is a reasonable inference from the testimony in this case, which the jury is capable and competent to evaluate."

Judge Ramos nodded. "Overruled."

Pancho turned back to the jury. "The testimony of Elie is that she went to Hong Kong on business to oversee the transfer of money from one of these dummy corporations to a bank in Nairobi. She's accompanied both to Hong Kong and to Nairobi by this mysterious CIA man named Donald, who travels under a false name.

"Consider the testimony of Elie, where she said that Donald had expressed concern over Laws' blatant thievery, which could bring everyone down, including the CIA, for using a common thief as a front man.

"Consider the fact that we lose the trail of Donald in Frankfurt, a few days before Reggie Bellows is in Paris and went to the restaurant where he allegedly took some matches, which were then left at the scene of a murder. Frankfurt and Paris are not far apart.

"Consider a frame up, ladies and gentlemen. Consider who or what is most capable of picking a disgruntled investor to frame. Who or what is —"

"Your Honor! I must object again. Counsel is alleging that the CIA framed the defendant and killed the decedent. This is pure, unadulterated speculation."

"Again, Your Honor," said Pancho, "I submit that this is all a reasonable inference from the evidence. I'm not making up the evidence. I note that

Mr. Chang has drawn the same inferences as I, since I've not yet accused anyone of anything. To disallow me to point out to the jury some of the reasonable inferences which they can logically draw from the evidence would be to change the burden of proof from the State to the defense."

Pancho absently rubbed his chest as he watched Judge Ramos deliberate. He knew he was walking the line, but he was gambling that the Judge would decide to err on the side of the defense. If there was a guilty verdict, the defense was sure to appeal, and the refusal to allow Pancho to draw such inferences may be grounds for reversal. No judge liked to be reversed on appeal.

"Overruled."

"Thank you, Your Honor." Pancho turned back to the jury, all of whom were clearly fascinated by what he was proposing.

"Who is capable of doing background checks on the investors, to pick a man with a military background? Who is capable of tracing Reggie Bellows to Paris, then taking a simple matchbook from a restaurant where Reggie had eaten? Who is capable of stealing Reggie's gun from his apartment, while he's out of town, to use at a murder, then dispose of at a place often fished and quite likely to be found?

"It wouldn't have done any good to plant the machete in a place to be found because there'd be no connection to Reggie, were it found. No prints, no ownership, no nothing.

"Who is capable of walking into Maynard Laws' house carrying a gun *and* a machete, or sword, without unduly alarming Laws until it was too late for him to run? A man Laws had worked with for years. A man Laws knew worked for the CIA and would be expected to have instruments of destruction, maybe to show off to Laws.

"And who is capable of disappearing into oblivion, having scared or seduced the one connecting witness into lying on the stand to protect him; for surely we don't believe that Elie Watson doesn't know Donald's real last name, where he lives, or anything else about him, other than the little she gave us? The answer to all of the above, ladies and gentlemen, is an agent of the CIA.

"Mr. Chang has objected to my argument, calling it speculation. His honor will instruct you that you may draw reasonable inferences from the facts in evidence. I realize what I propose is shocking and disturbing, for I'm talking about an agency of the United States government.

"But the reasonable inference from the evidence in this case is that my client was framed. Mr. Bellows has been painted by the prosecutor as a smart man, with military training. What are the realistic chances of such a smart man leaving a matchbook on the lanai table of someone he's allegedly just shot and cut up like a side of beef? What are the realistic chances that such a smart military man would dump a murder weapon less than a mile from the scene of a murder, in a shallow area of rocks?

What are the realistic chances of such a smart man not realizing that, as one of the biggest investor losers, he'd be a prime suspect in any murder of Laws?"

Pancho paused, walked over to his counsel table and took a sip of water. He'd begun to sweat, even though the courtroom was freezing. He wiped his brow and took a deep breath. The low hum of the air conditioner was the only sound that heard in the courtroom. He pushed aside the rising fear of a full-blown panic attack and turned back to the jury.

"Reggie Bellows had nothing to gain from the death of Maynard Laws. He didn't have something to hide, like the CIA did. If Laws' house of cards had come tumbling down, Laws would have been yelling for the CIA to protect him at the top of his lungs. Reggie's only conceivable motive was revenge. But isn't shooting someone to death revenge enough?" Pancho felt the onset of chest pain. He began to feel dizzy, and he could feel the blood drain from his face. He stopped talking and put his hand on the podium. The courtroom was deathly silent.

"Are you all right, Mr. McMartin?" asked Judge Ramos.

Pancho breathed deep and forced himself to stand tall. He nodded. "Yes, Your Honor." He turned back to the jury and forced himself to go on.

"I submit to you that the dismemberment of Laws was someone's bright idea of what a revenge murder would look like, filled with hate and anger. That's hogwash, ladies and gentlemen. If Reggie wanted to kill Laws for revenge and get away with it, he wouldn't have used his own registered gun; he would have bought one that could not be traced. He wouldn't have had a smoke at the scene of the murder. The record shows there wasn't time for that anyway; and he certainly wasn't going to lounge around having a smoke with Laws before killing him. And he wouldn't have tossed his gun away in such a discoverable location.

"No, ladies and gentlemen, the killing of Maynard Laws by Reggie Bellows simply does not make sense. What does make sense is that he was framed, framed by people who had much more to gain by Laws' death than Reggie Bellows."

Pancho admonished the jury to not read anything into the decision not to have Reggie testify. He concluded, noting what the Judge's instruction on reasonable doubt would be, and asked for a verdict of not guilty.

He sat down quickly, exhausted, fighting to remain upright. He knew what was happening, but, even so, it was hard not to think he was about to die. He felt like he would pass out any second. He'd give anything to get out of there. He knew he looked bad. Judge Ramos was looking at him with a questioning look. Pancho shook his head slightly, hoping to signal the Judge that he was okay. There was silence in the courtroom, until Judge Ramos finally turned to Harry and told him to proceed with his rebuttal.

Pancho barely listened as Harry tried to bring the jury back to the hard evidence, calling the CIA connection a red herring. Facts, facts, facts. Harry hammered them home. He talked for fifteen minutes, and then it was over.

The Judge said he'd give the jury instructions after lunch, and recessed. Again, the reporters made a mad dash for the door.

Pancho slumped back in his chair and closed his eyes. The attack was slowly passing. His breathing was back to normal and the pain in his chest was gone.

"You okay, Pancho?" asked Reggie.

Pancho opened his eyes, took a deep breath, and nodded.

"Yeah, I'm fine. Just got a little shaky there for a moment."

Reggie smiled then. "Well you did it, man, you fucking did it."

Pancho gave him a wan smile and patted his shoulder. "Let's not get ahead of ourselves." He stood up slowly and packed up his briefcase. "I'll see you this afternoon. Stay calm."

Chapter Forty

That afternoon Judge Ramos charged the jury with their duties and read the jury instructions as to the law they must follow in arriving at their verdict. Reggie's fate was now in the hands of twelve men and women. Pancho was surrounded by reporters as he left court.

"Mr. McMartin," one of the television reporters was virtually screaming, "can you prove the CIA murdered Maynard Laws?"

Pancho smiled at the man, whom he had dealt with over the years.

"Bob, if I could prove the CIA murdered Laws, the jury would already be through deliberating. Luckily, for any American citizen charged with a crime, he or she is presumed innocent until proven guilty. The State has the burden of proving guilt. I don't have to prove who did it. I can only hope that I pointed out to the jury the enormous amount of doubt as to my client's guilt."

"Do you think the CIA had Laws killed?"

"I think that it's a possibility, but it's up to the State to pursue that avenue further."

"Do you think your client will be found not guilty?"

"I hope and pray he will be. I have great confidence in our system of justice."

Pancho excused himself and made his way through the throng of reporters and spectators. The reporters turned their attention to Harry Chang, who'd come out of court a few minutes after Pancho.

Pancho again made the transition from the surreal world of the courtroom to the real world of people going about their daily lives. The afternoon was humid. It had rained in the morning and now the sun was sucking the moisture into the air. As he almost always did coming out of the over air-conditioned courthouse, he took off his jacket and slung it over his shoulder. He did not have his usual burden of files, as all he'd done after lunch was sit through the jury instructions. Now it was a waiting game, and he had to be by a telephone during deliberation hours in case there was a question from the jury— or a verdict.

He strolled back to his office, enjoying the feeling of powerlessness. A couple of attorneys he knew nodded to him as they made their way to court, trial briefcases in hand, worried looking clients at their side. A white egret walked gingerly on top of a hibiscus hedge, the twigs barely holding the bird's weight.

Pancho had made his way through the maze of this case the best he could. He tried not to harbor any great illusions about the outcome. When all was said and done, he'd ended up claiming that someone stole the gun from Reggie's apartment and used it to shoot Laws. The CIA involvement gave a new twist to the usual age-old and generally lame excuse, for one's gun being a murder weapon: 'I was framed I tells ya.'

Pancho could never help feeling excited and optimistic about a case while the jury was out. It was a time for hope. Even on dead ringer loser cases, it was a period of time when everything was up in the air, and optimism would sneak in and poison one's sense of reality. It was a feeling not unlike that which a gambler experiences on a role of the dice, a flip of the cards, or a spin of the wheel. No matter how bad it had been, no matter what the odds against winning might be, the true gambler had that hope.

Pancho felt both exhausted and exhilarated. The onset of a panic attack during his closing argument was scary, but he'd gotten through it. He hadn't died and he hadn't passed out. Dr. Ginsberg had told him that the more he realized and accepted what was really happening, the better chance he would have of the attacks just going away, just stopping on their own.

Now the survival of the attack and the adrenaline rush of the trial was replaced by a sense of freedom. No more preparation into the wee hours of the night. No more last moment decisions on trial tactics; objections to make or not make; questions to ask; traps to set. In the past, he savored it while it was happening and rejoiced when it was over. But now it was hard to savor the thrill of trial when the pall of a possible panic attack loomed. He wondered if his trial career was over. How could he continue to do what he loved if his mind and body wouldn't cooperate?

The office was empty. He'd given Susan the afternoon off. She had been a trooper, working the long hours without being asked, and he could see that she too was exhausted. Nothing much was going to happen today. He closed himself in his office and stretched out on the couch. He had about two hours to hang around before the Judge would send the jury home for the evening. He doubted that a verdict would come in. He closed his eyes and tried not to think about his closing argument; tried not to worry about things he should have said, or not said. That battle would rumble on in his mind for a few days, longer if he lost.

After ten minutes, Pancho temporarily won the battle and fell asleep.

Chapter Forty-One

Donald came out of the terminal at Dulles into a snowstorm. He was dressed for Mexico, not Washington, D.C., and the cold hit him hard. He swore under his breath and got in line for a taxi. It was night, and he would not have to face Oliver Wilson until the morning.

He had talked to Ricardo just before leaving Mexico City, and learned that Pancho McMartin had accused the CIA of murdering Maynard Laws. It would be all over the news tonight, probably already was.

He doubted that Ollie would be pleased about that turn of events. Donald hoped the jury would convict Bellows; it would make life much easier.

Sandy Foreman chuckled to himself as he watched the national news story about the Bellows trial. Bellows' attorney had accused the CIA of working with a con artist, and that allegation seemed to be borne out by the con man's secretary, Elie Watson. The attorney had gone so far as to accuse the CIA of being responsible for the death of Laws.

"Those fuck-brains paid me all that hush money for nothing," Foreman said to himself.

The balance of 'all that money' consisted of exactly one thousand three hundred fifteen dollars and forty-eight cents. Sandy was in Las Vegas, a venue he decided would be a pleasant place to avoid a subpoena. Unfortunately, his poker playing skills weren't what they used to be.

Sandy switched off the broadcast and allowed himself one last chuckle. He loved irony, which is why, when he was pleasantly stoned, he rather got a kick out of the twists and turns of his own life.

Now it was time for him to decide what to do with that life. His gig was blown in Honolulu, which was okay with him. He had some bad memories of Honolulu. It was time to move on.

He considered staying in Vegas, but prostitution and drugs were firmly in the control of organized crime, and a good independent capitalist like himself could get hurt. He liked the warm climate, but Florida was out; been there, done that.

He thought about Phoenix. He'd heard there were a lot of opportunities in the Sun Belt. Yeah, maybe Phoenix. Run a few whores, deal a little. Not too much, no point in getting greedy and bringing heat on himself.

Sandy counted his money again. The only question was, should he parlay this grand into some big cash, or should he buy some smack and get the hell out of Dodge?

Reggie Bellows sat in his cell. It was hotter than hell, and one of his cellmates had the most god-awful body odor. It had been an incredible ordeal the last couple of weeks, sitting through a trial, listening to people talk about him, accuse him of murder. It had been demeaning and frightening.

As trial progressed, he'd been able to make himself kind of numb. He would be led into court like a robot, sit quietly at the counsel table for hours on end, and allow himself to be re-shackled and transported back to prison at the end of each day.

He knew he'd gotten his money's worth out of Pancho, although he tried not to think of the fact that he'd lost everything: all that money to Laws, all his savings from Switzerland, his condo, his business. It was all gone. Even an acquittal could not bring it back. He tried not to think of the money lost because he could not yet deal with the anger that welled up inside him whenever he did so. He felt a rage more intense than anything he'd ever felt before, even when he'd faced people trying their best to kill him.

He tried to bury his face in his pillow to avoid the smell of his cellmate. He was fidgety and nervous. His entire life hung in the balance, hung in the decisions of twelve people he didn't know and who certainly didn't know him. *How strange to have it all come down to this*, he thought.

His cellmate farted, a loud, sickening fart that seemed to reverberate off the walls of the cell. Reggie buried his face further into his pillow. *Please let it be over soon.*

Chapter Forty-Two

The days turned hot and muggy. The trades stopped, and whatever wind there was came from the south, Kona winds. With the southerly wind came the 'vog,' the volcano version of smog, brought in on the winds from the Big Island. It hurt to breathe deep and it stung the eyes. Pancho took refuge in his air-conditioned office, waiting for a verdict, trying to concentrate on the backlog of work that had built up during the Bellows trial.

Every time the phone rang, he stopped whatever it was he was doing and waited for Susan to buzz him and tell him it was the court. Twice in the last three days, he'd received such a call, only to be told that the jury had a question. He trudged through the mugginess to court and met with Harry and the Judge to review the questions from the jury and agree upon a response from the Judge. Both times the Judge sent the jury a note saying they were to follow a particular jury instruction, as an answer to their question. Sometimes the response from a judge to a jury question was less than fulfilling to the jury, but there was only so much direction a judge could give.

Pancho tried to resist the temptation of reading between the lines of the jury questions. Were they leaning to acquittal or conviction? It was hard to tell. He'd gone back to his office to what felt like mundane administrative work. It was the post-trial letdown, he knew. After the excitement of trial, the paper work that comprised ninety-nine percent of an attorney's time seemed dull and boring. With a jury deliberating on a murder case, everything else seemed trivial. On the positive side, he hadn't had a panic attack since that last day in court.

Pancho wrote a note to Susan to set up a deposition of an expert witness in San Francisco. He'd already called Paula to make sure she could go with him. He picked a Friday for the deposition so they could go up to Napa Valley for the weekend.

He glanced at the phone. There were no lights flashing, so he turned to the next file in the stack. It was 4:30 p.m. when the intercom sounded and Susan told him Judge Ramos' clerk was on the phone. Pancho was told to be at court first thing in the morning, at 9:00. He wasn't told whether the jury had reached a verdict.

The word of a possible verdict had spread, and the courtroom was packed at 9:00 the next morning. Pancho and Harry nodded to each other as they entered the court at the same time. Reggie was already at counsel table. His face was sheet-white and he was visibly shaking. Pancho didn't have a chance to talk to him, however, as he and Harry were immediately called into chambers.

Judge Ramos had his feet up on his desk, and was playing with his usual cigarette. He didn't look happy. When he spoke, his lisp was pronounced.

"Well, looks like we're going to get ourselves a hung jury, boys." The Judge passed a piece of paper to Harry, who read it and passed it on to Pancho.

It was a note from the jury that said they were hopelessly deadlocked and needed help on how to proceed.

"I'm going to send in my standard form." He passed it to the attorneys to read.

> Is there any point to further deliberations on this matter?
> Yes____ No____
>
> Is this a unanimous decision?
> Yes____ No____

Pancho's heart sank. A hung jury meant a mistrial. A mistrial meant a retrial, in most cases. Dumbly, he nodded to the Judge, who handed it to his clerk to take to the jury.

The three men sat in silence as they waited for a response to the note. Pancho's mind was whirling. Would they prosecute again? Would they follow up on the CIA connection? How could he afford to do another trial for no more money? His practice had ground to a complete halt while he was preparing for and participating in the first trial. Cases had been turned down, and existing clients were barely appeased with the inaction on their files. Each client would, of course, demand the same kind of personal and complete attention that Reggie had received if their case went to trial, but since this was not their case, they were less than sympathetic.

He was jolted out of his depressing reverie when the clerk reappeared and handed the Judge the response. The Judge read it and passed it to Harry and Pancho. The jury had answered 'no' to further deliberations and 'yes' that the decision was unanimous. The Judge let out a big sigh. He didn't like it any more than Pancho or Harry.

"Well, I'm going to do it. Let's go on the record."

They returned to open court. Pancho whispered to Reggie what was happening as the jury filed in, followed by the Judge. He didn't have time to answer all of Reggie's questions, and Reggie was left looking confused and worried.

The Judge recited for the record what had transpired. He read the notes and asked the foreman of the jury if the responses were true and correct. The foreman said yes.

"I therefore have no choice but to declare a mistrial. This matter shall be referred back to the administrative judge for re-calendaring for re-trial or motions."

The courtroom erupted in chaos. Reggie was looking plaintively at Pancho. Pancho leaned over and tried to explain that Reggie would be tried again, before a new jury and new judge. If the State decided not to re-try, it would be a miracle.

"Can I get out on bail now?"

"We can move again for a reduction of bail, but I wouldn't hold my breath."

"How long can they do this to me? What the fuck? What the fuck? How long do I rot in jail?"

Pancho tried to calm him. "You weren't convicted Reggie. You could've been found guilty, but they couldn't do it. Take faith in that."

Reggie stared at Pancho. He'd built up his hope. He'd fallen into the trap of optimism that even attorneys have a hard time avoiding. He nodded, trying to gather himself.

"Are you going to still represent me?" It was more a plea than a question.

Pancho made an instantaneous decision, and nodded.

"Yeah, Reggie, I'll represent you. We'll work something out. Don't worry about that now."

For some reason Pancho flashed on his parents' friend telling him he was too emotional to ever be a good attorney. *Damn it*, he said to himself, *I wouldn't want to be any other way.*

He wouldn't abandon Reggie now, even though a new trial would cost him much more in lost business than he would ever hope to make; even though he needed time and relaxation to work through these damned panic attacks. He patted Reggie on the shoulder, not sure whether he was consoling Reggie or himself.

Reggie finally calmed down, and allowed himself to be escorted out of court, re-shackled in the irons binding his hands and legs, and led away to prison.

Pancho left the court and entered the horde of reporters who had been waiting for him.

"What do you think of the mistrial?"

"Are you pleased?"

"What does Reggie think?"

"Are you going to defend him again?"

"What about the CIA, are you going to make the same argument?"

The questions were hurled at him like a batting machine gone haywire. He raised his hands, and there was finally some semblance of quiet.

"We are naturally disappointed in the hung jury and the mistrial. We were hoping for an acquittal. My client cannot afford bail and sits in jail waiting exoneration. In light of the new evidence procured at trial, I am hopeful that the State will decide not to pursue the action against Mr. Bellows any further. If there is to be a re-trial, however, I shall continue to stand by my client. That's all I have to say, thank you."

He forced his way through the tight group, not listening to the shouted questions. He had too many questions of his own. His legs felt weak, almost numb. His head was beginning to throb. The joy of the trial being over evaporated, like the rain off the hot Honolulu sidewalks.

It was not over. It was just starting all over again.

Chapter Forty-Three

"I want to get this guy. I want us to find out who he is and I want to nail him if we can."

Pancho was sitting at his desk addressing Drew and Susan. It was the Monday following the mistrial and he felt better. He'd taken Paula to Kauai for the weekend, staying at a friend's house in Kilauea. They had walked on the beach, swam, made love over and over, and he felt rejuvenated. They did not talk about Reggie Bellows or the case. Pancho wanted to put the case completely out of his mind for the weekend, and although Paula had a lot of questions, she asked none.

On the plane coming home on Sunday evening, Pancho had made a decision.

"Drew, I want you to figure out what we can do to find out who Donald is. We have some time, but I don't know how long before the administrative judge will be putting the case on the master calendar to be assigned out for a new trial judge."

"Why don't we try to get Elie's phone records, see if she had called anyone who could be Donald?" said Drew.

"Yeah, I'll get a subpoena out. What else?"

"Why don't we hire an artist to make a sketch of the man Reggie met in Paris? It might help us determine whether or not it was the mysterious Donald."

"Couldn't hurt, call Rosie Akamine. She used to do that for the police."

"I'll do that," Susan said.

The three thought in silence, each trying to think of what they could do to find the identity of a man whose identity was apparently being protected by the CIA. Pancho didn't want them to get discouraged at the beginning of the new battle, so he told them to get going on what they'd come up with.

Pancho sat alone in his office once they'd gone. After a few moments, he picked up the phone and dialed the prosecutors' number.

"Harry Chang, please."

"One moment."

"Chang here."

"Hey, Harry, it's Pancho."

"Hi, Pancho. Howzit?"

"Oh, I'm okay, wondering if this case is ever going to go away."

"Not likely."

"You're going to re-try?"

"Of course. Why wouldn't I?"

"Well, there were just a few points raised at trial that you might want to investigate — in the interest of justice and all that."

Harry laughed. "What, the CIA thing? That's you blowing smoke, Pancho, that's not something for my people to investigate."

Pancho was getting irritated.

"Don't give me that 'blowing smoke' shit. Let's face it, the CIA was using Laws, a fricking con man. The CIA agent was boffing your star witness, who didn't tell you anything about it —"

"Pancho, relax brah. Don't be calling me up coming on heavy like this. If the CIA is doing stupid stuff that's one thing. Call your Senator and complain. But you're making a quantum leap from the CIA working with Laws to murdering him. No matter what you say, I simply don't believe that the CIA goes around killing its own citizens. Your client is guilty. You did a hell of a job, but I'm going to convict his ass next time. Period. End of conversation."

"You got it, Harry. End of conversation." Pancho hung up. The conversation depressed him. Maybe he *had* come on too strong. Harry was a good man, and didn't deserve it. It *was* a big leap of logic, and Pancho knew it.

He stared down at the figures he'd scrawled on a yellow legal pad.

He'd taken two hundred thousand in fees and costs. He'd paid Drew twenty thousand for his time so far, and spent another five thousand on other costs such as economic expert consultation, law clerk, paralegal, and the like. He figured he would pay Drew at least another twenty thousand, and possibly give him a bonus of ten grand or so. He'd also give Susan a bonus for her work beyond that of legal secretary.

That left him with about a hundred and fifty thousand for two murder trials. Dirt cheap. He couldn't quantify how much he'd lose in cases he'd have to turn away.

The silver lining was that he'd come across as something of a media hero. He'd taken what the prosecution was touting as a cold case of murder against Reggie, and gotten a hung jury. But it was only going to get harder the next time around. All the element of surprise would be gone. *This time,* thought Pancho, *I think I really do have to prove that the CIA murdered Laws.* He groaned and got to work.

Chapter Forty-Four

Donald Duerden sat in his economy Aero Mexico seat and stared out the window at the pouring rain. He was going back to Mexico, not on business, but to live for a while. The scene at Oliver Wilson's office on the preceding Friday had not been pleasant.

Wilson was sitting at his gray metal government-issue desk when Donald entered and he made no attempt to shake hands. He gestured Donald to a chair.

"I want a written report updating your previous, obviously bullshit, report on the Laws matter. You're under suspension without pay pending further investigation. Have the report to me on Monday morning."

Donald had been expecting suspension and didn't react. Wilson didn't say anything further.

"You know, Ollie, I'm sorry about not reporting the girl. I don't know how she knew about me. She was a great looking broad and I asked her out. One thing led to another and we started doing this thing. Laws must've told her what I did for a living. When I said everything was covered, I really thought it was."

Wilson said nothing.

"Honest. That's the way it was. I feel bad about all the heat the Agency is taking over this." He realized he was talking too much and he shut up.

Wilson continued to look at him with a cold stare. After a while, Donald shrugged and left without either man saying anything further.

Donald spent the weekend preparing a written report. He claimed that he didn't realize Elie knew he was CIA. He thought he had himself pretty covered. That is, unless Elie started talking again. If she did, and he was busted on these new lies, he figured it wouldn't matter much because he'd be fired anyway for breaking just about every rule of conduct for a field agent.

He left a forwarding address at the Agency and went directly to the airport to catch the mid-day flight to Dallas and on to Mexico City. The cost of living was cheap enough in Mexico that he figured he could weather a six-month suspension on his savings without any problem. It would be like a vacation.

If all this blew over with no more damage, he might even have a job left. He wondered whether he should give that divorcee another chance when he got back to Mexico City.

Chapter Forty-Five

It took a week for Rosie Akamine to complete her sketch of the man Reggie claimed to have met in Paris. She'd spent several days visiting Reggie at the Prison. He'd changed his mind numerous times, and was less than sure on many of the features. Finally, she had a sketch that he said was pretty close to the man known to him as D. Kendall.

Drew handed the sketch to Pancho, who studied it.

"How come all these police sketches make the guy look like a mass murderer?" said Pancho.

"Maybe he is."

"Good point. Well, I guess the next thing would be to try to find someone who might recognize our hypothetical Donald. Make a copy before you leave. I'm going to send a copy to Senator Ichinose and ask him to ask the CIA if this man works for the Agency. A little political pressure would turn up the heat a touch."

"Yeah, well, let's all watch our backs this time around."

Pancho considered Drew's words as he watched his friend leave. He'd all but forgotten about the attempt on their lives. It now seemed like some vague nightmare.

Susan bustled in and interrupted his reverie of paranoia.

"Hey boss man, you made *Time* magazine." She was beaming from ear to ear, the proud mother. She handed him a copy of the magazine, turned to the page and a headline that read, 'Mystery in Paradise.' The article recounted the murder case and Pancho's cross-examination that brought out apparent CIA involvement with Laws. Pancho read:

> Whether the speculation by McMartin of the CIA's role in the death of Laws is or is not correct, the revelation that the CIA

was using a con artist as a front man for dummy corporations to fund covert operations is serious. Sources tell Time that several lawmakers in Washington are calling for a full investigation into this latest disclosure of CIA dealings.

Pancho put down the magazine and smiled up at Susan. "Well, we be famous."

"I'm so excited, I'm going to copy the article and send it to my mother." Susan scooped up the magazine and left Pancho alone.

Pancho thought about the article. If Congress wants to investigate, maybe he really can get some political pressure going. He picked up his Dictaphone and began dictating a letter to Senator Ichinose.

Harry hung up the phone and swore to himself. What the hell was going on? He was fuming, and he had no outlet for his rage except his desk, which he proceeded to pound until his hand hurt.

The call had been from his boss, Ron Shigemura. It was brief and to the point.

"Harry?"

"Yeah, hi Ron."

"Harry, I want you to approach McMartin on a deal on this Bellows thing."

"What?"

"You heard me. See if you can deal it."

"Ron, I've got the gun. This CIA thing is crap and you know it. I can get him this time around."

"Deal it."

"Jeez, the only thing I could deal to would be manslaughter. That's ten year maximum."

"Harry, don't tell me what the sentence is for manslaughter. I know what it is. Just see if you can do a deal."

"But, why?"

"Don't ask questions. Let me know what happens." Ron hung up, leaving Harry confused and angry.

Harry called Pancho and asked to join him for a drink at Murphy's. They met at 4:00.

The restaurant and bar at Merchant Street was quiet. The *pau hana*, after work, drinkers, had not yet filled up the popular watering hole. They took a table in the bar area, glancing occasionally at one of the several televisions positioned around the bar which were constantly tuned to some sporting event.

Harry ordered a beer and Pancho did the same, trying to stifle his curiosity.

"Harry, I want to apologize for my actions the other day on the phone. You were right. I had no business jumping all over you like that."

Harry waved him off and took a sip of his beer. "Why don't we do a deal?" Pancho could see Harry was trying to be nonchalant, but it wasn't working.

"What do you have in mind?" Pancho kept a poker face, but his heart was racing with excitement. He was no dummy. Something was up.

"Manslaughter, and I ask for the maximum."

Pancho was silent. A million things were running through his mind. He knew the offer was a sign of weakness, but why? Was there some new evidence that had come up, or had they lost a witness, or, more likely, thought Pancho, had they been *ordered* to deal?

"What's going on, man?" Pancho's voice was soft, a gentle probe.

"We're offering to deal, that's what's going on. Save taxpayer's dollars and all that. Avoid another trial. Do you want to deal or not?" Pancho saw that Harry was too aggressively defensive. It was clear to Pancho that someone was pulling the rug out from under Harry.

"Come on, Harry," Pancho's voice was still soft, not taking offense at Harry's rudeness.

"You know that I know that something is going on for you to offer me a deal. I'm not some dip-shit just out of law school. Do you have some exculpatory evidence you haven't disclosed?"

Although it was an adversary system, the duties and responsibilities of prosecutors and defense attorneys were very different. The defense attorney's job was to defend the client with the greatest diligence within the ethics of the law. What a defense attorney knew about his client's guilt could not be disclosed to anyone unless the client pleaded guilty and waived attorney-client privilege. The prosecutor's job, on the other hand, was to seek justice. That meant if evidence turned up that tended to show innocence of the defendant, the prosecutor had a duty to turn such exculpatory evidence over to the defense.

"No," said Harry. "You should know me better than that. I'm not withholding any evidence. The evidence is the same. Personally, I think your client is guilty as hell. But my boss told me to look into a deal. That's what I'm doing."

Pancho took a sip of his beer and digested the information.

"I appreciate your candor. I do. I'll pass the offer on to Reggie, but I have to say I doubt if he'll take it. What if I could convince him to take assault one, with recommendation of probation?" Assault in the first degree and manslaughter carried the same maximum sentence, but Pancho didn't want Reggie admitting to being responsible for the death of Laws.

"Oh for crying-out-loud. You know and I know that Bellows shot Laws and cut off his damn head and arms. You want an assault and probation out of that?" Harry shook his head and took a big gulp of beer. He looked disgusted.

"I don't know that my client is guilty," Pancho said, his voice becoming slightly more aggressive. "I personally think he's innocent. Whether you think so or not, I think our protectors, the CIA, killed Laws because Laws was about to go under and would take the CIA with him. Think about it. Stop a minute and figure out why Ron told you to come to me to do a deal? Who the hell do you think put the pressure on Ron? Huh, Harry? Who?"

Harry was silent. He toyed absently with a cardboard coaster.

When Harry finally smiled, it was like a shrug. "Just because the CIA may be embarrassed about dealing with Laws, and doesn't want it paraded around in front of a jury and the media again, doesn't mean the CIA killed Laws. He was shot with your client's gun."

"Yeah Harry, and we got our little ol' selves caught right in the middle of some bizarre CIA cover-up."

They drank and stared at the televisions. Some hockey game was on. The silence was palpable. The door opened and the sun invaded the bar as several businessmen in Aloha shirts strode in. A moment later, the door closed, once again shutting out the brightness of the day.

"I'll talk to Reggie. That's all I can promise," said Pancho, his tone conciliatory.

Harry nodded. "Call me." He tossed a few bills on the bar and left. Pancho watched him walk out, shoulders hunched, deflated by unseen powers. The Pillsbury Dough Boy on downers.

Chapter Forty-Six

At about the same time that Pancho and Harry were having a drink at Murphy's, a federal grand jury was returning an indictment against Elie Watson for one hundred and three counts of conspiracy to commit fraud, as well as various other offenses. Elie's attorney, who'd been feeling rather impotent due to her obstinate refusal to follow his advice, had a friend at the U.S. Attorney's office who told him that the indictment was coming down. Bill Chambers called Elie and told her to be ready to be arrested. Chambers later said she seemed to take the news with quiet resignation. She thanked him for the call and told him she'd be waiting. When she hung up the phone, Elie turned to her Aunt and asked for some stationery and a pen. Then she retreated to her room.

Elie let the tears begin when she was alone. She went to the small desk below the window that looked out on a small backyard lanai, sat down, and began to write, stopping every few moments to wipe the tears from her eyes. She wrote for twelve minutes, then folded her finished products and put them in two separate envelopes. After she addressed each, she got up and pulled out the craft kit she knew her Aunt kept in the closet. She rummaged around for a few seconds and finally pulled out a double-edged razor blade.

Elie's tears picked up in intensity as she walked into the bathroom, turned on the water in the bathtub, and placed the razor on the edge of the tub. She began to undress. How had all this happened to her? She was just a small town girl who'd been looking to become something more than a meek, wimpy person with no self-esteem. Instead, she'd become nothing less than a whore and a criminal. She sniffled loudly. Worse, she thought, she'd done nothing to stop what she'd become. Instead, she'd actually tried to protect the two men who had made her what she was.

When she was naked, she tested the water. It was too cold, so she turned off the cold tap and let the hot water run while she sat on the edge of the tub, staring down at the razor blade. She finally let out a deep, animal sounding sob, turned off the water, and climbed in. The warm water enveloped and soothed her. She picked up the blade. She closed her eyes and wondered if there was anyone in Hilo she should've called to say goodbye. But she knew how they all felt about her now.

Elie put her left arm under the water, then watched, almost in a detached fashion as she ran the razor across the wrist. She felt little pain as the tendrils of bright red blood spread out into the tub water. She quickly transferred the razor to her left hand, and cut her wrist on the right. She let the razor drop and she let herself sink into the warm, deepening pink bath.

Two hours later, Elie's aunt came into Elie's room to have a talk with her. She was going to ask Elie to leave. It was just too hard on the family. They'd been embarrassed and humiliated in front of all their neighbors and friends. While family was family, they had done more than enough for her.

Elie's aunt never had to have that difficult conversation with Elie.

Frank Nishimoto sat across the desk from Harry Chang, a letter and an envelope lay on the desk between them. The letter lay open and the envelope was marked 'Donald Duerden - Personal & Confidential'.

Frank had been up most of the night, having been called in on Elie's death because of her involvement in the Laws case. Harry had been told of Elie's death the night before, but he hadn't known any of the details until this morning. He picked up the opened letter.

> Dear Auntie Kay and Uncle Steve:
> I'm real sorry to do this to you, but I just can't go on anymore. I've made a complete mess of my life and I know that I have embarrassed you and mom and dad. I love you all and I appreciate everything you did for me. I just can't cope with it anymore. It never seems over. Now that I've been charged with crimes I would probably have to go to jail. I couldn't take that. I thought that by cooperating with the police, they would let me off, but I guess not.

I'm just so tired now. This is better. I love you,
Elie

Harry put down the letter. It was in deliberate, neat handwriting on a lined piece of letter paper. It made him sad to read the last words of a tortured soul. He picked up the envelope addressed to Donald Duerden.

"Who's this guy?"

"My guess is he's the infamous Donald from the trial," said Frank.

"Yeah, well, it's part of the investigation so I think we have a right to open it." Harry broke the seal and took the letter out. It was on the same type of lined stationery.

'Dear Donald,

You have ruined my life and now I'm going to end it. I want you to know that you have killed me just as surely as if you had done it yourself. I tried to protect you and you threatened to kill me. I don't even understand why I tried to help you. I guess I thought I loved you even though I knew I hated you.

I don't owe you anything anymore. The police will now have your last name. Good. I hope you suffer like you made me suffer. Soon I will be free of you.

I wish I knew if you killed Maynard, like they are saying. He deserved to die, but I don't. Then why are you killing me?

Why have you killed me?'

The letter was unsigned. The handwriting not as neat as the first one. It was more like the handwriting of someone who knew she had moments to live. Harry sighed and handed it to Frank.

So they had a last name to go with Donald. Now what?

Frank read the letter, then put it back in the envelope and looked up at Harry.

"What now?" asked Frank.

"Contact the CIA and tell them we have a letter for one of their guys. Keep this second letter quiet for now."

"You going to tell Pancho?"

Harry sighed again. His chubby face looked pained. "I don't know what I'm going to do." He told Frank about the order to offer Bellows a deal.

Frank rubbed his eyes and yawned. "How come? You think the CIA guy really did kill Laws and it's a cover-up?"

Harry shook his head. "I wish the hell I knew. I don't know anything anymore. I just can't find it in me to think that the CIA had Laws killed and is willing to let an innocent man go down for it. Am I being naive?"

Frank smiled a grim smile. "Yes and no. I've seen too much to disbelieve anything anymore. But you and I both try to fight for what's right. So does Pancho, for that matter. Sometimes you start to wonder whose side everybody is on.

"It's all gotten out of hand. It's too damn strange. Maybe a deal is the best thing," said Frank. He stood up to leave, gathering the suicide notes to take with him.

"See ya, Harry."

"Yeah, see ya."

"Holy fucking shit! What? What? Son of a bitch . . . yeah, yeah, okay."

Oliver Wilson slammed down the phone and buried his face in his hands. *So much shit has hit the fan that it's clogging up the motor*, thought Oliver. He buzzed his secretary.

"Get Deputy Director Fuller on the line."

A few moments later he was talking to Randolph Fuller, explaining that Elie Watson had committed suicide and had left a suicide note addressed to Donald Duerden.

"No, sir I don't know what it says . . . no, sir they didn't say if they had opened it or not. Yes, sir . . . no, sir, I recommend having the note immediately classified and taken into custody . . . yes, sir I'll get right on it."

It had been Fuller's idea to pressure the Honolulu prosecutor's office into offering a deal to Bellows. Fuller reasoned that the sooner they could make the trial go away, the sooner everything would blow over.

Oliver had argued against it. It could backfire, making Bellows' defense attorney even surer of the CIA role than before. If word got out that the CIA tried to interfere in a local murder case, all sorts of additional shit would be hitting the fan in no time. But Fuller had been insistent, and Oliver had made the call.

Now the police had the full name of Donald. If they didn't have the suicide note classified for 'national security reasons,' it would be discoverable in the murder trial, and soon the entire world would have confirmation of the CIA involvement with Laws.

Oliver picked up the phone to call the Justice Department.

"Drew?"

"This is Drew."

"This is Wally Rodrigues at HPD."

"Hey Wally, howzit?" Wally was a patrolman who had his career saved a few years back when Drew had proven that a victim who'd alleged police brutality against Wally had, in fact, identified the wrong officer.

"This is super confidential," Wally spoke in hushed tones.

"Okay, man, I understand."

"This did not come from me. I'll deny it until the day I die, okay?"

"Sure, Wally. I wouldn't do anything to hurt you."

"Yeah, I know that, I just want you to understand. You heard about that Elie Watson person?"

"Uh huh, just heard this morning, poor girl."

"You hear she left a note?"

"Yes." Drew was getting excited. He hadn't heard what was in the note.

"You hear there were two notes?"

Drew's heart was beating fast. That, he hadn't heard.

"No, were there?"

"Yep. The second note was sealed and was addressed to a man named Donald."

Jackpot, thought Drew.

"Was there a last name?"

"Duerden." Wally spelled it for Drew,

"It was marked 'personal.'"

Drew was trying to keep calm. He didn't want to freak Wally by being too excited.

"Do you know what it said?"

"No. I was first on the scene, which is how I saw it. Frank Nishimoto took it as soon as he got there, and no one has seen it since. That's all I got. I owe you, thought it'd be helpful to you and Pancho."

"Yeah. It is. I appreciate it, man, and don't worry, it didn't come from you. Shit, we haven't even talked with each other since last Christmas, wasn't it?"

"Yeah, last Christmas. Gotta go."

"Aloha, Wally."

Drew let out a shout as he hung up the phone. He immediately began to dial Pancho's number.

Chapter Forty-Seven

"Duerden." Pancho said the name aloud for the first time. He smiled at Drew and complimented him for about the tenth time.

"Hey man, I didn't do shit. This one fell in my lap. Manna from heaven."

"Yeah, well, good work anyway. Now the question is, what do we do with the name now that we have it?"

"I've been thinking about that," said Drew. "I asked Susan to go through some back phone books to see if he'd ever actually lived in Honolulu under his own name. After that, we'll check the phone books of the suburbs in and around the D.C. area.

"I also called a friend of mine who works at United Airlines. He's going to do a computer check for me on passenger manifests to see what Duerdens show up. He's also going to see if he can check the Mileage Plus records. I don't know anyone at any of the other airlines, but if we're talking about the Pacific region, United's the main carrier, anyway.

"Other than that, I'm not quite sure what we can do. We're not even supposed to have this name so far."

Pancho thought for a moment. "Okay, we'll see what that turns up."

"You going to take the deal?" Pancho had told Drew about Harry's offer the night before.

"Don't know. I don't see why, right now. If we can find Duerden, who knows what'll develop? In any event, I do have to pass the offer on to Reggie. I'll go see him this afternoon."

They talked strategy some more, both feeling optimistic about the new development. Neither mentioned the death of Elie in concrete terms. They'd talked on the phone about it last night and there wasn't much more to be said. At first Pancho was inclined to blame himself for her death. He'd put her through hell and thoroughly humiliated her. What kind of life did she have ahead of her?

But Drew rightly pointed out that Pancho's cross-examination of Elie had taken place weeks ago. It was the news she was about to be arrested that sent her over the edge.

"Sad as it is, man, she brought this on herself," said Drew. "You were fighting to save your client."

Pancho spent a sleepless night and had gone for an early morning swim. In the end, he concluded that Drew was right. It wouldn't be fair to blame himself for Elie's death.

Drew didn't want to leave the office until he heard from his friend at United, so he pulled a chair up to Susan's desk and helped her go through phone books. There was no listing for Donald or D. Duerden for the last three years.

"Doesn't particularly surprise me," said Drew.

"Yeah, me neither," responded Susan.

"Got any other bright ideas, Suze?"

"Yeah, leave me alone so I can do some work."

"Oh, the thanks I get for helping you out." They laughed and Drew plopped down on the reception couch.

It was an hour before Drew's friend called.

"I could get in deep shit for this, Drew."

"You know I appreciate it. I'll owe you, and I'll always fly United."

His friend laughed. "Okay, all I could find was a Donald Duerdan, with an 'a', in Mileage Plus. He lives in Minnesota, anyway. There are some Duerdens, with 'e', in Mileage Plus, but all with different first names and none in the key geographic areas you mentioned.

"In terms of passenger manifests and reservations, all I could get into was within the last few weeks. I found a Donald Duerden that flew from Mexico City to Chicago to Dulles. Looks like he flew back to Mexico City too. Went through Dallas on the way back. D.C. was a key area, right?"

"Right."

"Nothing to or from Honolulu, with that spelling last name and D. or Donald first name."

"Okay, Gary. Hey, I appreciate it."

"Hope it helps. Call me next time you're in Chicago, we'll go get some of those ribs you love."

"You're on. Bye."

Susan looked at him expectantly. "Anything?"

"I don't know. Nothing to or from Honolulu, but we wouldn't expect him to be here anyway. There's a Donald Duerden who flew from Mexico City to Dulles, then back to Mexico City last week. I suppose that could be our man. Tell Pancho, will you, Suze? I'm going to the library."

"How much time do I do if I plead to either of those?" asked Reggie.

"Manslaughter is a ten year maximum, but it's probationable. You'd be admitting to having caused the death of Laws. Given the brutal nature of the wounds inflicted on him, I wouldn't like to venture a guess below the maximum in terms of sentence. The parole board then sets a minimum term to serve before you'd be eligible for parole. My guess would be that you'd get a three or four year minimum." Reggie's face was impassive as Pancho spoke.

"On assault first degree, you're not admitting to having caused the death of Laws, but you are admitting to having committed an intentional crime. The maximum term is the same, also probationable, but again, I wouldn't count on it." Pancho paused and leaned forward.

"I don't recommend dealing now, Reggie. We're finally making progress. I don't think we'll ever be able to prove someone else killed Laws, but I think we can build on our case against the CIA. Who knows, they may even decide not to prosecute again."

"Why not?"

"Think about it. They didn't offer to deal out of the kindness of their hearts. Someone is putting the pressure on them, probably the CIA, to hush things up. It may be time to play some poker, see how far they would go to avoid another high publicity trial."

Reggie nodded. Pancho noted that his affect seemed flat. This was no time for his client to be giving up, or losing interest.

"Well, Reggie, what do I tell them? No deal?"

Reggie picked some wax out of his ear. He examined it briefly, then flicked it away.

"What happened to my bail reduction? I thought you were going to try to get my bail reduced?"

"I have a hearing on that next week, but I told you not to count on it. You're still charged with murder and you have no family or ties to Hawai'i. I doubt we'll get much, if anything, in the way of reduction."

Reggie was digging around in his other ear. Pancho was getting irritable.

"I need an answer, Reggie."

Reggie looked at Pancho as if he'd just sat down, like he didn't know what Pancho was talking about. He looked quizzical. Then there was a change, like a cloud passing.

"Tell them I'm thinking about it."

"Let me tell them no. If you change your mind later, we can approach them."

"What if they won't deal again?"

"Why do you want to deal? There's all sorts of things happening now."

"I'm tired of jail, Pancho. I appreciate your excitement and your optimism, I really do, but you're not sitting in jail on a murder charge." Reggie's voice was flat again, almost quietly sarcastic.

"Reggie, you aren't going to get out of jail by pleading. The chances of you getting probation on this are slim and none without it being made part of a deal. If you ever do go down for something, you'll get credit for time served, but you'll have a long time before any minimum term makes you eligible for parole."

"Do what you want." Reggie waved a hand dismissively.

Pancho slammed his hand down on the table. "Goddammit, Reggie, I can't do what I want. I have to have a decision from you. I recommend you turn them down now, but if you want me to tell them you're thinking about it, I will."

"Maybe we should just take the deal."

Pancho was exasperated. He thought maybe he ought to get a psychologist out to see Reggie.

"I'll tell them you're thinking about it. Okay?"

"Okay."

Pancho left without saying goodbye.

Drew had no luck with the phone books in the Washington D.C. area. He went back to Pancho's office and called a private investigation firm that he'd dealt with a few years ago in Los Angeles. He explained what he needed and asked if they could refer him to a firm in Mexico City. He was given the name and number for Alberto Castillo at Castillo y Munoz.

Drew called the number in Mexico City and talked with Alberto Castillo, who, luckily for Drew, spoke passable English. He explained what he needed. Castillo seemed professional. Drew promised to send the agreed upon retainer by courier.

He knew that it was a big longshot, looking for Donald Duerden in Mexico City. But they had no other leads. A trip in and out of Washington, D.C. by someone with the same name as the one they were looking for was worth investigating. If it was the Duerden they wanted, and with all the flak that the CIA had to be taking over this story, it would make sense that Duerden would be called back to Langley for some kind of consult.

Chapter Forty-Eight

Donald knew he was being followed. At first, it was just a gut instinct, so he began to pay more attention. He walked through the thick Mexico City smog up Luis Moya, from his small budget hotel, the Estoril, to Avenida Juarez, glancing back as he turned left. He took in a quick overview of the people walking in his direction behind him. He picked up the pace, just another gringo in a hurry to do something, and headed toward Paseo de La Reforma, ignoring the ubiquitous Indian beggerwomen and their children selling Chiclets.

At Paseo de La Reforma, it was as if he were magically in another city. Beautiful buildings, impressive high rises, well-dressed businessmen, and a broad, expansive, tree-lined boulevard posed a welcome change from the abundant poverty so overwhelming just a block or so off Reforma. Donald turned left again, walking toward the busy intersection of Insurgentes. Though it was winter, and the air was cool, the smog was oppressive. Mufflers roared their disdain for environmental concerns.

He stopped suddenly to peer into a store, glancing back. He noted a Mexican man dressed in a well-cut gray suit and blue tie. It was the same man he first suspected when he'd left his hotel. That asshole Oliver Wilson was obviously keeping tabs on him. He smiled to himself and decided to have a little fun, see how good this guy was. He continued up Reforma.

He crossed the intersection of Insurgentes and saw a *pesero*, a communal taxi, stopping on Paseo de la Reforma, heading in the opposite direction, toward the Zocalo. It was crammed full of people, but he pushed his way on, ignoring the stares of the other riders. Few well-dressed gringos rode the ultra-cheap *peseros*. He got off at Hidalgo and walked quickly to Alameda Park. He was now just a few blocks from where he'd started. He sat down on a bench in Alameda Park and lit a cigarette. His tail was obviously local talent. Donald felt hurt that Wilson apparently figured he didn't merit wasting an agency man. With the peso's value being what it was, the poor schmuck they had following him was probably costing the Agency lunch money.

"*Senor* Duerden?"

Donald's head snapped up and he looked into the face of the man in the gray suit and blue tie. He was a round-faced man, with acne scars and tobacco stains on his lips.

"Maybe. Who're you?"

"My name is Alberto Castillo and I am a private investigator. I wonder if you would mind having a word with my client?"

"Your client? Who's that?" So it wasn't one of Wilson's men.

"He will introduce himself. Would you please come with me?"

"*Como se dice*, fuck you, buddy. Why should I go with you?"

"*Senor*, be reasonable. You are a smart man. I know that you spotted me as soon as you came out of the Estoril. But I too am a smart man. I found you in all of Mexico City. We know where you are living. We know who you are, how do you say it, banging, and we will continue to follow you and try to talk to you until you finally agree." Castillo had placed himself directly in front of Donald and smiled a pleasant smile. He looked pleased with himself for having remembered the American vernacular word for *chingar*.

"Are you not curious, *Senor*?"

"I gave up being curious about things. It's bad for my health." The fact was, of course, that Donald was immensely curious about Castillo's client. He figured it could be none other than that smart-ass lawyer who'd fucked everything up for him.

"But if it'll get you off my back, I'll meet your client. Where?"

"He is waiting in a Sanborn's, just down the street."

Donald got up, the Mexican backing off just a step or two. Together, they crossed the park, back toward Juarez.

Donald knew who Drew was as soon as they walked into the Sanborn's. A huge Samoan man sitting in the Mexican version of Denney's was easy to spot. He sat down in the booth opposite Drew. Castillo immediately sat next to Donald, blocking his exit.

"Okay, Mr. Client, here I am. What can I do for you?"

Drew took a sip of his coffee. He'd been waiting to meet this man and wanted a moment to take in his appearance and form an impression. He could see where a woman like Elie would be attracted to Donald, especially if Elie knew he was a spook. His angular face was ruggedly handsome, but his eyes and the expression he wore were cold and smirking. *This man thinks way too much of himself,* thought Drew. He'd seen the look, the way the head and body were held, many times before. There were many professional athletes who fit into the same mold. *Unfortunately,* thought

Drew, *these people rarely lived up to their own image of themselves, and they would eventually begin to self-destruct – always blaming other people for the collection of disasters that inevitably occurred.*

"My name is Drew Tulafono. I'm a private investigator working for an attorney named Pancho McMartin."

"Yeah, I figured as much. Go on."

"Ah, so I need not explain the interest that Mr. McMartin has in my discussing some matters with you. If you don't mind, I'd like to ask you some questions."

"I'm sure I do mind, but ask away. I'll answer what I please."

"Do you work for the CIA?" asked Drew.

"Pass on that question."

"Did you work with Maynard Laws on CIA business?"

"Pass."

"Did you have an affair with Elie Watson?"

"Maybe."

"Did you meet Reggie Bellows in Paris in early August of this year?"

Drew could see a trace of surprise register on Donald's face.

"No comment."

"You're being very helpful sir. Did you kill Maynard Laws?"

Donald smiled a full smile for the first time.

"You have some real balls, *cajones*, I think they call them here," he looked at Castillo, who smiled and nodded. "You followed me all the way down to Mexico and expect me to answer a bunch of bullshit questions? What kind of asshole do you think I am? You think I'm some dumb fuck that just got off the boat?" Donald shook his head in disbelief.

"You can't prove the CIA had anything to do with Laws," Donald continued. "The only evidence you did have is now dead. You don't have shit, and you want me to answer a bunch of dumb questions like that?"

Drew didn't react. He took another sip of coffee. Castillo looked like he was taking it all in, trying to remember all the good American swear words in just the right context.

"Why'd you try to have me killed?" Drew's voice was low and menacing.

"I didn't. I heard about it, but it wasn't me."

"I don't believe you. And I don't take kindly to being shot at. Neither does my boss. Now, I'd appreciate it if you'd answer some of my questions." Drew's tone had changed from that of polite interrogation to menacing threat. Castillo smiled.

Donald looked around. The restaurant was nearly empty.

"Hey man, I swear, I didn't try to have you killed. Or your boss. I was here in Mexico. This whole thing has fucked me up royally. I've been staying as far away from Honolulu as I could."

Drew stared hard at Donald for several moments before he spoke.

"Don't mess with me, man. You're on everybody's shit list, but I'm the one here. I get first crack at you if I want. You shouldn't have gotten me so pissed off, because ordinarily I play by the book. You know, no rough stuff, no breaking the law. But I can make exceptions where it's personal."

"Hey . . . just fuckin' hold it." Donald's voice had risen in anger.

"I don't know what the hell you think you're doing. You think I killed Laws? You're full of shit. Why don't you ask your client who killed him, huh? Your fucking boss is good; I give him credit for that. Just because he thinks the CIA is using Laws for some shit, he makes it look like the CIA killed him." Donald stopped and took a deep breath.

"I'll give you a freebie," he said. "You're interested in representing your client, right?"

Drew nodded.

"So I'll give you a little point in the right direction, then you leave me the fuck alone. Deal?"

"I'll listen to what you have to say."

"Okay, fuck the deal. Why don't you ask your client, Mr. Bellows, about the fifty thousand dollars I hear he got paid to knock off Laws. You do that Mr. Private Investigator, okay? Ask Bellows some of these bullshit questions."

Drew stared at Donald. Fifty? Bellows had said twenty-five thousand had been deposited in his account by the time he got back from Paris. The other twenty-five was to be paid when he killed Laws.

"You paid Bellows to murder Laws? And you're telling me he received the full fifty thousand?"

"Hey asshole, I didn't tell you shit. I told you to ask your client about some money I heard he got paid. You want to try to prove that I paid Bellows to murder Laws, you hang your client for murder for hire."

Castillo's eyes were large.

Drew stared at Donald, digesting the information.

"*Por favor?*" All three heads jerked up at the waitress in surprise. The tension had been so thick that none of them had heard her come to the table.

"*Más café?*"

"*No, gracias,*" said Alberto. "*La cuenta por favor.*"

"*Si.*" She turned and left to get the check.

"Now, if you're quite through, I have to get back to my ritzy hotel and change for a dinner date." Donald turned to Castillo. "And go *bang* my lady friend." He gave Alberto a million dollar smile.

Drew nodded to Castillo, who got up to let Donald out.

"One more thing, Duerden. If this turns out to be a load of crap and I find out it was you who tried to off me, I'll be back. I'll personally make your life so miserable you'll wish you'd confessed to murder, which, by the way, you pretty much did."

"I didn't confess to jack and you know it." Donald turned and walked away. Drew turned to the investigator, who was watching Donald leave.

"Alberto, I'd like you to keep watching him until you hear back from me. I don't want to lose him again."

"*Si*, Senor Drew. It is very fascinating, yes?"

"*Si* Alberto, fascinating as shit."

Chapter Forty-Nine

Drew went straight from the airport to the district court on Alakea Street, where Susan had told him Pancho would be. As they greeted each other, Pancho could tell immediately that his friend had some disturbing news. They waited to talk until they were outside the courthouse. The sky was dark and threatening. Pancho looked back, toward the Pali, and saw that it was raining in Nuuanu valley. He touched Drew's arm and nodded over his shoulder. "Let's try to beat the rain."

The two walked quickly down Alakea while Drew told Pancho about his meeting with Duerden. He recited the conversation almost verbatim. When he got to the part about Duerden telling Drew to ask Bellows about the fifty thousand dollars, Pancho's head jerked around to look at Drew. Drew finished the account.

The two men walked on in silence. The sun was shining *makai*, toward the ocean, but the darkness was creeping up on them from the rear, and now the wind kicked up, so strong they were almost pushed down the street. They stopped at Alakea and Merchant Street for the light.

"You think Reggie murdered Laws?"

Drew shook his head, more in doubt than in yea or nay. "I've been thinking about it all the way home. We never checked Reggie's bank account to see what money came in, or when it came in."

"Why would we? We weren't trying to prove Reggie murdered anyone, we were trying to prove he didn't."

"And the police had no particular interest in Reggie's deposits because it would never have occurred to them that this might be a murder for hire case."

The light changed and they crossed the street. Businessmen in Aloha shirts hurried past, trying to beat the coming rain.

"Duerden's right about one thing," said Pancho, "if this is a murder for hire case, and we prove that the CIA, or Duerden, hired Reggie to kill Laws, then we just bumped the charge against our client from life with possibility of parole to life without possibility of parole. That wouldn't exactly be effective representation."

"What do we do about Duerden? If we think he had Laws killed, aren't we supposed to turn him in?"

Pancho thought about it.

"I don't think we have any ethical duty to do anything about Duerden. We don't know what he did or didn't do. We have an ethical duty to defend our client within certain guidelines, and that includes defending him even if he's guilty. We can't convict our client by turning in a man we suspect paid him to murder Laws. I think that if he'd actually confessed, I'd be more troubled by the question."

They walked a block in silence. They had forgotten about the coming rain, and their pace had unconsciously slowed.

"Shoots Pancho, do you think it's true?" asked Drew.

Pancho expelled air, it could have been a sigh, it could have been a choked back laugh.

"No use speculating. I'm going to see our client. I think we have his bank records, so we'll have Susan dig them out and have a look see at the deposits."

They felt the first drops of rain on their backs and picked up the pace.

Twenty minutes later, they sat in Pancho's office poring over the bank statements of Reggie Bellows. Susan found it, letting out an involuntary gasp when she did so.

"Five days after Laws was murdered, there was a twenty-five thousand dollar deposit made to Reggie's account." She handed Pancho the statement page.

Pancho stared at it and said nothing. No one spoke. After a few minutes, Susan excused herself to answer the phone. Drew got up and went around the desk to Pancho, who looked depressed. Pancho had poured his heart and soul into representing Reggie. He'd believed in him. He'd put his reputation on the line for him.

Drew squeezed his friend's shoulder.

"One last thing, Pancho."

Pancho looked up at Drew standing over him.

"You know that artist sketch of Donald based on Reggie's description?"

Pancho nodded.

"Well, it didn't look anything like Donald Duerden."

Drew left Pancho alone.

Pancho folded the bank statement and put it in his pocket to take to the prison.

* * *

Reggie looked expectantly at Pancho as they shook hands in the interview room. Pancho looked grim as they sat down.

"Reggie, did you murder Laws?" Pancho's voice was soft.

Reggie looked at Pancho, a surprised look on his face. "No, I told you that."

"I know what you told me. You told me lots of things. Now I'm asking because I need to know."

"Well, I didn't." Reggie tried to sound indignant. "What's this all about, anyway?"

"Tell me about the twenty-five thousand dollars deposited into your bank account."

"I told you, Kendall said that he'd deposited twenty-five grand. I checked it out when I got back and it was there."

"I don't mean that twenty-five thousand, Reggie. I mean the twenty-five thousand paid into your account five days after Laws was murdered."

Reggie flushed and broke eye contact with Pancho. The two men sat in silence for a good two minutes.

"Reggie," said Pancho, his voice still soft. "I need to know. If I continue to press this CIA thing, and maybe try to bring Duerden back from Mexico—"

"You found him?" Reggie's voice clearly betrayed shock.

"Yes, we found him in Mexico. We talked to him. He told us to ask you about the additional twenty-five grand deposited in your account after Laws was murdered. So I'm asking." Pancho looked Reggie square in the eyes.

"If we push ahead with our defense, you could find the charges amended to murder in the first degree, which is murder for hire, which means life in prison without possibility of parole."

"Yeah, I know." Reggie's voice was low, almost a whisper.

"You know? How do you know?"

"I looked it up. I knew that if you found Kendall or whoever he is, that I'd be in even more trouble than I already am." There was a resignation in Reggie's voice. Pancho leaned in toward Reggie, knowing that he was finally close to getting the story.

"That's why you gave us the wrong description of Kendall, isn't it?"

Reggie nodded, "Yeah."

"Tell me about it, Reggie."

Reggie looked at Pancho. There was anguish on his face. He broke eye contact after a moment and looked back down at the table. Finally, he spoke.

"When I got back from Paris and found the money in my account, I was confused. Like I said before, I figured it wouldn't do any good to go to the police, it was such a bizarre story. And I thought that if I didn't kill

Laws, nothing would happen." Reggie took a deep breath, as if trying to keep himself under control.

"I didn't know what to do. My business was in big trouble and I kept thinking about all that money Laws had stolen from me. I kept thinking that Laws had to have been smart enough to stash some away, that he must have some Swiss bank accounts or something, but I couldn't even get him on the phone. I couldn't get past Elie."

"So you went to his house."

"Yeah, but it wasn't exactly like I told you. I didn't just go to his house, I was told to go to his house."

Pancho cocked his head. "What does that mean? Told? By whom? Donald?"

"No, no, no." Reggie waved his hand, dismissively. "Elie . . . Elie called me out of the blue and told me that Maynard was sorry for not being able to see me, but that he'd meet with me at his house the next afternoon."

Pancho sat back in his chair and rubbed his hand through his hair. He tried to process what he'd just heard.

"So you went to Laws' house because Elie told you that you could have an appointment with Laws, and you took your gun with you? Why?"

"I took my gun because I didn't know what was going on. Why was Laws so willing to see me now? After the thing with Kendall, or whoever he is, I thought it might be a setup of some kind. And, even if it was legit, I didn't know how Laws would react to me. I've been around. I've seen men who were trapped become violent. I knew Laws had to be desperate by then.

"I got to Laws' house and knocked, but there was no answer."

"This was on the day Laws was killed?"

"Yeah," said Reggie, nodding, still staring at the table.

"Then how come you weren't in the appointment book the cops found?"

Reggie shrugged. "My guess is that Laws didn't know anything about it, that Elie made the call at the request of Kendall."

Pancho thought about it for a moment. It seemed pretty convenient that Elie was dead and couldn't confirm the story, but it also made sense. If Donald was setting Reggie up, he had to get Reggie to go to Laws' house. Pancho nodded to Reggie. "Go on."

"So I got to Maynard's and tried the front door. It was unlocked. I walked in. I called out to Laws and I heard him say 'out here.' I went into the living room and saw Laws out by the pool, lying on a chaise lounge. He saw me and he kind of jumped up out of his chaise. He started yelling, 'get the fuck out of here, keep away from me you asshole,' stuff like that. I could see a rifle leaning against the table. I didn't know it was only an air rifle. The next thing I knew the gun was out of my pocket, and I kept walking toward him. He looked ridiculous. He was standing there, swearing at me, holding up his hands in a pushing motion, like he could push me out of his house from fifteen feet away.

"His big white belly was all greased up and he had some shit stuck to his right hand . . . it was the potato chips, of course, but I didn't know it then." Reggie looked at Pancho.

"You were wrong, Pancho. Laws' first reaction was not to wipe his hands. He stood there, swearing at me, belly shaking and glistening, shit on his hand. He looked foolish and so mean. Then I saw him look down at the rifle, like he was about to grab it. I shot him before I knew what I was doing. I didn't even aim, but the bullet went into his stomach.

"You should have seen his face. He looked so surprised. I think he thought he was invincible, like he thought he could just steal from everybody and get away with it. He kind of sat back down on the chaise, staring at the blood coming out of his stomach. Then he started screaming, and I panicked and ran. I left, Pancho. I shot him and left."

Reggie looked up at Pancho with eyes that were pleading; one of the saddest faces Pancho had ever seen.

"The doctor said the shot didn't kill him. Didn't she say that? I didn't kill Laws, because that shot didn't kill him."

Pancho was silent; trying to digest everything Reggie had just told him.

"You mean you didn't cut him up?"

"No. I swear to God, no. Why the hell would I do that? Maybe I would've shot him again if I hadn't run — maybe not, I'll never know. I've killed lots of men before, but never in cold blood like that. This felt different, so . . . personal."

"So you threw the gun into Koko Marina?"

Reggie shook his head. "That's the weird part. I didn't throw my gun there. I agree with what you said at trial. That would've been a stupid place. I may've panicked and run, but I still had *some* wits about me. I've been in combat too many times to lose it altogether. I drove over to the windward side. I threw the gun into Kawainui Marsh. Then I drove up to the North Shore, like I told you I did."

Pancho mulled over the question of the gun.

"What about the matches?"

"I didn't leave those matches at Laws. I didn't smoke. I was only in Laws' place a total of about two minutes. I walked in, he started swearing and yelling, I shot him, and I left."

"You must have known you'd be a suspect."

"Shit, Pancho, everyone who ever invested with Laws would've been a suspect. I hadn't gone there to kill Laws, but when I did shoot him, I knew I hadn't touched anything except the front door knob, which I wiped on my way out. I hadn't left anything there. I threw the gun away in the damn marsh where I thought it would never be found."

"But you ran away while Laws was still alive. He'd seen you."

Reggie looked at Pancho again. He looked better, like it had been a catharsis to tell the story and finally be able to discuss all the things he'd been wondering about since.

"Yeah, I thought about that, of course. My figuring was that either he was dead, which is what I thought, or that he'd be able to get help. If he got help, what would he do? He's a thief who hadn't been caught yet. If he turned me in for having shot him, it's all over for him because there'd be an investigation and a trial and he'd be proven to have been a fraud. He'd go to jail longer than I would. I figured he'd say he was shot by a burglar who got scared and ran away.

"The next morning I even went to the law library at the UH and looked up the alternatives. I hadn't gone to his house with any intent to kill. When he was shown to have been stealing from me, and everyone else, I figured that even if he turned me in before he died, a jury would believe I'd shot him in the course of a heated argument. Or that maybe I could get off on a self-defense argument if the jury believed I thought he was going for the rifle. I figured assault second, maybe first, at the worst. And I figured that given what Laws had been doing, I'd stand a shot at probation."

He looked at Pancho, who nodded. "Of course," Reggie continued, "at that point I hadn't heard that Laws had been butchered. When I heard that, I freaked out. I didn't have to worry about Laws anymore, but I worried about who had cut him up. If he wasn't dead when I left, did Laws tell his killer that I'd shot him?

"Once I heard about the butcher job, I figured I was home free, except for that one worry. Naturally, it crossed my mind that it might've been that Kendall guy, but I couldn't figure out why. The most likely thing I could think of at the time was that someone came to see Laws after me and found him shot, but not dead. That person hated him, worse than I even, and found something to cut him up with. Maybe it was another investor, who knows?" Reggie stopped talking and took a deep breath.

"And five days later you find that the balance of the money Kendall promised you had been deposited." Pancho said, more as a statement than a question.

"Yeah. Of course, I still didn't know if my shot had killed him or not. But he was dead and Kendall paid off, apparently assuming that I'd done it." Reggie shook his head in wonder. "I still can't figure out the gun and matches business."

Pancho shrugged. "Assuming you're telling me the truth this time, the answer has to be what we'd thought all along. You were set up. Let me take a wild guess: when you were meeting with Kendall in Paris, he let it be known that if things went wrong and you tried to nail him, you would nail yourself on a murder for hire charge, right?"

Reggie nodded. "Yeah. That was his protection. If I didn't do it, chances were I wouldn't say anything because I had twenty-five grand for nothing, and, besides, no one could trace him or the money he'd deposited anyway. If I did it and got caught, I wouldn't turn him in because I'd go down on murder one."

"So all along, this Kendall, or Duerden, planned to have you caught and convicted, thereby short-circuiting any prolonged investigation that might turn up the CIA connection."

"What happens now?" asked Reggie, his voice soft and pleading.

Reggie was watching Pancho intently. Pancho knew what Reggie was thinking.

"Don't worry, I'm not going to run out on you now. I'm pissed, but I'll stick with you."

Reggie let out a sigh of relief. "I know you're mad, Pancho, and you have every right to be. But don't you see that if I'd told you what had really happened, you wouldn't have believed me? It wouldn't have made any sense without the CIA connection, which I didn't even know about. You wouldn't have found the CIA connection and wouldn't have almost won at trial. None of this would've made any sense."

Pancho grudgingly admitted to himself that what Reggie said was true. How could he have believed Reggie's story without first knowing about the CIA? He would have taken a completely different tact at trial, and probably would've lost the case. If what Reggie said was true, he wasn't guilty of murder; but thought Pancho, he wasn't exactly innocent either.

"Do we take the deal?" Reggie asked.

Pancho understood now why Reggie had been willing to consider the deal. He'd been prepared to accept the consequences for what he'd done, but he hadn't wanted to go down for a murder he didn't commit.

"I think so," said Pancho. "Let me see if I can get assault. It'll have to be assault one, though. I'm pretty sure about that. And, unless we can figure out a way of showing that you're only guilty of assault, the Judge, who knows it's a deal, will still assume you're guilty, so the sentence will be harsh."

Reggie nodded. "I know."

Pancho sat still for a moment, not getting up to leave. He admired the fact that Reggie wasn't pushing to get him off completely. Reggie was willing to take responsibility for what he'd done.

Without saying anything further, Pancho left, slightly less confused than he'd been in many months.

Chapter Fifty

Pancho finished telling Reggie's story to Drew and Paula and sipped some Silver Oak Cabernet Sauvignon. They were at Michel's, at the Colony Surf, having dinner. One of the big dinner cruise ships worked its way slowly across the horizon. The ship was ablaze with lights, and looked alluring. There was only a breath of wind and the ocean smelled strong and fresh.

"But what about the gun being found in Koko Marina, and the matches from the Paris restaurant?" asked Paula.

"Let's say that Duerden, who we'll still assume is Kendall, based upon Drew's conversation with him, had been following Reggie to see if he was going to kill Laws. He followed Reggie to Laws' house and waited until he saw Reggie come out.

"Duerden decided to go in and make sure Reggie did the job. He found Laws still alive. He found a machete, maybe he had one in his car, more likely Laws had one at the house, to trim the coconut trees. Duerden whacked-up Laws and left—" Pancho paused. It still didn't work.

"But how would he kill Laws and still catch up to Reggie to see where he'd thrown the gun?" Pancho asked out loud.

"He couldn't, unless he had help," volunteered Drew.

Pancho and Paula looked at him. They were drawing a blank. Drew smiled.

"You folks seem to forget that someone tried to kill us. It wasn't Duerden, but I don't believe Duerden for one second when he said he had nothing to do with it."

"Sure, of course," said Pancho, slapping the table. "Duerden had to have someone helping him. Even after he was gone, he'd have had someone watching the trial, keeping an eye on the evidence, and doing whatever dirty work needed to be done."

"So," said Paula, "Duerden, or his helper, cut up Laws while the other followed Reggie, saw where he threw the gun, and retrieved it to plant in a more discoverable location?"

"I think she's got it," said Pancho.

"By George, she's got it," said Drew.

"You guys are going to get it," said Paula.

"Anyway," Pancho continued, "Duerden had followed Reggie in Paris and copped a book of matches from the restaurant Reggie ate at. He figured the matches would be the fastest way to put the police on to Reggie.

"He knew that all the big investors would be the prime suspects. The cops would find a book of matches from a faraway location at the scene of the murder and immediately run a check on which of those investors had been to Paris recently. Up pops Reggie's name. The fibers on Reggie's slippers, which he would ordinarily have taken off before entering someone's home, were a bonus for Duerden in the set up.

"But he still needed the gun to be found, so he planted it where it's not absurd, but still stood a good chance to be found. Koko Marina Bridge is perfect, since there're people fishing there almost every day."

Pancho took a bite of his venison and looked to Drew and Paula for comments.

"How did Duerden, or his friend, have time to hack-up Laws before the police came?" asked Paula.

Pancho smiled, proud of himself.

"Remember how Drew found out that the neighbor lady, I forget her name, hadn't reported the gunshot right away? That left plenty of time between the gunshot and the arrival of the police for the job to be done.

"Of course," continued Pancho, "whoever did it still took a big chance on going in and cutting up Laws after there'd been a gunshot. He didn't know there'd be a fortuitous delay. I reckon he knew his business and went about it with dispatch. It probably didn't add more than five minutes, and probably less, to the scenario." Pancho grinned. "Turns out I was right about the timing being important, I just didn't know it."

Drew had been listening intently, chewing on his steak with a vengeance.

"I'd still like to get the motherfucker, pardon my language, who shot at us. That really irritated me."

Pancho thought about that.

"I don't want you looking for that guy, Drew. He shot at us twice, coming awful close, and he may've been the one who butchered Laws; probably was the one. It just isn't worth it." He paused for a moment.

"Besides, I still can't figure out why the murderer would want, or need, to butcher Laws. That seems a little over the top to me."

Drew frowned. "Yeah, I guess I wouldn't want to run into that maniac in a dark alley." He drank some wine and tried to let the anger drain out of him.

Paula asked Pancho if he was angry at Reggie for having lied to him.

"You know, Reggie pointed out that if he'd told the truth, we would've had a hard time believing him and would almost certainly not have found the CIA connection. It's that connection that makes his story plausible." He paused and sipped his wine.

"So, yeah, I'm angry, but by the same token, I can kind of understand it in this case. I mean, can you imagine what must have been going through his mind?

"He shot Laws, only to hear the next day that Laws' head and arms had been cut off. He threw his gun into Kaiwainui Marsh, only to learn at the preliminary hearing that it'd been found at Koko Marina. He didn't leave anything at Laws' house, only to learn later that a book of matches from a restaurant he ate at in Paris was found at the murder scene. He didn't dare say anything because he thought it would only hang him higher.

"Besides," he said, and smiled, "I'm in the business of hearing lies."

Chapter Fifty-One

Oliver Wilson once again sat across the desk from Deputy Director Fuller. This time he'd sat down without asking. Fuller seemed to have recovered from his embarrassment over paying off Sandy Foreman. No one had heard from Foreman and he'd dropped from sight. With Elie dead, there was no one with sufficient evidence to positively link the Agency to the Laws fiasco.

"What's the status on the Laws case? Did the defendant take the deal?"

"Not yet," said Wilson. "According to my contact, he's 'thinking about it.'" Wilson made air quotes with his fingers as he said this.

"Well, how the hell long is he going to think about it? When's this scheduled to go to trial again?"

"In about two weeks, from what I understand."

"I don't want this going to trial. Do you understand that? This thing has caused us enough grief and embarrassment already. The Director's all over my ass because the President is all over his ass because the Congress is all over the President's ass. Do you get the picture?"

"I get the picture, sir, but there isn't much I can do. We've put about as much pressure as we can on this. The prosecutor over there has a bunch of angry deputies who think they can get a conviction."

"Well, I want results, and soon."

Oliver Wilson got up to leave.

"Oh, and Ollie, how long are you going to keep Duerden on suspension?"

"As long as our internal investigation takes. He should be fired. He broke some serious rules. And you know my suspicions about Laws' murder."

Fuller waved his hand, as if waving away the suspicions.

"Seems to me, he's a pretty good man. He just got his dick caught in a wringer. You've nothing to prove his involvement in Laws' death do you?"

Oliver couldn't believe the Deputy Director was sticking up for Duerden.

"No, sir nothing concrete. But there're all sorts of irregularities and breaches of conduct turning up. For instance, we have a report from one of our African rebel groups we'd been funding that the last shipment of arms they received was negotiated directly by Duerden. That's against policy. He was supposed to arrange for the transfer of money, so it could be called humanitarian aid, if necessary. Instead, he acted as intermediary between the rebels and the arms dealer. Now it turns out that the shipment is supposedly fifty thousand dollars short."

"According to the Africans."

Oliver inwardly fumed. "Of course, according to the Africans. According to the men we're backing in a civil war."

"Oh, well, keep me posted." Fuller waved an angry Oliver Wilson away.

Harry Chang stared in disbelief at his boss. He couldn't believe his ears.

"Say that again, Ron."

"I said, do whatever you have to. Make whatever deal you have to make. This Bellows case can't go to trial again."

"Are you saying to dismiss it?"

"I think you're overreacting a bit. You can get a deal of some kind out of McMartin. He just lost a main witness in that Elie person, hasn't he?"

"He has her sworn testimony from the prior trial. It'll be admissible because of her death."

"Yes, yes, I know, but there's nothing like a live witness, eh? Look, I know you're mad. I don't blame you. But just do this thing for me, okay?"

"Since when do we let the feds tell us what to do?"

Ron let his irritation show. "Look, Harry, we try to work together. There's some national security stuff involved here and it won't do anyone any good by parading all this stuff about the CIA in front of another jury. Go strike the best deal you can."

Ron got up and left Harry's office, leaving his subordinate to sit and wonder what was really going on.

Pancho came to Harry Chang this time. It showed respect, and Pancho hoped it would serve to make Harry feel like he'd already won a small point. He sat down across from Harry in Harry's small office. There were files and boxes of documents stacked everywhere. Harry's diplomas and Bar admission were framed in cheap plastic fake wood frames, and hung crookedly on the wall behind him. If there were any personal photos, Pancho couldn't see them through all the files.

"Looks like they're working you pretty hard, brah."

Harry shook his head. "We lost two prosecutors last week, Adams and Chinn. They both went to big civil firms. Said they were tired of criminal law, so I had to take some of their cases." He gestured to the files. "As if I didn't have enough to do."

Pancho allowed a few moments of amicable silence before saying, "So, we start trial in two weeks, huh?"

"That mean no deal?" Harry's voice was flat. He hadn't tried to hide his disappointment.

Pancho smiled. "No, I mean we start trial in two weeks, if we don't have a deal. I have some authorization from my client."

"And?"

"We can do assault second with an agreement for probation."

Harry almost flew out of his chair. "C'mon man, you've got some balls. Assault two? Probation? "

"That mean no deal?" Pancho mimicked Harry's earlier question.

Harry settled down.

"Is manslaughter out?"

"Yes," said Pancho. "No negotiating on manslaughter."

"How about assault first, and we stand silent on sentencing."

"Standing silent on sentencing in this case is tantamount to my agreeing to the maximum term, and you know it."

"And why shouldn't he get the maximum term? Your client killed Laws and you know it. You did a great job taking advantage of the whole CIA bullshit, but don't you think we can squeeze some semblance of justice out of this case?"

Pancho leaned forward, toward Harry. "Reggie didn't kill Laws. You've got his gun, but he didn't kill Laws. Believe me or don't, but I want probation or I won't deal." Pancho knew the prosecutors were getting pressure from Washington, or Langley, to be more accurate, to deal, but he didn't know how far they'd go.

Harry sat in silence for a few moments, doodling on his legal pad.

"Assault one with recommendation of probation." Harry said it quietly, hating himself, hating Ron, hating the system.

Pancho didn't press his advantage. He would later wonder if he should have, and why he didn't. He knew he could probably have gotten a petty misdemeanor if he wanted. Hell, he could probably have gotten the case dismissed. He knew he probably should've pressed. But he didn't. Perhaps, at the back of his mind, he still had doubts about Reggie's story.

"Done," said Pancho. Harry looked sad.

* * *

The following week, Reggie stood in front of Judge Ramos and pleaded guilty to Assault in the First Degree. The Judge lectured Reggie about the sentence he could be given, regardless of any deal that he may have entered into with the State.

Pancho had briefed Reggie on what would happen, and told him that, in extraordinary circumstances, the judge could choose to ignore the deal entered into with the prosecutors. It was not binding on the judge unless the judge specifically agreed in advance to be bound by it. In this case, there was no way Judge Ramos would agree to be bound by a deal in advance.

Reggie told the Judge that he understood.

Ordinarily, the Judge would refer Reggie to the probation office for a pre-sentence report. Over the course of the last week, however, Pancho and Harry had several conferences with the Judge. The secrecy Harry had insisted upon was almost comic, but Judge Ramos had gone along with the unusual requests. None of the conferences were listed on the Judge's calendar or docket. The meetings were all held either before or after the clerks and bailiffs were at work.

Harry explained the deal to the Judge Ramos, who expressed a great deal of concern over the probation part of the deal. He would take some serious heat in the press over that. Harry asked to talk to the Judge alone.

"Judge, I'll be frank about this. If we can't get this deal through, I may be ordered to dismiss." Judge Ramos's eyes widened.

"Pressure from the CIA?"

Harry nodded.

"Did Bellows do it?"

"I don't know, Judge. I think so, but maybe you and Pancho can talk a little about that."

Pancho and the Judge spent a half hour together without Harry. Pancho explained Reggie's story. Reggie was guilty of assault, but not murder. Finally, the Judge agreed to go along with the deal if Reggie would submit to a confidential and sealed psychiatric exam. The Judge wanted to be sure he was not putting some psychopath on the streets. Pancho agreed.

Judge Ramos found Reggie guilty of Assault in the First Degree and sentenced him to time served and probation.

The Judge looked out into the spectator gallery, where scores of reporters had been furiously scribbling notes.

"For the record, I want to say that this plea bargain, which included the sentencing, has been accepted and approved by me after a number of off-the-record chamber conferences with the attorneys of record, and after a comprehensive psychiatric examination of the defendant, performed with the consent of the defendant and his attorney. That report has been reviewed by me and is compelling in its conclusion that the defendant is not a risk to society. That report is, by stipulation, hereby sealed and not to be made a part of the public record of this case."

Pancho had the paperwork ready, and Reggie was released from custody within two hours after appearing in court. He was a free man.

The case of State of Hawai'i v. Reginald Bellows was over.

Chapter Fifty-Two

At his parents' restaurant in Chinatown, Ricardo Baguio looked up from his plate of lumpia to see his grandfather motioning to the telephone. Ricardo sighed and pushed his plate away. He got up from the counter and walked to the back of the little restaurant, ducking through the curtains into the kitchen area. Confused aromas from pots of boiling stews assaulted his senses. The extreme heat of the kitchen hit him like a body blow. He never understood how his family could stand to work in this hellhole, day after day. Of course, he thought bitterly, now that Laws had bilked his grandfather out of his life savings, they would have no choice.

He picked up the phone.

"Ricardo, is that you?"

"Yes. Sandy, that you?"

"Yeah, it's me. I need your help, man." Sandy Foreman sounded down, very bad, thought Ricardo.

"What you like for me to do?"

"I need some money. I'm broke and I'm desperate, man. I wouldn't have called you, but I've got to get away from this place. I—"

"Where you stay?"

"Vegas."

Ricardo smiled. He'd always wanted to go to Vegas. He had an almost genetic love of gambling.

"You in Vegas? And you no like?" Ricardo's voice showed his astonishment at such a concept.

"Come on, man, quit fucking around. I'm all fucked up here and I need some help. Can you send me something?"

Ricardo did some quick calculations in his head.

"I come Sandy. I come and bring you money."

"Oh man, oh shit man, that's great, that's just great. You're a hell of a dude Ricardo." The relief in Sandy's voice was palpable.

They arranged a place to meet in Las Vegas the next day and hung up. Ricardo looked at his mother bent over the stove, sweat dripping off her frail body. He shook his head. Fucking Laws deserved everything he got. He went back out to the dining area. The tables were scarred and scratched orange Formica, the customers, mostly older Filipino men.

He sat back down at the counter to finish his meal. He saw his grandfather playing some game of chance with an old friend at the end of the counter. His grandfather was the only one who he could relate to in the whole family. Grandfather had been an old friend of Ferdinand Marcos from Ilocos Norte, and had had a good life in the Philippines. He wished his grandfather hadn't let himself be talked into putting money with Maynard Laws.

Ricardo finished his food and told his grandfather that he was going out of town. Grandfather nodded, showing his toothless grin that Ricardo had offered to pay to have fixed. Grandfather had vehemently refused.

"No like go, no like go doctor."

Ricardo had given up.

He glanced back at the kitchen area, wondering if he should say goodbye to his mother. He decided against it.

Ricardo walked down the sidewalk on Hotel Street, which was quiet in the mid-afternoon. He headed downtown to First Hawaiian Bank, where he drew out twenty thousand dollars. He hadn't decided how much he would give Sandy, but he certainly needed some gambling money for himself.

He smiled as he walked back to the restaurant. He was looking forward to going to Vegas. He would help Sandy. He'd never forgotten how Sandy had come to his aid when Ricardo was being assaulted by the Marines. He thought back to the day he learned how the *haole* man had humiliated Sandy, the same man who had ripped off his beloved grandfather, he'd wished there was some way of exacting revenge.

Ricardo's chance had come sooner than he'd ever expected. Donald Duerden called Ricardo at the restaurant one afternoon and told Ricardo he had a job for him. Two days later, they'd met at the restaurant. At Donald's instructions, they rode in Ricardo's old Honda Civic to Makiki, a highly populated section of town near Punchbowl Cemetery, where Donald told Ricardo to park across from a large, modern condominium. Donald explained that they were going to follow someone. An hour later, as Ricardo nodded out in the driver's seat, he could sense Donald had seen their prey. Ricardo opened his eyes and was surprised to see the man he'd known as a mercenary in the Philippines, Reggie something.

The man began driving out toward Hawai'i Kai. Donald told Ricardo to follow, explaining to Ricardo what he wanted him to do.

"The house this guy is heading to is owned by a man named Maynard Laws." Donald looked over when he heard a gasp from Ricardo.

"I think this guy is going to kill Laws. The people I work for want it to happen—pull in here." Ricardo drove into a long drive. One side was bordered with oleander bushes and the other side by a dilapidated wood fence. He saw a circular drive appear to his left, fronting a large house.

"Drive past the driveway, turn the car around, and park next to that Acura." Ricardo did as he was told. "Now we wait."

Less than two minutes later, they heard a shot. Donald smiled. "Looks like you may have it easy today, Ricky. When the guy comes out, I want you to go in and see if Laws is dead. If he's shot, but not dead, kill him—however you want. If he's not shot, make up some excuse for why you're there—a mistake or something, and get the hell out. Don't do anything until I get back."

Donald handed something to Ricardo. "If Laws is dead or you kill him, leave this near the murder scene. Don't leave it unless Laws is dead."

Donald started to get out of the car. "If Laws is fine, come back to the car and call me, I'll be back as soon as I can. If you have to move the car for any reason, call me."

Donald walked around to the driver's side and leaned into the open window. "Of course, if Laws is already dead, or if you have to finish him off, get the hell out as fast as you can, then call me."

"Where you go, Donald?"

"Just do your job, Ricky. You clear on it? Any questions?

"What if other people stay in the house?"

"There aren't, but if there are, do what you have to do to protect yourself."

Ricardo shrugged his assent: *whatever*.

Donald patted Ricardo on the arm and walked away. He got in the Acura that had been parked there when they arrived.

A moment later Ricardo saw Reggie's car pull out of Laws' long driveway, turn left on Portlock Road, and speed away. Donald followed him in the Acura.

Ricardo got out of his car, walked to his trunk, and took out his machete, which always came in handy when he needed to do some intimidation work. He'd not had occasion to show what he could do with it on a human being since fighting in the jungles in the Philippines. He hoped Laws was still alive so he could have some fun. He'd pay Laws back for what he'd done to Sandy, and for what he'd done to his grandfather.

He walked around the side of the house. On the pool deck, he saw a man hunched over, sitting on a chaise lounge. The man was moaning, holding his stomach. Ricardo smiled. The man was still alive. Good. He'd have an opportunity to avenge Sandy and his grandfather, earn some extra money from Donald, and once again test his ability with the machete.

As he approached the man known as Laws, the man looked up, glassy eyed. He'd been crying. He held out his left hand. It had potato chips stuck to it. He nodded toward an object on the deck, at his feet. Ricardo looked at it. It was a greasy cell phone that must have slipped from Laws' hands. He wondered if Laws had been able to call 911. Just in case Laws had made the call, Ricardo figured he better hurry.

Ricardo looked back to Laws and they made eye contact. The look in Laws' eyes was pleading, begging. Ricardo had seen that look many times before. Laws stood up, still holding out his hand, almost as if he were offering Ricardo some potato chips. Ricardo raised the machete, and the look in the eyes changed from pitiful pleading to abject horror. The machete swung through the air, making a whistling sound as it did so. The sound of ripping skin and crunching bone was lost in the formative scream as Laws' arm fell to the deck.

Ricardo quickly grabbed the right arm. He almost lost his grip on the greasy arm, but he held tight and held the torso upright. He swung the machete again, this time at the base of the skull. The head teetered on the body, but did not fall off.

He'd lost the edge of his skill—he used to be able to decapitate a man with one swing. He swung again. It was almost severed. The body was swaying now, as he held it up with the one arm. It made the job more difficult. He chopped a couple of times to finish the job. Finally, the head fell to the pool deck, and Ricardo nonchalantly booted it into the pool, as if it were nothing more than a soccer ball. Blood spurted out the top of the torso, which was now leaning toward the pool.

He held the arm out straight and swung the machete one more time, expertly cutting through the shoulder joint. He tossed the arm to the deck. Almost simultaneously, he pushed the teetering, blood spurting, torso into the pool.

He had a lot of blood on him, but he didn't worry about that. He checked his bare feet. They were bloody, so he dipped them in the pool, one at a time. He did the same with the machete. He used a clean handkerchief to drop the book of matches Donald had given him on the lanai table, then walked around the side of the house to his car.

Ricardo tossed the machete in the trunk, took off his shirt, and quickly wiped his face and body. He looked around to make sure no one had seen him, then he casually got in the car and drove out the long drive to Portlock Road. In Hawai'i it was commonplace for men to drive shirtless. He turned right at the next block, then left on Lunalilo Home Road. At the intersection of Lunalilo Home Road and Kalanianaole Highway, he turned left and drove slowly back to town. There was no traffic. When he called Donald's cell and told him Laws was dead, he could tell Donald was on the road somewhere. He didn't ask where; it was none of his business.

The next morning, when the accounts of the Laws murder were confirmed by the press, Donald called Ricardo.

"What the fuck, Ricky, what happened in there? My man only had a gun."

Ricardo smiled to himself. "I wen finish job for you, Donald. I neva have one gun. Besides, you setting up that man for murder, yeah? I know that guy—from Philippines. He knows how to kill with a machete. The cops gonna find that out, so I wen help you set him up, yeah? You send *da kine* bonus to me, okay?"

"Holy crap. Yeah, okay, Ricky. Remind me not to ever fuck with you, okay?"

"Okay," said Ricardo, then paused for a beat. "Oh, and Donald?"

"Yeah, Ricky?"

"Don't ever call me Ricky again."

Chapter Fifty-Three

Pancho put the client file aside and swiveled to look out the window. He rubbed his chest with his right hand. A jumbo jet was taking off from the reef runway. A Coast Guard cutter was pulling away from the dock. The sky was a deep blue, with only a few wispy clouds. He was restless. He thought about calling Drew to see if he wanted to go surfing.

It had been three months since Reggie had pleaded to assault and Pancho wondered if he would ever know the truth about what happened. There were so many unanswered questions. He pretty much accepted Reggie's last version, but if it was true, who had cut up Laws? Why the dismemberment? Who was the presumed accomplice of Duerden? What had happened to Foreman? And last, but not least, was the CIA really behind it all?

The questions plagued him, and he, Susan, and Drew had spent many hours asking the questions and speculating on the answers. But it was becoming increasingly clear that the real story would never be told. Someone had gotten away with murder.

He thought about his life. When he was in trial, he lived and breathed it. It was tiring, stressful, scary, and sometimes it was heartbreaking. But he admitted to himself that he also loved it. He'd had only one short panic attack since the trial. He was cautiously optimistic that they were on the wane, and that they wouldn't interfere with his career.

When he wasn't in trial, he was bored and pressured out at the endless reams of paper work and telephone calls. He was restless, as he was now. If he couldn't continue to do trial work, he didn't think he would want to continue to be an attorney.

He was looking forward to the deposition trip to the Bay Area with Paula. She'd been great during the trial. She seemed to sense when he needed her to be with him and when he needed the space to think and work. Could she be the one who'd be willing to share him with the law?

Pancho swiveled back around to his desk, opened the *Star-Advertiser*, and read the lead article. The police had just arrested a suspect in the murder of the schoolteacher whose husband had disappeared the same day. It had been a big news case, and everyone had been assuming that the husband had murdered his wife and fled. But the suspect wasn't the husband. It was a neighbor, a man who had supposedly been a friend of the family. They lived in a ritzy area called Waialae Iki. The man's name was William Chatfield, Jr.

Pancho skimmed the rest of the article and moved on to a piece about Japanese investors in Hawai'i. *The selling of Hawai'i*, some people called it.

The intercom buzzed. Susan's raspy cigarette voice sounded tired, almost sad.

"New client on the phone, Pancho."

"What's the name?"

"William Chatfield, Jr."

Pancho felt his pulse quicken.

AUTHOR'S NOTE

Although all of the characters and events depicted in this book are fictional, the character named Maynard Laws is inspired by an old and bizarre case in Honolulu that once again proved that reality is often stranger than fiction.

On October 21, 1985, a man named Ronald Rewald was convicted by a jury in federal court in Honolulu of 94 counts of mail and securities fraud, tax evasion, and perjury. He'd been accused of bilking some $22 million from 400 investors, who had placed money with his investment firm with dreams of huge interest returns.

Rewald's defense was that he was a front for the CIA, which allegedly wanted him to live a lifestyle of the rich and famous while using his company and dummy corporations for CIA operations. Rewald's trial was a bizarre circus, replete with tales of sex for money, classified documents, hob-knobbing with celebrities and politicians, Arab arms deals, and ex-CIA employees as investors.

It is interesting to note that volumes and volumes of documents which the defense sought to have admitted at the Rewald trial to support his allegations of CIA involvement were deemed 'classified', and were excluded from evidence. The defense attorneys were required to have national security clearance to represent Rewald.

Additional Notes and Acknowledgements

Writing dialect is always a tricky business, and there are those who advocate staying away from it altogether. But Pidgin English in Hawai'i is so prevalent and such an integral part of everyday language, I felt that it was essential to include some very basic elements of the language. It is not uncommon to hear lawyers, wealthy businessmen, and even politicians employ some level of pidgin in everyday conversations. Real pidgin is almost like another language altogether, such that *malihinis* (newcomers) may find it impossible to follow a full-on pidgin discussion. I apologize to pidgin purists, but I hope the readers got the general idea.

Likewise, Hawaiian words, such as *pau* (finished), *okole* (butt), *mauka* (mountain), and *makai* (ocean), are all incorporated into everyone's day-to-day dialog. I have even used many such words in open court.

I want to thank my array of 'readers' who generously gave their time to read my draft(s) and comment accordingly: Nancy Tetenbaum, Lee Roberts, Tom Work, Gary Sprinkle, Ron Ward, Larry Stubblefield, and my former law partner, Dan Chur. There are several doctors, including a medical examiner, who were kind enough to review some of the medical testimony, but I won't disclose their names in the event they do not approve of the medical literary license I took in a few small instances. But you know who you are and I thank you.

My wife, Marcia Waldorf, is a retired Honolulu Circuit Court trial judge and was therefore my go-to expert for criminal procedure and rules of evidence. Just the fact that she has put up with me for almost forty years should be sufficient reason to get down on my knees and thank her, but it's a bonus situation to have an in-house expert.

Unplayable Lie

A Novel by David Myles Robinson

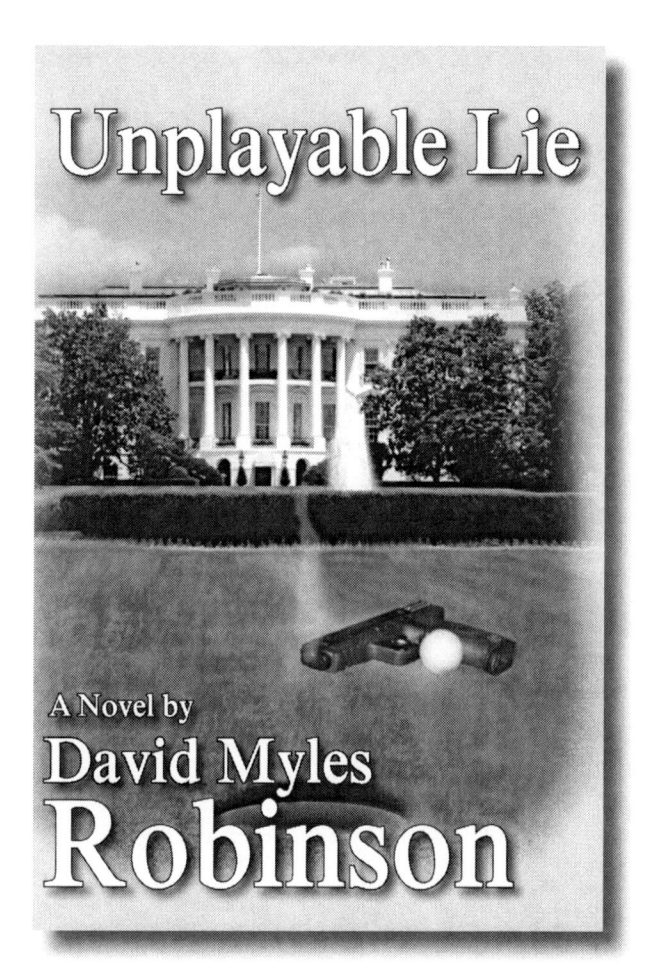

We hope that you thoroughly enjoyed David Myles Robinson's *Tropical Lies*. If we may suggest, his other book published by BluewaterPress LLC is just as thrilling and exciting.

In *Unplayable Lie*, Eddie Bennett began playing golf as a way to bond with his father. He quickly displayed a rare talent for the game. After a long and at times tragic road to the PGA Tour, all of the hard work appears to have paid off when it looked as if Eddie would be a sure candidate for Rookie of the Year.

Then Eddie sees something he should not have seen on the back nine of the Congressional Country Club. During a practice round for his first U.S. Open, he witnesses a murder. The killer is the man who will probably be the next President of the United States. He quickly understands his golfing career is ruined, but that is not all. The event forces Eddie underground while he tries to prove what he saw in a bid to get his life back.